Born to an American musician father, and English mother, **Jemma Wayne** grew up in Hertfordshire and studied Social and Political Sciences at Cambridge University and Broadcast Journalism at the University of Westminster. She began her career as a journalist at The Jewish Chronicle, and later as a columnist for The Jewish News. She is now a regularly featured blogger at The Huffington Post and continues to contribute to a variety of other publications. Her first play, *Negative Space*, was staged in 2009 at Hampstead's New End Theatre, receiving critical acclaim.

Jemma's debut novel *After Before* was longlisted for the Baileys Women's Prize for Fiction, longlisted for the Guardian Not the Booker Prize and shortlisted for the Waverton Good Read Award.

Visit Jemma at
jemmawayne.com
or on Twitter
@writejemmawayne

CHAINS
OF
SAND

JEMMA WAYNE

Legend Press Ltd, 175-185 Gray's Inn Road, London, WC1X 8UE
info@legend-paperbooks.co.uk | www.legendpress.co.uk

Contents © Jemma Wayne 2016
The right of the above author to be identified as the author of this work has
been asserted in accordance with the Copyright, Designs and Patents Act
1988. British Library Cataloguing in Publication Data available.

Print ISBN 978-1-7850797-2-6
Ebook ISBN 978-1-7850797-3-3
Set in Times. Printed in the United Kingdom by Clays Ltd.
Cover design by Simon Levy www.simonlevyassociates.co.uk

For Audrey and Alice

I will not cease from Mental Fight,
Nor shall my Sword sleep in my hand:
Till we have built Jerusalem,
In England's green & pleasant Land

William Blake
'Jerusalem'

Prologue

The house is on top of me. Under me. Around me. Darkness is everywhere. Like a coffin. I am not scared. I am used to darkness. In Gaza, when blackouts come as often as they do, you have to get used to it. My mother's hand is on my ankle but it has not moved for at least an hour. She is dead, I think. In our coffin. Above us, I can hear them scrabbling through the rubble. Their voices are muffled but my father knows we are still here, he is the one who told us to stay. Where could we go anyway? They will be calling our names. I think I hear mine: Farah. I cannot answer. The second I open my mouth there will be dust in my throat. I must concentrate on shallow breaths, on staying calm.

Stay calm, says my mother, *be good*. Now that I am 12 she takes me with her to her cleaning job. If it is quiet I am allowed to help, if not I have to do my homework in the back room. The health centre where she mops the floors is run by the UN. The manager is Swiss. She wears a covering on her head, too, and my mother points this out to me – *see, even this woman* – but I still dislike the hijab. I am made to wear it, but I would not choose to. Then again, choice is not a staple for me. I do not choose to live with a father who now that he is back home beats my mother. I do not choose to hide weapons under my mattress. I do not choose to be trapped in a place where such lack of choice is commonplace, all I should expect. When I was a child, I disobeyed my father. I would not say the Jewish soldier had hurt me. He had given me chocolate. And he had smiled. And I did not feel like laying still. So my father taught me the importance of the cause.

At the centre, I talk sometimes to the American nurse. He does not seem like a criminal. He is not the way the TV shows say. He has an iPad and on days when it is quiet, I see him take it out to play games upon. His favourite is a strategy game. There are objects you have to find and then codes and puzzles and riddles to decipher. I am good at this and he lets me help, though I am not meant to be noticed, because I am not meant to be there. He has started bringing me tokens from his trips into Israel. Sweets. A magazine. An iPod. My mother tells me I am jeopardising things. She tells me this money is vital. She tells me the UN centre stands less than 100m from land once tilled, and owned, by her grandfather. She smiles. Unlike my father, she does not want to quash my disobedience. Disobedience, she tells me, is the beginning of free thought. When she can, she feeds me with books, and pretends that one day these will be my route out, away, up.

Up. Above me, a shaft of light blasts through the darkness. I cannot touch it but it illuminates my mother's rigid fingers at my feet.

Farah.

I hear my name again. It is my brother Saad. The one at university. The one who tells me I can go there too. The one who has sat with me every night for the past two weeks as missiles dot the sky and cars explode outside our door and soldiers rip through the streets. Saad is the quiet one. But he is shouting. Shouting for me.

The shaft of light grows thicker. It is a tunnel now. A lifeline straight to the sun.

Farah.

I open my mouth to reply.

The dust hits my lungs.

***

10

Now

1

Udi sits hunched over a pile of papers. It isn't his natural stance. His neck aches and his finger has calloused from where the pen has been balanced too long. Still, he has spread the sheets carefully across the wooden table on which he used to do his homework and now contemplates his life. His mother, Batia, is in the next room so he opens the first booklet quietly. She'd be sure to ask what it is he's studying so intently, thrilled that he's finally interested, focussing. He doesn't want to disappoint her. Besides, he has to complete the forms before anything of substance can be announced. He has been pouring over them for days but is yet to concoct what to write in the box that calls for the title of the occupation he's meant to have already secured but hasn't, or the section that asks how long he intends to reside in the UK. There is no option, it seems, to write 'forever'.

He peels the sticky white vest from his back and closes the Entry Clearance application form. The air conditioning isn't working, again, so he's resorted to a fan propped up next to the window, which seems only to move the hot air around the room in an ever-more oppressive cycle. Ramat Gan is less than five miles from the sea but there is no breeze in the city, no movement, only this constant, unyielding heat. It is 34 degrees outside, a typical summer, but this year it feels hotter, harder to bear. Udi re-opens the guidance booklet that came attached to the form for a UK work permit and offers little real guidance. He abandoned it in frustration the day before but perhaps there is a note of explanation he missed. If there is, he will find it. He has always been good at tracking down things that are hidden, like cockroaches in his mother's kitchen cupboard, or tunnels in Gaza.

He could have asked for help – Tomer's brother is a lawyer, he would have done it for nothing – but Udi isn't yet ready to tell his patriotic friend about his intention to leave. To deconstruct it. The economy's shit and that's all there is to it. He has been living at home with his parents since he left the army two years ago and of course there have been jobs, and more jobs, but: 'The only way to make a fortune in Israel is to come to Israel with a bigger fortune.' This is the joke bandied around to new immigrants and still he laughs, though he no longer finds it funny. His mother wants him to study, but the army left him dumb. It leaves everyone dumb. They arrive aged 18, finally adults, still in the throes of working out what they believe, who they are, what they will and won't do; and the army erases them. They are taught to say yes. Only yes. Udi's commander had been clear: *You don't question, you don't think. You say yes and you do.* And then, three years later, they were all given tests for college and they had to learn to think again and to dream again, and by then Udi was unable to imagine that. He said he wasn't interested anymore, which in some ways is true because what's the point in spending money and energy and time, or even trying to start his own business which is what he really wants, when at any moment until he's 45 the army can intervene, calling him away to the reserves for months at a time and leaving him with fuck all? His father thinks he should return to the army permanently. "You did well there," Oz reminds him. But Udi has had enough of Gaza and Nablus, and every other shit hole they send him to. He's ready now for the rest of his life. To live it. He has a cousin in London.

Udi hears his father arriving home and quickly sweeps the papers into a drawer. He has never been able to persuade Oz of the virtues of knocking, or of locks. Hurriedly he adopts a posture of nonchalance at the empty desk, then feels ridiculous; he is 26. Oz's footsteps linger in the kitchen and he considers retrieving the forms, but Oz has only paused to talk to Udi's mother, or perhaps to eat one of the sambousak she has spent all day cooking, and suddenly he appears at Udi's door.

"*Y'allah*," Oz tells him. 'Let's go,' it means in Israeli-appropriated Arabic, this time as a practical instruction, often as an accentuation, sometimes when there is a silence and nothing else to say. He nods only fleetingly at Udi before returning to the kitchen, suspecting nothing.

Udi gets up and reaches for a cotton shirt to wear over his jeans. He chooses long trousers always, no matter the heat. The scars on his legs have faded now but he prefers not to see them, or, perhaps, he prefers others not to see. He rolls his shirtsleeves up to his elbows and slips his feet into the worn sandals that have taken him to Thailand, to Mexico, to the park where he and Ella once made love. They are tattered and Ella wants him to throw them away, but these shoes know the shape of his feet perfectly; they understand the length of his stride and the slight roll of his big toe that has carved out a comfortable dent in the leather.

"*Y'allah*!" Oz shouts again from the kitchen.

Udi appears in the doorway and Oz nods: "Good. You are driving."

They walk together towards the road and climb into Udi's beat up Subaru. The exhaust fell off yesterday for the third time since he bought the car second hand a month ago, but he is glad that he no longer has to rely on his parents, for transport at least. Oz does not fasten his seatbelt. He is rounded these days, his chest always a little wheezy from too much smoke, his skin as dark and impervious as ever. He hands Udi Batia's plastic container filled with sambousak. Udi surveys the perfect savoury pockets and takes two.

13

"Abba, I still don't know about this," he ventures, nevertheless starting the engine.

"What should you know?" Oz slaps his hands together then flicks them towards the road. "You haven't tried yet. First you try, then you know."

Oz has arranged an interview for Udi at a friend's construction company. It isn't the kind of career that Udi imagines for himself, but Oz thinks it is better than the bar jobs he has been working so far. It is strange to Udi. Strange that his father, with his dark skin and his Farsi tongue and his lifetime of closed doors, should suggest this, this manual labour. Strange that he should not wish to end the cycle, believe things have changed, see it as possible. Strange that he should not notice that all of the other construction workers at the company are black, a band of Ethiopian Israelis who Udi is sure will not be paid as much as him. A new breed of Sephardim.

"Okay, so we'll go in. I'll introduce you," Oz says as Udi parks in the lot adjacent to the building. It is a tall, white structure, one of a host of impressive architectural creations that have sprung up in Ramat Gan over the past few years and somehow merge seamlessly into the city's eclectic malaise: tree-lined streets covered with graffiti; a diamond district next to tired, un-landscaped parks; new ones, with colourful playgrounds beside modern, 'affordable', 'family' apartment complexes; neon lights; boarded up buildings; wild scraggy cats perching like crows atop the boards, surveying it all; black-hats almost rubbing shoulders with the illegal casinos of the night; 'Baghdad Town' in its full, amalgamated glory.

Yacov, the owner of the company and Oz's friend from back in Baghdad, is standing outside the entrance shouting orders into his mobile phone. He raises his hand when he sees them, then waves them inside. Udi and Oz find Yacov's office and help themselves to water. Udi notices a photo on Yacov's desk: a boy, younger than himself, and two women, neither of them as beautiful as Ella, who all wear army uniform and

14

share the same muddy eyes. Eventually Yacov enters and sits on the other side of the photo. Twenty minutes later they emerge together. Yacov is making jokes and also laughing at them. Oz is smiling, and Udi has a new occupation. He is expected to start on Sunday.

"Good," Oz declares. They are back in the car and driving towards home. Oz has opened the container of sambousak and is eating with renewed gusto. He has un-tucked his shirt and his growing roundness spreads contentedly outwards. "This is good for you. This is something."

Udi doesn't speak. He knows he is meant to thank his father for the introduction, for the opportunity, but silent assent is the best he can manage. He takes his sunglasses out of the glove compartment and puts them on.

"*Qus!*" Oz shouts as the car in the neighbouring lane pulls in front of them.

Udi's foot is quick on the pedal. The driver of the car in front flicks his hand out of the window unapologetically and speeds off. Udi glances at his father whose own hand is still raised, his mouth still tasting the end of the profanity. It isn't Hebrew, but Udi understands such insults, guesses that they feel comfortable on his father's tongue. It is only a guess because Oz has worked hard over the years to become a new, true Israeli, to lay this foundation for his children, and it is only at moments like these – base, instinctual exchanges – that he will speak Farsi in front of them.

Before, long before Udi was born, when Farsi came easily, Oz fled Baghdad. And was welcomed by Israel.

This is the entire mass of knowledge that Udi has gathered about his father's youth. Even these details have been gleaned from his mother, but at moments like these, traces of Oz's carefully trampled former self resurface. Udi guesses it is easier for him to swear creatively in the language of his formative years. It is easier for Udi, too. Somehow he understands his father better in this foreign tongue.

15

"And fuck yourself!" Udi adds for good measure. He lifts his chin out of the window as he catches up and swerves around the offending vehicle whose driver returns the gesture. They pull to a stop at a crossroads and now another car to their right tries to inch forward. Udi flashes his lights. It is a signal everybody understands: 'Do not dare go under any circumstances,' it means. 'I am going. Get out of my way.' The car stays where it is and again Udi hits his foot to the floor.

Oz seems satisfied.

Oz and Batia met in a kibbutz in Dafnah. This much Batia has revealed. This much Udi knows. They had been living in the same refugee camp in tents just meters apart, but they didn't meet until Dafnah.

Oz shifts in his seat. Without speaking. Udi has long ago given up trying to talk to his father, his own high-pitched questions long since faded, and the demanding tone of Oz's queries making any answers seem insufficient.

Oz is not his name. It wasn't his name. He chose a new Israeli one. A fresh name for a fresh identity. Once, when Udi was 11, on the day the news came that their grandfather had passed away, he had witnessed from a darkened window his mother caressing his father's lowered head. She had slipped seamlessly in and out of Hebrew and a language he didn't understand, and she had called his father Bekhor. Sometimes Udi thinks about saying it, using it, just to see.

It is almost four o'clock so, for his father, Udi switches on the car radio. The final bars of an American song die out before the familiar hourly beeps herald the latest news: the Iron Dome has intercepted another rocket, this time fired from Sinai toward the southern resort city of Eilat; the government has announced another tax increase; there has been a four-car pile up on the motorway heading into Haifa. There have been no bombs. This is what they are listening for. Still. Music returns. It is a song with a Brazilian beat that reminds Udi of his time in Central America. Oz switches it off. There is silence again. Except for the sound of pastry between teeth.

"Good," Oz says as the house comes into view and Udi parks, badly. "So you should be early on Sunday."

"Okay, Abba," Udi replies.

"So okay. We'll tell your mother. *Y'allah*." Oz heaves himself out of the car, squinting in the sunlight as he looks towards the house, and then, glancing back at Udi, he almost smiles. The expression sits absurdly on his lined face.

"You tell her Abba," Udi replies. "I'm not coming in." He hands his father the empty tub of sambousak.

"You are working?"

"No."

Oz's smile fades. "Don't drink too much Udi," he says, before turning again towards home.

***

Batia is in the kitchen alone. It is a luxury she used to long for, but now the house is empty too often. Avigail has been married for seven years already. She has two daughters of her own and lives in Jerusalem. It is too far to travel daily. Ari's apartment is only three streets away but he is never there. Usually he is stationed near Gaza, where again the air is tightening, where Batia's mind wanders when she cannot sleep. She is lucky if they see him once a month. Then at least it is for whole weekends at a time – he doesn't flit and float across her radar like the others, he allows her to pin him down – but she isn't privy to the daily nuances of his soul. Udi is the only one left at home, exposed. Udi, her baby. Whom, when he *was* a baby, so much younger than Ari and Avigail, she gave the time she hadn't had for the others. By then the older two were at school so if the housework was done and Oz was at work, she would bypass the cot and bring Udi into her own bed for an afternoon nap. There she would inhale the gloriousness of his chubby hands and curled hair matted with heat across his forehead. And later, sit with under sheets propped up by kitchen chairs. Or sing into the whirring fan to hear their voices transform into reverberations. It is strange for her now to regard his tough, sharply contoured frame lifting things she cannot manage. And she has to check herself often not to enlist him in sharing some small wonder – the first flowers of spring, a sequel to the cartoon movie he once loved, his favourite chocolates now in mint flavour. Sometimes when she collects his washing from his room she senses that her presence is an irritation to him, and that he would rather be with Ella.

Oz thinks he should return to the army. He is proud already to have one highly ranked son and he would be prouder still to have two. Batia however cannot weigh any amount of national fervour against anything that could see him again on the front line. Again in a hospital bed. But Oz hasn't asked her opinion. He says Udi lacks focus.

The sound of a car engine disturbs the silence, intruding on Batia's pondering, and a few moments later the front door scrapes across the worn tiles of the floor. Batia remembers when Oz laid them. It was the final job in making the house habitable and he had stood back and admired his work with a puffed-out chest. Ari and Avigail were only children then, Udi not yet born, but she had gathered them around their father and served tea on the front step where they had all stood, gazing inwards. Now the grout needs refilling and one of the tiles has been replaced by a new one that creaks when it's stepped on and doesn't quite match. Batia hears only one set of footsteps crossing.

"Udi is not with you?"

"He has gone out." Oz sits on the stool in front of the kitchen counter and stirs a generous helping of sugar into the glass of Arabic tea Batia has already poured for him.

"He is working?"

"No."

"With Ella." This is not a query. "So?" She runs her hands quickly through her cropped hair then reaches for the sugar to flavour her own brew. "Does he have the job?"

"Yes."

"It is good?"

"Yes." Oz stares into his tea.

"So?" She leans over to touch his hand. "We can smile." She kisses his forehead. He smiles.

"He will be okay," Oz decrees suddenly, firmly, leaving his calloused hand under Batia's. Only she would be able to detect that this is a question.

"Of course. He is strong," she affirms.

They drain their cups in silence. "*Y'allah*," he says.

***

Udi grinds his foot hard into the accelerator as he speeds away from his father. "*Qus!*" he hears himself exclaiming more than once in Oz's voice, this in itself an irritation.

The car behind him beeps impatiently and Udi adds his own horn to the racket. There is traffic. Nobody can move and it is impossible to progress. It makes Udi uncomfortable. He bangs his fist again on the horn and offers a few belligerent hand gestures out of the open window. There will be at least another 20 minutes of this. He is only at the first of the three giant billboards he and Chaim use to mark the distance between each other's homes. When they were still in highschool and the 'Hello Boys' Wonderbra campaign first appeared on the billboard closest to Udi's house, they began assigning names to each of the signs depending on which advert was adorning it. Neither of them used to mind getting stuck in traffic if they were close enough to Eva Herzigova and her splendid breasts. Eva however has long ago disappeared and there is an old image of the Prime Minister, Bibi Netanyahu, occupying the 20-foot space out of Udi's right-hand window. Udi lights a cigarette and thinks instead of Ella. He imagines her in a Wonderbra.

Finally the traffic begins to move but by the time he reaches Chaim's house he is hungry and needs to take a piss.

The house is similar to the one in which Udi lives, except for the extension Chaim's parents have recently completed turning unused lawn into a larger, granite-topped kitchen. White floors meet white walls, the paint a little old, a little sun-soaked, but the idea of freshness still perceptible. The furniture is an eclectic mix of aged patterned fabric and crisp Ikea leather. The main rooms are open plan and seem to melt into each other, despite the cool tiles underfoot and Chaim's working air conditioning. Every ornament – of which there are many – is polished and cared for, the surface dusted underneath. Chaim is watching TV when Udi enters. He is the only person Udi knows who would do this in the middle of a Thursday afternoon. Udi himself only finished his bar shift at four o'clock that morning and would have been working in the café now had he not had the interview with Yacov. Chaim however has just returned from India and will work only to save enough money to go travelling again. In the meantime he insists on a day off – *God promised a day of rest* – laughing when someone responds that the day of rest was also promised on a Saturday. Chaim would never rest on Shabbat. It is by far the best day to earn extra cash.

Udi slaps his friend's hand in greeting then goes to the bathroom where he thinks again of Ella. When he returns, Chaim is standing in the new kitchen eating from a vat of salad his mother has prepared. Udi takes a Coke from the fridge and finds a piece of pita bread into which he spoons some salad. He adds hummus and a couple of meatballs he discovers in another tin-foiled bowl readied by Chaim's mother, then slaps Chaim hard on the back.

"*Y'allah*," he says, and Chaim grabs his own pita, which he fills deftly before following Udi out to the car.

Loud American music smacks them as soon as Udi turns on the engine. He likes to listen at such a volume that all other sounds are muted and doesn't need to turn it down for Chaim's sake, but there is only one song before the hourly news beeps sound again. Chaim turns off the radio and inserts an old cassette full of Indian tunes. He takes a small bag from his pocket and expertly rolls a spliff, licking the paper and carefully moulding the end into a cone before lighting it. While Udi drives, they take it in turns to savour long, deep drags.

Udi's phone rings.

It is his home number. He has been gone barely an hour but it is probably his father checking he's not drinking or remembering another pre-job pearl of wisdom. Udi ignores the phone. It rings again and he turns the whole thing off. Chaim nods. He never leaves his phone on and is stubborn in this rare, disconnected eccentricity. Udi takes another drag of the spliff. Drummed bass pushes through the windy melody of Indi-pop. If he closed his eyes, it would almost be possible to believe they were somewhere else.

Eventually they reach Tel Aviv and wind their way through the busy streets towards Ha'Carmel. Parking is never easy but the shuk is worth the extra stress. Without the need for consultation they amble their way past the stalls of fish and meat, kitchenware and designer knock-offs. Narrow alleys are buffered on both sides by rails of tablecloths for the locals, and gleaming Judaica for the tourists, and between them wafts the smell of cooking. Antiquity and practicality clashing, or converging, on sustenance: hummus, schwarma, fresh falafel. Udi quickly slips a strong mint into his mouth, but he is too slow. The scent never fails to upend him. The passage of 20 years has choked off some off the pungency, but still…

He is six years old. He is excited over some object he can no longer picture but he feels vividly the rush of adrenalin in ducking through the stalls to grab it. He reaches up, climbs on something to unhook it, he has it in his hands. Victorious. Turning to show his father, Udi is smiling. The object – whatever it is – is something he is sure will please Oz. But suddenly in front of him are legs he does not recognise, a moving sea of limbs that hem him in, and his father, who had instructed him to stay close, is not smiling back at him but is nowhere to be seen. The object – which must have been something hard because it clatters on the cobbled stone below – tumbles from his hands. Udi's throat is gripped by a surging, shameful, terror. And he cannot move. He feels tears welling. He hears voices around him – the language of his cousins and his aunts and his grandparents, but not his father who will not speak it. And still he cannot move. At last an Iraqi woman at a falafel stall takes him by the wrist and encourages him to chop parsley. For him who can't, she shouts across the bustle. She does not seem concerned. And a moment later, nor does Oz. It has been merely minutes and as he appears like a mirage through the crowd, he ruffles Udi's hair casually, laughing at his poor attempts with the parsley, purchasing for him a falafel. But Udi cannot eat it. He is too ashamed, shamed by his terror that remains stuck in his throat, shamed by his failure to act, his inability to be as strong as his father.

It is this shame that to this day the smell of falafel conjures, despite the intervening years of obsession with action movies and superheroes and ambition to be chosen for the most elite of combat units, and success in that. Shame still smells of falafel. He has at least grown better at shrugging it away.

It doesn't take long to reach the nut stall. After a token barter, Udi digs into the bag of pistachios they have purchased, dropping the salty shells underfoot until they reach the coffee house that is their final destination. This is a relatively new part of their shuk routine. Café Carmel opened only a few months ago but they are addicted. Udi orders a coffee and sits down at a table outside. It is in the shade, there is a slight breeze, and at last the air is bearable. While Chaim is still ordering, Udi turns his phone back on to check for messages. In the space of an hour he has acquired 12 texts and three voicemails. This is excessive even for him, but before he can open any of them the phone rings again. The number flashes across the screen. His sister.

"Yes, Avigail," he says into the phone, spitting another pistachio shell out of his mouth and starting a pile of them on a paper napkin.

"Udi. Thank God. You're not in Tel Aviv?"

"Yes, I'm at the shuk."

"You are okay?"

"I'm fine." He says this with practised patience. If it is not his father hounding him, or his mother, it is his sister Avigail. He has no siblings but multiple parents.

"Then why the hell aren't you answering your phone?! Ima has been going mad."

"Why?" he asks, sitting a little straighter. "What's happened?"

"Udi, don't you even listen to the news?"

Udi puts down the nuts. Peering now inside the café he notices a close huddle of people near the till, Chaim amongst them. One of the women is gesticulating wildly. Everybody is on their phones. Udi spins back to look at the market. In front of him on the pavement there is a woman around his mother's age standing unmoving. She has been there for a number of minutes, Udi had noticed her already. But now he sees that her eyes bore into the empty space just above her own head. And that the fingers of her right hand have contracted into a claw.

"You should listen," Avigail scolds him. "You should listen." By now she barely needs to say the words, but does: "There's been a bomb."

Udi exhales so sharply that the sound is audible, and he is glad he is alone. His throat contracts, but he attempts to ignore these spasms, that shameful terror.

"Udi?"

"Where?" he croaks. "Where was it?"

"Shaul Hamelech street."

Udi's mind races through his mental address book, checking through the people he knows who live or work nearby, or who simply could have been there.

"Dana and David are alright," Avigail pre-empts him. These are their cousins. "So is Uriel."

Udi's voice eases a little. "Where did it happen?" he asks.

"On a bus, but-"

"How many?"

"They haven't said yet, but, Udi, there is something else. Ima can't get hold of Abba."

"Abba? But he's at home."

"He was meeting Uriel."

"What?" Udi's throat closes in on him again. Rapidly this time. Like hands around his neck. "But no, I just saw him. Anyway, he would be in his car."

"Yes."

"He's probably just caught up in diversions."

"Yes."

They pause again. Udi pictures his father parking his car at the mall near Uriel's house. Heaving his expanding belly out of it. Taking Batia's advice and walking the extra distance because there are no parking restrictions at the mall *and anyway, the exercise is good for you.* Lighting a cigarette as he walks. Stopping as he always does to say hello to the old men at the café behind the bus stop. The bus stop. Seeing an arriving bus.

"I'll call when I hear," says Avigail.

"Okay," says Udi, but he doesn't want to put down the phone. Across the café, Chaim is walking towards him, his own phone to his ear.

"Okay," says Avigail, but she doesn't hang up either.

There is another pause.

"He'll be okay, Udi," she says finally. "Just call Ima. And answer your phone."

Chaim sits down and Udi hangs up. "Fuck the Arabs," Chaim declares, banging his coffee onto the table.

Udi places his phone carefully on the table in front of him, screen side up.

Chaim notices his gaze. "Hannah and Noam are okay."

"Good," says Udi. But he looks at the screen again. The same screen that just an hour ago he turned off, to avoid his father. It has been less than a minute since he hung up on Avigail. She would barely have had time to call him, to call anyone. Still... All around them other phones are buzzing, buzzing.

"You okay?" asks Chaim.

Udi nods and waves his hand dismissively, but he looks down again. He can't speak. He can't breathe. They sit, the pistachio shells forming a small mountain between them. Chaim begins saying something about the bus and where they think the bomber boarded, but Udi can't concentrate.

What was the last thing he said to his father? That he was not coming in? That he was not working? That he clearly didn't want the job, or his help? When did it happen? When did admiration turn to suffocation?

Would it be suffocation? He has read that losing vast amounts of blood feels like suffocation.

Udi pushes the pile of pistachio shells closer to Chaim. They smell of falafel.

Inside, the owner of the coffee house switches on a television and customers gather around to watch it. Udi cranes his neck, but he can imagine the visuals without even looking. Shattered glass, screaming people, rage, devastation. Humanity pushed to its farthest edge and scrawled upon faces. No bodies are shown, no dismembered arms or legs, no close-ups of dead children, though this is what the Palestinians like to show when it is their dead, their disaster. And though these are the images hovering just beyond the filmed visuals, emblazoned in Udi's mind, in all of their minds, even now, eight years since the last intifada when there was no fence and so these scenes came often. The news cameras show the orange-vested volunteers, the paramedics and the hundreds of people who run towards the site of the tragedy to help.

To lay a hand, perhaps, onto the wrist of a hapless child. Udi stares hard at the orange blur but he can see no rounded stomachs. No un-tucked shirts. *Y'allah. Y'allah.*

Udi's phone rings.

He snatches it up, but it is Ella. "Shit," he says to Chaim. Then to her, before hello: "I only just heard."

"I've been ringing you, Udi." She is wavering between rage and tears. "I've been worried."

Udi forces an even tone. "You knew I was going to the shuk. I'm nowhere near Shaul Hamelech."

"I didn't know for sure." Her voice cracks with the hint of a scream. "It's selfish."

"I'm sorry," he says, and for a moment he contemplates telling Ella about his father. About the hands around his neck. "Are you still coming to meet us?" he asks instead.

There is an extended pause, and then a sigh, but eventually she answers. "Yes. Where are you?"

"Still at the shuk."

"The roads are a mess. They've closed off the motorway. I'll be a while."

"So okay, we'll meet you in an hour or so, at the beach."

"Okay."

"Okay." Udi wonders if he can hang up. He wants to hang up, Avigail may be calling. Or his father. But Ella often pauses without meaning to say goodbye.

"I love you, Udi," she says finally.

"You too."

"Leave your phone on, okay?"

"Okay."

Udi hangs up and turns his phone off. "*Qus*," he says, and turns it on again.

"Fucking Arabs," Chaim says and digs his hand deeply into Udi's bag of nuts. He offers them to Udi, but Udi pushes them away.

They wait.

They wait.

26

It is clear they are waiting and Chaim says nothing. He sits. Udi does not take his eyes off the screen. Around them other diners are draining their coffees, paying their bills, continuing on. Chatter is returning to the market. Udi drums his thumb against the table in quick, successive pulses. His throat tightens and releases. His shoulders spasm upward. He wills his phone to ring.

At last it does.

"He's fine." Avigail breathes this as soon as Udi picks up. "Lost service and was stuck in the jam near the site. He's fine."

A gulp of suppressed air rockets out of Udi's throat and surprises him with a high gasp. Chaim raises an eyebrow.

"He's fine," Avigail says again, gently.

"Of course he is."

"Okay." She pauses. "Are you okay?"

"Yes, Avigail."

"Okay." She stops again. "Udi, call Ima."

They say goodbye and now Udi turns off his phone.

With effort, he steadies his shoulders, his throat, his hands, and reaches for his cup, taking a long gulp of his cold coffee. For a moment he holds the liquid in his mouth and closes his eyes. For another moment. And another. Then he swallows, grins, and claps his hand onto the table-top. Chaim nods.

Now that nobody they know has been killed they are free to be angry only, un-tempered by fear or grief.

"Fucking dogs," declares Chaim. "These are not people. I mean what kind of person sends their son out to kill himself? I'll tell you – the same kind of person who hides behind his women and children when we come looking for him. And hides rockets behind them too. These people are crazy. They are not rational. How can they be human?"

Udi cannot answer. Unconsciously he touches his leg, rubs the scars beneath the denim, but even in the aftermath of sudden fear his rage isn't as pure as his friend's. Chaim didn't go to the army. He wasn't in Gaza.

27

A newsreader appears on the television screen. Twenty-eight people have been wounded, the families informed. Celebratory gunfire is shown in Gaza. Hamas praise the attack as a natural response to the occupation. The Israeli government announces that there will be reprisals.

Udi and Chaim order another coffee.

"I'm fucking going to leave all this shit," Chaim announces after they have arrived. "Enough, you know?"

"Where to this time?" Udi asks.

"I'm not sure yet. Maybe Guatemala. Maybe Brazil. You want to come with me?"

"I have to work," Udi answers instinctually, but then reassesses. If any of his friends will understand, it is Chaim. "Actually," he restarts, "I'm planning on leaving too. On moving. To London."

"What?" Chaim sits forward. "You mean for good? To leave Israel?"

"Yes."

"When will you go?"

"As soon as I can."

"Wowee." Chaim lights a cigarette. "Have you told your family yet? Ella?"

Udi shakes his head.

Chaim takes a deep drag of his cigarette, then sends the smoke swirling. "Israel is the greatest country in the world," he tells Udi. "You'll be back in six months." Udi says nothing and Chaim looks at him harder. "You know what, forget Brazil. I'll come with you," he declares, raising his coffee cup. "My friend, next year in London!"

***

Ella drives solidly and with determination. Her eyes do not leave the road. Her hands do not leave the steering wheel. She doesn't look up when a car behind her hoots its horn.

28

She should not go to Udi. She should not do this. She should, at some point, make a stand. It isn't unreasonable, she doesn't think, to expect him to worry, to care. She deserves that. After four years she ought to be worthy of that. But she knows that expressing himself is alien to him, that he cannot bear to make himself vulnerable.

Ella sighs and momentarily allows her right hand to unclench the steering wheel in order to reach into her bag for her lipstick. She paints on a fresh coat that barely alters the appearance of the two she has already applied and glances fleetingly into the mirror. She notices that her cheeks could do with a little more blush. Also that she has again pursed her lips inwards. Opening her mouth wide, she makes herself relax these muscles. She has read that unhappy expressions will lead to downward-drawn wrinkles.

Ella turns the radio on and tunes it to an all-music station that Udi loves. A song starts that makes her think of the summer they met, the first time they locked eyes, then lips.

Perhaps it is not that they don't want the same things, only that he doesn't know how to show her that they do. Or realise that this is necessary. Ella has been dropping hints about marriage for over a year now and every day her mother asks her if he has proposed. He hasn't and she can feel the resentment brewing within her. But there is little more she can do to force it and she feels powerless, obliged to sit and wait for him to decide her future. The waiting makes her angry. It tempers their love. Even when they are out with friends, or at the beach, or having sex, there is a part of her that remains bitter, hating him for refusing to make her happiness whole. Yet there is nothing she can think of to do: she has been supportive, patient. She is even working hard at her studies now – something she doesn't find easy – all to make herself more desirable to Udi because the only thing she really wants to use her business degree for is to manage a home. She is ready already. She wants a husband, to be a wife, to have children. She wants to get on with life and live it now. And she wants this with Udi. She is still hoping to be married by the New Year.

The beach comes into view.

She could still turn around.

***

Udi spots Avi and Dov crossing the street towards them. Dalia is dismounting her bike a little way down. This is the way evenings emerge for them. One person calling another, who calls another, congregating on the beach, falling into someone's house, out again for food, to a bar, to a club, always together, always moving, always active. The promenade extends all the way to Jaffa now, shiny and new. Tel Aviv never sleeps and nor do they.

Ella looks up from her conversation with Yael and smiles at Udi. He still finds her beautiful, even after four years, though he prefers her just-woken-up self to this made-up version she presents to the world. She wears a low-cut black top over tight blue jeans with just a hint of red escaping above the waistline. Udi knows it is the red thong she wore for him on his birthday. His favourite. He wishes they were alone. Chaim kisses her and Yael hello and Udi watches as Ella smiles with pursed lips in the way that makes everyone who meets her believe there is something even more beautiful behind them, held back. There is. Though it has been a while since he's heard that unbridled giggle he loves.

Ella kisses him discreetly on the cheek and slips her hand into his. She has graciously adapted to his aversion to public affection, though he knows she would like him to sweep her into his arms or lean her backwards like the kisses in the Hollywood rom-coms she forces him to see. He would like to surprise her with this, with some kind of extravagant romance, just once, but he cannot for long enough forget the lessons he has learnt. Lessons of concealment and anonymity. Udi no longer carries a gun or wears his army uniform to meet Ella for snatched hours on too-short leaves, but still he worries that someone will be watching him, and noticing the beautiful girl that he loves enough to lean backwards and kiss.

Ella squeezes his hand and they greet the rest of the group together. Chaim lights another spliff and they pass it around, settling into a circle on the sand until it is decided they'll go to Dov's place. Unlike the rest of them, Dov did not grow up in Ramat Gan. In fact he is nothing like any of them. He windsurfs. And he hardly swears. But they met at a music gig a few years back, shared a spliff, and became firm friends. Through his connections, he gets them free tickets to concerts. And he is the only one with an apartment in Tel Aviv. He is Ashkenazi. At Dov's, a bottle of whisky is opened and poured straight. Ella requests a beer instead and Yael follows suit. They talk about nothing: the movie they went to see last week; the camping trip they're planning to take in the North; the existence of God – all topics to which Udi contributes with willing fervor. But then Avi mentions the bus and suddenly everyone is sitting forward on their seats.

There was a time when Udi would have been just as impassioned as the rest of them, would have argued over Bibi's policies and the Palestinians' tactics, and *what should be done*. Now, he fidgets and taps Ella's hand. She has been sitting quiet too and smiles at the interruption. He signals to the door and together they disappear into Dov's bedroom.

The space is of sparse design, free from the remains of childhood that cling like smoke to the walls of Udi's room, or the flowery flourishes that adorn Ella's. It is not dissimilar in fact to the room in which they first made love at the army base where they had met. Dov's uniform is even thrown over a chair in the corner. He is off to reserve duty the following day. Ella sits on the bed.

"I've missed you this week," she tells him. She has been studying for her Fall exams with a seriousness that has surprised him.

"I've missed you too."

She purses her lips. "How was the interview?"

"I got it."

"That's good," she smiles. "It's more money," she cajoles him when he doesn't agree. "Soon we might be able to rent somewhere."

Still he doesn't say anything.

"I was worried today."

He sits on the bed next to her. "I know. It's okay."

"It's not okay." There is silence. "Weren't you worried about me?"

"Why would I worry? I knew you weren't there."

"I didn't even cross your mind?"

"Of course you did." He backtracks. "I had only just found out when you called."

She shakes her head. "Udi, you never think about me."

"Of course I think about you."

"You don't, Udi."

"I'm thinking about you now." He places his hand on her thigh. Suddenly the red thong is glinting at him.

"Udi, you can't just-"

"I'm thinking about *all* of you."

Her lips are still pursed, but she smiles.

Udi needs no more of an invitation to push her backwards on the bed. He kisses her hard and there is barely a pause before she reaches for the buttons of his shirt. He loves that foreplay no longer has to last more than a minute and unbuckles her belt while she wriggles to help him peel off the tight denim that clings to her thighs. She has shaved her legs – no longer an expectation – and her bra matches the thong. She is dressed for sex. This excites Udi and he drags off the thong, climbing on top of her. She doesn't try to remove Udi's jeans. He pushes them down himself, half way, above the mottled skin. Now she lets him roll her over and he nudges her up onto her knees, pulling her head back gently by her long dark hair. She confessed to him once that this is her favourite position, though she will never volunteer it herself; he is happy to oblige.

When they are finished she lights a cigarette and they share it between them. Ella rests her head on his chest, her dark curls rising and falling with his breath as though anchoring it. His hand is on her smooth, bronzed stomach. With her finger she traces the outline of his own torso until it begins to tickle and he laughs. She tucks her hand beneath him and snuggles closer. She smells of peaches. This is the nearest they ever get to privacy. Ella's parents do not allow Udi to sleep over, and though Ella is officially welcome at his home, he knows his mother doesn't like it when she appears from his bedroom in the morning. Someone in the next room laughs loudly. No one will disturb them here but still they reach for their clothes. Ella adjusts her hair and smoothes down the bed until both are impeccable. Udi reaches underneath the bed for his sandals, and looks as dishevelled as he did before. Casually they return to the sitting room.

Dov is talking now about the new route he has been offered by El Al, better hours, more pay. Everyone is impressed. Chaim clocks Udi and Ella entering.

"Udi has a new job too," Ella announces to the group.

Udi rolls his eyes. "In construction," he explains reluctantly, settling into a chair and making room for Ella who perches next to him on it.

"With management potential though, right?" she adds.

"Sure."

"If you're there long enough, huh Udi?" Chaim chips in.

Ella's eyes flash towards Chaim, and Udi shoots him a warning look, but if he notices he doesn't understand.

"If you're not a British millionaire by then, right?"

"Chaim," Udi grunts, gently shaking his head and flicking his hand as though to brush away the indictment of nonsense.

Ella is staring at him.

"It's nothing," he attempts to say flippantly. But all eyes are upon him. Ella's are practically burning him with their heat.

"It's not nothing, it's big," Chaim encourages. "Ella, it's big, no?"

33

Ella opens her mouth, but no sound comes out.

"So okay, I guess I should tell you all," Udi rushes. He locks his eyes onto Ella. "I'm getting ready to move to London."

***

Ella is determined not to cry, not in front of the group. She nods at them, smiling as Udi fields their questions, pretending she has heard the answers before. He does not stop glancing at her but she refuses to make eye contact. When the lump in her throat pushes higher she swallows it down with a swig of beer.

After what seems like an age, the conversation shifts. She can feel the pull of Udi's eyes but throws herself into a combination of fiddling with her phone and paying intense attention to talk of the evening ahead. She dares not speak. Without her input, they decide to grab a schwarma on the way to a new bar on the beachfront and as they leave the apartment Udi tries to catch her arm, but Ella attaches herself to Dov and Yael, burying herself with their chatter. As they walk, she observes their teasing flirtations, the considerate way they listen to each other talk, the kisses they give each other in public. She does not look back for Udi who is talking to Chaim some metres behind, does not give him the end of her schwarma, and does not wait for him to enter the bar. It is not a desire to punish him, she simply doesn't know what to say. Plus a little punishment wouldn't hurt. Or rather it would, which is the point. She and Yael open their bags for the security guard and walk in at the front with Dov who knows one of the bartenders – a good-looking Russian who waves a greeting and finds them a table by moving some other patrons away. The rest of the group follow, the blare of music and the fog of smoke – despite the ban – absorbing them as one by one they squeeze through the crowd. Ella counts them as they appear. Six… Seven… *What will she say to him?* Seven… Seven…

Udi is not there.

Nobody else seems to have noticed and she doesn't want to ask, but she strains her neck to peer for him through the crowd. He is nowhere. She looks again. She cannot help it.

"Doorman says the place is full." Avi is the last of their group to reach the table. He hovers next to it, hands raised in exasperation. "Udi's still outside."

They all look to her. Ella has to consciously command her legs not to stand. They obey, but her heart wrenches. This is not the first time a bar has turned out to be full when Udi has tried to enter. He is darker than the rest of them and she cannot count the number of evenings that have been ruined this way. Ordinarily she would attempt to bat her eyelids at the offending doorman, and then, later, try to convince Udi that ethnicity is not necessarily the cause, not always, not now. But such obstacles lurk heavily in Udi's blood and claw at him.

They look to her.

Ella remains seated.

Dov stands.

**

The doorman is waving in another group of French men. Two are light-skinned with long, non-wiry, non-black hair. The third is tall, blond, looks as though he should be German. Behind them enter two girls. They are almost as dark as Udi but they have legs to their necks and are wearing skirts that barely cover an inch of them. Udi attempts to breathe. He has tried shouting before, he has even tried punching. Neither are effective. He would not care. He would go home. But Ella is inside.

"What the fuck is your problem?" he asks the doorman for a second time in as composed a tone as he can muster.

"It's full, man," the guy shrugs.

A girl carrying a clipboard and wearing a headset now sidles up to the doorman who points at Udi. She glances up, then contorts her lips, shakes her head, looks elsewhere.

"This is fucking bullshit," Udi says, loudly. The doorman turns towards him and seems to broaden. Udi moves closer and is about to add that the doorman is a piece of shit and the girl is a piece of shit too when from the door behind them Dov appears, and quietly places a charming, light-coloured hand upon the girl's shoulder, and whispers a charming word, and flashes his charming blue eyes. And she looks at Udi again.

***

"So they didn't find his bomb," Dov jokes when some minutes later he and Udi return together. Even today, the group laughs. Udi laughs too, but is unconvincing. There is vulnerability in the strong-set stance of his arms. Ella wants to go to him. He looks at her. She looks away.

Dov goes to the bar and Udi sits down in the empty seat. His neck is slightly hunched, he seems tired, defeated, but he places his hand on Ella's leg and because everyone is watching, she lets him. She doesn't, however, cover his hand with her own as she usually would; she doesn't gently press his cuticles. And now that he is there next to her she finds it is no longer difficult to restrain herself in this way. She is not concerned, but angry. So seethingly angry. The others are asking him questions about London again and she wants to hit him as he reveals that his greatest worry is adjusting to the cold. Dov returns with drinks and Ella sips hard on her schnapps. A new song starts and Yael sings along. Avi notices a girl he used to go out with on the other side of the room and Chaim reminds him that she was crazy, he tells him not to go over. Ella can feel Udi watching her. She won't look at him. The heat of his body is stoking her rage. As soon as she is sure they are not being observed, she removes his palm. Now she is going to get up. She is going to move away. She is going to leave. She is-

Udi reaches for her hand. He fastens his fingers around her own, gripping her, turning her towards him, forcing her to look.

"I want you to come with me," he whispers.

Ella is not sure if she has heard him but there is a flicker in her stomach and she allows him to keep hold of her hands as he leans through the chaos of the bar to say it again.

"I'm still figuring the whole thing out, that's why I didn't tell you, but I want you to come."

She does not answer. The music blares.

"Ella? Did you hear me?"

Silence. Cacophony.

"Ella? Say something."

"Bullshit, Udi."

Ella is a little surprised to find that this is what she says, that after her protracted silence these are the words that spit out of her, but she cannot help them coming in sharpened whispers through the air. And it is right. She should be sharp. She should be strong.

"What?"

"I'll never leave Israel. You don't even talk to me about it and you think I'll come? You are crazy if you think that, if you think I would leave my home, my studies, my life."

"Ella-"

"You are crazy. My whole family is here."

"We could start our own family," he tempts her.

Ella doesn't mean to, but a giggle escapes her mouth.

***

Now

2

Udi cannot delay any longer. The uncertainty is killing him. He kicks through the dusty streets, glaring at tourists who with their cameras collect the ruins and the sleek Bauhaus architecture, and the dust. Late one afternoon on his way to his shift at the bar he finds himself caught up in a teenage tour group. Many summers ago, he kissed an American teenager from just such a group. She was two years older than he was then. He liked her accent, her breasts, her enthusiasm for him. They ate bubble-gum ice-cream on the beach-front and held hands looking out over the port, and ignored the sewage floating just feet away. Now the chatter of these teens charges him with an acute claustrophobia. They jostle. Their hair braided with coloured thread, a couple of the boys sporting fresh tattoos in a Hebrew script they don't understand, one of the girls clearly watching him, her eyes wide and welcoming. He is, he imagines, part of her envisioned escapade. Tensing his arms he attempts to plough through, but the rest of the group are oblivious to all but their adventure together, their false snapshot, and do not disperse. He moves left and then right but they hem him in. A surge of rage rushes up his spine. He will have to speak, to tell them, to do something. But he says nothing.

Udi has not felt this way, this paralysed, since he was six years old smelling falafel. Not amidst the fire of bullets, or the melting of flesh, or the madness of an angry people: familiar terrors, routinely overcome. At the back of his throat, shame mingles with anger and incomprehension. But there is no real surprise to it. What lies before him is simply far more immobilising: he must decide whether or not to wait for Ella.

She has said that she wants to come to London. By giggling, she has tempted him. And in so doing she has both handed him his freedom and tied him tightly, jealously to herself. Because emigrating together has unveiled a whole new set of obstacles. It is not only double the cost, double the time spent deciphering double the application forms, and double the headache, it is the navigation of circumstances entirely different from his own. She is a student, her studies important to her.

"And I can't transfer in the middle of a semester."

"But if we get you a student visa-"

"We should wait until January."

"Wait?"

"What if I don't get a university place in London?"

"You will."

"Would you want me to drop out if I don't? Udi, should I?"

"I don't know."

A sigh. "Then I should wait for the transfer."

"But I cannot wait. Ella, I cannot wait."

"My professors will help."

"When will you talk to them?"

"Tomorrow." "After this paper." "After this presentation."

Her application is stagnant. And he is waiting. But each day he wakes with a pounding headache and knows it is this, this, this constant, unbearable unknowing.

Why is he waiting?

He had been prepared to mourn her. He had been going, he was almost gone.

Even if she manages the transfer, she will only be a student, it will only be temporary.

But temporary is better than nothing.

Screw temporary – with or without her he will not be able to move at all if he can't find proof of a job waiting for him. It is the only section still empty on his own application form.

'*Y'allah*,' he shouts with a flick of his open palm at the still-milling teens. Surprised by his aggression, the girl who had been eyeing him steps aside.

Before his shift begins, from inside the bar's office, Udi decides to call Ben, his British cousin. The two of them have grown up in parallel. Different countries, different cultures, different climates, languages, expectations. But they are the same age and share the same last name so they feel no distinction. Or at least they didn't used to. When they were small they spent whole summers together, Ben's family making their annual trip to Israel and Ben slotting fluidly each time into Udi's life. Mornings were spent in darkened rooms in front of computer games followed by afternoons at the beach, or as they got older, in cafés, by schwarma stalls, at parties talking to girls. Ben used to tell him repeatedly that Israeli girls were the most beautiful girls on Earth and back then this fit easily into Udi's philosophy: Israel was the greatest country on Earth so why shouldn't it be home to the most beautiful girls? He and Ben flirted with them equally, with equal luck.

Since the end of high school however, things have been less equal. The divergence is not enough to stop him calling, but there is a moment of hesitation.

It is 2005. Ben is in his first year of university and has invited Udi to visit. Udi is on leave from the army, a welcome break from a month in Gaza during the long awaited disengagement. For months, blue and orange flags have been flying from car antennas. Half the people he knows are hopeful that it is a step towards peace, the other half think it is a betrayal, and his sister, Avigail, thinks the unilateral mode of the disengagement is a conscious manipulation by the Israeli government, outwardly giving back land while in real terms fating the Palestinians to failure. All Udi knows is that it is shit, it feels shit, he feels shit. It is his first real assignment since his training finished a few months earlier and not what he imagined, not what he has *been* imagining. Making it into one of the army's elite combat units has been his dream since he was 13 years old. Time had passed since he was six and lost in a market; by 13 he had watched *Die Hard* and *Mad Max* and *Mission Impossible*, and decided that hell yeah, he wanted to shoot guns and jump out of planes. And so on his 13th birthday he'd set his alarm for 4am and every day since then he has run hills and done press-ups and readied himself for this. For defending his country, the country that saved his parents. Somebody once told him that if you don't have what to live for then you don't have what to die for, but he did, he had both, he'd thought. And so he'd shined his boots and packed his bag, and carried his heavy gun to Gaza.

He hadn't been naïve. He'd known this was what the training was for – real stuff, real war, real danger. But still…

Ben picks him up from the airport and takes him straight out to a club where they drink vodka and Red Bulls that are two-for-one for students and three-for-one for a mad 20 minutes at midnight. Around them, barely-clothed girls do body-shots, Udi steps in something sticky, and sometime after three they tumble agreeably comatose into Ben's student flat. The following day they consume a fry-up breakfast at two in the afternoon and smoke weed with Ben's four flatmates well into the night. It is a Wednesday, but Ben explains that he has only one lecture that day and it can be missed – they spend most of the next 24 hours high.

The blur of this is a pleasing rest for Udi, he is glad of the film, the hazy edges, the sharp, flashing images softening just a fraction in his mind. He lights another spliff and enjoys the usual sense of edification when talk is laced with weed. He sleeps. He sleeps.

Yet it is a jolt.

The nothingness.

The length and extent of the apathy.

Nobody seems to care. Not about studying. Not about their future, their life plan or lack of it. Nobody talks politics or worries about British defence policy.

One evening, during a brief lull in the partying during which they are consuming seven pizzas between five people, Ben asks, "So how are things over in Y'Is-ra-el?"

But he says it while selecting a computer game from his stash of them, and while his flatmates are ranking girls on a 'Hot or Not' website. And it doesn't feel right to drag them down. To tell them how it felt to prise sobbing, screaming settlers from their homes, or about the marks left on paint by clinging fingernails. It doesn't feel right to describe the surprising sadness of dismantling synagogues, of cracking stained glass. Or how sick he was, how physically sick when he had to dig bodies from graves, bodies too Jewish to remain in Palestinian land. It doesn't feel right, and so he says nothing.

And on his return to the army he says nothing too, not telling Shimon or Tomer how his British cousin wastes his time at university, time they would kill for. Time they do kill for. He talks about the clubs and the girls, but not his cousin by whom, for the first time, he is embarrassed. They are both 18, only 18, but Ben seems so woefully immature.

Udi glances at the phone in his hand and shakes his head. It took years before he had appreciated the beauty of Ben's naivety then: British families send their sons and daughters to university to learn, but also to grant them a few extra years in which to figure out what will come next – a gentle transition to adulthood. Israeli parents send their children straight to the front line. This, he sees now, is the idiosyncrasy. What *he* did back then, not what Ben did. This is the oddity. The injustice. He didn't ask for the heaviness that has been foisted upon him. He didn't agree to the intensity he still cannot shake.

When he was 18 he had not yet even voted. Yet he learned his country's lessons, the too-direct education about the shortness of life and the quickness of death.

In any case, last time he saw Ben, two years ago now, everything had flipped again.

Ben is staying at The Hilton, not on Udi's bedroom floor. His girlfriend is with him. She wears Prada sunglasses and wants to spend most of her day by the pool or shopping at the Kikar, a place mobbed by the French and Russians and where Udi can afford exactly nothing. Ben has been out of university and working now for over three years. Last year he and his older brother, Jonny, opened a restaurant in London and it is doing well. There is talk of expanding into a franchise. Ben speaks of this with the confidence of success. He has a bank manager. And a title. And staff under him. Udi is working for tips in a café.

They go for lunch at a fancy restaurant on a cliff-top. Their conversation is as fluid and joking and probing as ever; but Ben pays – it is, he says, his invitation. Udi allows it only because there is no way he can afford the meal. He feels young next to Ben. Too young and simultaneously too old.

Udi picks up the phone. Things may have changed, but still they stay in touch and think of each other as close cousins.

Ben answers after a single ring. He is with Jonny who shouts myriad swear words down the phone in light-hearted, broken Hebrew. Udi throws some more imaginative ones back and hears Ben and Jonny laughing. The two of them are tight, always have been. They work together with their father and after work spend more time in each other's willing company. Ben has told Jonny about Udi's plans, although Udi has yet to inform his own family.

"So?" Udi asks after they briefly catch up on each other's news. He is attempting to sound not too pushy, or too needy. "Is there anything?"

He will take anything: builder, waiter, gardener, anything. The only requirement is that he can write it down in the accusatory blank space of his immigration form, and that it offers him some kind of wage, some kind of beginning.

"Are you ready to come?" Ben asks plainly.

"You've found something?" Udi does not want to allow too much hope, but finds himself standing up from the desk he has been leaning on.

"How soon can you be here?"

"Ben, have you found me a job?" From outside the office, Udi can hear the swell of a large group entering and his manager shouting for Udi to hurry up.

"How long do you think the application takes?"

"Stop fucking with me you cooney. Did you find something? What is it?"

Ben laughs. "We need a new manager," he says. "At the restaurant. Jonny and I are starting some new projects so we can't be there all the time, and we need someone we can trust. The only thing is," he continues, "we like the manager to be close by in case anything needs attention, so you'll have to stay in the flat above the restaurant. No rent obviously, but that's the deal. And you'll have to drive the company car cos it has our logo on it. What do you think? You okay to drive here?"

As though to provide illustration, the first honks of evening traffic pierce the walls of the bar. In the next room, the volume on the sound system is turned up to its usual deafening level. But inside Udi's head there is an unfamiliar quiet.

"Udi?" probes Ben after Udi is not sure how long.

Still he cannot answer.

"Udi?"

"Get a move on and get your Israeli arse over here!" Jonny shouts abruptly, and Ben laughs, and now finally Udi manages to say okay, okay, yes, and soon the three of them are exchanging insults again and Udi is teaching them how to say 'go screw a goat' in Hebrew.

Ella breathes in as she pulls at the top button of her favourite pair of jeans. They are a size smaller than the rest of the trousers she owns and they pinch when she sits down, but she likes the way they hug her body like a second skin, painting her curves with a thin brush of denim. Udi likes them too and this is why she has rooted them out of the closet. He has phoned to say he is coming over even though she is due at his house in less than an hour for Shabbat dinner. He says he has something to tell her.

Ella's mother is almost more excited than she is and is the one who instructed her to make sure she looks good for this seminal moment. To make sure her nails are painted, her fingers unadorned, ready. Now her mother is pottering around downstairs, pretending to put the finishing touches to the Shabbat meal she is creating but making more trips to the sink underneath the front window than is necessary, conspicuously peering out. Finally Ella hears a door open and her mother's voice rise followed by another at a lower cadence, then Udi's unmistakable lilting footsteps on the stairs. She shakes her dark curls about her shoulders and waits.

He is smiling as he enters. She gets up from the bed and he immerses her in an oversized hug. It has been many months since she's seen such an untainted expression on his face, and she doesn't think he has ever been so voluntarily affectionate. She giggles freely and they kiss. It is as if they both know without speaking the joy that the next few moments will unfold. She wants to savour the anticipation. But he begins.

"Ella, I need to talk to you about something important. Something great." He digs his hand deep inside his jeans pocket, reaching.

"What is it?" She pretends not to know. He grins broadly and she feels her stomach leap in expectation.

"Something we've both been wanting. I've been wanting it for a very long time."

"I have too, Udi. For so long." His brow furrows but she knows he finds it hard to express the true depth of his love. She sits on the bed and waits for him to say it his way. Hesitating, he is nervous, and she feels another giggle pushing its way through her chest. Finally he begins again.

"I'm going."

"What?"

"I'm going, Ella, to London. Ben's found me a job, I've even got somewhere to stay, it's…look." He pulls the immigration form from his pocket and unfolds it carefully before presenting it to her, like a gem. "Look," he urges again. "It's finished. No gaps!"

Ella's mouth feels painfully dry. She can hardly concentrate on what he's saying; she can't grasp it. "But- I don't understand. I thought we were going together."

"We *are* going together. Not at first maybe. Maybe you'll stay here and finish the semester and then join me. But I can finally send off my form." His face is alight. He wants to be congratulated. She wants to be sick. Her jeans are suddenly suffocatingly tight.

"How- When- How can you go without me?"

"Only for a while, Ella. I still want you to come. As soon as your application's ready, you'll come too."

"Bullshit, Udi."

His smile has waned slightly. "Only at first, baby."

For a moment she stares at him in silence. Clutching the bed where she is still perched, she sees the fragility of his enthusiasm, and there is a part of her, even now, that wants to make it solid, wants to shore him up. But, "I don't want to go," she whispers.

"What?" He steps away from her.

"I don't want to go to London, Udi. I don't want to leave Israel. I thought you were going to ask me to marry you."

"But you said-"

"I said that because you promised me a family!" She is no longer whispering. "For fuck's sake Udi. How can you just

46

move to another country without me?! I thought you were about to propose."

"So you've been lying to me all this time? You never wanted to go?"

"Of course I didn't want to! Are you stupid? Why would I want to? Only for you, Udi. I was going to try it for you. But now, again, you don't even think about me. Do you even hear what I'm saying to you: I-thought-you-were-going-to-propose! Don't you care? You never think about me."

"Have you been thinking about me?" he shouts back at her. "Do you care that I want to leave? That I'm going mad here? That my life here is shit?"

"Thanks."

"You know I don't mean-"

"You're so selfish, Udi. You only think of yourself. You think you're the only one whose opinion counts. You are just like your father."

"*Qus!*" He bangs his fist against the wall and a picture of them that he once framed for her smashes to the ground. They both stare at the shattered pieces.

"Udi." She moves towards him. "Udi-"

"Okay," he says, putting his hand up to stop her. "Enough." And slams the door as he leaves.

*****

In the car, Udi stuffs the large, brown envelope he has already addressed, with the form, and drives rebelliously to the post office. It is closed. He had forgotten that it is Shabbat. Udi swears at nobody and slams the car door. Checking his watch and driving furiously back towards his home, he anticipates the inevitable complaints of lateness that will come from his mother, and he pushes the accelerator harder against the floor. Tonight it will matter more than usual. Ari is home. At least it will please her that Ella is no longer joining them.

Udi sighs.

Even now, even at this red-raw moment, he cannot agree with his mother's barely hidden indictment that Ella is not good enough for him. Ella has always been better than he deserves, stronger and more bolstering than others know. She is, during Udi's darkest moments, a reason to hang on for the light. A reason, he considers again, to wait...

He will say she is ill.

And then he will tell his mother about London.

He wonders what Ella is telling her own mother.

It is not his fault. He did nothing to make her think he was going to propose. He shakes his head and concentrates harder than he usually would on the journey ahead.

It will not be long now until he is home. The roads have begun to empty – despite the fact that most of the people Udi knows do not keep Shabbat – and there is only a short line of traffic, a sea of still-angry motorists flicking open palms out of windows. Udi adds his own hand in practiced impatience, but does not append a verbal insult. Soon, even these late-comers will be at home, lighting candles, blessing bread, sharing traditional dinners that older generations cling to and the younger ones pretend not to love. That he pretends not to love. That he doesn't think he'll miss. Brief, inconsequential lulls. Later, the roads will fill up again. With stomachs and souls lined, determined youth will spill back out into clubs and bars and other activities of which the rabbis would never approve. And Udi will be among them. And Udi will be leaving them. And the thought of this sustains him for the length of the protracted journey home.

***

Batia cannot sleep, even after Avigail and Ari have left, and the last of the food has been carefully wrapped and taken home with them, or packed into air-tight containers in the fridge. For a while Oz had been sleepless too, his tossing and turning a comfort to Batia's own restless state, but now he has released her hand from his sleeping palm and she is left with silence, which is no longer any solace at all. Noiselessly she slips out of the thin sheet she likes to wrap around herself at night, despite the heat, and pads barefoot across the bedroom floor. She does not want to wake Oz. He has been working too hard lately and is tired all the time. She worries that one day he will simply dissipate, melted by the sun he refuses to heed, or beaten by the grass he is adamant about mowing on the days when Udi forgets. She tells him to leave it, let it grow a little messy, but she says this only gently. Once you have lived in a tent it is difficult not to treasure those small things that neaten one's life. She opens the door quietly and lets him slumber.

In the kitchen Batia heats up the kettle and sprinkles some tea leaves into a glass ready to be watered and sweetened. She has no idea how many pots of tea she has brewed in her life, she drinks it constantly and as much from habit as desire, but it reminds her of her mother, before she was frail and forgetful of the strength for which she was once renowned. Batia stirs the golden liquid and casts a discerning glance around the dimly lit room. Everything is in order: the washed plates are stacked next to the sink ready to be put away in the morning; the over-used dish-cloth is hanging from the tap to dry out overnight; and the fridge is respectfully adorned with the picture Avigail's daughters drew after dinner. Batia straightens the brightly coloured paper remembering a time when Udi's sketches covered every inch of the metal underneath and she, without savouring them, stuck one on top of another. She removes a shopping list to give this drawing more prominence, and stands back. Only one kitchen object lies out of place to disturb her: a coffee cup still upside down on its saucer in the sink, stained dark by the thick, coagulated contents. All of the others have been washed and put away, but this one is Udi's, made specifically for him.

49

Batia was barely ten years old when she realised she was able to read coffee cups. It is a gift inherited from her mother and one she believes Avigail has a talent for too, if only she would allow herself to embrace it. She doesn't understand why all three of her children fight so hard against their spirituality. Avigail is religious, but only in the rule-keeping sense, and mainly she believes for Ezra. She wears modest clothing and is strictly kosher, but her writing is dominated by secular philosophy learned at university rather than faith learned in the heart. The boys are even more detached. Batia tries now, as much as she can, to re-invoke old customs, to encourage the boys to think about their Judaism, to understand it; but for them, for most people she knows, it is enough to be in Israel, to be a living people in a Jewish land. They have no need to cling to memories of a nation that exists only in the bible, like her family did. No need to practise the rituals that once bound them as descendents of it – a prayer, a hat, a candle in the window – small gestures but enough to distinguish them from their non-Jewish Iraqi hosts. No, her children are Israeli. There is no secret identity beneath the public one, no Diaspora otherness for them to explore and safeguard. To them, ancient practices seem irrelevant and immature. Practicalities are what they talk about, what they care about: the fight to defend the country, the struggle to survive within it. What was their conversation this evening? The Kerry talks, the hopelessness, or not, of them, the benefit, or not, of releasing Palestinian prisoners to get the talks on track. Ari and Oz disgusted; Avigail full of Israel's culpability, visions of peace; and Udi, even Udi, joining the others in crushing such visions. 'They would kill you in a minute,' he'd told his sister, he who barely speaks when the topic is politics, he who is a baby still. 'We need to just extend the fence and not speak to each other for 50 years.' Practicalities. Pragmatism. Politics. Batia fears that something has been lost in this, this abandonment of spirituality, this neglect of religious pursuit. There is much to gain from using one's imagination as well

as one's rationale. There is so much more one can know.
There is a lot that even one upturned coffee cup can tell her.
She moves over to it now.

The first time Batia grasped the truth of her own
interpretations was just before she left Iraq. Until then she
had been making vague prophecies from the random shapes
in the cups of friends who would place their saucer over
their finished coffees and give her the leftover grinds to read:
prosperity, she predicted, when she saw a ladder leading to
coins; good news in the wings of a bird in flight; obstacles
foreseen by a coffee-coloured mountain. Her mother used
to listen carefully and nod at her interpretations, but it was
only when she read her mother's own cup that she first
became certain of her accuracy. In it, she saw a tent which
she interpreted as travel, an upside down baby for a birth that
will take a while to appear, and a raven – a symbol of death
leading to new beginnings. Batia had whispered this last
foretelling, not wanting to tell it. And this time her mother
had closed her eyes as she nodded, for a long minute holding
them shut as though preparing for what she would see when
she opened them again. Within three weeks, her husband,
Batia's father, had been arrested and hanged. A fortnight later
each of them packed a single bag and fled by foot to Israel.
And by the time they were in the camp and Batia's mother
discovered she was pregnant, none of them were surprised.

For a while after that, Batia had refused to read the cups
again, but slowly she grew used to the gift she possessed
and she became comfortable enough to look deep inside the
imagery. It has been years however since she has read the
cups of either of her sons. Ari refuses to let her; he doesn't
want to know what is destined to happen during his next stint
in the army. Udi has simply not asked. But Batia wants to
know what is in store for him, what might happen in London,
what tragedy might come from his decision to leave. She
knows it is wrong for him. She is sure of it. Avigail agrees.
Yet she cannot look at the cup and stands paralysed, almost

more afraid that she will see a journey leading to a new life filled with joy in a place far from her, than a disaster that brings him rushing back. Quickly she turns on the tap and runs the coffee cup under the water that bursts powerfully through the evening heat.

It is almost an hour before she returns to bed, but this is only the beginning of an insomnia that plagues her for weeks. She tries everything to rid herself of it: hot baths, lighter meals, calming oils. She even puts on some old Arabic music that Oz complains is too disturbing to his own sleep and switches off. Nothing however is loud enough or strong enough.

Udi has begun to make preparations in earnest. He has not yet heard back from the immigration office and worries that his application will be turned down, but still he is on the phone every day to Ben, making arrangements. He does this in their company now. He must have been hiding for many weeks. Hiding under her nose. Oz asks him how things are coming along and she can see Udi basking under the approval of his father, his chest broadening. But she cannot believe that Oz has let her down, that this moment should be the time he has chosen not to put Udi straight. 'It is good you want to make a success of yourself,' he told him. 'Go fast and come back fast. And then buy your house. And then maybe get married, yes?' He doesn't understand the danger. He won't believe that Udi would ever leave Israel for good. It makes the dialogues between he and Udi impossible for Batia to bear and while they talk she retreats to the garden where she waters the neatly cut grass with her tears.

"What about Ella?" is all she herself can manage to ask Udi, as many times as she feels he will stand.

One Friday, Avigail remarks that she looks tired. Or perhaps she is ill? She feels ill. With every passing day the dread in the pit of her stomach grows a little, consuming her, consuming time, which contracts as the moment to mourn her son approaches. In preparation, she begins to wear black.

She tries not to look forward each morning to the moment that he emerges from his bedroom into the kitchen where she waits. She experiments with not buying Coke – he is the only one in their house that drinks it. One afternoon, she does not call him to ask what time he'll be home. Then one Sunday, there is a letter. It arrives unencumbered on the top of a small bundle so the horror strikes her as soon as the postman, who she has taken to waiting for, delivers it into her hands. Seeing the official typed envelope amidst the pile of bills, she knows at once. Or, she thinks she knows. Because in fact, as she inspects it more closely, she realises that it can't be from the British immigration office after all, for she has seen this kind of envelope before, many times, and each occasion has been accompanied by this same, familiar dread.

She will have at least a few more months with her son. Batia's hands shake, but for the first time ever she carries this letter to Udi's desk without the feeling that with it she is delivering his death warrant. The envelope feels lighter than usual, like it contains life. And that evening, Batia sleeps.

***

Now

3

I don't know, is it weird to think about this right after fucking Sara? Sorry, having sex with. It's not making love is it, we've only just got together, but as always I can hear Mum and Gaby in my head. Anyway, this is the random event I am thinking about while also hoping these aren't the sheets with the chocolate stain and listening to Sara breathe...

It was, I think, the first term of my second year at senior school. So I was 12. Definitely still 12 since I distinctly had not yet had my barmitzvah. If I had then I would already have kissed Nicole Blatter and entered into a profound six week relationship and may have told her instead of my father. As it was, on the day that Mr Pike made me dress and undress continually for the entire length of a lunch break because I'd been too slow, again, at getting dressed after football, I stormed from the coach stop into the house, and then told the tale to my father. It was pre-Internet, pre-email, but he worked from home three afternoons, his office stacked with A4 binders, his desk littered with highlighters and perfectly sharpened pencils with rubbers on the end.

"He didn't even give me a warning. Just straight away gave me the lunch detention."

My gripe, I clearly remember, was the unfairness, omitting then from my own consciousness the fact I recall now, which is that Mr Pike had told me to hurry every week for the entire term. Although, I never actually tried to be slow. Rather I couldn't fathom how some boys didn't seem to mind not drying between their toes after a shower even though everybody knew that's how you picked up verrucas. Which is what I told Mr Pike.

"What exactly did he say to you, Daniel?" my father asked, putting down a stack of papers. My father even now has a way of speaking that bestows the most serious of conversations with a sprinkling of humour and the lightest exchanges with a dash of gravitas. He was wearing MC Hammer-style trousers that we had absolutely banned him from sporting in public but he insisted upon at home, believing himself to be the epitome of cool. Or maybe not caring that he wasn't. He pushed his glasses higher up his nose.

"I dunno. Something about all of us being spoiled and he doesn't care if we are 10 per cent off we can get ready 10 per cent faster."

"What?"

"And then he just fired the detention at me. And Dad, literally the whole lunch break I just had to get dressed, get undressed, get dressed. Ridiculous."

"Right," said Dad. "Right."

The following morning my father walked with me up the path to the school. Since we were usually late (my mother busy dropping Gaby at her girls' school 20 minutes in the opposite direction and Dad and I thus left to our own devices), I consented each morning to a ritual we'd had going since prep: I would walk ten metres or so, turn around, wave to Dad who was still in the car at the bottom of the path, see Dad wave back, walk again, turn, wave…and keep doing this until I'd rounded the corner at which point I had to sprint the rest of the way since the whole production clearly added to my lateness. Dad is probably entirely unaware that I still do this: I look back for his waving arm, I stop at least twice on my way to my car. I don't even care if passersby see. Back then of course I would have cared, but since we were so late, nobody else was around to bear witness, and my reputation was safe. Following one's Dad into the actual school building, through the halls and to the staff room, is a different matter altogether.

Luckily, it turned out that my father is a legend. Actually. Not just to me. He's tall, genuinely, not just for a Jew, and back then his hair was still jet black, his frame not exactly muscular but badminton-strong. Mr Pike barely resisted when Dad yanked him up from his seat and just centimetres from his face told him that if he was going to perve on children he better do it somewhere else and if he ever EVER heard of him harassing his son again, he'd be slapped with a lawsuit for racial discrimination as well as abuse and he didn't care if Pike did have a fetish for circumcised penises, he'd better stay away from mine. He followed this of course with a formal letter to the headmaster – which, let's be honest, Dad was far better at than physical violence should it have come to this – and I'm sure subsequent correspondence followed; but that day my father went down in school history. It was revealed to me that he did, sometimes, shout, and all of us in Year 8 learned the meaning of '10 per cent off'.

So, is it strange to remember this after having sex with Sara?

She is breathing heavily. I actually hadn't thought she would stay but we've been flirting casually for a couple of weeks – ignoring the fact that when we were 15 I went out with her best friend – and, well I wasn't going to say no.

Sara is no stranger to 10 per cent off. Approximately 30 per cent of my school year were 10 per cent off and Sara has been out with approximately 15 per cent of them. She was part of the 'yeah you' crowd too. We, the cool Jews – not the geeks or the introverts or the religious, or in hindsight the better occupied – drawn from North West London's vast array of private schools, and of course the Jewish Free School. With gelled hair and bomber jackets we gathered as 13 year olds on Saturday evenings outside Edgware Station, then at 15 with curtain cuts by the all-night bagel joint in Golders Green before graduating in our later teens to Hampstead Maccy D's. 'How 'you?' Air kiss. 'Yeah, you?' We were too cool and there were too many people to greet, apparently, to utter a properly punctuated salutation. Anyway, since there were 100 boys in my year, but for a while we didn't do much below the waistline, and in later years our relationships began to last, I reckon that Sara has seen two and a half circumcised penises that I am familiar with.

"What's the time?" she whispers.

It is four in the morning. Sara turns away drowsily. We collapsed into bed for the first time two hours ago, but I can't sleep.

Maybe it's my mother. How Freudian would that be? But she probably has no idea that I still do this nightly, this trick she taught me, that I can't sleep, apparently, if I don't. 'Imagine each person you're worrying about in a space-suit,' she told me; me aged eight, reading novels too adult for me, watching *The X-Files*, listening to my parents talk about the IRA; she sitting patiently at the end of my bed, holding my foot in the dark. 'Do up all the zips. Put on the gloves, the boots, the helmet. Okay? They all in? Good. Now visualise each person smiling at you, waving. They're safe. Nothing's going to happen to them. The suit will protect them. The power of the mind, Dan, is an amazing thing.' It became habit. Like counting sheep. Ignoring Sara's breathing, I try now to put everyone into their astronaut suits. There is Gaby, her helmet is on, she waves. Check. Next, Dad. Check. Now my mother. I can't quite visualise it. She will not wave. She furrows her brow, gives me that look, the one that tells me she's on to me.

I turn back towards Sara and caress her bottom, hoping she won't mind being woken. Hayley did sometimes. She'd hit my hand away and pull the cover tighter under her. Sara stirs, smiles.

There hasn't been anyone I've been really into since Hayley. We broke up almost three years ago now, but eight years with one girl will do that to you, I guess.

Sara turns to face me. This has the disadvantage of removing her bottom from view, and introducing middle-of-the-night breath. The smell of hers makes me suddenly paranoid about my own and I close my mouth.

I'd thought for a while that I would marry Hayley.

I haven't actually articulated this to anybody, not even her, but I suppose really it was never because of a passionate, uncontrollable need to. Rather, we'd been together since school, we were getting to that age and I couldn't think of a reason why not. Apart from getting dumped, of course. Which I hadn't anticipated. Nor the impact with which that would hit me in the gut. She'd been there through my boyhood. She was the only person I'd slept with. Her rejection felt like a reproof – of who I was, of everything I'd become, forgetting she'd had a hand in shaping me. There have been a stream of weddings ever since where we bump into each other. Of course she never fails to look gorgeous, and assured, despite no longer sitting at the couples tables where we used to feel smug and sorted, but with singles cobbled together, taking sips from the wine that's passed around to us only, the unattached, the unloved, to bestow luck that we will marry next. *Please God by you*. Clearly a custom invented by some enterprising Yenta. Next, as it happens, will be my flatmate Robert. And I'll have to arrange the stag in some Eastern European destination. I'll do it with appropriate gusto, obviously, I mean it's Robert, but in truth I'm getting a little bored of these dos. They are condensed versions of what, I think, is the problem, my problem: irrelevance, routine, excess.

I give Sara's breasts a squeeze, since they are there, and accept her kiss. Attempting not to breathe on her as I do so.

I know a lot of it's down to my own choices. One of my uni friends works for the UN in Tanzania and posts Facebook pictures of himself on what seems like permanent safari. I wonder why I never considered a career like that. I think sometimes that I would have enjoyed living amongst expats and elephants. But not mosquitoes. I wouldn't be good with mosquitoes. Besides, I've always wanted to be a banker. God knows why. I took the right A Levels, did the right degree, and spent enough summers doing the right internships. Now, I'm damn good. Mum of course boasts for me – *my son the banker* – irking the friends whose kids turned out to be not as high flying as their A*s once suggested. Though of course it's never too late to be a doctor, Mum likes to remind me. She's joking, I know. She wouldn't have cared what career I'd chosen so long as I was happy. Dad too. They're supportive, I'm lucky. In fact, I'm lucky in everything, always have been. And grateful for that. My life is nicely padded, nicely, nice. So why, why, why am I not, actually, happy? In spite of everything, there is dampness where fire should be.

Sara's hand has moved downwards.

I look at her and feel a pang of guilt. There's nothing wrong with Sara. She's pretty. She's smart. She's Jewish. But she is, like the rest – like the rest, given away by that first twang of her slightly affected, slightly imperious North London accent. Though actually, there is a little less confidence in some of the girls these days; as 26 has given way to 27, then 28, the desperation to snag a Jewish man before they're all taken has become more urgent, less easily concealed.

Sara reaches for another condom.

Not that I don't enjoy confidence. I do. It's just that they are all so similarly confident. Similarly... similar. Or else they are unavailable, or I've dated and rejected them in the past, or they have rejected me.

Taking the condom from Sara, I put it on swiftly.

"Are you sure?" I whisper. She told me she wasn't looking for a relationship, she was bold about it, but aren't all girls, really? Is it fair to pretend I don't realise this? That I haven't benefited from the insights of having a sister? Is it fair to wake her up at 4am for a second round when I have no intention of calling? I'll definitely make her breakfast. And book her a cab. Sara smiles and pulls me towards her.

Of course there is Safia. Safia. Intelligent, feisty, beautiful in a way that even after all this time surprises me, and elegantly spoken – a mixture of St John's Wood and Tehran – from underneath a dark fringe that covers half of one eye and that she continually hooks behind her left ear. We've been friends since our first year at Warwick but as far as romance goes, she isn't Jewish – worse, she's Muslim – so there has never been a point. For her as much as for me. Plus until a few years ago I was with Hayley. In any case I couldn't do that to my parents. Not again. Gaby has just gotten engaged to a non-Jewish guy and it's killing them.

Sara's hair tumbles over her breasts in dark curls.

Safia's hair is dark too.

I'll shower after this. Mr Pike isn't here so there'll be time to dry between my toes.

***

For some reason I can't stop thinking about that year – the year I became a man. It's wrapped in a strong smell of leather and old books on account of the unprecedented amount of time we spent in synagogue; barmitzvah boys must attend every Saturday, *every Saturday, Dan*. Dad would often sneak off to the loos mid-service, loosen his tie, break out a novel, ostensibly not-pray, and once slip into the room laid out for kiddush and pilfer a fishball. But I have a memory of one Saturday, post shul, being in a field somewhere with him – I think it must have been the park, or maybe at school after a cricket match – and the two of us sharing a warm Coke while we pored over my portion, which I'd taken to carrying around with me in the weeks preceding The Big Day. It's actually pretty hard work learning a Torah portion. First you have to decipher the Hebrew letters fast enough to read them without sounding like ET, then you have to learn the tune, and then you have to sing that tune with your non-choirtastic voice to everyone you know including all the girls you're hoping to get off with at the party the next day. When I see barmitzvah boys being called up now, I still feel such empathy. Gaby, of course, being a girl and not having had her own portion when she was 13, learnt mine in half the time it took me and while I was practising, yelled corrections from her room down the hall. One afternoon this led to an all-out physical fight. But on the day of my barmitzvah I kept catching sight of her up in the ladies' gallery, and even though she was with a gaggle of friends too adult to be much interested in 13-year-olds, she didn't take her eyes off me. Her smile didn't waver for the entire portion, even when I hesitated on the second verse and turned bright red, and though she later scoffed at the idea, I'm pretty sure that there was a moment when she cried.

It was also Gaby who, a few days later, guided me through phone protocol with Nicole Blatter during that crucial week after the first kiss.

I have never kissed Safia. It's worth clarifying because a lot of people who see us together presume we have, presume we're a couple, increasingly so in the years since Hayley. It isn't unusual for me to rest my head against her like this. We sink comfortably into the worn leather of the sofa at our favourite café. There is only one such sofa, the rest of the room dotted with wooden chairs around long, sharing tables, but this Sunday we have scored it. Safia playfully flicks my head off her and leans forward to turn the page of my *Observer*. I raise an eye in mock irritation.

"Too slow," she shrugs into her coffee.

I take a sip of my own: milky and sweet, two sugars. Safia's is a more mature black. We have long since finished dissecting each other's week, I have re-told the tale of Mr Pike, and we have slipped now into easy silence. A slightly wavy tendril of hair has escaped the bunch scooped onto the top of Safia's head and is now caressing the nape of her neck.

I'm going to tell her. I've been thinking about it for months but with the beginning of autumn there's been a new imperative. There is something about the remembered smell of freshly sharpened pencils and newly laminated exercise books that renders autumn, the period of nature's demolition, for me prime pickings for new beginnings. I have to tell somebody to make it real, to make it happen. And it was always going to be Safia. It's about completeness, I'll tell her. About feeling whole, and part of something, important to something.

She glances up and catches my stare. With uncanny muscle control she upturns first one corner of her mouth and then one eyebrow into a familiar question mark. I look back to the paper laid out between us onto which we are dropping crumbs of banana bread. It's not like she's my girlfriend, but I know her blessing will be the hardest. Mostly because my hankering is not for New York or Singapore or Sydney or somewhere else easy to explain, but for a place I know she'll never understand, never condone, never feel for as I do. I train my eyes to the words on the page: *Disaster of scrapping HS2 rail link*, reads the headline. We both skim, then without consultation turn the page. *Peers plot to revive plain cigarette pack law*. Safia is a reformed smoker. We read the whole piece then spend a moment rating the collage of models' off-duty style at Paris fashion week adorning the page opposite. Safia is not mean with her critique, just funny. She could be an off-duty model. I turn the page again. *Israeli run shop divides Brighton*. Safia's breath changes, almost imperceptibly. Underneath the headline there is an article about a small Brighton store selling ethical products – such as soda from a tap into customers' own bottles – that has unwittingly become the site for anti-Israel demonstrations. The company's factory, apparently, is located in a settlement on the West Bank. I'd like to read the rest of the article, not just because of what I'm about to announce to Safia. But I don't feel like a debate.

Safia turns the page.

In the end I don't say anything. The sofa is too comfortable. And there is either everything or nothing more to say.

***

I used to wonder whether everybody behaves differently outside of their all-consuming work microcosm, or just me. Of course I know I'm still me, Daniel, but at work I'm a different me, a louder, cockier, sharper version. Am I putting it on? Am I that false? Or perhaps it's real, perhaps the bank brings out the full Daniel Incarnate, harnessed at home by things like parents who remember me crying when I discovered where beef came from, and a sister who used to dress me in her tutu. Or maybe there isn't a solid, tangible 'me' at all. At the bank, socialising takes place at bars and clubs where wives and girlfriends aren't welcome or invited so I've never seen any of my colleagues in the context of their families. I haven't seen if they've been able to find a workable way to split the paradoxical pieces of their souls. I worry that there isn't a way. I worry that sleeping with the secretary isn't what my mother expects of me. And that there's something more important than the size of my bonus. And that no matter how quickly I am promoted I will never be as successful as my father who made his fortune from nothing, or as worthy as my grandparents who Survived. And that in my attempts to staple all the scattered fragments of myself together, I will never truly see the 'me' that others see or know what that means or who I am or why it is that something is missing.

It's not that this quandary disappears in Israel. The longest I've ever stayed there is for a month and that was when I was 16. But there's something about the dry, dusty heat that gets under my skin. There's something about the history of the geography. There's just a whiff of, something, that makes me feel centred, and connected, and different and –

63

There's a dream I keep having. Some of it really happened but I've had the same dream so many times now that I can't quite pick real from imagined. It's nothing special, just me sitting on Rothschild Boulevard outside a café. The same kind of café that has flashed across news networks in previous years, devastated by a bomb. (Or rather bomb-*er*. Sorry, I've watched too much BBC and am removing the actor.) But there I am. Across the road are a group of fledgling soldiers decked out in olive green. To my left are French people, to my right Russians, the waiter is from Brazil. They speak in Hebrew and in their various languages and at fast fever pitch. And I, somehow, understand everything. Just sipping at my perfect upside down cappuccino. Not speaking myself but intuiting that something important is on the tip of my tongue. And I just feel this sense of getting it. It's exciting, that feeling.

At the end of August I have this dream three times in one week.

As usual however a flurry of work means that there is no space to dissect any of it, and by the time I have another opportunity to breathe I have still not told Safia, or anybody, about Israel; it is thus no more real than my fantasies of taking up surfing, it is September, I'm back in my parents' house helping my mother lay the table for the first night of Rosh Hashanah, and lazing around in the rooms I grew up in making resolutions for another New Year.

My favourite part of Rosh Hashanah is my mother's honey cake. Mum – hair blow-dried to perfection and wearing heels instead of her usual indoor-Uggs – catches me peeking under the silver-foiled shell and slaps my hand away, directing me instead towards the dishes of fishballs, pickles, egg and onion, chopped liver, and olives, dotted everywhere about the room despite the fact that only four of us are coming. Most years the house is full by this point in the evening – grandparents, cousins, wives and husbands of cousins, a kid or two and a stray friend whose family are spending the festival in Israel. But this year, for one reason or another they are not attending.

Also not attending – or rather, not invited – is Gaby's fiancé Pete. For the previous two years he has politely taken part; wearing a yamaka during the blessings, dipping apple into honey, and commenting more than once on the deliciousness of Mum's cuisine. But those were in the days when Mum and Dad believed they were merely tolerating another of Gaby's phases, like piercing her bellybutton. When Pete was this year officially not invited, Gaby suggested that perhaps Mum would be happier if her flagrant daughter was missing from dinner too. Mum promptly spent the next three hours alternating between raging and crying and in the end, Dad persuaded Gaby to change her mind. But she has not yet arrived. Even as Dad returns from work, late, and dodges Mum in the kitchen, she is yet to be seen.

Dad dashes upstairs for a quick change before unloading himself into the chair next to mine. He has been less frantic about the whole affair than Mum who calls every morning just as I'm stepping on the train to work, urging me – for the entire length of my journey until I go underground – to reason with Gaby; but even he, between mouthfuls of fishballs, emits an air of desperation.

Dad's hair is these days a rainbow of thick, untameable and uncoordinated greys. To complete the effect he has this evening adorned his head with a bright purple yamaka he got from Mum's friend Elaine's grandson's bris. And jazz shoes that he swears are slippers. It is hard not to smile at the ensemble. Dad grins and leans over me to reach for a pickle.

"Have you spoken to Gaby?" he whispers.

"Not today." We are talking quietly so as not to agitate Mum further. "She'll be here though."

Dad nods. "I know Mum's being a bit extreme Dan, but look, there are real practicalities. I mean, if they have a son, will he have the snip?" Dad mimes. "You don't know. Pete might want him to look like him."

"Is Pete not 'snipped' then?" I laugh, noticing how frequently I have thought recently about the status of penises. "I can't say I've been looking."

"You know you do look though," Dad says, unintentionally waving a pickle as he talks. "When you're a kid at least, at school, you look. Richard Zelden: huge. Barry Gardiner: a little wonky."

"Dad!"

"Won't he wonder why he's not like his friends?"

"You're assuming his friends will be Jewish."

Dad lifts his hand to respond but then takes a bite of the pickle.

When we were kids, I hated pickles but loved olives. Gaby the reverse. There was always a selection of them and nuts too at the Wednesday night meetings Dad took us to. He was a founding member of a cross-cultural London dialogue group and, as young teens, he would drag us along with him to listen to a local Imam or Vicar, until demands of GCSEs and A levels granted us Mum's backing to stay at home, which I did while Gaby continued to join Dad out of choice. When he stepped down last year, Gaby took over his role. Perhaps this is why he speaks now like a man clutching desperately to a stream of water escaping from a tap that he himself turned on.

"You know I don't care if my hypothetical first grandchild's friends are Jews, or gentiles, or the sons of storm-troopers. But will he know what being Jewish means?"

"*I* don't know what it means. You're Jewish because you're Jewish, that's it. Don't worry, if there's another Holocaust, Gaby's kids will be just as high up on the list of people to chuck into the gas chamber."

"Daniel-"

"You know what I mean. I'm just saying, Gaby's Jewish so her kids will be Jewish."

"They'll be Jew-*ish*."

66

"Actually," says Gaby. "I've already put my non-existent offspring's names down for a place at a nunnery." Gaby has appeared at the door. "Hi family," she sings in falsetto.

The thing is, Gaby is a collector. She collected Sylvanian Families way past the age it was socially acceptable to do so under the pretence that she was playing with me. She discovered Holocaust literature aged 14 and spent the following six months reading everything from *I Am David* to *Schindler's List* before moving on to a fascination with, I think, all things Russian. At Oxford she studied Politics, Philosophy and Economics and she collected ideas, giving us a sample over the dinner table as she moved swiftly from socialism to liberalism and finally landed as a signed up member of the Conservative party. But she is a hoarder too. Her Sylvanians are still intact in a box under the bed in her old room, her bookshelves are lined two books deep, and although she swears it is irrelevant to her whether her husband is Jewish, she forgets that the summer of my barmitzvah she signed herself up to a Chabad Lubavitch camp and declared herself Shomer Shabbos.

"*Chag Sameach*," says Dad, standing up in his jazz shoes to kiss her.

Mum appears from the kitchen with a glass of wine and hands it to her as though the liquid is made not of grapes, but olives.

"So..." I venture, with exaggerated inflection. "How's Pete?"

Half an hour later we have somehow managed without argument to sit ourselves around the dining table in the places we've spent years cultivating. I have visions of Gaby opposite me in her green school uniform. She wore her hair in a ponytail tied with a dark green scrunchie for three years straight before she suddenly cut in a side-parted fringe with the kitchen scissors and brightened it with Sun-In. Despite Mum's outrage, she persuaded me the same day to bleach just the tips of my own spiky do. In hindsight, I looked like a skunk, but back then I thought it was coolness personified. My school didn't agree and suspended me until I cut or dyed it, and Mum blamed the whole thing on Gaby who was older and should therefore have known better. But she also booked Gaby in for an appointment at the hairdresser and allowed her to have her hair properly highlighted. This marked the beginning of an obsession with hair colour and opened the door for myriad discussions between the two of them as well as justifying the tandem religious study of *Vogue*.

Now Gaby and Mum speak to each other only to ask for the passage of potatoes or other such foodstuffs. That is until Dad begins a clever 'what's-going-on-in-Dan's-life' diversion tactic and neither of them can resist. Dad kicks off with questions about work but Mum wants updates on my friends, the boys who used to come for play-dates, then sleepovers, then crash three to a couch after a night clubbing; it isn't apparent but my mother is actually far more relaxed than most, very much of the 'better at home where we can see than God-knows-where' variety. "What about that clever one who used to wet the bed?" she says, "And what ever happened to Toby? You know the one, he was very tall, good-looking thing. What happened to him?"

"Tony, Mum. He's called Tony."

"So who are you dating?" interrupts Gaby.

"Nobody."

"Anyone you fancy?"

"No."

"Geez, Hayley did a real number on you." Gaby raises her eyebrows. "Are you at least sleeping with somebody?"

Dad grins.

"Perhaps he's waiting to find a good match," Mum intercedes, taking a mouthful of roast chicken.

"Well I wondered how long that would take," smiles Gaby.

"What?"

"For you to turn passive aggression into a more honest attack."

"I don't think-" Dad begins.

"It's not an attack. It's nothing to do with you, Gaby. There are other people in this family to think of besides yourself you know."

"There you go again. You think just because I won't do what you want that I'm not thinking about you."

"Actually," I say. "I thought maybe I'd meet a girl in Israel."

This isn't the exact manner in which I'd intended to tell my family about Israel; it doesn't have the careful, gentle introduction, the preamble of ponderings, my intangible feelings of yearning, and I still haven't tested the idea on Safia. But for some reason I find myself thinking about the time when I was 17 and got bottled in a club, and Gaby was the one to take me to the hospital and confirm my ridiculous story about a sharp-cornered table and a loose bit of carpet.

"When are you going to Israel?" asks Gaby, taking a deep breath and with obvious effort turning her attention away from Mum. "Weren't you just there in the summer?"

"I'm going again in a few weeks for a friend's wedding."

"So you're giving yourself the length of a wedding reception to find your wife?"

"At least he'll know she's Jewish," Mum mumbles.

Gaby throws her napkin onto the table.

"Well maybe a bit longer than that. Actually, I wanted to talk to all of you properly, because I've been thinking about Israel a lot lately…"

Gaby places her napkin back onto her lap and reaches for another slice of challah.

Dad absent-mindedly tops up his wine.

Mum waits. She has that on-to-me look.

"Not because of this wedding. More… Well, I've been thinking that I might actually try living there for a while, or, actually, maybe even move there, make aliyah."

"Are you absolutely mad?" Gaby's napkin has again landed on her plate, half of it swimming in gravy. "Do you want to get blown up?"

"Gaby-"

"Israel is under attack Dan, constantly."

"Not in Tel Aviv-"

"And you're still army age. You'd have to go to the army for God's sake. What are you going to do, *talk* Hamas to death? You've got to be joking."

"He's joking," Dad laughs. "Can you see Mr Banker here giving up his flash career? I don't think so."

They all laugh nervously.

"Guys, I'm serious."

"Oh my God." Mum gets up and starts collecting the plates from the table, as if by cleaning the scene she will be able to erase the truth of it.

"Mum-"

"You're not moving to Israel, Daniel. Don't be so stupid."

I look around the table but nobody contradicts her. "I get that you'll miss me, I'll miss you too, but-"

"It's nothing to do with missing you," says Mum. "It's where you're moving to. Is your brain in your arse?"

"Mum!" I can't help but laugh. "Seriously? You were there yourself last year. And you know about ten different people who've made aliyah. Rachel Fleischman's daughter. The Wolfsons. Your second, third, whatever he is cousin. Tony's there, Mum! You know, tall, good-looking thing."

"Israel is the ghettoisation of the Jewish people," Mum explodes. "You've been raised in a multicultural world Daniel. Why do you want to cut yourself off from that, for the sake of what?"

"Exactly," Gaby tells her.

"Oh you can shut up," Mum screams. "What's wrong with this family? I don't know what's worse, my daughter marrying out or my son going frum!"

"He's not going frum," Dad interjects. "You're not, are you Dan?"

I shake my head, thinking of my friend Josh who has not moved to Israel but to Hendon where, eight years ago, he shed his old school friends and love of Big Macs in favour of yeshiva, a black hat, and a 19-year-old wife with whom, allegedly, he has sex through a sheet.

"Then why the hell do you want to move?" says Dad. Lightness and gravitas.

"Because I like Israel. I like how I feel there."

"I like how I feel in New York!"

"I like how I think there. How I-"

"Here's dessert," Mum declares, slamming the honey cake onto the table. She has removed her heels and storms in stockinged feet out of the room. The stairs thump one by one beneath her. Her bedroom door slams, loudly. It used to be Gaby and me who made such exits.

Slowly, Gaby stands up and follows her.

Dad shakes his head, but says nothing. We listen for the bedroom door opening again and then closing.

After a few minutes we each take a slice of cake.

It is meant to symbolise a sweet new year.

***

The festivals come too close together and in the wrong order.

I have never been able to understand why Yom Kippur – the Day of Atonement – comes a week *after* Rosh Hashanah, Jewish new year. Surely it would be better to atone for one's sins before the fresh zeal of resolution?

And all three of my annual shul visits landing within the same autumn week? My first year at Warwick this meant me returning home two days into Freshers'. When I was 15, I missed the semi-finals of my local tennis club tournament and Guy Johnson (who I'd beaten every other time we played) got a walk-over. Now, I have to explain to my colleagues why I – a non-yamaka-wearing employee – suddenly need a succession of days off for religious reasons. It marks me as different, and a type of person I'm not sure I am.

I try nevertheless, sitting in the uncomfortable wooden pew, to concentrate on the sermon the rabbi is giving. It has been 19 hours since anything has passed my lips (except for toothpaste, though strictly that is forbidden too). I know the idea behind the fast is to help me concentrate on praying without the distractions of life's food-oriented timetable, and also to afflict myself; but I can't help but feel that if I had just a small bagel I'd be able to furnish my repentance with a far greater level of fervour.

Or some spring rolls with soy sauce.

It's the only time of year we actually walk to shul, the rest of the time cheating by driving the short distance and parking around the corner for shame of being seen. But it's as though my favourite Chinese restaurant knows I'm going to be passing and intentionally sprays out volumes of spring roll scent.

Despite the unusually balmy September weather, my hands are cold. I've only just come back inside and underestimated the need for a coat at the beginning of my shift. This is the sixth year that I've been doing security for the shul. Checking coats, bags, tickets, keeping an eye on passing vehicles, on passing people, on thrown words. I described the organisation of Jewish security once to some uni friends who couldn't believe such a thing existed. *It's not like you're in Nazi Germany*, they say. It is true that thus far I have seen no violence and only been called a Yid once.

I blow on my fingers to warm them up and attempt to catch up with the sermon. The rabbi is talking about the responsibility of Jews as citizens of the world, how those of us gathered, we who know what it is both to be attacked and discriminated against, we particularly must stand up and reach out to heal the fractures that divide. It is a time, he says, to reflect, to repent, to make peace with first ourselves and then others. I feel my neck get hot the way it used to if I was told off in school assembly, singled out. I think of Sara, whose last text I still haven't replied to. Then of Mum and Dad and Gaby. But then I realise that the rabbi has not noticed my late arrival and is not actually talking about the divisions I personally have caused. He mentions Egypt, Syria. There are murmurs of agreement, but then the rabbi switches to Hebrew and only the most learned understand the text he reads. Like most, I push my finger along the page of my prayer book, managing to recall the Hebrew letters I finally mastered for my barmitzvah, and join in at most of the moments in which participation from the congregation is required. Not having a clue what the words actually mean.

The men in front of me sit down so Dad and I follow suit. Now there is silence, a pause reserved for personal prayer, for inward-looking. I exhale, a little too loudly. I often find myself exhaling when I'm home in Mill Hill, not just now in synagogue. It is only a short drive from West Hampstead but far enough North for urban sprawl to give way to the odd green pasture, to space. I breathe again. Actually, I suppose it's more a simultaneous exhalation and inhalation, at once swapping the proximity of people for the proximity of memory, and familiarity. My dentist is three rows in front of me. To my left is the father of Ricky Greenblatt's TV presenter cousin.

I see my own father closing his eyes and I recognise the posture, the sorting, the measuring, the recharging. I'm not quite sure when I lost the knack for it. It used to feel real, this reflection. It used to buoy me up through the rest of the year's busyness. Despite the fasting and the things I was missing, this brief moment, this pause, this fleeting second of sincerity – it was something I looked forward to, treasured even. I want it now. But when I close my eyes, my university degree sits on Dad's highlighter-laden desk, and means nothing.

My Mercedes sits outside my West Hampstead flat, and means nothing.

My vote for one party only marginally different than the other, and my opinions about issues other people seem to care about, and my 'passions' (do I have any?), are mainly constructed from clever-sounding things Russell Brand or Stephen Fry have said, or occasionally Gaby's hypotheses, and mean nothing.

Hayley and I, and Sara and I, and me and every other girl I meet, mean nothing. Safia and I refuse to mean anything.

And as the rabbi begins another prayer in Hebrew, I still have no idea what the sacred words to God mean.

"And so we should look to Israel," the rabbi says.

Opening my eyes I glance up towards the women's gallery where Mum is sitting in front of stained glass whispering to some of her girlfriends. They are all meticulously made-up, despite Talmudic instructions to the contrary, and despite today's show of wearing trainers instead of prohibited leather. *To Israel*. Thud. Perhaps the rabbi is talking about me after all. Mum doesn't give away her anxiety, but I see how she repeatedly touches her hand to her face and fidgets with her prayer book. "Fine," she told me yesterday as we were devouring the pre-Yom Kippur meal she'd prepared and downing a third glass of water. "It's your life. Go then. Get blown up. I'm just your mother, why should you listen to me?"

Gaby is not sitting with her. This is not because of my announcement, thankfully, or because of Pete. Gaby left the congregation quite of her own accord five years ago. She goes instead to a Liberal shul that allows men and women to sit together, and where she openly wears leather shoes. Mum has filled the gap with three women she went to school with, the owner of a local boutique who gives Mum a discount, Dad's partner's wife, and, awkwardly, Hayley's mum. She's okay without Gaby. She'll be okay without me. She is surrounded. But alone.

Now the rabbi makes reference to the peace talks in Israel; he expresses hope. It is a controversial topic for a sermon. Too political. Too much to disagree upon. There is some shaking of heads. Mum doesn't shake hers but she lowers her eyes to the men's seats below. She locates mine.

Tucking her stare away, I add it to the list of things for which I must repent.

***

Safia is at a table by the window. It is unusual for her to have texted for a meet-up mid-week. Sundays are our thing, with coffee and croissants and daylight debate. But we haven't been in touch since I texted her after the disastrous Rosh Hashanah dinner – casually dropping into my message the reason for my mother's meltdown – so I knew it was coming. As I hesitate outside, it's possible that she sees me spraying breath freshener. I grin as I enter and plant a kiss in the air to the side of her cheek.

"Mmm, minty fresh," she smiles, one eyebrow raised.

I grin again, settling myself into the wooden chair opposite and noticing that I haven't seen her in a skirt since a wedding we both went to a year ago. She has come straight from work. "What are we drinking?"

"Shiraz. How was the fast?"

"Not bad. I'm so stuffed now." A waiter is hovering nearby and I signal for a drink to match Safia's, then on second thought add some olives. You can't really have wine without nibbles. "I saw Hayley at shul."

"Oh?"

"It was fine, actually."

"Progress," smiles Safia.

"Saw her mum too. Apparently she and my mother are bosom buddies now. Starting some culture club together. There's a bunch of them in it. They're going to go to the theatre together and then discuss what they've seen, or something." I am aware that I am talking about totally irrelevant topics. My wine arrives and I take a long sip. "Sorry I couldn't talk last night, fast was coming in. Was there anything urgent?"

"Oh you know, I got given the Tesco account, same old same old."

"Saf, that's incredible."

"Thanks."

Safia pretends to be nonchalant about most things, but she is totally driven. She completed two different Masters before landing a job at one of the most elite advertising firms in London. In less than a year she worked her way up from researcher to planner. Now she runs workshops, and presents to teams, and strategises, and brings in business. Tesco is a big deal.

"To Tesco!" I raise my glass and Safia clinks it. We both drink at length. She tells me a little more about the Tesco brief and I enjoy watching the pride dancing at the corner of her mouth, too modest to occupy the foreground. I wish I could be as simultaneously unpretentious and brilliant. Conversation lulls. We stab a couple of olives with toothpicks.

"So... Israel?" Safia says eventually.

"Israel."

"Israel?"

"Israel is a small country located in the Middle East that-"

"Hilarious, Dan." Safia takes off her blazer and hangs it on the back of her chair. "You're really moving there?"

"Apparently so."

"You say that like it's not your decision."

"It's totally my decision."

"Any illumination as to what's prompted this decision?"

"Hmm, not really."

"Great reason to up your entire life."

"Thank you."

Safia takes another olive. "Seriously, Dan."

"Seriously, I can't properly explain. But, I don't know, don't you ever get, I don't know... I feel like I'm missing something."

"Well we all know you're missing something," she smirks, though with not quite her usual lightness.

"I don't feel like that when I'm in Israel."

"In Israel, or on holiday? Because you know real life is different from sitting on the beach."

"Not if you happen to live by the beach."

Safia pulls a face. "Is this all so you can take up surfing?"

I laugh, but she's right. I sound flippant, whimsical. That's the whole problem. "Mum hates it," I tell her. "So does my sister, 'cos of the army."

"You'd have to go to the army?"

"I *might* have to."

"And fight? Against Palestinians?"

I shrug.

"Seriously?"

I shrug again.

"Dan."

I'm not sure what to say. I'm honestly not. I'm not trying to be evasive. Safia sucks on the end of a toothpick, waiting. She has always been able to pry details from me with the minimum of effort.

"Okay, you know what, I think I can explain," I say.

"Okay?"

"So, basically, I feel old."

"You're 28."

"I know. But I *feel* old, cynical. Like everything here has already been done. Built already. Worked out. Everything in London's so structured, so planned."

"Only if you choose to follow the plan."

"Okay I'm not articulating it properly. I mean, are you a feminist?"

"What? Of course I am. I mean, not an out and out burn your bra kind of feminist, but as in I think women are equal to men."

"But you're not burning your – very nice by the way – bra."

She grins and adjusts the black strap that has nudged its way into visibility. "No."

"Why not?"

"Because there's no need to. I can vote instead."

"Aha."

"What are you aha-ing about?"

"Because it's not an issue anymore."

"Actually-"

"Okay I know there are feminist 'issues' but it's not the big Issue, for you, here, today."

"Okay…"

"And nothing is. It's done. We play at adventure. We pretend passion. I just don't care."

She raises an eyebrow again.

"No but I want to care," I clarify. "And I know you've never been to Tel Aviv-"

"And will never go to Tel Aviv."

"Okay. But the city is amazing. Tripping over itself with newness, dynamism, fire. None of this watered down damp squib nonsense."

"So now you're moving 'cos of the rain? Daniel, have you ever considered that you can find your fire here? You just need to look for it."

She drains the last of her wine and gestures to the waiter for another glass. I catch her up and raise my hand to signal for two. Despite a friendship that spans more than ten years we have never actually been out drinking just the two of us. Safia leans forward and rests her chin on her hand. Her hair tumbles about her face. She is truly beautiful, not merely sexy or cute or hot or pretty, but beautiful, more so now at 28 than a decade ago. Her eyes are a deep green and bore into me.

"Too complicated," I say.

"To look for fire?"

"Maybe to find it." I touch her hand. I have no idea what I'm doing, but for a moment Safia doesn't move. For a moment, I think I feel her fingers underneath mine responding. For a moment, her eyes don't look away. But then we are in the next moment and she gives my hand a friendly squeeze, placing it perfunctorily onto the table.

"I meant look inside yourself. Not look at me!"

"Yeah yeah, I know," I grin. "Stop throwing yourself at me then."

"Too complicated, Dan," she agrees.

And then we kiss.

***

By the time I arrive back at work the next day I have already eaten my way through an entire plastic container filled with Break Fast leftovers and masturbated twice to the thought of Safia. The kiss was short, quick to dissolve, candyfloss on the tongue. She likes me, always has, and I like her, but nothing is ever going to happen. We established this, agreed upon it. It was in some ways a relief to finally voice the quandary, admit it to each other. On the other hand, we fucked an hour later. On her couch, her heels and skirt still in place, her black bra and excitingly matching knickers peeled off, our normal back and forth banter replaced with a new physical repartee. Now I can't stop thinking about her. Physically can't stop. My morning moves with an uncommon intensity, like trying to sleep at gunpoint, everything brought into fiery focus. I call during lunch, but she doesn't answer. I check my phone three times that afternoon and so many times that evening that I lose count. I text her once, but there is nothing.

Over the next few days I don't sleep well. I am dreaming again but for once not about Israel. My head is full of her. Hot, fiery sensations that when I wake leave me drenched in sweat. But on Sunday, Safia finally texts, and tells me she can't make coffee.

It shouldn't matter. It can't matter. But even as the weekend passes things remain different. I am different. I am awakened. Or alert. Or something else I can't quite place. But I can't get her to pick up the phone. I start to feel foolish trying. But try anyway. One morning I forgo the tube and run to the office in an attempt to ease out the knot in my stomach. But it doesn't work. I still feel knotted, tied. The only remedy is busyness. And as another week trudges by I force myself back into bank chitchat, the rush to finish a report, the calls to clients, the questions from journalists whose inquiries I have to deflect even though I know the answers because I don't have media training. *Structure. Parameters.* Entanglement. Slowly, that feeling of fire starts to dwindle. Most nights the following week I am still in the office at 9pm, dinner ordered to my desk or wolfed down much later in front of recorded episodes of television series I will never have enough time to catch up with. Safia cancels another coffee. By the time I get around to washing up the mouldy Yom Kippur remnants, I can no longer smell her perfume on the shirt I was wearing and can barely remember that fleeting feeling of prayerful pause. I begin dreaming again of beaches.

Most Fridays over the subsequent weeks I make it to my parents' house for dinner. Sometimes Pete is there with Gaby, sometimes he is not, and occasionally neither of them is present because Gaby has had another row with Mum and is refusing to enter the house. I try a few times to talk with Gaby. Despite her conviction, and despite my recent wading into her kind of water, I'm not certain she's certain. Though, for the record, I like Pete, and tell her so. We go to TGI Fridays ordering potato skins (no bacon), and nachos, and try to describe to the young waiter the ingredients of a San Francisco cocktail, which no longer appears on the menu. These days, neither of us would select this restaurant as a place to dine, but when Gaby passed her driving test she would sometimes pick me up from school and bring me here. I think she was on some kind of mission for a while to make sure I was okay. Dad's business was floating and Mum was flat out with the dental practice, and it was just after Grandma Adele died, and nobody seemed to notice that I was getting more migraines again, so I suppose she felt like somebody should check in. It feels therefore like the right venue for checking in on her.

We don't unravel anything shocking. She loves Pete, that's it. *In a 'Can't live without him' way, Dan, and don't want to. You'll know what I mean when you find it.* Besides there is not enough time for elongated probing. Some weekends I spend every daylight hour and part of the night at the office. Others I smoke with Robert or party hard at clubs with money I rarely have enough time to spend, on girls who are never as perfect as Hayley or imperfectly perfect as Safia.

For another three weeks straight Safia cancels coffee. The last time, when pressed for an explanation, she gives the simple response: *2 complicated*. I have ruined everything and I text her this. She doesn't reply. I decide not to push, I don't think I can bear another cancellation, I don't know why it is frustrating me so much anyway, I don't know how we got here. Then late one evening she texts when I am already in bed and suggests dinner. We cannot find a date for nearly a month but I type the arrangement into my phone, I set a reminder, and for a while I abandon my Internet searches about making aliyah. This is not intentional, but I am busy searching for restaurants where I can take Safia. A week or so before our meeting I discover in the inside pocket of my suit jacket the crumpled admittance ticket I'd needed for the first Rosh Hashanah shul service. I discard it and replace it with a lottery scratch card.

Without noticing, the memory of autumn begins to fade. I buy a new coat and wrap myself deep within its woollen protection, then fold it carefully on my lap making a good Kindle rest for tube journeys that remain too hot. I am reading a book Safia suggested months ago and use the notes function so that I'll remember the witty commentary I am constructing inside my head. At the beginning of November, the world prepares for Christmas and I dutifully buy greetings cards for the people who will expect them before arranging to be out of the country for as much of the season as possible. In the end, work commitments meant that I never made it to Israel for the wedding in October, but Robert and Debbie are going out to visit Debbie's sister over Christmas and have invited me to join. When I tell my parents they raise their eyebrows but do not comment. They are spending a week in New York themselves and Gaby is going skiing so it is comfortable to interpret my choice of destination purely as a desire to seek out the sun. Plus, they are tiptoeing, as though by not mentioning Israel I might forget it was ever something I wanted. But of course I haven't forgotten. Even with the whisper of Safia I haven't forgotten. I carry it with me like the smile I can never quite muster for a 6am tube journey; an emotion I know I'm capable of, but don't, yet, have the inclination to express. I wonder if Safia will mention it, but on the day of our dinner she cancels again.

***

Now

4

It is difficult to concentrate on the whiteness of the slopes, their purity and unblemished surface. Pete wanted both of them to rise early to appreciate this newness and Gaby is trying hard to embrace the snowy clarity; but even at the top of the run, standing on the tip of the world, she is distracted and cannot escape the feeling that something serious, something important, is about to be lost.

She assumes that it is Daniel. She didn't say anything to her parents about his trip to Israel. She didn't want to say anything because their father is insisting that the whole moving thing was a whim, like Daniel's teenage sherbet straw empire or the surfing malarkey. He thinks there's no way Daniel would give up the life he's jumped through a million hoops to construct. Their mother thinks so too. Despite the current volatility of their own relationship, Gaby has had enough conversations with her mother to see that she is easing into a new confidence regarding Daniel, one that increases in direct proportion to the amount of time lapsed without the subject of Israel being broached. But they are wrong. Daniel does not just forget things. He thinks. He plans. When he was eight their mother offhandedly told him that he could only have *Mortal Kombat* for the Playstation if he bought it himself – a ploy to make sure he never got one – and she didn't think of it again until almost a year later when Daniel produced the necessary sum from money he had apparently earned from relatives or found down the crack in the sofa. It is not just a holiday. It is a test, a trial. But it is not a fair one. The sun always has a satisfying flavour and disguises as sand the dust beneath one's feet.

Gaby digs her poles into the fresh snow and begins her descent. She has skied since childhood and the movement up and down comes naturally, the letting go, leaning forwards even when trepidation warns to lean back. Pete however has picked for them an icy black run and she should be concentrating. She fell hard yesterday and it has jolted her confidence, it has made her more aware of the rocks to the side, to the edge of their posted path. She imagines Daniel navigating similar rocks but in a deep blue sea and on a different sort of skis. She wants to tell him that this leisure, this feeling of flying, this is not how life will be, not the reality. The reality is bombs, explosions, guns. He does not understand what it means to have real enemies. He says things have changed, things are calmer, that the whole world is a warzone now. He reminds her that he was only two trains ahead of the one that was bombed on the 7th of July. But how can he fail to see that this way, he is choosing to put himself on that train? He is Jewish but surely he is British more. He is not one of those fanatics who clothe themselves in the garb of another century and refuse to see that the world has moved on. He is not an untrammelled Zionist unable to see the faults of the Jewish State. He is not religious. Not without success. Not without anything. Why does he want to trade it all in? For what? Israeli girls? Heat? God? Is there even one?

A snowboarder swerves past Gaby, too close, and she falls hard for the second time in as many days. It doesn't hurt, but now Pete is out of sight and one of her skis is half way across the run. She will have to pigeon step to it slowly. She has never enjoyed this element of skiing; having to push on because there is no option to go back, knowing all the while that an apparition may suddenly appear from behind and knock her down.

When she reaches the bottom of the slope, Pete is waiting for her. He has lifted his goggles to peer towards the run and his normally bright eyes are a clouded blue. "What happened to you?" he asks. "Are you okay?"

"Fine." She leans over her skis to kiss his sunburnt nose. "I just fell again. Lost my ski. I don't know why I'm going so badly."

"You've been in another world since we got here. Are you sure you're okay?"

She nods but he insists that they take a break, have some coffee, which really means a weak shot of caffeine swimming in milk and smothered in cream. How can she resist? They prop up their skis and move without consultation to the café they both love. This is not their first trip to this resort in Val-d'Isère and they are no longer careful to explore, accepting quietly that they are happier with the comfort of known pleasures than the risk of places still obscure. She cradles a hot mug in her slowly defrosting hands and tells him she has been thinking about Daniel. Pete nods sympathetically and lets her vent, but he is not as concerned about her brother as she would like him to be. To be fair, it is not the first time she has brought Daniel up and she is relaying nothing new, besides which Pete finds it difficult to understand why she is spending so much time obsessing about a sibling who is grown up and has a mind of his own. Pete has lived away from his family since the age of seven when his parents sent him and his twin sister to boarding school, separate ones. They speak regularly, but it doesn't bother him that his parents live in Singapore or that his sister has recently moved to Dubai. It makes their gatherings more special, he says, the time they spend more precious. She can see that there is some truth to this. They have been sharing the small chalet Pete's parents own with all of his family – which is now extended to include a brother-in-law complete with bouncing baby boy –

85

for almost a week and they are yet to have a single argument. Pete's mother fusses too much over everybody's warmth, his sister Jane's smoke-scratched voice directs traffic too often, Pete himself has regressed into what she assumes is a teenaged insistence on leaving wet towels on the floor, and his father is an inordinately loud snorer; but nobody has said anything. It is as if each one of them knows the fragility of their relationships, the short time they have to work on them, and so they treat them with extra care. Either that or they simply don't know one another well enough to be brazen with their opinions, interacting as she would with her friends not her blood, always with just a thin veil of civilisation and restraint. Perhaps this is how she will become with Daniel if he moves away. Perhaps they will finally stop squabbling. Perhaps it will be good. Suddenly however she longs to be small again and running madly through the house, chasing Daniel who has stolen her diary, both of them being shouted at by their mother to be quiet, to just stop.

Pete finishes his coffee and signals to the waitress to bring the bill. "Ready to go up again?" he asks her. "We should try to get in a good morning 'cos you know we have to stop early this afternoon."

She nods. She has remembered. It is Christmas Eve and they have promised to be back by three to help decorate the tree. It is a hallowed tradition for Pete's family and she has been part of it for the past two years, mucking in as they hang the decorations they have wrapped in tissue paper and packed away the year before, smiling at the explanations they gleefully offer about when each one was picked or how a particular china reindeer came to have a broken leg. Her freshness to the gathering is almost becoming a tradition in itself, she the reason they are able to tell stories of times she wasn't present at to remember for herself. She wonders if it will always be this way, if she will always be a little bit on the outside, or if in time they will forget that their histories are not the same.

They manage to arrive back at the chalet only a few minutes late. Susan and Keith are already drinking eggnog while their daughter Jane struggles to contain baby Henry who is attached to her breast and grasping the feeding apron she is attempting to use for modesty and with which Gaby can't imagine ever bothering amidst family. She will have to adjust to this she supposes, when it is their baby, her boob. Or else shock them. "Tree in five minutes," Jane tells them. Pete helps Gaby to lift her skis onto the rack in the hallway then they shake the last bits of snow off their jackets before stripping down to their matching thermals, and joining the rest of the family in the lounge. Susan hands them both a glass of eggnog and quickly the room fills with discarded pieces of tissue paper, multicoloured shards of tinsel littering the floor, and anecdotes Gaby pretends not to have already heard. When the last of the sun disappears, they turn on the fairy lights and marvel at the way they set off the tree. The twinkling reminds Gaby of the remnants of the candles her own mother burns on Friday nights until they have disappeared, and suddenly she realises that today is Friday. Usually she would be preparing to drive the short distance to her parents' house where they would break the challah, drink wine. The image makes her feel uneasy, detached slightly, like when she was 11 at some sleep-over at a girlfriend's house and it was finally time to sleep and the sugar was wearing off and all at once she was acutely aware that she didn't have her own bed or the stuffed animal she was too old to admit to wanting. But it is strange now to find herself missing such small customs, such trivial, irrational, antiquated things.

"Gaby," Pete cuts in. "What do you think?" The tone of his voice tells her that he is repeating a question. "Are you daydreaming again?"

"It's lovely," Gaby answers, touching one of the sparkling lights. "It's beautiful."

"You're tired sweetie aren't you?" Susan says, pouring her some more eggnog and smothering her with a blanket.

"We've had a hectic few days haven't we? You need a good night's sleep."

"Susan's eggnog will see that you sleep well!" Keith chuckles.

"Give some to Henry then," Jane jokes.

They all laugh, and Pete slips his arm around her, and Gaby takes a sip.

***

Now

5

I've never been to Israel at Christmas. Menorahs are everywhere but not one Santa Claus. No Frank Sinatra, no Bublé 'Jingle Bells', no bombardment of shoppers and greeting cards and adverts demanding me to be happy and bright. Instead there is a quiet dissolution of prejudices, a slowing down and toning down. Old men smile as they pass me and say '*Chag Sameach*'. Children grip paper menorahs they have made at school. In the market, here in Tel Aviv, people don't push me out of the way to lay their hands on the fattest turkey. Into the calm, a revving car complete with megaphone crawls the streets announcing when each giant menorah will be lit, but there is no frenzy, at least no more than the usual Israeli tumult. There is a casual acknowledgement of communal pleasure, but not a race to stockpile happiness for oneself.

The whole thing is weird. I don't know how to behave. Christmas is mentioned only on the international news and instead my festival, the one I never even got days off school for, is being nationally recognised as a reason for joy. There is something liberating about this, like shouting in the library. Still, more than once I find myself humming 'Jingle Bells'.

Robert is quicker to adjust. London doesn't seem to have followed him in the same way, or perhaps with a lifetime of Christmases abroad he's just more adept at shedding it. Debbie and her sister are similarly at ease – they have their favourite clubs and boutiques and restaurants and beaches and select them casually, knowledgably, just as they would at home. But none of them actually want it to be home.

One afternoon I set off alone and seek out my café on Rothschild Boulevard. The one from my dream. I must have been there before to have conjured it though I have no idea what it's called. When I see the orange canopy shading a cluster of street-side tables, I sit down. A bus passes and, at the abrupt splutter of its exhaust, I hear Gaby and my mother cursing my negligence. *Buses. Cafés. Markets. Shopping malls.* These are the places that have been frequent targets, places they'd want me to avoid. I study the traffic that has come to a halt in front of me. Next to the road a man stands to attention, staring up. I have a sudden premonition that he has spotted a missile the Iron Dome has somehow missed and it is about to land square at my feet. I picture my mother and sister again. But when I follow the man's line of sight I see that he is looking at the construction across the road. I laugh at myself, to myself, and look. There is construction everywhere. It is sometimes hard to know whether this city is half-crumbling or half-built but either way it is a seamless amalgamation: pristine newness and ancient stone; shiny designer boutiques covered with Banksy-esque graffiti; and building, building, everywhere building. It is tiring to look at. Exhausting. But exciting too. There is a coolness here, a confidence, an edge, an unapologetic show of progress, innovation. My coffee is smooth and satisfying.

I listen now, waiting for the foreign voices that I will somehow understand. Here they come. Strolling by with phones glued to their ears are businessmen speaking a loud, dynamic Hebrew. They wear short-sleeves and trainers. Weaving past them, children are cycling and calling to each other – unaccompanied and un-hooded. Around me, at almost every table, smokers puff away, as if they are in a place too innocent to know better or too stubborn to care. I listen. Definitely some Russian to my left, some French to my right. A lot of Hebrew…

I do not miraculously understand.

Obviously.

I must admit there is some disappointment to this.

But then, some French grandmother-type leans over and asks me if I have a girlfriend, she has a granddaughter. And a few minutes later the Brazilian-born waiter tells me about a club opening I should go to. And then a middle-aged gent at the table next to me hears that I'm English and starts telling me about the year that he lived in Willesden Green. So okay, I may not understand their various languages, but in London strangers rarely speak to each other at all. And what is the point of language if we don't use it to interact? What is the point of money if I have no time to spend it? What is the point of living if I don't know what I'm living for? And dreams are symbolic aren't they? It's not about literally speaking the language but feeling like I understand it, feeling understood. And the mind is a powerful thing you know, my subconscious is telling me something.

I think for a moment of Safia. She would tell me to stop being overdramatic. But I bet she would like it here if she ever consented to come. I have always thought of her as a little bit not completely British. A fragmented soul. Like me. She'd like the warmth of these people, she less constrained than through-and-through Brits, less compelled to personify the cold climate.

The waiter interrupts my pondering to encourage me to leave; there are people waiting for the table. I get up to let them sit down and immediately regret my chivalry. Now I have no seat and must loiter near the cash register in hopes of catching a waiter's attention long enough to allow me to pay. I ask three times and am nodded at, but nobody brings me my bill. Other customers are calling more loudly than me and nobody has time for my politeness, my deficiency of resolve. In the end I physically restrain my waiter by placing my hand on his arm.

"I've been waiting to pay for half an hour!" He is unbothered. I thrust the cash at him. "Half an hour. It's ridiculous."

He takes the money calmly. "See you at the club tonight?"

"That's longer than I was sitting down!"

He smiles. He will not apologise for my weakness. And I have to laugh because now he has my money and I will have to wait another half an hour if I want change.

On Christmas Eve I text festive greetings to my family strewn across the world. Also to Safia. And to Hayley. Gaby and Mum reply within seconds.

Mum has recently got the hang of text-speak and her response is a rapid-fire list of instructions: *U 2 D. Dnt 4gt 2 b SAFE. Call ur cousin. Pls buy me 2 ahava body moisturiser. Txt me ur flight deets*. She ends with a heart emoji.

Gaby's text is longer, telling me how wonderful her holiday is but that it's just a holiday and it's hard to remember that sometimes but she is looking forward to coming home and seeing me in the real world. And Merry Christmas too. I suspect she's had one too many Christmas cocktails.

Hayley's says: *R U hanging a stocking?* With a winky face. Our first year together we filled stockings for each other and it became a tradition between us to slip in one racy item. Our last year together she bought me red, furry handcuffs.

Safia does not reply.

As I'm getting ready for the evening I think about texting her again, something witty, something she can't ignore, something that will get us back to normal if not more than normal.

I miss her.

The realisation of this infiltrates my otherwise enthusiastic preparations. I am at least ten minutes in the shower and it takes me an inordinate amount of time to select a pair of jeans and shirt. Dressed, I lay on the bed. It's ridiculous – our situation, my melancholy. What do I miss? Not the sex, that was once, brief though brilliant. It's her. Admittedly we only used to meet once a week, we were never 'together', nor could we be, but we were connected. We texted all the time or called on the way to and from work. We had confidence in ourselves I guess, in our friendship, in our mutual desire to value that friendship. There was no concern about over-sharing or phoning too much or being unwanted. And now I miss her humour, and her feisty jibes, and her question-mark eyebrows. And the reliability of a reply to my texts. More than that, I miss being the one receiving hers. The one she will allow herself to be sad to, honest with. She'll have her whole extended family descending on her over the holidays. Her parents will have offered out her flat and she'll be sharing it with an aunt and three cousins. One of them has always been a bitch to Safia. I want to tell her to stick it to her. But it's hard to think of a way to say that after our weeks of silence. It's hard to summon our previous intimacy. And by the time I think of a perfectly phrased text, my hands are thick with hair gel and Robert is rushing me out of the bathroom into a cab and the blaring throng of the Yemeni driver's hardcore house music.

We head towards the sea. Most nights we go to the sea, often congregating at a beachside bar or club following dinner in a cool new Neve Tzedek restaurant, but sometimes simply sitting in circles on the sand with expats who ask with sadistic relish about London's cold weather. Always near us, or with us, are slim, sun-kissed girls, each apparition more beautiful than the next as if they are being manufactured somewhere, the mould edging ever closer to perfection. Christmas Eve is no exception and as we enter the bar, Robert reminds me that I am not with Safia, I have never been with Safia, and she clearly has no interest in being with me. Plus I am in Israel, and hey, look around. I nod, he's right, she won't even reply to my texts, and so I accept the vodka shot he hands me, the two of us taking a quick scan of the room before situating ourselves near a group of women who could easily all be related to the Israeli supermodel Bar Refaeli. Perhaps they are. Our English is an advantage. I play up the poshness. Robert, under Debbie's watchful eye, is a good wingman. But these women aren't easy to impress and we have to work hard to keep their attention. When they listen, it is a demanding silence and I feel sometimes an unfamiliar desire to scurry. When they speak, it feels like a challenge, exacting from me "*Ma*? *Ma*?" (what?), but never as a question, never anything as feeble as a question. They talk and stand and demand with absolute assuredness, their eyes telling me that, unlike me, they are complete, and certain, and need no affirmation of themselves. They agree with me only when I'm right. They laugh only when I'm actually funny. They will not follow my lead blindly. They will never be like lambs.

Orli arrives on her own just as I am about to call it a night. I don't at this point know her name but I know that I will. I spot her as soon as she walks in, see the way she stands boldly by the door, oblivious to the rows of eyes on her, see how she considers the room carefully, see how her face lights up as she locates her friends. See that she is not Safia. Orli's beauty is different, and mesmerising. I can't believe my luck when she walks towards our group and kisses a greeting to two of the women at the table, clasping one of their hands and conveying some sincere joy that makes the other woman hug her. Her blonde hair is loose and dishevelled – *tousled* is the word I feel like I've heard Hayley or Safia or maybe Gaby use. She has luminous blue eyes. She is slim yet curvy, and tall enough to wear flats. Her black jeans are tight but her top relaxed, effortless, her face seemingly bare except for a strident coat of bright red lipstick. One of the girls whispers something in her ear and she briefly raises her eyes in my direction. Somebody hands her a beer and she takes a sip.

"Hi," I say.

She takes my extended hand with circumspection. "Hi."

I don't start well.

Trying to impress, I order one of the gigantic cocktails with sparklers that arrive carried above the head by a team of clapping waiters, but Orli only grimaces and sticks to her beer. Then I insist that we all down shots, eagerly passing them out to the group, and she laughs, covering her eyes as though cringing on my behalf and eventually taking one but only, I imagine, because she is tolerating me. And when I try to compliment her, I find myself saying something schmaltzy about her eyes reflecting the depth of the sea, and she uses those ocean eyes to give me a look of utter disbelief and perhaps pity. Which would be about right given my material. But then, suddenly, she leans forward, offers me her hand and leads me outside.

The night is cold. She has a jacket, otherwise I would offer her mine, and I follow her to the edge of the promenade. The waves lash against the barrier and the wind whips us in the face. Orli's hair shoots out around her like a mermaid, or sea witch.

"So," I say. "Now that you have me here what are you going to do with me?"

Orli rolls her eyes. "What is it with you, Daniel?" she laughs. "I have been told that you are a good guy. My friends say this. An interesting guy. An honest guy. Where is this guy? Why are you always acting?"

"Acting? Ah yes, you may recognise me from such films as-"

"Why can you not be yourself?"

She is still a near stranger, she doesn't know me like Safia, but there is something about those eyes that enchants me, and I find myself answering, "I don't know who 'myself' is."

Three hours later, we haul ourselves up from the café round the corner from the bar and locate our various friends. I have consumed four cappuccinos. We don't kiss as we part but the taste of the sea air is almost as good: her sea, the colour of her eyes.

Just as I am getting into a cab my phone beeps. It is finally a reply from Safia. As I see her name flash across the screen my stomach twists – it is the first time in weeks that hours have passed without my thinking of her and I am wracked with simultaneous guilt, shame, longing, and something steelier too, something defiant. I read her message. A single: *X*. Complicated. Or uncomplicated? There is no question, no entreaty, no lifeline. I lift my phone to text her back anyway, I try to remember the message I had concocted earlier, I wonder if, now, there is something else I should say. But while thinking about this I get sidetracked wondering where to take Orli for breakfast, and by the time I have sent Orli a message to tell her, we are back at the hotel, and Robert is suggesting one last drink and a game of pool, and when eventually I am alone and remember Safia's unanswered text, I am in bed, and my phone is plugged in on the other side of the room, and the alcohol and the coffees are wearing off, and then I am with Orli and nothing is the same.

We sit close. There is no need to hide how intimate we have become. Safia is not here to see, besides which it is clear she would not care. That space still echoes a little inside me, and for the first day or two with Orli I tried to listen to the reverberations, if only to check there was no whisper I had missed. But in mere days Orli managed to peer deeper into the chaotic workings of my mind than anyone I've ever known, even Safia. And I let her. I let go and let her. We talk constantly and it is more sensual than any sex, any grand romantic evening I've previously concocted. There is something about the way she speaks to me, in her impressively proficient English, that makes each conversation seem poignant. As if, because she so assiduously selects words from her learned vocabulary, they are never careless. Never just banter. They are meant, considered, and require an equally considered response.

"So? Why do you keep working there if it's destroying your soul?" she asks one afternoon when we have laid out a blanket a few metres away from the others. We are at Sarona, Tel Aviv's new cultural hotspot. We have picked up a picnic basket from the aptly named Picnic restaurant. Later we are going to check out the galleries. In a few weeks there will be a jazz festival here. Orli scoops up her long wavy hair and ties it loosely behind her head so that it won't fall across her brow and disturb her sketch. She looks up and scrutinises my face, perhaps to test the truth of my response, or perhaps to work out how much space there is between my eyes. Orli is an artist, though this is something I've only belatedly discovered. She is famous actually, one of her friends informed me. Her work has shown in galleries all over Israel and she's beginning to gain a following in New York. It is all there to read on her website, there for public consumption, but not something she told me at the start. Most of our first conversations were about me, my life, as though I am a puzzle we have decided between us to put together. Now that I know about her art, I ask question after question and she tells me her style is a mixture of surrealism and pop art, smiling because I am quite clearly not versed in these matters, a fusion, she says, of the imagined and the real, the spiritual and the gross. I like hearing her talk with such conviction, such passion. I envy it. Now she has demanded to draw me. "So? Why do you do it?"

"I like the thrill, I guess, and I'm good with numbers. It's easy for me."

"Hmm," she says.

"I make a lot of cash."

Orli looks up to capture what I suddenly notice is a frown. She never actually condemns me, but she listens hard, and she looks, and makes me look too. "But what is it about it that you love?"

"I don't know, I guess just that, the money. Or the power maybe. The respect. I mean it's a really high-powered job, competitive, and I'm good at it."

"You mentioned that." She smiles.

"And it's what I always planned. So it's just what I do now, you know?"

"Do you look forward to getting up in the morning?"

"Only at the weekends. But that's normal. I mean, who actually loves their job?"

"I do."

"Well, you're lucky."

"You could also be so lucky." She finishes the sketch and shows it to me, turning the canvas and laying it on the blanket. "It is rough," she says. "I would add colour."

The picture is more accurate than any photo and renders me speechless. I both know and don't know the man staring back at me. Orli has managed to capture both my melancholy and my happiness, my uncertainty and my longing for passion, my entire fragmented self. "You are incredible," I tell her.

"So are you."

On my last Friday in Israel, Orli invites me to her parents' house for dinner. She no longer lives at home but in a small apartment in the centre of Tel Aviv. There is a living area that has perfect light and she uses as a studio. All of her friends live close by in similarly artistic venues and gather at the coffee shops that litter the streets until late into the night before working until even later. By now I've met most of them. Each is more fascinating than the next: this one writing a script, another directing a play, all creating. They wear timeless black jeans, classic t-shirts, and a hat or a pair of shoes that are a stylish thowback to a previous era. Their talk is filled with energy, a natural disposition to explore, to analyse, to dissect. Their vibe is confident, engaged. I feel like I've stumbled upon an intellectual rat-pack, a tribe of young Israelis embodying the now of the country, constructing it, building it, thinking it, directing its future. And while I'm sure they're fully aware of their own appeal, they are not selfish in commandeering it; they are happy to share it with me.

"Danny, when are you going to forget this cold weather rubbish and come make some money for Israel?" Ittai, one of the men in the group, asks me that Friday when I arrive at Orli's. Ittai has been there to show her the plans for the new building he is designing and welcomes me with a slap on the back. He is dark skinned, of Moroccan descent, and slim-built, wearing jeans that slip below his waist. "Or you could be *my* backer Danny? Handle the business while I create brilliant architecture. What do you say?"

"*I* say no," Orli interrupts. "He is going to open a gallery for me."

"Let's do it, all of it," I joke, noticing Orli smile with a qualification that I cannot yet interpret.

"So come to Israel," Ittai presses. "It's a good time. The shekel's growing strong now. It is crazy what's happening. And you know, Danny, Israel is the greatest country in the world."

Orli drives us to her parents' house. I am yet to take the wheel in Israel despite my many trips here and am glad to avoid it still – the drivers are nuts. Occasionally pausing to add her own horn to the bedlam, Orli is telling me about her family. "My mother will be offended if you don't eat much," she warns me. "But don't wait to be offered everything like you did when you first came to my apartment, otherwise she'll think you are arrogant. When you go to someone's house, you must help yourself."

"But I don't know them. I can't just make myself at home," I protest.

"So you'd rather make my mother get up and serve you? No, you should help yourself."

"Okay, I'll be sure to snoop in all the kitchen cupboards."

"My father will want to talk politics. He was a great man in the intelligence you know. He only retired last year. He likes Britain. He used to like your Tony Blair."

"I did not used to like my Tony Blair."

She senses me mocking her speech and prods me in the ribs. "He was a great friend to Israel."

"Really?"

"You don't know?"

"What about Cameron?"

She laughs. "Ask my father. I will enjoy it."

"Will your brother be there?"

Orli has talked a lot about her brother. He is younger than her by just over a year but she speaks of him as if they grew up in tandem, as if every experience she's had is one he's shared. I can't help but feel a little jealous, cheated that I've met Orli so late.

"No, David's still away on miluim. Reserves," she explains. "His call up is always for a long time because he's a pilot, but he'll be back at last next weekend. I wish you could stay to meet him." Her face has grown animated at the mention of her brother. "He's a songwriter too, of course. He plays guitar. When he's not working at the airline he writes the most wonderful songs. Here, listen." She inserts a CD into the car stereo and beautiful, sad music spills out of it. We are both silent as we listen. There is something about David's song that demands silence. I don't know what the words mean but they make me want to embrace Orli, to protect her, and simultaneously they make Orli withdraw, as if the music is pulling her away, or she is remembering something, or trying to figure something out. I don't interrupt. We listen to the rest of the track and then turn the CD off. By the time we arrive, joviality has been restored.

Orli parks and watches with amusement as I climb out of the car, balancing the bunch of flowers I've spent almost half an hour choosing, convinced irrationally that my selection will define her family's impression of me. Orli's mother Ariella smiles generously at the conservative tulips. It is the same smile as Orli's. She pours me a drink before I have a chance to fetch it myself but Orli nods that this is allowed. Then the two of them show me around the house and I spend a long time inspecting the photographs: a practically blonde infant-Orli clambering on top of her smaller brother; the two of them aged ten or 11 running through a park somewhere; an already-beautiful teenaged version of herself standing proudly next to her now gangly but athletic looking playmate, the two of them always grinning, always with their arms around each other, tangled like spaghetti. I can see that it will be hard not to like David.

We sit down and a boy around 12 years old saunters into the living room. "Muaz!" Orli declares, enveloping him in a hug. The boy is clearly happy to see her but he leans away slightly, patting her back with exaggerated slowness. In a year or two he will not tolerate such a display from female relatives. He grins though as she ruffles his hair.

"So short?" she demands in English.

"So cool," he answers.

She kisses him firmly on the cheek leaving a smudge of red and he rolls his eyes but allows her to pull him near to her on the couch. They are comfortable together. Close. "Danny, meet my nephew," she says.

But he is not her nephew. He has dark hair quite unlike hers, dark skin, and even darker eyes. Plus she has only one sibling, David, unmarried, without a son. Ariella looks to me for reaction, but I try to give none other than to say, "Shalom".

Orli has warned me about Muaz. He is adopted, taken as a baby from an orphanage on the border. "His name means 'protected'," Orli has explained. "That's what my parents wanted to do." It is noble, but from the way Ariella is watching me I can't help but wonder if they sometimes experience prejudice about this, if it was a decision they have had to defend.

It is a good half an hour before Orli's father, Nadav, arrives with both of his parents and their Filipino carer in tow. As soon as he enters the house it is all noise. Muaz is excited to relay something to Nadav that I don't follow, but Nadav wants to make sure his parents are seated comfortably, and he takes seriously the role of host – bringing out the wine, telling me about the Israeli groves where the grapes were grown, pointing out a new piece of art and relaying the story of the artist behind it, the architecture of the shop from which it was bought and the history of the man who sold it to him. He has an incredible memory for detail and I marvel at the interest he shows in everything. Nothing is dull to him. Nothing overlooked. I am glad that I am able to say *Amen* at the appropriate pauses when he leads the Shabbat prayers, and both he and Orli smile approvingly when I get up to help Ariella bring in the dishes from the kitchen. Nadav carries dishes too, though in his hands the full bowls look small and irrelevant. He is tall and appears more European than Israeli, a pair of glasses and blazer making a change from short-sleeved shirts. He takes a pocket watch out of his jacket before removing it to sit down. I would like to call him Doc, or Prof. But I don't yet.

We eat. And while we eat, we talk. They seem both interested and a little pitying of my life in London. I am not used to this. 'Investment banker' is usually enough to tick parental boxes. There is rarely a presumption that I should want anything more, or different. It endears me to them. I feel strangely at ease.

"You should come to Israel," says Nadav. "For the young ones here, it is difficult – computers, science, technology, yes. But it is hard to make money if you don't have some money. It's different for you. There is much opportunity for someone like you."

"I'm thinking about it," I say, not asking what kind of person Nadav assumes I am. "I am thinking about it."

"Your mother wants to keep you?" asks Ariella.

I laugh. "And my sister."

"Of course!" She pats my hand conspiratorially. "Orli and I plan to keep David forever."

"And what about Orli?" I laugh. "Is she free to go, or shackled too?"

"Ah, but daughters never really go," says Ariella. "A daughter is forever."

"It's only us men who disappoint," says Nadav mischievously.

"I am a constant disappointment," I agree.

"Constant," smiles Orli.

The evening rolls on and soon it is late. Orli has suggested going out after dinner, perhaps to meet Robert and Debbie at a bar, or to a salsa club where some of her own friends are heading. But I am happy sitting with her family. The conversation has moved to politics, to the Kerry talks, to the third group of Palestinian prisoners just released, to the anger about murderers walking free. I don't know enough to offer much of an opinion, especially not to a man in the intelligence, but I am asked. My sources for information are limited to the particular slant given by news reported in British nationals, and to the pages of the *Jewish Chronicle* that my mother buys. My gut feeling is that the release is tough, but necessary.

"You are right," says Nadav. "But you can understand the hysteria. These are criminals, terrorists, with Israeli blood on their hands. We spent a long time finding these men."

"And for many people it is very emotional," interrupts Ariella. "Imagine somebody killed your wife, your child. Brutally killed, hacked to death, lynched. And then they are allowed to just go."

"And arrive to a hero's welcome," adds Nadav.

"But not all of them are murderers," says Orli.

Nadav waves his hand. "Three. Three on this list were not murderers. We send our children out to fight, to protect us, and then we give them back their killers. It is crazy."

"There are of course many factors that lead us to this situation," says Ariella. "Many difficult, uncomfortable factors." She looks at Muaz and smiles reassuringly. I had forgotten about Muaz and wonder if he minds, if he even knows where he is from, who his parents were, what they may have thought of this conversation.

"But, you are right, Danny," Nadav continues. "It is also necessary. For peace. The problem is, too many Israelis don't understand this. There is Tel Aviv. And then there is the rest of Israel. And this stupid Bibi-" He shakes his head. "It is so complicated." He looks up at Orli.

"Abba-" Orli interrupts, but he continues.

"Do you know, Danny, some boys now refuse to join the army at all, or they find some reason to get out of it. They pretend to be mad, or disabled or something like this. My generation, we fought to secure their future and now they refuse to protect it. It's something every Israeli must do, for his people. A man who doesn't go to the army is not a true Israeli man." He stops. "That's all I want to say," he assures Orli.

She nods assent. "I could never respect someone who didn't go to the army."

"Did you go?" I ask her, realising we haven't spoken about this before.

"Of course," she says, glancing at Muaz.

Ariella holds up her hands. Have we eaten enough, she wants to know.

Collectively we clear the plates away and conversation returns to lighter topics – the new restaurant that has opened on the other side of Tel Aviv, the play Ariella saw the night before, how much they all miss David. But I only nod now and then and let the talk continue around me. My mind is stuck on what Nadav said about the army, how it is a defining part of being Israeli, of being a full, whole Israeli. How it is something each family does, for his country, for his people, a gift of one's own to protect all. To protect me, too. If I come here. Or even if I don't. Because of course it is my haven even now, it is all of our havens, even my mother's and Gaby's, just in case.

"I want to join the army," I say, as we sit down with coffees in the lounge. "To come here, and join the army."

Orli furrows her brow. Nadav turns towards me and Muaz rolls his eyes. But before anybody speaks, the phone rings and Ariella goes to the hallway to answer it, so I'm not sure if this is the reason for the silence that follows or if I have said something offensive, something stupid and naïve.

And then it comes.

A scream. So loud that, at first, I think it is a siren.

It is shrill and circular, laced with urgency. It impels me to get out of the way, to move, to run. But around me people are already running: Orli and her father. They are racing out of the room, hurrying to the source of the wailing, rushing to Ariella.

A moment later there is a second scream. Tortured, twisting. Rising and falling. Gasping for breath.

And below that, the haunting sound of heavy male sobs.

Across the table, Nadav's parents are rising to their feet, Muaz is already at the door, even the carer has mobilised. I don't want to be rude, to intrude, to impose myself in family disaster, but I have to go to Orli.

She is sitting on the floor with her arms wrapped around her mother.

Orli's father – Doc, Prof – is on his knees. His tall back is hunched, his head lowered, grey dipped downwards. He holds the phone weakly against his ear.

His parents are caressing Ariella's head. Muaz is trying desperately to grasp her hand, but she is pushing him away. Her cries are still loud. So loud.

Orli looks up.

"What's happened?" I mouth to her silently.

But she shakes her head. She gasps again for air, for a breath. Tears leave tracks down her previously unblemished cheeks. And there is something else, something lost. I kneel down, put my hands around her face, let her weep into them. And of course I know.

I delay my flight until after the funeral. David's body arrives wrapped in blue and white. There are tens of people willing to carry him and hundreds to help Nadav suffer the sound of the first thud of earth that it is his duty to pile on top of his son. Ariella clutches his arm and half-stands, half-sits, as if she is no longer sure if the dirt is above or below. Orli stands alone. I wanted to be with her at the funeral but she refused, determined to be strong, like her brother. Now the empty space next to her – the space I know David has always occupied – makes her look so vulnerable that I inch forward.

The earth builds up slowly as the closest relatives add their contribution to the grave, but then a line of men, Ittai and some of Orli's other friends among them, swell forwards and as quickly as they can they finish the job, piling up the dirt until long after the last blue of the flag can be seen. Some of the men weep. They carry the world as they have carried David, but their strength is not enough to mediate calmly between life and death, even when the clash between them is so frequent. There are no suits or ties, no formalities to protect them from the rawness of what they face. Only I am dressed smartly and it makes me feel removed, an outsider. Orli glances behind her to where I am standing. During her eulogy she managed to speak without flinching, to tell of David, to do him justice; but now her legs shake and I am only just able to catch her before her knees buckle. She feels slight in my arms, as though the tip of a breeze could blow her away, but by the time we reach the car my arms are aching. Heaviness is something that has crept into us.

I place Orli into the passenger seat. I have accepted the challenge of driving her green Corsa and attempt to turn the key with confidence, but the news comes on as soon as I start the engine. The rocket attack on David's helicopter has been all over the bulletins since it happened. I switch it off. Orli has asked me not to tell her what is being reported, what reprisals are being carried out in David's name.

"Find me some music, Daniel," is all she says through the silence.

I am afraid of hitting the news again so I switch the stereo over to CD. A soft melody sings out of it, peaceful, soulful, appropriate. I am pleased with my selection. But a moment later Orli lets out a strained sob, she clasps her hands to her stomach as though she has been punched there, as though once again she cannot find a breath, and I realise that the music is David's. Again I reach for the dial but this time Orli steadies my hand.

"No," she breathes with difficulty. "Leave it. Listen. I want you to meet my brother."

So we listen, and though I still cannot translate the sad, haunting words, it makes sense, like in my dream, the feeling makes sense, and I am sure that I understand it, this song, that Orli loves, and her dead brother wrote.

***

Now

6

Udi hauls his army uniform down from the top shelf of his cupboard and sets about shaking it free from sand. It hasn't been washed since he took it off 11 months earlier, despite his mother's hunt for it. He doesn't quite know why he stuffed it up there so rapidly but suspects it has something to do with the blood stain on the sleeve and a desire never to wear it again.

It wasn't this way the first time he prepared for miluim. Then, less than a year after he'd quit the army, it hovered before him like a college reunion, a chance once more to be brothers-in-arms. Now he has been to funerals of such brothers who thought they were invincible. Now he seldom sleeps a whole night, the churning of a pipe or the whirring of a fan reminding him of other sounds, noises that Ella cannot know. It is not PTSD. He doesn't wake from nightmares in a cold sweat and his heart rate doesn't jump up when he thinks of it, when he thinks of what happened. But it is in his mind every day, exploding afresh. And miluim seems now like something that should be less ordinary than a trivial item of post.

He picks an encrusted lump of something he cannot identify off the bottom of his combat trousers and pulls them on. His mother has insisted on driving him to the base and she will be hovering outside his room any minute now. She has been treating him like this, like a piece of wedding china, ever since his call up arrived, or maybe it has been since he told her about London but the weeks that followed were so full of planning that he didn't have time to make the distinction. A month on, he is still waiting for a response from the British Embassy and her attention is beginning to suffocate. One evening he told her this, told her that she was smothering him, told her that she was interfering.

But was it her, or them? The army? Interrupting him, stopping him, controlling him again.

They tiptoe around each other now.

Udi takes a deep breath as he hears her voice from the hallway and pulls on the last of his uniform before slinging his bag over his shoulder.

"Udi? Are you ready?" comes her entreaty again, shaky in her uncertainty of him.

He hates that this is what he has reduced their relationship to. He can still remember what it felt like to be smaller than her, encased in her arms. But he cannot help prickling and he doesn't thank her enough when she parks the car at the base where he has to register, nor grants her more than a fleeting wave goodbye.

Tomer is standing at the entrance to the base in front of them. Tomer lives in Neve Tzedek, perhaps the most sought-after sector of Tel Aviv. His father is a politician, his mother a doctor, he is studying for his own doctorate. They are not natural friends. But in the army trifling matters like wealth or ethnicity are unimportant. Character, that's the thing. When there is blood on the floor and bullets in your ears. Character. When he spots Udi, he grins. It has been many months and they leap into each other's open arms before smacking hands and squeezing shoulders as they make their way to the registration room. Udi doesn't look back for his mother, but as he walks away he imagines that she might be there still, lingering next to the car, also holding her arms open for him.

They are assigned to the Nurit base at the Lebanese border. Udi tries to mask his relief that they are not returning to Gaza, but Tomer too seems pleased with the result. They room together along with Shimon and Yoni and five of the other men in their unit who they like in varying degrees and love absolutely. Their room is at the far end of the underground base, a coveted location because it is further from the noise of the canteen, and they sleep in bunks, each tower of three less than a foot away from the next. The room stinks. This is better than it can be. There are camps where nobody has their own bed because there aren't enough to go around and sleep is grabbed in a rota fashion on any mattress vacant, so nobody complains, not even Tomer. Udi still jibes Tomer about his comfortable, Ashky upbringing and Tomer calls him a stinking Arab in return.

They are issued with their guns, assigned duties, and within hours it is as though he has never been away. Already his back aches as if in anticipation of discomfort from heavy guns and long patrols and too hard bunks. Already he craves music to sustain him during lone watches. He has eaten just one army meal consisting of something that pretends to be rice and something else that professes to be chicken and already he misses his mother's sambousak. But routine kicks in and numbs him, quietens his mind. Their unit is responsible for 5km of border. If they do not watch, if they are not vigilant, then somebody could cross over. Carrying what? Planning what? They do not know so they must anticipate. Each morning begins at the barbed fence. Udi has to check that no one has crossed during the night, that it hasn't been cut, that there are no footsteps in the raked sand. He talks to the soldiers who have been on guard behind the sandbag lookouts and those finishing their eight hour stint driving up and down in a Humvee, then he inspects the area carefully, trying to give nothing away to the Hezbollah men who from the other side observe things just as keenly. After that he boards a Humvee himself or takes up a post, and that's what he does hour after hour, watching, watching, watching. At least once a day he is interrupted and called to a specific point along the fence. There has been a disturbance. A sensor has gone off. Now he must be alert, and sharp, and not dreaming of other things. Sometimes he is called two or three times and on each occasion goes through the long process of meticulous checks. More often than not it is a rock thrown, or another small incident, barely worth mentioning. But as he works through his checklist he is aware that his reaction is the purpose, not the offending rock. He feels the men on the other side watching him – to see what he will do, what they will do, which parts of the fence are faulty, which cameras are broken, where their weaknesses lie. Watching. He remembers this feeling: when he was a new soldier in uniform stopping in an Arab neighbourhood for a schwarma; and later out of uniform in Mexico but speaking Hebrew; and always when watching international news. A lab gorilla may feel the same. Observed. Scrutinised. He works with one eye on the border.

At the end of his shift he is free, but now there are chores to be done: the laundry, the weapons checks, the cleaning. He has spent an unknown but significant amount of his time in the army cleaning. Sometimes the smell of disinfectant takes him back here, to these corridors, these bunkers. He has only eight hours before his next shift begins and he must sleep, and shower, and eat, but occasionally there is time for a round of cards, there are bets and banter, and then it is almost like boy scouts. Occasionally, Udi even manages not to think. Days pass. More days pass. Udi ticks them off, grateful for the relative quiet. Hopeful that it will stay so. Counting down time. Tomer however grows restless and is therefore the first to volunteer when three men are needed for a surveillance mission on the other side of the border. Shimon is the second – he is still eager for a cross on his gun. But Udi goes only because of Tomer, and because they all expect it of him.

They leave at night and crawl through the sand until they reach the dense shrubbery they have aimed for. There is a smell of darkness, a soil-sodden, mountain-tipped coldness that creeps up their nostrils and under their skin. They know now that they have left the comfort of their thin, hard bunks. Now it is time for truth and reality, for the reason that any of them are here and not flying to London, or at least safe at home with wives and girlfriends, parents and children, lives they are here to protect but not to think about; for now only this, only each other. Udi signals to the others that it is okay to stand and, still hunched, they climb into the bush.

This is every soldier's nightmare. Turning into a rock or a bush and just laying there, laying still for days on end, trying to grab your tuna sandwich from your bag and peeing into a bottle and just waiting, waiting. But there has been intelligence that Hezbollah are about to do something. Something is going to happen. And eyes are needed. Eyes only, they are not to shoot. They are never to shoot without higher authority to do so. Udi wishes Hezbollah were tied by such a restraint, slowed in a similar way.

As though filled with falafel, his stomach churns unhelpfully.

This didn't happen when he was first a soldier, not even here in 2006, during the conflict. Lebanon was his first war and he remembers the solemnity with which he packed his bag for that mission, carried his gun, marched forwards. His neighbour had nodded at him as he'd left the house at the crack of dawn in his fatigues. He was a friend of his parents, another Baghdad immigrant, and that nod, that unspoken recognition, appreciation, it was something he carried with him. Tomer tied an Israeli flag to the antenna of their vehicle. And as they had walked, Udi remembers telling himself calmly that this is what he always knew his training was for – war, conflict – that if something happens, it happens, if he is killed, or if he loses a leg…it could happen in a car crash. He was so philosophical, he thought. And justified in being so because nothing did happen. Not to them. Not that time. He saw things of course – a Lebanese man with a hole in his neck, a small child standing atop a house reduced to rubble, a Humvee on fire – but by the end of the war, that war, Udi still retained a sense of the unassailable. He was young. Yet Tomer has this even now. Tomer remains interminably idealistic about everything, unfathomably unconcerned with the 'ifs' of life. He will worry when the worst happens and not beforehand. Besides, he as well as Shimon is after a cross.

A cross is an honour. A cross shows bravery, proof of contribution made.

It is tough to remember ever believing this. But he did. Back then he was invincible and *they*, the Arabs, the enemy. *They* were the reason that recovery centres in Haifa were filled with children with missing limbs, and he was the protector of those same children. It was an honour to kill one of *them*, and he was honoured to commemorate it. He marked his gun carefully, as though carving in stone. Once. Twice. His third and fourth crosses were heralded by his entire unit: a group of Hezbollah fighters had crossed the border and attacked a Northern kibbutz. It happened at night. They'd found a hole, and footsteps. Udi had tracked them with a Bedouin named Ishmael and after seven hours they had finally spotted the men, lying in the night, blending in with other raised lumps of sand. Ishmael had been sure and Bedouin are never wrong, so Udi had radioed in and secured authority to shoot. They had shot. And they had killed. The unit had cheered when they returned, cheered the deaths of two men who will never again break through the border, never kill another Jew, and Udi had felt proud as he marked two new crosses onto his gun. The pride stayed with him as he received his certificate for courage and placed it carefully in the box of treasures he still stores under his bed. Even when he slept he felt no sadness, no guilt. But that was almost a decade ago. That was before Gaza, before he earned his fifth cross, before Mordechai was blown to pieces trying to prove that there is a God.

The churning comes again.

Udi wishes he had kissed his mother.

He thinks of Ella, imagines her flower-flourished bedroom, the peach-tangled smell of her wet hair.

They sit in the bush for five hours before anything happens. Udi has curled himself as far as he can into the hollow crevice of a tree whose feet their bush adorns, its wooden surface marginally more comfortable than the sharp edges of the hostile shrubbery. They dare not speak since they cannot see who they might be speaking to. They have night vision goggles but these outdated versions rely on starlight to work and in this undergrowth there is none. Udi feels the occasional tap on his boot from Shimon who thinks he has spotted something, then a double tap to indicate it is nothing. Probably just another creature of the night. Tomer's breath is warm on his forearm, but the rest of his body is cold, frozen into numbness by the dark and the activity of staying still. Eventually a dull light creeps through the undergrowth, painting shapes that once were black a ghostly, unsettling grey and transforming masses of mysterious matter into objects still indiscernible before suddenly flooding everything around them with glaring, oppressive colour. Now they can see the terrain before them and they let their eyes adjust to the hub of forest activity. They are hot now and this is worse than the cold. Tomer's breath smells and Shimon's tap is harder to distinguish because other creatures are tapping at his boots, and his legs, crawling all over him. His legs itch. Sometimes it feels as though they are burning again.

Suddenly a group of Hezbollah fighters appear in front of them.

Udi says nothing, but without conferring all three are alert, and listening, with fingers on their triggers, oblivious now to the heat. Tomer and Shimon look repeatedly to Udi because, despite his father's insistence to be rid of it, he is the one who understands the most Arabic. Tomer speaks it also – he has studied and is more proficient than Udi when it comes to business or grammar or proper conversation – but Udi has a knack for the slang and the colloquialisms Israeli professors are unlikely to teach but they are likely to hear. There is, however, nothing much to report. Only four men brandishing guns, speaking of people they do not name and a meeting they do not place. The three of them stay quiet until the men pass, then Udi radios the non-news in. Slowly he feels his muscles un-tense, his shoulders un-stiffen. He feels Shimon and Tomer do the same. He imagines Ella digging her palms into his aching neck.

Now that it is light, they are able to talk, though only in whispers and without moving their eyes from the areas for which they each are responsible.

"When do you think the fuckers will be back?" Shimon asks quietly.

"That's probably not even them," Udi answers to calm him. Shimon has been a liability before; a good soldier but too easily riled.

"Damn. I want my cross," says Shimon.

Neither Udi nor Tomer respond. They both know Shimon too well, know where this passion for blood is coming from. It is almost 15 years since he lost his brother Isaac to a bomb in Jaffa. This is how Shimon describes the perpetrator – a bomb. But it is merely a way for him to depersonalise the individual who strapped on a vest and crossed the border and, because back then there wasn't a fence, strolled unchecked towards a café where Isaac was sitting, just reading the paper and sipping a coffee and maybe thinking about a game of basketball with his kid brother who was on his way to meet him, and exploded Isaac's body so completely that he died right there, on hot Jaffa concrete, and not even in a hospital, on a clean bed, where 11-year-old Shimon who wasn't allowed through the police line might have said goodbye. The ordinary man who did this, this is a perpetrator Shimon will never know, but a bomb… The semantics allow him to hold a whole people to blame and salvage at least some opportunity to put things right: a tooth for a tooth. But Shimon has never killed a man.

"You'll get your cross," Tomer appeases. "Be patient, Shimon. These were not our men."

It is only possible to talk with such gravity when hiding in a bush.

Hours pass. They see nothing but this is where they have been instructed to wait. Occasionally a voice in the distance disturbs their conversation and silences them all until they are sure they are alone again. Sometimes the silence lasts into the minutes and hours that follow. Sometimes it is only an uninvited interlude to a debate that continues unabated as soon as the voice has gone. Eventually it is dark again and now they must be more careful. They take it in turns to sleep, though none of them are able to do so in a restful way; it is always with the thorns of the bush catching an arm or a leg, reminding them how fast pain can come, how vigilant they must be. Shimon is the one to wake them. The glare of the new day is beginning to break through and again four Hezbollah fighters are in front of them, the same men as yesterday, hazy in the dim light but speaking as before in conspiratorial tones that are of no help to listening ears. Udi thinks that he hears the words 'fence' and 'guns'. Tomer thinks they have said 'tomorrow'. Shimon does not speak Arabic beyond a few swear words so cannot know but repeats in a barely audible whisper the words he has heard. One of the men turns and stares directly at the bush the three of them are occupying. Udi freezes, smells falafel. But the man looks away. There is no indication that he has seen them, yet there is that feeling again, that sense of being watched. Then the four men disappear. Again Udi radios in the news and they are told to remain in position. Shimon is excited. He wants to discuss what they have heard and Tomer humours him, but Udi wants only to sleep. He thinks of Ella and how comfortable he is when lying with her, how she squeezes his palm and absent-mindedly prods at his cuticles, how she called him to tell him to be safe during his miluim, though they hadn't spoken in weeks.

"What do you say, Udi?" Shimon demands, kicking his boot. "Is it proof?"

"Huh?" He hasn't been listening. "Proof?"

"That there isn't a God," Tomer explains. "He's talking about Mordechai."

It was inevitable that Mordechai would be brought up at some point, he always is, though Udi has never mentioned him in his civilian life, not even to Ella, and even amongst his unit, amongst these brothers, for almost a week they have been afraid to say his name. It has taken two days of meditation in enemy shrubbery before any of them have been bold enough to brave it.

"Mordechai is proof that the Gazans hate us," Udi says. "That's it."

"He is proof that there is no such thing as God. Or if there ever was that He abandoned us a long time ago," Shimon rebuts. He is one of a growing new tribe of Jews: fierce Zionists, adamant defenders of the Jewish people, and absolute atheists.

"You cannot *prove* that God exists," Tomer sighs, as if this is something he has spent much time working out for himself and is now weary of explaining. "Haven't you read any Rambam, you heathen? Look, you can't prove the positive, you have to disprove the negative. You have to show what God isn't to see the converse, what He is."

"God *isn't* letting His most loyal servant be blown to bits," Shimon says, spitting on the ground in punctuation, a fly quickly descending onto the welcome, unexpected fluid.

"Exactly," Tomer answers. "That wasn't God. That was Hamas."

"You're so damn blind," Shimon argues a little too loudly. "So where was He? Taking a fucking day off?"

Tomer looks to Udi for support, but Udi cannot offer it.

"We have free will, Shimon," Tomer says finally. "We have the ability to choose, to choose our actions, and our actions have consequences. So do the actions of Hamas. It was them who set the bomb, Shimon, not God. And it wasn't God who killed your brother."

"I'm not talking about my brother!" Shimon explodes. He kicks the tree Udi is still sitting in. Udi doesn't take offence. "I'm talking about Mordechai, okay? Remember him? The kid who wore a yamaka and grew his hair into those stupid curls? The kid who could have stayed in yeshiva like everyone else he knew, but didn't. The kid who hated nobody and prayed for everybody? The kid they sent to fight because he was a brilliant shot, our best, better even than you, Udi, and didn't care that every battle was eating away at his soul that he still kept clean from pork and fucking prawns? Do you remember him? Yes? So where was his God? Where is your God now?"

"Shimon, Moredechai stopped in the middle of a back yard, in the middle of Gaza, in the middle of a war." Udi finally contributes. "We should never have been unloading the explosives there. I wanted to go to the wall."

"He was a believer. He thought God would protect him. Isn't that what he said, Udi?"

"He was stupid," Tomer says. "He thought his faith made him invincible. But you can't test God like that. And Mordechai above all people should have known this."

They fall again into silence. Udi stares through the leaves of the bush and tries not to think, not to remember. But Tomer speaks.

"You know, Shimon, God *was* there that day."

"Yeah? Well he didn't do much good."

"But maybe he did." He pauses. "Udi is here. Alive. He had a miracle."

"Not a miracle, Tomer," rushes Udi, unable now not to remember, not to speak. "You can't tell me I had a miracle when right next to me, on top of me, Mordechai was killed. Was that also a miracle? Was it the same one?"

"It was a miracle to see you live."

"I don't want to talk about it."

There is another long pause, tension thrusting through it. Udi's leg muscles contract. He feels again as though they are on fire.

"You know," says Tomer carefully. "Rambam says that really there is no evil, there is only good. We see things as evil because we can only see the effects, not the cause, and because we can only see things from our insignificant perspective of the universe. We can't see the whole plan like He can. Israel is part of the plan. And maybe there was a good reason for-"

"Oh fuck off with your philosophising you fucking Ashky," Shimon says, and puts his hand to his eyes. "Fucking sun," he murmurs. "I can't see a thing."

They remain in silence now for hours, interrupted only by Udi radioing in the news that there is none. Still they are required to wait. Two women in full Arabic dress walk past their bush, gossiping loudly, but other than that there is nothing to distract them from themselves. Udi radios in the sighting and it sparks conversation between them, of their current girlfriends, girls they have slept with, and girls they would like to. Udi enjoys this conversation. He feels closer to Ella. It occupies them for most of the day. They move only to stretch a numbed leg, or to pull a portion of inedible food from their backpacks, or to piss. The rest of the time they sit and allow the sun to melt them. It is almost a relief when night falls again, despite the vulnerability it carries in its dangerous black shield.

It is Udi's turn to sleep first but he cannot. Memories of blood, of fire, of limbs, of screaming veiled women, and of a Gazan man now dead, explode through his mind like fireworks. He had felt no honour in this killing, his fifth, not even the satisfaction of avenging his friend's death, though others had been envious, because probably this was the man who set the bomb, or exploded it, or was at least there to shoot at those still able to crawl from the fire. He had felt only sadness, as he burned, as flesh melted from his legs, and as he was choppered away, only sadness.

They had been checking houses. Looking for tunnels. Searching for Hamas, like cockroaches. They couldn't walk through doors that were probably booby-trapped so used more explosive means. Udi would have felt sorry to damage property in this way and at first they tried to keep it clean, but every house contained weapons, guns, ammo. Many had IDF uniforms – to hide in? To use to infiltrate? To fool? For a young soldier it was like a slap in the face, a repetitive slap. Nobody was to be trusted. And then they'd come to one house where they hadn't found a thing.

It looked nice, like it could be in a quiet suburb in Israel, and the man, the father, was warm, almost welcoming. A grandmother offered them water, children played cautiously. One girl, maybe four years old, looked a little like one of Udi's cousins and he had offered her a bar of chocolate. She was gregarious. She'd smiled and moved towards him before looking to her mother for approval, and when the mother nodded she had taken it. At once her brothers had clamoured, two of them loud and forceful, a third quiet, gentle, singing her name: *Farah, Farah, Farah, please give to me*. Graciously, Farah had shared the sweet between them. And then, hands sticky with chocolate, she had blown Udi a kiss. Which had made him smile. In the middle of a war he had actually smiled at the enemy.

Offering thanks in Arabic to the father, they had left then for the house next door. But a few minutes later, sirens sounded. An ambulance came tearing down the road and Udi and Tomer rushed out of the new house they were checking to see what had happened, who had been hurt, if they could help. A press van was in tow with the ambulance and a man jumped out of it, camera poised. Watching them again. The man from the nice house ran up to Udi. At first he thought he was asking for help but then he started to shout in Arabic and broken Hebrew, to swear, to berate. He waited for the camera to move closer and then he accused Udi of kicking his four-year-old daughter down the stairs. Udi remembers feeling confused, standing confused, like a comic book drawing where question marks are popping out of somebody's head. What had he missed? What had happened? A stretcher was rushed into the house and a moment later it returned, the young girl, Farah, on it. Udi's first idea was that she had been hurt by the father, but thankfully she was sitting up, not hurt, as gregarious as before. She blew him another kiss. And at this the press man shook his head. It didn't work, he told the father. The girl was removed from the stretcher, admonished, pulled roughly inside. The stretcher followed and a moment later it returned, this time the grandmother upon it, more appropriately sprawled, more appropriately wailing and wailing. Now the man of the house went up to Tomer. The camera followed. 'You pushed my mother off the roof!' he insisted.

Now Udi understood. And now he should have felt validated in his mission, in what he had to do. It should have convinced him that civilians were not innocent, that everybody was complicit. It should have freed him to do his job and not think of the factors that lead to it. Just say yes. Say yes and do. But Farah's kiss had bounced through the dusty Gazan air to him. And as she was pulled inside, crying, he felt a wrench, like something vital was being yanked away, plucked from his soul, as though this one small person was important, symbolic, crucial to everything.

After the ambulance had left they returned to the 'nice' house and searched it again. This time they did not try to be clean. They yanked open drawers and pulled clothes out of closets, and that's where they found the opening to the tunnel, and brought it down along with everything on top of it, which included the man's flat screen television, and the grandmother's ancient sewing machine, and Farah's four-year-old's bed.

"And that's what you get when you mess with the IDF," had said Shimon.

Half an hour later, Mordechai had bent down in the middle of a backyard.

Udi is glad they are not back in Gaza. Still, they are here and he needs to sleep, he has to, soon it will be his turn to be alert and watching. Tomer's breath is steady beside him and Shimon is quiet. There is no sound from the undergrowth around them. At last, Udi begins to drift. He dreams of course of Ella, of her determination to distract him when he falls into silent reverie, of the disappointment in her eyes when he did not propose, of her slim, tanned limbs wrapped around him, of the giggle that wakens his soul. Does she know that it is her who sees him through this? Has he ever told her? He sees her dark eyes looking through him, searching him, holding him, willing him to make the moment last forever. And he can feel her hand gently stroking his arm, his back, his leg, stroking, tapping, growing harder, too hard. He wakes. It is Shimon. His eyes are like flashlights. Their whole bush is illuminated.

Udi lurches for the radio and requests backup. The three of them huddle as low as they can while bullets whistle past their ears. Their enemy is the night, the night with guns, but Shimon points slowly in two directions. Tomer adds another, Udi a fourth. He is scared, but it is not the first time he has been shot at and as always their training kicks in. The radio crackles and they are told that backup is at least half an hour away.

"Great, so we're a three-man army," Shimon whispers, though whispering is no longer necessary.

"I've got your back," says Tomer. "Have faith."

They open fire. The guns are so loud that it is impossible to tell which sounds are incoming and which they are producing themselves. The bombardment collects in their eardrums as one continuous explosion. Udi strains to see in his night vision goggles and thinks of Ella, then of his mother and her open arms. And his always-strong father. The fire continues to rain down. Tomer curses. He has been hit, but it is only his calf and only a graze. They battle on. More bullets. More explosions in their ears. More moving shadows they cannot identify darting out in front of them, running towards them. Shimon throws up. The vomit smells, but not as much as the gunfire with its smoky, ashy stench. One of the shadows in front of them falls to the ground. They do not hear the thud, but each of them feel it, like dropping a weight. They continue to shoot. They continue to be shot at. Then Udi raises his hand and they stop. For a few minutes the clatter of bullets continues, but less than before and from only two directions. Then there is silence. It is louder than any noise of the last 30 minutes, heavy with the certainty that it will not last. Udi's radio crackles again and he is told that backup is arriving. It does, from both sides, and in less than ten minutes the sharp, tiny missiles come afresh, though now they fly from what seems like everywhere. Occasionally there is a pause, but only a pause, and then more of that jarring sound, on and on and on, until eventually, it is light.

Slowly, Tomer, Shimon and Udi stand up. Holding hands to eyes they see five of their fellow soldiers emerge from shrubbery nearby. There is no one else. No bodies clutter the ground. No enemy fighters stand ready to shoot them in the dawn hue. Only the empty shells littering the earth tell that there has been a battle and only the blood soaking the soil and quenching the thirst of the morning flies reveal that anyone was hit.

"Do I get a cross? How do I know if it was me? Fuck," Shimon says despairingly. "Fuck."

"It was you," Tomer tells him. He points to a pool of blood. "See there – I remember when he went down. It was early and you were the only one firing that way. It was you, Shimon."

He looks to Udi for confirmation. Udi nods and Shimon lets out an obscene laugh. "I fucking got him," he shouts.

Then he laughs again, before falling silent, his mouth hanging in a fixed, wild, unnerving grin.

Neither of them approach him. Tomer tends to his own wound and Udi returns to the bush for his backpack. They are in a state of shock, euphoric in their continuing existence and quietened by the same. They need to hurry, return to their side of the border, but Udi sits for a moment in the hollow of the tree that for three days has been his shelter. He leans back against the bark where just hours before he rested his head and dreamt of Ella. And he thinks of her again.

"Wowee," Shimon says, still smiling as he walks over to Udi and points at the bark just above his head.

"What?"

"Look."

Udi kneels up and looks at where Shimon is pointing. The whole surface of the tree is indented with metal, plastered with it, practically forming a circle around the space where Udi's head has been. For a moment he cannot move. His limbs feel paralysed. It hurts to breathe. But slowly he takes out a knife and one by one he digs out the pieces of shrapnel. They are still warm in his hand, the edges sharp and deadly. Udi finds himself unable to speak. Shimon too is quiet. But to their left there is a breaking of twigs underfoot.

"There!" Tomer shatters the silence as he limps towards them. He points fiercely to the pockmarked tree. "There, there is your proof you damn atheists. There is God."

The following day their unit is abruptly re-stationed. Udi can only guess that security along the Lebanese border has been tightened, that the incident is being explained to the press. He can only hope that the small information they provided is useful, that it will aid protection, that there was some point to it all. He does not know, but he hopes regardless. They spend much of the morning driving south. Attached to a petrol station they stop at is a small supermarket. It is a 'peace' market, one of a chain that employs Palestinian baggers and Jewish cashiers. In perfect harmony. Of course it will not bring peace. It is the kind of leftie idea dreamed up by idealists like his sister, an example to prove the possibility. Unconvincing to men who have just spent three days inside enemy territory. Still, Udi overhears two of the baggers talking about football and he weighs in with his assessment of the season's best goals. Even Shimon joins the conversation. And Udi notices a young Jewish boy listening to the four of them. His eyes pass from one man to the other – soldiers, Palestinians, equally good sources of football passion. This store will not bring peace, but Udi smiles. The same smile he gave Farah all those years ago in Gaza. Yet, back on the bus, the football talk is over. Shimon is excitable again and wants to relive the gun battle for their friends. Tomer has been despatched home (though only for the weekend) so Udi turns to the window on his own, fingering the drink he bought from the Jewish cashier, packed by the Palestinian bagger, and the shrapnel still in the pocket of his fatigues. He closes his eyes, but does not sleep.

They are only at the base long enough to unload their bags before leaving for the flying checkpoint. It is not Gaza but the West Bank has its own challenges. Not external danger in the same way, not that feeling of each moment being precarious, each second demanding absolute attentiveness, but an internal wrestling with one's soul. It would have been easier to be at Ezra even, or Qalandia with their glass cubicles and steel-door mazes, and long scrutinised walks, and miles of traffic: precious meters of disconnection. Instead, Gazan men and women file towards them: some in cars that they stop, others on foot; some with the correct documentation, others without; some granted passage, others denied it; some proud, defiant, others bent by the exhaustion of every day explaining themselves to soldiers young enough to be their sons. There is a Jewish settlement nearby, so extra explanation is demanded.

Shimon and Udi stand together, guns poised. Shimon seems to grow in this role, to broaden. He is still pumped from their experience the day before, his eyes alert, hands twitchy. Full of his own might. On a cigarette break he expresses to Udi the magnitude of responsibility he feels here. 'We could be the ones, you know, Udi? The ones who stop the bomb. The last line before Israel, before some fucker gets close enough to my town, to my house, to my family to- you know?' Udi nods. Yes, he does know. But he is preoccupied watching a family some way in the distance who have exited their car, perhaps because of the jam their checkpoint is causing. There are four children, three boys and a girl. The girl is maybe four years old. Of course Udi knows it is impossible for the girl he saw in Gaza all those years ago to have remained the same size, the same age, and of course it is unlikely she would have made it here to the West Bank, this is not Farah, but there is something about her that is familiar. As her parents and another two adults ignore her, with her sandal she draws lines in the dirt. Udi is too far away to make out what she is drawing, but he would like to see. Next to him, cigarette finished, Shimon shouts for somebody to stop.

Udi does not want to watch. Shimon is not physical with the people he interrogates, not cruel, but he is not polite and he will not make things easy. He will not let a car pass without first checking underneath the baby seat. He will not accept an identity card without scrutinising the corresponding profile from both sides. He will always ask the women to lift their veils. Even without Shimon, Udi hates this kind of assignment. It makes him think back to his childhood of action movies and superheroes. What was it Spiderman's uncle told him? *With great power comes great responsibility.* But it is remiss to without challenge wave people past. And he knows that for Shimon, every fence, every checkpoint is for his brother.

"Fucking Arabs," Shimon says as one of the men flashes him a smile.

Udi nods again. He nods a lot when he is a soldier. Nods. Assents. Shimon tells the couple who are next in the queue to

126

open and empty their suitcases. They are young, handsome, a little reverential towards each other, perhaps just married. White, neatly folded garments are placed onto the dusty ground. Then a washbag. Then a pack of sanitary towels. The couple keep their heads lowered as they unpack these private possessions. Udi turns away. He returns his gaze to the young girl. She has stopped drawing and is being ushered back into the car by her mother. The father and other men remain outside but they will all drive this way soon. Udi will tell Shimon to let them through.

As he is imagining this, an ambulance drives fast towards the checkpoint. Shimon puts his hand out to stop it and the Arab driver jumps out, frantically explaining that he is driving a pregnant woman who is about to give birth and the nearest hospital is on the other side of the checkpoint, on the other side of this obstacle they have created, on the other side of them.

"Let him through," Udi says quietly.

"Wait a minute." Shimon walks around the van and peers through the window. A woman is lying inside clutching her stomach and at the sight of Shimon she starts to scream. Now the man shouts wildly too, gesticulating to be allowed to move forwards, to be allowed to move. Udi thinks at once of the lecture Avigail gave him a few years back about pregnant women at checkpoints. It had been in the news too: Delays by IDF soldiers at one of the crossings had resulted in tens of women giving birth at the checkpoint, in the dirt, a number of them miscarrying, some of the women dying.

"Shimon, just let them through."

"Okay, okay," Shimon relents, waving the ambulance on and turning back to the young couple who are now repacking their dusty clothes. Udi signals to the soldiers a little further along to allow the ambulance to pass and watches as it hurries forwards. He feels better. A little better. He turns his eyes back to the girl and her family, but the car she was in has turned and is driving away. Away? The father has remained with the other two men outside. They are standing, touching one another on the shoulder, bowing slightly, looking towards the ambulance…

"Stop!" Udi spins towards Shimon and then to the soldiers whom the ambulance has almost reached. "Stop! Don't let it through!"

Two soldiers quickly move in front of the vehicle, guns ready. A third gets on the radio. Udi glances to the men in the distance and sees their heads raise defiantly, their stare unflinching. Udi and Shimon race to catch up to the van. Together they throw open the doors. The pregnant woman is still lying, still screaming, but there is something else in her eyes, something more salient than pain, or fear. Udi climbs into the vehicle and makes to help her up. She waves her hands at him and begins to wail hysterically, motioning him away, clasping her arms around her belly. The driver tries to intervene but is stopped by Shimon. Udi moves forward again and roughly pulls the woman to her feet. Something hard and metal falls from underneath her dress.

***

He does not cry but Ella can see in his eyes the boy who wants to, could hear it in his voice when he called to say he had a one-day leave, asked to see her. They have not met in many weeks and spoke only once before he left for miluim. She has been mourning him, mourning their lost future, wearing nothing but black. But she could not say no.

He looks strong standing at her door in his army fatigues. His body does not shake, or fail, or ask to be held. His hands are sturdy when he puts down his gun. His words are sure when he says he wants her. But when they are in bed he will not take control, will not bend her forwards, he wants her to be on top, dominating him.

Afterwards, she raids the fridge for leftovers of her mother's cooking and stacks them up on a plate that she brings to him in bed. Her parents had left that morning for their annual visit to their cousins in the north so for once they have space and they are alone and could, if they chose to, undress their intentions and desires as well as each other. But Ella tells of the essay she is struggling to write, and of a funny incident with a customer at work, and of the latest gossip from their friends. She does not ask about where he has been sent or what he has seen. She does not ask about London. She does not once mention marriage. She tries to smile frequently, to feed him lots, to run him a bath despite the water shortage, to make sure he knows that he is loved. It is what he needs and she has grown used to putting him back together, though she has always kept such handiwork to herself. And will do. Even now. Despite her shattered heart, it is better for Udi to believe that she is the insecure one, she the one who depends on him.

***

"Let me tell you a story," says Tomer.

They are back on the Lebanese border, playing cards on top of their bunks. Shimon has already lost his stash of cigarettes and stormed out to buy more. The rest of their roommates are occupied in other sections of the base. Udi has just told Tomer about London. He hadn't wanted to think about it. Not now, not while there is nothing he can do to make it happen. And not since seeing Ella. But the topic has materialised and Tomer has taken issue. Udi tried to explain: it is the money, the economy, the shitty jobs. "It's different for you," he had urged. "What do I have?"

"You have Is-ra-el."

"I need more."

"There is no more. Israel is the greatest country in the world."

"Come on, Tomer."

"Let me tell you a story."

Tomer lays his hand of cards on the mattress. It is a full house and Udi cannot beat it. Tomer takes the cigarettes from the pool in the middle and shuffles the deck. Udi takes one of the cigarettes back from Tomer's hoard and lights it. "Okay," he says. "Enlighten me."

"So okay, do you know the story of Joshua and Ulla?"

Udi almost chokes on his cigarette. "Fuck off, Tomer. You're going to try to talk me out of this with biblical mumbo jumbo? I don't even believe in God." He says this while unconsciously reaching his hand to his pocket where tiny pieces of shrapnel still remain. It is only out of habit, but he has become used to rolling them in his palm, like prayer beads.

"This is basic talmud," Tomer insists. "Just listen, it's a good story."

"Okay," Udi says, waving his hand impatiently. "*Y'allah*."

"Okay. So Joshua ben Levi was a rabbi who lived in a time when the Judeans were being persecuted by the Romans and being denied their independence," Tomer begins. "Ulla was a freedom fighter and Joshua hid him in his attic." Udi nods to convey that yes, he is still with him. Tomer is studying for his philosophy doctorate at the Tel Aviv University and sometimes supposes that others will not understand the things he has already learned. "So when the Romans knocked on Joshua's door they told him that if he did not turn Ulla over to them, then many others would be captured and executed. So, what should he do? It was legal, according to the biblical precedents, it was legal for him to turn Ulla over, but was it right? In the end, Joshua let Ulla decide, and on hearing the predicament, Ulla chose of his own accord to give himself up. Good, right? He saved everyone's skins. It was the best outcome for the masses. Well maybe, but then Elijah stopped talking to Joshua."

"Elijah the prophet?"

"Right. And he used to talk to Joshua okay, but now he tells him that acting legally wasn't enough, he would only communicate with people who were truly moral. And he stopped talking to the rabbi. So you see, it's not enough to act according to the law, or even to be good. Jews must aspire to be perfect, in even the smallest of interactions, and Israel must aspire to be a true light amongst nations."

"Okay. It's a good story," Udi says. "Now what the fuck does that have to do with me?"

"Because you can see it. And I can see it, in your face, all the time, Udi. You don't like it when what we do here doesn't feel just, even when we're well within our rights to do it, and we *are* well within our rights, we are the most moral army in the world."

Udi raises his eyebrows.

"I know that's why you want to go. But that is why you should stay. So that we can build Israel."

"Have you seen Tel Aviv lately?" Udi coughs. "Israel is built."

"Not shovels and hammers, Udi. Real building. We're 66 years old, that's nothing. We need people like you."

"Tomer, I want to go to make money-"

"Bollocks, you want to go because- "

Shimon comes rushing into the room and the blackness of his face hushes them. He lifts his hands into the air. "You haven't heard?" Their own expressions reveal that they haven't. "There's been an attack on Kibbutz Malkiya. A Katyusha rocket. They don't know yet if people are hurt."

Udi and Tomer need not look at each other. Without consultation their cards and philosophy are abandoned and their minds are back here, again, back now, again, narrowed again to this.

Malkiya is a small community a short drive away. Udi was there two days ago.

Nobody will blame them, but the town is on their border, the border they are patrolling, responsible for, the border the three of them crossed just weeks ago to find out if something was being planned.

131

His parents will know already. They'll be watching the news, worrying, waiting for confirmation that no soldiers were involved, hanging on for the beeps. They will know the politics. The context. The reaction of the world.

Udi, a soldier, knows nothing. He will do. He will say yes and do. But there are no orders yet.

He takes his mobile phone outside of their underground base. He has not spoken to his parents since being away. Despite the insistent image of his mother hovering by the car, he has not picked up the phone. He could not. Staring at it now he sits on a pile of superfluous sandbags without dialling. He fingers the shrapnel in his pocket. *Qus. Y'allah*.

Batia's voice is full of panic and relief. "Thank you for phoning, Udi," she tells him, too profusely. "Thank God you are okay. When can you come home?"

"Four days to go," he tells her. Prickling and softening. "I'll be back for dinner on Friday."

"I'll make tabyeet," she says. "And sambousak."

Instinctively, Udi smiles. Although his body is pumping with the adrenalin of impending action, although he is exhausted, and also fearful, and also ready, and although he has so far resisted the pull of his mother's voice, the danger in calling her, for a moment he allows himself to hear it, her, home. She continues to talk and he lets her. He imagines his family standing around a table filled with food. He can feel his sister kissing his cheek, hear her children careering wildly around the garden. Catch Ella in the corner, smiling. His mother talks on and he tastes sambousak. He can sense his father's solid, decisive presence, and hear his brother's laughter. Batia continues. Something about making sure he eats enough and has he spoken to Ari and…He closes his eyes…

Then suddenly there is the sound of bullets.

"What's that? Udi, what's that? Udi? Can you hear me?"

He can hear, but he is no longer listening. Or tasting, or dreaming. Stuffing the phone into his pocket, with gun in hand, Udi races from the sandbags to the trenches that lead to the lookouts at the top of the hill. One of the men from his unit is flat on the floor. Another is on the radio crouched behind a sandbag and indicates for Udi to stay down. Udi crawls towards the overhang and waits for the signal. He sees Tomer running out of the base below him, Shimon just behind. Tabyeet and sambousak and the gentle nagging of his mother are already a million miles from his mind. London is even further. There is only sand and dust and Israel, and the need to survive.

***

Then

7

They are in the east of the city. In a narrow street where the angle of the sun on stone cobbles gives the whole place a coating of rust. There is a faint smell of sewage, and something else, something cooking, deep-fried with a lot of oil.

They shouldn't be there. Dara slips a flattened pack of cigarettes out of the wallet in which she has squashed it and offers the crumpled sticks to Naomi and Rachel. They each take one, in unison, then spark the lighter and inhale a shallow drag. Resisting the splutter, Dara leans against the rust-tinted wall behind them, her pert bottom and golden head just grazing it, allowing her back to arch and press forward her breasts. She is wearing her regulation school t-shirt, but she has shrunk it by leaving it overnight in a sink of hot water and it is now tighter than it should be. She cannot help glancing into the window of the building opposite to regard her curves. Dara is 15 and already 'developed', as her mother would say. Her legs have shot up, and her breasts have shot out, and her hips have somehow softened. Her hair is long with sun-bleached blonde strands streaking through golden brown and she has been told by Shmuel that she looks a little like Julia Roberts, when she was younger, in her *Pretty Woman* days, though without the red. Unlike Julia Roberts, Dara is not wearing makeup and knows she doesn't need to. Not because her skin is clear and her lips are full without it, although they are. But because she is acutely aware of the unspeakable allure of sexuality mixed with youth. It has blinded the boys in her class, the teacher too; she is able to do anything.

Naomi, Rachel and Dara have bunked the last lesson of school so they can come here. They have told each other that they want to see this worn down, worn in, worn out part of the city. All three of them are studying art and have grand ideas about finding truth in humanity. They have decided that this is where they will find it, in East Jerusalem where the Arabs have not built high-rise apartment blocks like the ones they live in, where poverty is abundant and written on faces they can paint. It is only incidental to them, they say, that this is a neighbourhood their parents have banned them from walking alone, that the Arab men here stare at them with an intensity laced with danger. This is their second visit. They speak to each other here in English instead of Hebrew. They come early, before it is dark.

Dara's brother would kill her if he knew where she was. At least he would if he were older. She has grown up quicker and suddenly he looks like a little boy to her. He is athletic and lanky, but not filled out, his face not yet really in need of a shave, although he runs the wet razor encouragingly over his fluffy cheeks, in preparation. In just a few years, even if his hair hasn't come in, he will be considered a man and he will join the army. But for Dara he lacks the appropriate masculinity that is now required for her to take him as seriously as she used to, to talk as they once did.

When she has finished her cigarette, Dara takes out her sketchpad. Her mother is a psychologist and has told her about *collective trauma* and *mob mentality* and so Dara does not fear or despise the Arabs as much as some of her friends do. They see them often enough although they are invisible – working on construction sites, as cleaners, the dark faces in the mirrors of taxis – but that is on the other side of the city, where their presence feels controlled and sanitised, and tallied in blue card. Not here. Here they occupy the foreground. This is their territory. She can smell their open drains.

Naomi and Rachel have spotted a young Arab boy playing amongst a pile of rubble and they are scribbling furiously, but the image feels patronising to Dara, offensive somehow. She has moved away from them, a little further up the winding street that bends to the left and darts off like a rabbit warren. She sits on the dusty floor and stretches her legs out in front of her. She is wearing cut-off jeans that come to her ankle, but they ride up as she balances her sketchpad on her knees and reveal a glimpse of the slim curve of her bronzed calf. Passers by in full-length skirts and covered heads glance at her disapprovingly. Dara looks up. She is trying to catch the shadow that the canopy opposite is throwing against the cobbles, but the light won't stay still, the shading is wrong, too stilted. She scrutinises the image on her pad before finally turning the page to begin again. When she looks up this time, a man has walked into the shadow. Out of the canopy. From under it. Behind him, she now notices a selection of tired posters pasted onto the window below. She cannot read Arabic but sees pictures of computers. The man stands still, territorially marking the shop's doorway. He is looking directly at her.

Dara does not move. She has an urge to stand up, to run even, but she doesn't. The man is wearing dark jeans and a dishevelled white t-shirt. Unlike her brother, his arms pull at the sleeves as though the thin material is struggling to contain a masculine power that simmers underneath. The man's skin is dark, his hair short, almost shaved, matching the generous stubble around his mouth from which a half-smoked cigarette is hanging. It is one he has rolled himself. Unbranded. Imperfect. He breathes deeply and does not splutter.

Dara pretends to be consumed by her sketching but after a few moments she cannot resist lifting her head again. The man is still looking at her. She can feel the heat of his eyes tracing her exposed calf, her denim-clad thigh, her developed chest. She feels that she should cross her arms to cover herself, but instead, she adjusts her stance so that he can see her better and rests the end of her pencil between her lips. She is testing herself, or him, or something: the complexity of the city, or her womanhood, daring to touch it. She feels his eyes linger, then slowly they move again, upwards, until finally they reach her own. Dara does not look away. She never looks away, never allows herself to be the first to buckle, it is something she has been practising. The boys in her class have such an inflated sense of themselves, all machismo and testosterone; she likes to assert for them a challenge. Shmuel calls her *difficult, high maintenance*. Dara waits for this man to lower his eyes. His stare, however, is rubber-banded. It stretches on, tugging tighter and tighter. He takes another casual drag of his self-made smoke and there is amusement in the way that he watches her, as though he is sure of himself, here, and knows that she isn't. There is something else too. Something elemental. Hot. Dara feels it bouncing between them across the rusty, dusty ground, though it is possible too that it is simply the beginning of the long summer heat. Her tight t-shirt feels a little damp at the armpits.

When Naomi and Rachel fall giggling into her, Dara watches as, at last, the man loosens his stare, glancing down to the ground where he stubs out his cigarette. Released, she allows herself to be dragged up from the floor and back down the narrow road in the same direction from which they have come. Her friends are giddy, and loud, and in a rush. If they are late their parents will ask questions. Understandably, she supposes, since the bombs.

Eighty-two Israelis murdered in one month. Dara's father says this over and over, his hand touching his head, as though it needs holding up. Another 15 in the past two weeks. The last bomb at the market where her mother shops.

When Dara glances back at the man she cannot help but wonder what he thought when he saw the bloody Jerusalem chaos flicker urgently across the news channels. He, one of them. When he stares at her this time, her chest tightens, her voice dissipates, fear touching her tongue.

And then in the same moment, he smiles. With that same hint of amusement as before, that same air of confidence. She doesn't smile back. She tosses her light-licked hair over her shoulder and links her arm through Naomi's. But later, when she is home, watching TV with her too-young brother, she remembers that smile only, and not the other thoughts that for a tainted moment exploded inside her head.

It is almost a week before Dara returns to the east of the city. This time she is alone. It is Friday lunchtime and her mother thinks she is at the mall with Naomi and Rachel, but she has not even told these best of friends where she is going. All week the tail whip of excitement has lingered in the pit of her stomach, and it feels as though this visit should be kept clandestine, coiled. In the depths of her backpack lie a rapidly warming can of Diet Coke, her school pencil case containing drawing pencils, a battered sketchpad, *Don't Call it Night* by Amos Oz, a newly bought, un-crumpled packet of cigarettes, and her wallet. These are Dara's tools. She has anticipated both a long wait and none at all; for either she is in need of occupation.

She walks for a long time before she finds again the winding road and the computer posters and the canopy. This part of the city feels maze-like to Dara, riddled with turns and archways and unfamiliar alleys that seem to rise and dip and flow into the next as though they are all connected, and all lead nowhere. She strides forward however and imprints each bend purposefully into her mind: the cracked parts of stone walls, and graffiti, and half-erected houses, and windows without glass; crumbs for her to track back by. As she progresses, time evaporates, centuries unravel, modernity turns to dust.

He is there.

Standing exactly as before, smoking, he sees her as soon as she rounds the corner, though it is not clear whether he watches her so closely because he remembers, or because he would watch any girl with fair skin and light hair. Despite her preparations, Dara is not ready. She wonders if she should walk on a bit, pretend that she has passed this way again only by chance, on her way to the Arab market that for a blonde-haired tourist – which she could easily be – is a thing to do. But in the end she refuses to fluster and sits resolutely opposite the canopy, delving into her backpack for her sketchpad and pencils. She can feel the man observing her again and in the small alley her movements seem suddenly exaggerated and disproportionate. She glances up purposefully, squinting through the sun as if to study the shadows before her. The man is still standing, amused, in her periphery, and it is difficult to pretend that she hasn't noticed him. Or intended it. He crosses his sandaled feet and leans an elbow against the shop front, regarding her with an absolute nonchalance that is laced with lightning. Dara squints again. With determination she makes a series of fluid markings that are still too stilted and she forces herself to stare at them on her pad, slowly counting a minute, two, three, before looking back up. She has waited too long. He is gone.

Unsubtly and with uncharacteristic frenzy, Dara now glares up and down the road for a glimpse of him, but she cannot make out his white t-shirt amongst the lethargic throng. Dara stands up. As she does so, her pad falls from her lap and sends up a cloud of dust, her pencil rolls slightly down the road, and the shadows are still in front of her and not possible for her to pin down. Dara crosses the road and walks defiantly into them. She touches the canopy, an object at last, solid, firm. And then suddenly, the man is by her side.

"What are you doing?"

He has appeared again from inside the shadows, inside the shop, and he speaks to her in Hebrew, not Arabic. Also not in

English or French or Spanish. He knows she is not a tourist but an Israeli Jew. His Hebrew is flawless. Dara spins around. Up close, the man is younger than she had imagined, she guesses 21, 22, although he leans against the wall again with the same mixture of assurance and weariness that had fooled her. His eyes are almost jet black, unnerving in their absence of light. It is as though they are able to pierce right through her, to look but not be looked at. To see but be unseen. Dara wishes that her pad, her explanation, was in her hand and not languishing in the dirt across the path. Nonetheless she answers confidently.

"I am drawing, of course." She says this in Hebrew and waves her hand towards her abandoned tools. "You were watching me draw, no?"

The man smiles, his teeth imperfect but casting whiteness against his dark skin. It seems to uplift him. Dara flicks her golden hair over her shoulder. His eyes have not left hers and they follow this movement as though he is a cat and she his plaything, or prey.

"I am an art student," she tells him.

Now his smile prickles at the corners with laughter. He takes a roll-up out of his pocket and taps it on the end of his lighter. "A student? Yes, I saw you here last week. With some friends, no? You were in your school shirt." Dara blushes. "How old are you? 16?"

"I'm 17," she lies quickly. "I'll be finished school next year, I'll be going to the army-" She stops, but if he's offended his face does not betray it. "And then to university."

The man nods and seems to stare at her harder, as if waiting for the last flicker of her untruth to pass between them. His black eyes continue to pierce her own and occasionally they brush downwards. Dara feels intensely aware of her sun-kissed shoulders, exposed in a white vest since she removed the t-shirt she'd had on top, and of the red bra she is wearing underneath it, the material hinting with a pink hue at the generous area it is covering, the straps escaping altogether.

She grapples for something else to say and feels a need to impress him. An unfamiliar compulsion.

"I'm going to study art and art history," she volunteers.

But the man ignores this. He puts his hand on the wall behind her and tilts his head down, close to her face. "What is your name?"

"Dara." She pauses. "It means compassion."

"Dara." The man accepts the name and seems to consider it, to consider her, as he lights his cigarette and inhales the strong smoke, holding it in his lungs for many seconds before relinquishing it to the heated Jerusalem air. Air that feels closer here, where people are closer, where there is less of it to share between them. "Dara, what is it you are trying so hard to draw?" he asks her finally.

"The shadows. From the canopy. But the light is difficult."

"You don't have shadows near your home?"

Dara flinches. Of course she has shadows. It is not even a beautiful part of the city. "Art is everywhere," she replies assuredly.

The man smiles. His eyelids bat a few times in quick succession as though he is a camera readjusting his focus, then he lets his hand slide down the wall so that it is almost touching her shoulder. "You should come back in the evening," he tells her.

This time, Dara does not have a quick response on her tongue. She can smell the smoke on his breath, feel the warmth of it, see deep into the black pools of his fortress eyes. In the reflection they provide, she can also see her own wide stare and wonders if he has noticed the fear in them. The fear and abrupt, surprising longing.

He has seen something, for he laughs. "The light is better in the evening." Standing straight and a little back from her, he removes his hand from the wall. "You can own it then. At this time of day it is too high, too harsh, too bright to see the colour. It is hard even to capture the form it illuminates. Or to break it." He grins. "Even with compassion, Dara."

"You know about art?" she asks, surprised.

"I know about many things." He takes another puff of his cigarette.

"I know. Of course. I didn't mean-"

The man laughs again. "I am Kaseem," he tells her. "And you, you are very beautiful."

***

As she walks away – taking in the crumbled walls and the angry graffiti on them – she glances back again over her shoulder, her golden hair swishing to the side, her skin pale and pure.

Come back in the evening, he said.

Beautiful, he said.

But she is an enemy, as well as a beautiful thing.

***

Then

8

She goes three times a week. Sometimes Naomi and Rachel are with her but then she and Kaseem have to stick to niceties and he cannot show her how to de-emphasise her lines, or how to transform shape into form, or illustrate how the space in her sketchings is just as important as the content. How to own the light. He has been teaching her about gradation and her latest pieces seem to contain more movement, more rhythm than before. Kaseem says that art is about knowing oneself, or at least about the quest to know. Once, he dug out one of his old canvases and revealed a city landscape that had overwhelmed Dara with an uncomfortable feeling of claustrophobia. "Why have you painted the sky black?" she had asked him. "And a blue and white sun?" And he had answered that a blue sky was something he knew, but black was what he felt. Adding colour, he said, adds the truth.

When they are alone, he traces that truth for her. He translates extracts of Arabic love poetry, *ghazals* he calls them; unfamiliar words sounding smooth on his tongue, as though uncluttered by grammar and rubble. He shows her inside his computer shop. If his uncle is there then they examine the broken machines it is Kaseem's job to fix, his fingers moving fast and deftly over their insides. His uncle calls Dara 'beauty', but there is something about the way he says this that feels threatening, degrading almost, and often it is on his arrival that she makes for home. When his uncle is not there, it is Kaseem who tells her she is beautiful, and when he says it it has an altogether different effect. He cups her baby-faced chin in his hands, pushes streaks of gold behind her ears, and brings his ever-amused smile close to her soft, longing lips. He hasn't kissed her yet. Dara feels this as both a compliment and an insult, and of course it makes her want him more.

This time, Naomi and Rachel are with her. They have stopped outside Kaseem's shop and Dara knocks on the window for him. Naomi wants to know why they must always stick to this same part of the city. She wants to explore, she says, to dig deeper. Neither of Dara's friends are interested in talking to Kaseem. At first they thought him handsome and exotic; but he does not smile at them in the way he does Dara, he does not pay attention to their flirtations, his Hebrew University education is not Arabic enough for them, and his offers of water (laced with the risk of diarrhoea) are too much so. They are anxious to return to the children with no shoes swinging their legs on the half-built or half-destroyed stone walls. Nevertheless they wait for Dara. They would not be so irresponsible as to leave her alone with him.

Kaseem emerges into the light, smiling. He has had a job interview and thinks he will get it. His confidence is soaring. "A Coke for my beautiful artist," he says, handing a can wet with condensation to Dara, and then presents one each to Naomi and Rachel. They look at Dara questioningly.

"*My beautiful artist?*" repeats Naomi.

"How very… possessive," says Rachel.

And now Kaseem has to backtrack. Nothing yet happened but without conferring, she and Kaseem seem to have decided to keep whatever is not happening solely between themselves. "I see you all the time with your sketchpads," he says casually. "You are all beautiful artists, no? What are you always drawing?"

Now Naomi and Rachel are tempted into conversation. They like this about Kaseem, they will concede later, that he seems interested in their distractions, that he will let them talk without them having to shout over men who think this is their prerogative. 'Emotional intelligence', they will call it. But this is long after they have whispered to Dara in urgent, anxious tones on the windy road home: "What the hell are you doing? He's an Arab. You can't trust them. You know they only want one thing." This is after Dara has denied her secret, tightly coiled crush.

Kaseem and Dara exchange glances as Naomi and Rachel talk and sip their drinks. It is a scorching, airless day and she is wearing a dress that flaps about her thighs when she moves. She can see him watching it, chasing the cotton with his jet-black eyes. She wishes it was possible for her to peer behind them, behind the darkness, but she does not yet know how. Nevertheless, there is something noble about the way he carries himself, something mysterious and heroic. And poetic. He is a weary warrior, he is a challenger of inequality, he is not the kind of Arab others may expect. They finish their Cokes. Dara agrees to go with Naomi and Rachel to find the market where Naomi wants to buy a special Arabic bread they can't get at home and Rachel wants to draw the vendors, and when she hands Kaseem her empty can, their fingers touch.

"The light is better in the evening," he whispers.

That afternoon, the sketches Dara draws at the market are full of texture and clashing shapes. When she gets home, she seeks out her coloured pencils and adds hue upon hue of red.

***

"It's so sad, the girl was 23. The entire family has been devastated," Dara's mother says, pausing between mouthfuls of new potatoes. It is dinner. Dara has been back from the market in East Jerusalem, fondling her reds, thinking of Kaseem, for three hours. Downstairs, her mother has been locked behind the heavy door of her study where she runs her home practice on the days that she isn't at the hospital. It had been left to Dara to make dinner and distractedly she had thrown together this concoction of new potatoes and salad with a casserole re-heated from the previous night, not really paying attention, knowing that neither will her family when they eat it. Conversation has always been more important than food; it is the sustenance of their lives.

Dara's mother has been counselling some of the families of the latest Egged bus bombing. It is work she has done before over the years but the heavy fist of this time seems to have hit her harder. Perhaps because it was so close. Perhaps because so many died. Perhaps because it was the third time on the same route and because she has a husband and a son and a daughter who take the buses and who could have been one of the dead or one of these grieving relatives she is counselling. Never before has she restricted Dara's movements, issued curfews or warnings; but she's told Dara twice this week not to get on any buses, and after another bite of potato she shakes her head. "They are a cruel, brutal people."

"They?" asks Dara. "Who are *they*? *All* Arabs are fanatics?" She knows this is not what her mother thinks, not really. Both of her parents have been vociferous in challenging just this kind of prejudice, they have written papers and letters and held meetings to that effect. And though there are no Arabs in her school, there are times when they pass them in the street and Dara's parents do not mutter the insults or cautions she has heard other parents pass on. Dara's father even speaks some Arabic and sometimes when they have come across Arab families when they have been hiking in nature reserves, he has struck up conversations with them, and Dara has seen them laughing at each other's jokes. "*All* of them are suicide bombers?" she presses.

"Of course not. First it depends what kind of Arab we are talking about: Christian, or Bedouin, or Muslim or... But the Muslims, there is something in them, I think, now. Something, violent, that makes them, that makes them send their children to murder ours. It's a psychological phenomenon."

"That's ridiculous. You can't judge a whole people from a few," Dara insists. "You're being racist."

"Not racist," Dara's father intercedes. "Realist. I don't like to say it either, Dara, I want to hope too, but more than 82 Israelis murdered in one month... And you see, even right here in Jerusalem, the Arabs who are citizens, who have rights, who enjoy the benefits of being an Israeli, even they celebrate when we die." He looks tired, older somehow. "Maybe Sharon has it right."

"You hate Sharon," says Dara's brother. He has been playing basketball and is still in his sweaty vest. It is too small for him now. He is growing fast, though still only upwards. "You said Sharon is too hard-line. You said he'll only cause more violence."

"I know." Dara's father reaches for some more stew. The bowl is too hot but he quickly tames the heat with his napkin. "But, maybe we need him to be." He dollops a spoonful of the thick beef and carrot concoction onto his plate, then carefully returns the bowl to its place on the heat-proof mat in front of Dara. His glasses are hanging around his neck and his long, newly greying hair gives him an aura of wisdom. He is wise, Dara knows this, but he is also wrong. It is terrifying. "So," he says, breathing out heavily. "Dara, how is school?"

But Dara is not ready to accept the crumbling of her parents' liberalism. "Ima, you always said that these bombers did it as, what did you call it? A form of self-actualisation? Because of their sense of power-loss, of impotency. Because of their poverty. Don't you still think that?"

Her mother sighs. "Yes, I do." She puts down her fork. "But that's not all of it. It's not poverty, is it, that drives people to this? There're plenty of Jews who live in poverty too. That's not it on its own. You can't ignore the other things, the politics, the lack of autonomy, the history, but also the *religious* motivation, this is the thing, the promise of virgins in paradise… it's, it's primitive."

Dara thinks of Kaseem. Of his proud face after his job interview, of his knowledge of art and poetry. "It's not true," is all she can mutter.

But now her father speaks again. It is as though having finally given each other license, both of her parents are letting escape a lifetime of stored up, pushed down loathing. "Look at how they treat their women," he says. "Dressing them in these ridiculous shrouds. Keeping them in the home. Beating them. Polygamy. It's of another century. How a society treats its women is revealingly indicative of the progress of that society."

"Some of the women are very well educated, and successful," Dara battles.

"Few and far between," her mother declares sadly. "And I wouldn't be surprised if even those ones went home to violent husbands."

"No. You're wrong," says Dara, but her usual fight has left her. Colours flood her head. But what she needs is words. Her brother rolls his eyes at her sympathetically, as if to say, *they don't know, they're older, they don't see how things have changed*. But they used to see. They used to see every shade of the debate. Dara's parents are liberals, peaceniks. They've taken abuse for it. They've campaigned for it. They've taught it to her. If they cannot keep hope then who can? She does not want to listen to their words that taint them and fill her with guilt. It is only dinner conversation, but suddenly, Dara cannot breathe.

In the dark, the streets look different. It is not evening but night. What little light there is comes from inside homes that Dara would never wish to disturb. Around them, archways and alleys are littered with men who materialise from nowhere and in groups threaten her with their shadowy presence. She runs the whole way to Kaseem's shop, realising only as she nears it that this is not where Kaseem lives but where he works; he might not be there, she might instead end up alone with his uncle, or with the Arab night. Dara runs faster, her fists clenched tight. She is not carrying a bag, she has no sketchpad or book or other modes of camouflage. She is here only to see Kaseem. She has to get to him.

The shop is lit. Dara sees him sitting behind the counter, reading. She taps softly on the window and he looks up, unsurprised. He stands and for a moment they stare at each other through the dirty glass, rust-tinted no longer, the dirt black and definite. Smeared by her own hand. As he crosses the room towards her and unlocks the door's series of latches, they do not smile, but neither do they take their eyes off each other. It is a serious business and they know this. There is no middle ground between loyalty and treason. They are crossing over.

***

Kaseem is gentle but determined. He does not pause between a kiss and what comes after it. Dara tells him that she is a virgin and sees him try to slow down but this pronouncement of her purity excites him further. Perhaps there is something about sullying something so clean that makes him feel powerful. Dara feels fragile under his hard, dark frame. She wants to feel fragile. She is nervous, shaking, but also liberated. It is he who tugs at her t-shirt, but she who unhooks her bra.

He says, "You are as luminescent as I imagined."

He says, "I care for you, you know. My baby."

He says, "You are squinting at me as you squinted at the sun that day, you are studying me, no?"

He says they are adding truth, adding colour, creating upon a clean canvas.

He says it is many years since he has felt this free, this uplifted.

She feels uplifted too. But Jerusalem is a heavy place. Everything is complicated.

***

Then

9

Dara's parents have no idea. It has been almost two months that she has been hiding her dashes across the city. There have been bombings: Patt Junction and French Hill, and the massacre at the Hebrew University (where it turns out Kaseem studied engineering because his father wouldn't let him study art), and even on these days she has routed around blood to see him. But Jerusalem is calmer again now. It is still heavy, always riled, but the terror of the summer folded away, like prayers in the wailing wall: desperation scrawled on bits of brick-padded paper, flattened in crumbling crevices of stone, assigned to history and addressed only by God. It is the only way the people can move forward. Not forgetting, but crumpling up and squashing memories amidst the fabric of the city, lining the foundations, layering them.

Over the last week or two, Dara's mother has finally stopped lecturing and restricting and is busy again in her investigations into other people's minds. Both of Dara's parents trust her to make good decisions and have never demanded a regimented accounting of her time. They believe her when she tells them that she is with Naomi, working on a project, or that she has begun an oil painting class, and her brother is away at camp so not there to spot the ruse and tell them otherwise. Their only concern is that Dara is so young to spend so much time with the same people, or pursuing the same thing. She is a brilliant artist they know, but they remind her that she also used to like to dance and to sing. They are worried that she is narrowing life down, too quickly closing in.

When she is with Kaseem however, the world is at its widest.

Naomi and Rachel know now. Subsequently they have stopped accompanying Dara to East Jerusalem. They think this will deter her, they tell her it will only lead to trouble, that Kaseem is an Arab, a *Muslim* Arab, that it will never work, that she is making things hard for herself, that she must be careful. She listens to their cautions but ignores them. Kaseem is different. He is worth the risk.

His family pretend to like her. They make her stay for dinner and often she leaves smelling of rice cooked in a lot of oil. They do not ask her age, or perhaps are simply unsurprised by her youth. It is her way of life that is novel. Kaseem has five younger sisters who all wear head-scarves and want to know how she weaves gold into her hair. His mother makes flattering comments about her 'modern' jeans, and asks about her ambitions – will she work, she wants to know. Can she cook? Kaseem's father died three years ago but his brother is often there to check in on his sister-in-law, and he still calls Dara 'beauty'. It still makes her uncomfortable, though she has learnt to laugh in a way that confirms the compliment as a friendly jest. Kaseem tells her he is glad that she laughs at him, he is glad she is not shy when she is amongst his family, he is glad she speaks as he has learnt to love, boldly and with honesty. It pleases her that he is glad, but secretly Dara suspects that his family's smiles and inquiries turn to mocking as soon as she has closed the door. She knows they think she is promiscuous and immoral. She sees them stare at her rolled up jeans and exposed knees.

It is to the shop that they escape. To the room at the back where there is a single lamp whose bulb blows often and where faulty parts are stacked up in boxes. The floor is old and needs retiling. Ants scurry in and out of cracks; Dara once discovered a line of tiny red bites at the top of her thigh. There is no fan and the room is boiling, but they shed their clothes quickly and remain that way as they listen to each other, and touch each other's skin, and gather proofs of their dreams.

At the end of August, a few days before Dara's brother is due to return and a week before school restarts, she and Kaseem plan a trip away. They want to get out of the city, out of the thin, built-up streets where the dry heat rises in columns of dust and confuses old and new with its equal coating of sandy white. Dara's parents are remodelling the house so even inside she cannot escape the disconcerting clouds. Builders and electricians and plumbers arrive early to begin the day-long moving about of noise and mess, and Dara's mother locks herself and her patients in the office that can be accessed from a door at the side. Dara's father works late. Neither of them bat an eyelid when she announces that she wants some quiet too, somewhere in the countryside, away. She tells them she is going camping with Naomi and Rachel.

They take a bus to Tiberius. From there, despite the heat, they are planning to hike to the Jordan River. Kaseem is carrying a tent and sleeping bags, Dara has a deflated lilo and the food. They are both dressed in jeans and t-shirts, and sitting close to him on the bus Dara feels that to outsiders it is possible that they might seem a match. He is very dark, but not black, he could be a Sephardic Jew; she is 15 but developed. She hopes that at the camping ground they will not know anyone and at last they will be able to be together without worrying about who might see or what those who do see might think of them. She glances up at Kaseem and squeezes his hand, but Kaseem is staring out of the window and does not notice her excitement. He has just returned from another job interview. It is his fourth of the week, a good position, but he no longer seems to harbour much enthusiasm.

When they first met he had only recently graduated – fifth in his class despite the exams being in Hebrew. He had wanted to do art, it was all he had ever loved, but his father had told him that more important than love is survival, advancement, and so he had risen to it. And was about to reap the rewards. The computer job was only temporary, a high-tech career was around the corner. "You'll get the next one," Dara often tries to encourage, but such declarations irritate him now. He waves his hand at her, dismissively, and tells her she doesn't understand. Or he mutters something below his breath in Arabic. Dara forgives him because she agrees. He is the only one from his class who has not yet secured that high-paid job from the high-tech course that cost the high price of his soul, and she can see the discrimination. She tells him this. But she cannot feel it, he tells her, and nothing she says can atone for what is. This time she says nothing. She lets his thoughts simmer in the heat of the bus, bumping over roads that are unevenly made.

Dara has never been here before though she has camped many times. When she and her brother were children their parents would often camp out with them, taking them to nature parks and beaches and harsh desert regions so that they would learn to cope. Hiking for miles at a time despite little legs, they would stop at lakes where their parents would let them swim, cook burgers on makeshift barbecues they would be allowed to light, unwrap carefully cellophaned bread and pickles and salads, drink squash from plastic cups, climb trees, run, play, scream. It was an outdoorsy kind of childhood, open to the sky. When it got dark, their father would help them name the stars. She has forgotten most of the names however: they have not camped in a while. And Dara has never been here.

It is beautiful. The banks are shaded by a canopy of eucalyptus trees that seem to hum as they sway. A hot breeze whistles gently through them, rubbing past the leaves and carrying off a scent of green. A little upstream, there are a row of neatly pitched tents, but Kaseem and Dara have hiked down a little and there is nobody else nearby. They are on the edge of a part of the river that feels like an isolated bay. The water is high and laps at the greenery; it does not *seem* to be shrinking, it does not tell of water wars, of dams built and resources diverted, of politics; it is only wet and cool and inviting. They throw their bags beneath a tree and shed their clothes. Dara is wearing a yellow bikini and even though he has seen her in less she feels Kaseem's eyes appreciating her curves within it. They keep on their sandals and climb over un-cleared branches and late summer nettles to reach the old, wooden steps that weave down to the water. They are unofficial, some are broken and the rope that once was taut and there for balance is decaying, unsecured on the floor, but Dara, unafraid, tries to descend first. Kaseem stops her. "What?" she demands as he pulls her back. "What? I am lighter?" But Kaseem will not let her risk her unblemished perfection, and secretly Dara likes this insistence on her protection. Still, after dutifully abandoning the steps she picks her way down the snake of rocks that diminish in size until they are just pebbles by the water's edge. She and Kaseem arrive at the river simultaneously. He shakes his head and pushes her in.

In the water, they dance. It is a mating ritual almost as old as the river itself: she splashes, he chases, they kick their feet and race, she rides on his shoulders, they dunk one another, she dives under the water and re-emerges next to him, a mermaid, an enchanted thing. They are aware of their unoriginal romantic silliness, but continue nonetheless. In the end, she wraps her long, lean arms around his neck and in the dying sun they sway back and forth like a slow, water-logged waltz, gazing undisturbed by land into the equally deep pools of each other's eyes. Dara is beginning to be able to read his, finally. When she gets really close she can see that at the very far edges they are not jet-black after all. Between the pupils and the whites, there is the thinnest line of grey.

***

Later – dry, hot, full – Dara and Kaseem lay close in their shared tent. They have not had time like this, time to lay uninterrupted, time to learn the hills and valleys of each other's bodies, the scars and their stories. He traces hers with his quick, engineer's mind and deft, artist's fingertips, at his leisure, carefully, and she cannot look away. He makes her feel nervous and safe all at once.

They talk about everything that is not important. They talk about art, her dream to go to the Bezalel Academy, the uselessness of his own painting, his longing for it. They talk about friends they do not have in common; Rachel's new obsession with nightclubs and ecstasy, Naomi's parents who are getting divorced, Shmuel who she suspects is gay. They talk about Kaseem's 12-year-old sister Hadiyah who has told Kaseem that she wants to dye her hair like Dara's, and wear jeans, and go to university. Kaseem does not tell Dara that he doesn't approve of this, and although she can see it in the way he flicks his finger and waves his hand as he talks, they do not for now dwell on the subtext of their opposing views. This is their moment, their escape. They can smell their freedom on their river-scented skin. Dara remembers that this is the same river that Joshua once crossed with the Israelites. But for she and Kaseem, their freedom is not from Pharaohs or shackles. Dara's parents are not the sort who would call Yad L'Achim and seek intervention to drag her away from her Arab love, her father would not lock her in her room, she would not become a news story. Her mother would pretend it was okay, like Kaseem's mother does. Their escape is from glances and opinions, unmovable barriers of the mind, quirks of law and perception that stop Kaseem from finding work and unless one of them converts, means they will never marry. Their chains are made only of sand. Soft. Elusive. As hard as steel.

It is different by the river. Here, the water carries their manacles away, and instead it is only they who clasp each other's wrists and hands and bodies. Still, it is after midnight before they pick their way towards the topic of his job, his situation, Israel's situation, their opposite sides of it.

"You know, I feel like my house."

Dara raises herself up onto her elbow and looks at him quizzically. "Your house?"

"I have some land, I have good, solid foundations, but I can't build, I'm not allowed to build."

"Your permit hasn't come through?"

Kaseem laughs a little, but not because it is funny. "This is the third time we've been refused," he says. "On the other side of Jerusalem the buildings are touching the sky, but for me, no, it's not allowed. I must stay in my one storey house with five sisters and a mother who tells me every day that she needs more space. And I have the tools, you know, that's the thing. I can get the materials, I can imagine it and build it, and I would do it well."

"I know you would."

"But I don't have permission. I am not permitted to advance."

"And you feel like that? You feel like your house? Unfulfilled?"

"Unfulfilled is nothing. I am limited. Belittled."

"But things are changing, no? You told me yourself, you said the job in the computer shop was only temporary."

Kaseem tuts at her, a little aggressively. "It's not for want of trying," he says.

"Of course," she answers quickly. "I know that, of course." She has not meant to upset him, or offend him, or make him mad. "But don't you still believe you'll find success in the end? Don't you feel that?"

"I feel humiliation," he whispers. "And resentment. And also yes, I still believe."

Dara nods. "I believe too," she tells him.

Now he smiles, and kisses her softly. She takes his hand. She is in awe of his strength. And his sensitivity. And the way he is both at once. "When will I meet your parents?" he asks her.

Now, without intention, it is Dara who tuts, though she manages to disguise hers in a heavy exhalation of breath. It is not for want of desire that she hasn't introduced them. It is not because she doesn't long for it or dream of it, or sketch it in her pad. It is only that when they are not here but in the city, he is an Arab and she is a Jew.

His friends will be stopped and asked for identity cards; hers will do the stopping.

His history lessons have been filled with occupation and deprivation and injustice; hers with survival and terror.

And when they are back in the city, back folded amongst the layers, these differences between them rise like the dusty Jerusalem billows, and there is a haze around them, a stifling, far-reaching fog.

Only at the river, under a cloudless, star-lit sky, does the air feel cleaner. She lays back into Kaseem's arms and turns to face him. They are cleansed here, cleansed of their histories. It is possible to explain, at least a little, to talk of now, and from now, and of each of them as beings, separate from their different Jerusalems. When she speaks, the water helps her words to flow. She promises that she will introduce them, when she is a little older, when the time is right. And just as she did, Kaseem listens. He lets Dara rekindle his hope. He does not flick his fingers and wave her away when she tries to encourage him. He lets her tell him how smart he is, how intelligent, how destined for greatness. He smiles when she talks about his art, how it has influenced her already, how *he* has influenced her, how she loves him. He listens, and understands, and takes her in his strong, dark arms and holds her tight. And lets her believe that what they feel for each other cannot, unlike the river, be dammed.

***

Now

10

The package is in the drawer of Udi's desk underneath a stack of *Playboy*s with a thin piece of tape across the join. He hasn't opened it and he has told nobody. He thinks of it though at least once every few minutes, and Ella has noticed. She is complaining that he's not paying attention, that he is distracted, *why is he distracted* she wants to know.

They are back together. Or rather, for now they are together. For now they have chosen to release their issues into the spring air. Marriage. London. The words float around them like the city dust, but they have not settled, not yet. For as long as they can they are pretending these pollutants are simply part of the atmosphere, part of the tumult they breathe. He is not sure what he will do without Ella's chatter. It will be hard in London. *If* the package contains a visa. It will be harder here if it does not.

Since miluim things have been better. There were only two options – wait or work – and it seemed stupid to cling to a dream likely to fail. Besides, his mind needed occupation. So he worked every hour he could and less than a month later was promoted at the construction company. The change has suited him. He is good at practical tasks, at organising others, at making things happen. He enjoys the illusion of being in control and he likes that slowly, very slowly, the funds in his bank account are growing. Nevertheless, the old disquiet has returned. Ella charges him with it daily, demanding to know what is wrong so that she may help him, desperate to keep his mind with her.

"Udi," she prods now. He looks away from his desk, away from the closed drawer containing the unopened envelope, and back towards the swimsuit Ella has bought that afternoon and is modelling now for him. "Don't you like it, Udi?"

He finally looks at her properly. Her hair is loose and pulled to the side so that it falls thickly over one shoulder and covers half of the white bikini top that illuminates her deep olive skin. The bikini bottoms are miniscule and perfect. He feels himself stirring and for once his mind is fully concentrated on her. She sees it in his eyes and walks smilingly towards him, pursing her lips as she straddles his lap. She pulls at his trousers, gently passing her hands over the scars beneath them. In the next room, Batia is preparing dinner, and the sounds of cupboard drawers opening and closing waft underneath the door. Ella presses herself against him and undoes the single thread of material that seems to hold her entire top together.

"Shall I stay over?" she asks in a whisper.

He nods.

The envelope will still be there tomorrow.

***

But he cannot wait.

Ella is fast asleep but Udi has been alert for hours, even after a spliff. Every time he attempts to close his eyes they simply fall open and he finds himself staring again at his drawer. Climbing out of bed he creeps across the room and in one swift movement breaks the tape and pulls the brown envelope free from the magazines on top. Ella stirs. She calls him back to bed and he sits next to her. The space beside her is still warm, welcoming. He contemplates telling her about

160

the package that is in his hand, that he is about to open, that is about to decide their fate. But her tousled hair swathes the pillow, her delicate, tanned arms are folded beneath her restful face, and her body is tranquil, her breath steady, steadying.

"I'll be right back," he tells her, squeezing her hand when she reaches for him to stay. "I'm just getting some water."

"There's some right here," she murmurs as he opens the door, but he pretends not to hear.

In the hallway he opens the seal of the envelope but doesn't pull out the documents inside. More than anything he fears that it is the application forms returned with a section they have spotted that he hasn't filled in, or has filled in wrong, or is not able to. He decides to eat something first, for fortification. In the kitchen he turns on the light and moves without any real decision to do so to the pita bread and hummus in the fridge. He is being careful to be quiet, concentrating on opening the door softly, not rustling the packages, and he doesn't at first notice Batia sitting, sipping tea at the table. It is only when he closes the fridge door that he sees her in the shadows, but even then he doesn't jump. Instead he turns on the tap until it runs cold and fills a glass with water before taking it to the table where he sits opposite his mother.

"It has arrived," she tells him.

"Yes. I haven't opened it."

"So you should open it."

He raises his eyebrows.

"What reason is there not to? Open it, and either you'll cry or I will. At least then maybe one of us can sleep."

"How long have you been sitting here, Ima?" he asks her.

"Just two hours." As if in proof she taps the half empty pot of tea next to her, the remaining contents of which have now been brewed too long and have turned a dirty, mud-like colour that will taste bitter on the tongue. He nods and moves to the counter where he fetches the envelope. Sitting back down, he places it between them.

"If I can, I will go," he tells her, fingering the open seal.

"If I can, I will stop you," she replies.

"You can't stop me, Ima. Even Abba isn't trying to."

"Your father doesn't realise you plan to leave us forever."

Udi drops his head. He stares at the envelope. Suddenly he feels tired, as if he is back at the base and has been fighting all day, or wading through sand all night. "I can do better in London," he tells her carefully.

Batia shakes her head and makes a distinct tsking sound at the back of her throat.

"I won't have to go to the army," he coaxes. "You won't have to worry about me when there is another war."

"Life is a war," she answers, but her eyes have softened.

Udi picks up the envelope and pulls out the contents. It bodes well, he thinks, that the bulk is thick. Neither of them speak as he reads the covering letter. Batia holds her small glass of tea in both hands but doesn't sip it. Eventually he reaches the end. He re-folds the paper. He looks directly at her.

"I'm going," he says.

Batia exhales deeply. She stands, collects her glass and teapot and takes them to the sink where she pours out the stale contents and washes the containers meticulously. Then she returns the sugar to its airtight container and wipes the spot on the table where she has uncharacteristically spilled a drop of tea. All the while Udi waits for her to speak.

"You will do well in London," she says eventually. He opens his mouth to respond but she puts up her hand. "Time to sleep, Udi," she says, and kisses him on his forehead in what might be blessing, or else goodbye. And then she is gone. And it is silent.

Guilt comes first.

Then relief.

And then an unfamiliar sensation that washes over him and creeps slowly into a growing exultation that culminates finally in a loud clap of the hands that he cannot resist, despite the late hour. He feels an urge to run or jump or hit something, though all he does is stand and let the energy shoot through him, cracking, an undetectable amount more, the broken tile beneath his feet. And then he returns to his room, replaces the envelope in his desk drawer, and climbs into bed next to Ella who wraps her lean arms around him.

***

Avigail strides angrily through the Jerusalem streets. She is late for her writers' group and cannot concentrate on the relationship between gender and peace about which she is supposed to be speaking. She is thinking instead of Udi. And their father's unfathomable support of his desertion. And their mother's unprecedented silence. And the fact that with Ari away, it was left to her to argue with Udi alone.

Had his reasons been different she might have understood. Not liked it of course, but understood. If he had political motives, for example. But for money? He is not destitute, he is not scrabbling for food like so many in Gaza, or living in tents in mud fields like their parents once did. He is a strong, capable, Israeli man in a society where strong, Israeli men rule. He has choice, and responsibility, and no excuse. But, 'Don't tell me what I owe to my country,' he had argued angrily. 'It's my blood on this land, not yours. I don't need you telling me what I owe.'

It is the first time he has ever mentioned what happened to him in Gaza. Avigail thinks about it at least once a day, more when he is on miluim. And she thinks about Ari. And Ezra, even though he was a jobnik and has never been in actual combat because still he wears a uniform. And she thinks about her children.

They did not stay at her parents' for dessert. The children were disappointed but there was a lot of traffic, Avigail explained to them, and to her mother, unprecedented jams. They left before coffee, before Udi could talk any more about Ben and the job and the flat, before she had to observe another minute of her mother standing silent and stoic. But in the car, until the girls fell asleep, she and Ezra were silent too. Udi's departure was not the announcement they had been planning that Friday. For weeks they have been discussing their own declaration, plotting carefully the manner in which to reveal it, and Friday was supposed to have been the night they told her family that she is pregnant again, this time with a boy. Avigail has filled many days imagining the thrilled creases that will flood her father's face. It is not easy to make him smile, not a true, through and through smile; but this would. A boy. During long bus journeys or queues in the grocery store she has been drip-feeding herself these daydreams, hugging them to her. Occasionally expanding into visions of her mother's simultaneous excitement and panic, the entreaties to attend this doctor or that pre-natal class, or to read a particular new book that will help her control and protect every detail of the pregnancy and birth of her unborn son, since she will not be able to protect his life. All the mothers she knows are the same, no matter the generation. They cling to the small influence they have, while they have it.

"We'll tell them next week," Ezra had consoled.

"But we're telling your parents tomorrow."

"We'll wait. It's just a week."

She had nodded. And stroked her slightly protruding belly, and cheered herself at least with this. Another week of keeping the future to herself, a possession of her own.

She puts her hand on top of her stomach again, now, as she nears the old converted church where her writing group meets.

Several women are already gathered and they greet her with chatter and enthusiasm. There is the playwright Gal Shwartz, who during her last production was hounded by critics for daring to explore the relationship between victim and oppressor; there is the religious poet Ronit Esther, badgered by her own community for daring too much and by the left-wingers for daring too little; there is the activist Mira

Peled who spent three years living in Hebron attempting to protect the remote dwelling Palestinians who lived there from settlers, soldiers, stones, guns, raids on their land; there is the Palestinian feminist author Layla Habash; the Mizrahi journalist Liat Gov, the Ashkenazi graphic novelist Dana Kuntsler... Avigail cannot look around the room without being overawed by the talent and bravery it contains. She might, if she was so inclined, feel dwarfed by it. But this is Avigail's favourite hour of the week, a fleeting pause in which she can stop being a mother, a daughter, a wife, even a woman, and simply be a writer, a thinker, Avigail Shammash, whose words are judged for their accuracy and insight and not in the context of the roles she as their creator plays. They are doing something here, she feels. They are extending the feminist discourse into a multi-cultural context, and they are filtering the political conversation through a feminist lens. Their exchanges are exciting.

The format is for each of them to take turns presenting an issue for discussion by the group. So far they have dealt with everything from feminism in Israeli art to modern slavery. Avigail has led the group twice, the first time exploring the pinkification of young girls, the second time the psychological consequences to Israeli society of the Hannibal manoeuvre. Today she is supposed to be talking about peace and the unique relationship that women have to it. It is a topic that has fascinated her for years – the basis in fact of her postdoctoral thesis and the thread that links much of her published works – so it is not difficult for her to think on her feet; but she is distracted. When she had considered the topic originally, she had planned to approach the issue from a psychological stance, an exploration of Israel as a society in collective trauma and an analysis of the female role in healing it. But that was before Udi's disclosure, and now, sitting forward in the empty chair the others have left for her in their circle, she finds herself talking instead about the Women in Black.

Avigail has been a member of the Women in Black since she moved to Jerusalem after leaving the army aged 20. It had felt then like penitence. Now it's an imperative. Ezra doesn't like it. Or rather he does like it, he admires it, respects the aims and the principles, but he doesn't like Avigail putting herself so physically on the line. He has grown used to her doing so in her writing, on paper and in the ether, and he supports her throughout the Twitter storms and the newspaper letters; but this is different. This is a protestation of body as well as soul. One of the other women in the room is a member too – a Palestinian historian from the east of the city. Together they have stood on street corners to mourn the lives of those lost in war, they have held vigil to protest the occupation, they have worn black and clasped placards Friday after Friday ignoring curses and comments and occasional globules of spit. Her parents do not know. Ari and she avoid the topic – to him, it is traitorous. And Udi has, she is sure, seen the occasional photo she has posted on Facebook, but he has said nothing. For her it is not every week. Life is busy and she supposes that this is why these days there are not so many of them – even the founders are getting old – but it remains so simple, and so beautiful: women from across the divides shouting silently together. Peace is more important. Life is more important. We refuse to be enemies.

Everyone here is familiar with the group and it is a good starting point for discussion. It sparks debate about why it is intrinsically a women's group, whether it would exist if it was not, and then onto why so few women have occupied leadership roles at Middle East peace summits, and how many of these women were Sephardi, and how many female leaders around the world have actually given the command to go to war, and a raft of other issues that rile and enthral them. In the midst of it, Avigail wonders whether she has underestimated her brother, whether Udi's decision to leave Israel is actually a protest against its patriarchy, or the occupation, whether for him this is the only way to escape it because with a father like Oz, it is too hard to stay and say so.

It will be a challenge to bring up a boy. Ezra is practically doing cartwheels at the thought of it, but Avigail feels troubled in a way she didn't when she was carrying the girls, challenged with a responsibility to equip her son, his generation, with the tools to be different from the rest. Again, she puts her hand to her belly. A couple of the women in the group notice and smile knowingly, but Avigail leaves it there, gently stroking the life inside of her as she leaves the church and walks towards the bus that will take her home.

Avigail would rather not ride the bus – she far prefers to drive, her destiny in her own hands – but this section of Jerusalem is difficult to negotiate by car so she has taken to using the Egged line for the weekly journey. Today she takes a seat near the front and ignores the raised eyebrows of the men around her. They are all dressed in black. Black trousers, black coats, black boots, black hats, black beards. Black eyes examining her. But it is not a *mehadrin* line, which have thank goodness been discontinued. It is not necessary for her to board through the rear door and sit with the other women at the back. It is not her responsibility to uphold their lingering, self-enforced segregation. The first time that Avigail took this bus she didn't even notice the division and it was only when one of the men told her to move that she became aware of it. Now she sits in the front out of protest and refuses requests to relinquish her seat for any man. Avigail is orthodox but this is not a synagogue and she will not accept discrimination. Still buzzing from the meeting she takes out a notebook and while they are fresh scrawls a few thoughts she may incorporate into a future article – *persistence of 'the other', feminism as a way to universalise plights of marginalised, possibility of progress*. Then she digs into her bag and opens a book she has just started reading entitled: *Raising Sons*.

The bus jolts as it comes to the first stop. She looks up. Everybody does. It is unthinkable not to check who is

167

boarding, what they are carrying. But when she sees only another black-shrouded Haredi man and his similarly clad son mounting the steps, she relaxes and buries her head again in warnings about the dangers of early day-care, the double edged sword of competitive sports, and the importance of a present father figure. She is lucky, Ezra is present. Even her own father attempted to be so. In his own way. She looks back up. The man and the boy have not sat down but are standing over her. The man's expression is surly, impatient, but *at least here is a present father*, she hears herself thinking, glancing quickly at the son before taking a breath to receive the predictable instruction.

"You should be at the back," the man informs her. "Women sit at the back." He strokes the white, fringed *tzitzit* at his waist, a garment worn to help remember God's commandments. "We will sit here."

"No," Avigail replies, smiling. "I am happy here, thank you."

"Get up," the man repeats, louder this time.

"Thank you, I am fine here."

"You should not be sitting amongst men."

There is a murmur of concurrence from the other men around them. Mutterings about her stupidity and about not knowing her place. This is new for Avigail. She has been confronted before on this bus but those times were brief altercations with single irate men, curt but fleeting reprimands, disdainful looks but no further words. No vocal derision from the collective. *The collective against the 'other'*. Avigail closes her book and sits up straighter in her seat.

"This is a public bus," she says slowly, loud enough for the onlookers. "I can sit wherever I like. There are plenty of empty seats for you." Determined to retain an aura of composure Avigail now reopens her book and trains her eyes to it. For a moment there is silence. It is over. She is sure it is over. In a moment she will take out her notepad and write down that thought about the collective. But suddenly she feels a wetness on the side of her face.

The man has spat at her.

The man has spat at her?

"I am not asking you, I'm telling you. Get to the back, slut."

Avigail's chest feels suddenly tight and her voice stuck somewhere below her throat, but she does not move, she cannot move for this man. Besides, she cannot quite believe what has just occurred. The disbelief is sticky, disabling. But she notices the calmness in the eyes of the man's small watching son, the opposite of disbelief, certainty, as though such aggression is nothing new, for him. Nothing wrong. Underneath her book her hand moves protectively to her belly, and then to her cheek where she wipes away the hot liquid.

She should go to the back. Ezra would want her to go to the back.

But she should not go to the back. None of the women in the church she has just left would ever go to the back.

Slowly she puts down her book, turns once more towards the man, reaches hard to the back of her throat, and she tells him: "No."

"Move."

"I will stay here."

His voice is growing wilder. "Move."

Avigail looks away. She stares straight ahead, unbreathing. There is silence.

The bus pulls to another stop and somebody gets on. Momentarily everybody turns to see who it is.

She has triumphed, she tells herself, she has remained calm, dignified. She has remained true. She holds still. The new passenger sits down, a woman, at the back. The bus starts again.

Then all at once the headscarf she wears when travelling to religious parts of the city is flying through the air.

169

Avigail spins around but for a moment disbelief takes hold again. She cannot work out how, why, what has happened. Her mind is slow. She sees the scarf land on the arm of the man's son and in her mind she wants to reclaim it but she finds that her body cannot reach out, and now she realises that her hair is being tugged, tugged, the book is falling from her lap, and she is being yanked from the chair, pushed to the floor, and dragged into the aisle by this man, and by other men too who are still muttering at her, and decrying her stupidity, and have taken it upon themselves to enforce their interpretation of God's will.

Only when the bus stops and the driver moves to disperse the group is she able to escape from the black, leather boots that have been beating rhythmically, as if in prayer, against her body, leaving their marks on her back, her limbs, and her belly.

The driver calls for an ambulance and orders everyone off the bus, and obligingly now they traipse past, off, away. Not one passenger stops. Not one person comes forward to help her. Not even the women, in black, at the back.

Even the driver wears a look of disgust when he spots the blood streaming from between her legs, contaminating the seats meant for men.

***

She will not weep.

She tells nobody. Except for Ezra who weeps for her. For them.

She does not write. It is the first time she has withheld her life from public consumption and she knows that on the one hand this is the time she should most thrust it forwards. This is the event that should make her voice impossible to ignore.

But then Udi would stay.

And now she wants him to leave. To escape. To be rid of this place overrun by religious zealots who are taking over government, and taking over the army, and taking over buses.

She cannot stop placing her hand onto her stomach. Though it is empty.

It is the first time she can remember that Ezra stays home from shul on Shabbat.

They do not visit her parents that Friday. Her daytime imaginings are no longer full of her father.

And she cannot see her mother who she knows she will tell if she does. Besides, there are bruises. And her mother's eyes upon them will make Avigail see what she does not want to see. And then she will weep.

And she will not weep.

She will stay.

And one day, she will write.

***

Now

11

Orli is coming to London for my birthday. I haven't seen her in over a month though we speak daily, usually twice. Sometimes I get a call from her mother, or occasionally from Ittai. They let me know when Orli is down, more down than usual, because she won't tell me herself. She began a new series of paintings the day after the shiva ended but she won't let me see them, won't let anybody see them.

Safia tells me not to push. We have finally got back to normal, sort of. I suppose it could have been difficult – my coming back from holiday with a girlfriend. But Safia was the one who didn't want to complicate things between us, the one who enforced this, and she was right, it would have been far, far too complicated. If Gaby's example wasn't enough, being with Orli's made me see that. Orli challenges me but our relationship is not the challenge. What we have is uncomplicated. As though she pushes me but from behind, from my side. Whereas with Safia it is like jousting. In any case Safia's been fine, more than fine. We have been coffee-ing. I am again the recipient of her daily anecdotes. She is again the analyser of mine. It was she who told me to send the plant. An idea she got from a TV programme apparently, but specifically a plant, not flowers, not a quick fix but something that would need care and take a while to bloom, when it did

172

bringing that long awaited freshness. I wrote something to that effect in the card and Orli loved it. I didn't tell her it was nicked off TV.

After the funeral I stayed in Israel for another two weeks. Orli didn't ask me to be there, but during those first seven days of shiva she gripped my hand as she greeted the constant stream of friends paying their respects, wishing her long life. I've always found that an odd thing to say to the family of the deceased: *I wish you long life*. It's handy to have a proscribed script, something to say, but it feels sometimes like rubbing salt in the wound. After Papa died I remember watching my Nana closely. People kept wishing her this long existence and I could see all she wanted to do was curl up next to her not-existing husband and join him in his sleep. But as I stood next to Orli that week I uttered it in my head again and again – *I wish you long life, I wish you long life, I wish you to get through this, to look to life not death, to remember to live.* Orli's eyes revealed that she had not yet remembered. Her heart was with David, and on the morning after the seventh day of prayers, she told me to go.

I took her at her word. I told her I was there, that I would be there, but I drove her to her apartment and hugged her goodbye and for the whole of the following week I didn't call. Robert had gone home by then and I spent my time looking at antiques in Jaffa, examining graffiti, stumbling across vast modern sculptures and ancient fortress ruins, eating sushi in the middle of wide boulevards, and walking, walking, walking along the river, watching people cycling and boating and running, noticing how landscaped and green the banks were, marvelling at the life, life sprung from desert. Towards the middle of that week I thought about going North for a night, or South, visiting a border town, swept up in a compulsion to see everything. But while I was fondling a map in a Jaffa bookshop, an American nurse peered over my shoulder to encourage the trip. He worked in Gaza, he said. He was buying the book in his hand for a young Palestinian girl who lived there. 'Bright as anything,' he told me. 'Farah. Mother's a cleaner. Father's just released from an Israeli prison. Bright as anything. And without a hope in hell, to get out of hell, you know? You should venture out of Tel Aviv,' he urged again. But I didn't then. It felt precarious and too ambitious. Besides, Tel Aviv had plenty more for me to see. And of course I didn't want to be far from Orli. One day I visited her apartment and stood for a while outside her door listening to the sad music that seeped from under it, smelling fresh paint. I didn't knock, but I stood there.

She finally called on the day I was leaving for home. She insisted on driving me to the airport in her green Corsa and when we arrived, we sat together until the last moment possible, drinking coffee, slowly, allowing the caffeine to quicken our pulses, the hot liquid to loosen our tongues. I tried to give a humorous account of my week detailing an exaggerated version of my forensic hunt for the perfect hummus, my encounter with a clowder of wild cats, and my failed attempts to navigate the purchase and setting up of an Israeli phone. Occasionally, Orli's face would illuminate in the way it had been as a matter of course before, and two weeks later when I flew back for the weekend I noticed that these periods of illumination were growing. When I was there at the beginning of March it had lasted a whole day.

Safia wants to meet her. We talk about it over our reinstated Sunday coffee. Same café, same newspaper, a little less brushing of thighs and leaning on each other's shoulders. We have tactfully turned the page on a story about the floundering peace talks between Israel and the PA. Israel has failed to release the last batch of prisoners, rockets have been fired from Gaza, and now Hamas and Fatah are reconciling, apparently. Bibi says Abbas has a choice between peace with Israel and peace with Hamas. Safia says I have a choice between introducing Orli to her, or her turning up unannounced with pictures of me stoned out of my mind at Warwick.

"Okay, but you can't do your interrogation thing," I say, turning another page of the newspaper.

"What interrogation thing? I don't interrogate." Safia smiles from behind her coffee cup.

"No question mark eyebrows."

"What are you talking about?"

I realise I've never actually articulated to Safia that her raised eyebrow reminds me of a question mark. "You know, that one eyebrow thing you do," I say offhandedly. "Weirdo."

"I will be perfectly polite," Safia promises.

I give her a sceptical look. It feels like flirting, so I stop.

Safia scoops the foam off the top of her second coffee. She looks at me while she does this. Our eyes lock for a little too long. "Dan, you love her, right?"

I nod.

"Okay. So I want to know her."

On the morning of my birthday and Orli's arrival I wake up at 5am and crane my neck every few minutes to see the clock on my bedside table before finally allowing myself to get out of bed. It's a Saturday and Robert is still asleep. Not even my parents will be up this early. It is like being a child again, counting down the minutes before I am allowed to drag everyone down to the kitchen for birthday pancakes and presents. But Orli is not due until 11. The plan is to go straight from the airport to lunch at my parents'. Mum has invited Gaby *and* Pete. Also Nana. And Robert and Debbie though they can't make it. I think she wants as large as panel of judges as possible. Over the past months she has expressed a mixture of enthusiasm and contempt for the girl I've described. Orli is beautiful, smart, talented, *Jewish*; but Mum is convinced she's the only reason I'm talking again about Israel.

For the sake of her sanity I've tried to tone it down, but I can't help it. Every time I return to London it gets harder and harder to tread the dreary streets, to concentrate on pointless work, to muster enthusiasm. I find my mind wandering to beaches, to coffee houses, to relaxed, unstuffy art exhibits, to exciting new architecture, concerts, museums, markets, to Hebrew words that are alive, vital, and mean something. And yes, to Orli's bed. But she hasn't once pressed me to come. She is determined to fill the void around her with light of her own making.

When she rounds the corner of the arrivals gate at Heathrow, the triumph of this is all over her face. She carries a single bag that looks heavy – and even when I lift it from her shoulder she remains just slightly weighed down – but she holds this load now as though she controls it. And her eyes are ablaze. In the car, she gazes keenly out of the window. Her eyes dart left and right. Looking. Looking. Finally we pull up in front of my parents' house.

"So," she smiles, squeezing my hand. "Should I get my own drink?"

Gaby's wedding is planned for June. Mum seems to have lost the will to do battle with what seems an inevitable course – she does after all have only one daughter for whom to plan a wedding – and Pete is back at family gatherings. Still, she can't help dropping occasional clangers. "You seriously don't want a chuppah?" she is asking Gaby as Orli and I nudge through the front door. "Correct me if I'm wrong, Pete, but Jesus was Jewish, even he would have had a chuppah."

"As far as I know, Jesus hasn't sent out his wedding invitations, as yet," Pete parries. He is getting the hang of our family dynamic. Dad laughs.

"He didn't get married, he just got it on on the sly with that Mary Magdalene didn't he?" Gaby chips in. "We could always do that Mum. Just skip the wedding."

"Oh ha blooming ha," Mum retorts. "Fine, no chuppah. I'm just saying, all of our friends are going to find it pretty strange. No rabbi, no shul, now no chuppah. It's only like making a little stage for you anyway. Your lot wouldn't even notice, Pete. Just a little canopy with flowers, nice no?"

Pete grins at Mum with amusement. "I don't mind a chuppah, honey," he says to Gaby, managing to pronounce the guttural 'ch'. Gaby throws up her hands in exasperation. "This is like a master class in negotiating," Pete whispers to Dad.

I cough to announce our arrival.

Everyone turns to face us. I notice the communal approval that sweeps across each of their faces at their first sight of Orli. She is wearing simple skinny blue jeans, flat shoes, and a long beige silky coat cardigan thing. Her hair is loose, her face fresh – I can never tell if girls are wearing makeup unless it's obvious, but it is not obvious. She looks effortlessly lovely. I remember the first time Hayley came to our house for dinner. To be fair we were 17, our dress sense less cultivated, but Gaby was particularly scathing of Hayley's teetering heels and too-heavy eyeliner.

"Anne Hathaway had a chuppah," Orli ventures. "So did Drew Barrymore."

"I love Drew Barrymore," says Gaby.

By the end of the afternoon, not even Gaby or Mum can fake resistance. Nana is at home with a cold but the rest of the panel are won over. She has them laughing, listening, talking, confiding. Then come the presents. Gifts are funny things. I know you're meant to try to think of something the receiver will like, something they would want, nothing to do with you, but it never works that way. There's always a not-so-subtle hint of the giver in there, an intimation of their perception of who the receiver is, or who they wish them to be. Dad's indictment of me comes in the form of an Arsenal season ticket, with another for him, Mum has selected a variety of smart dress shirts, and Gaby and Pete present me with a briefcase, perfect for a continued existence in the city. Orli goes to the car for her contribution. She digs into the bottom of her holdall for a thick green tube and allows me to spread the canvas out on the dining room table. I have examined her work extensively, spent time browsing her website, clicked through all her old pieces, read her blog. But I am unprepared. The vast painting is an enlargement of the sketch she made of me that day in the park, the etching that even when she hardly knew me caught so marvellously the unease in my smile and the entire dichotomy of my life. Now it is even better. It is as though with brushstrokes she has revealed me. Nobody speaks.

"I added colour," she says when even I say nothing.

For a while the silence continues and I notice that Orli, who I have never seen seem nervous, is looking at my family with what I'm sure is anxiety. But then Dad claps his hands onto the table and stares deliberately first at the canvas, and then at me. "Well then," he says. "When will you go?"

There is no need to explain the reference. "I've been thinking about September."

"You're coming?" Orli asks. "To Israel? To live?"

"Of course he is," Mum answers. "Look at your painting. He's already there." She cannot hide her resentment but puts her hand on Orli's arm despite it. I could kiss her for that gesture, and do.

"Not September though," says Gaby. "Dan, promise to wait a year okay? Wait until you're 30. Until you're exempt from the army."

She taps Pete's shoulder to indicate she is ready to leave and they stand up, hovering next to Mum and Dad who are waiting casually for me to assent to this small, reasonable condition.

But I don't want my new year to begin with a lie. I'm starting to feel that that's part of what the whole thing's about – finding my true self, a true path, one I've actually chosen. "I'm not waiting," I say.

All eyes shoot towards Orli, but she holds up her hands. "Danny, it makes sense," she says. "If you come before, you may not have to serve but you'll still be in the reserve pool. If there's a war you may really have to go to the army."

"I'm going to volunteer anyway," I tell them. "I want to fight for Israel. Remember what your dad said, it's part of being a true Israeli, it's something everyone does for everyone. It's something I owe."

"Not to me," she replies quickly. "You don't owe it to me."

"I'm not waiting," I say again.

***

As we drive back to my flat, I can feel Orli brewing. With Hayley, by the end, I'd only need hear the slightly shallower intake of breath to know she was angry, or see the almost imperceptible flaring of her nostrils to know she was about to ask a favour, or weigh the heaviness of a silence to realise that I was about to get sex. I like that I'm beginning to navigate Orli in this way. She's had me pegged from the start, but I'm catching up. Now, she has cocked her head ever so slightly to the left, as though balancing an emerging thought on her jaw. I wait.

"Don't do this for me," she says at last.

"The army?"

"The army. Israel. You shouldn't do it for me."

"Don't you want me to come?"

"Not for me."

This isn't quite what I'd expected. "Hang on. You don't want to be with me?"

"Of course I do. But…Things are… I don't want to be your reason." She puts her hand over mine and I like the warmth of it, the electricity from it, but I'm forced to shrug it off as the road narrows, littered with parked cars, and I have to shift into first gear, flashing my lights to tell the oncoming car to go.

"I'm coming for me," I tell her.

She pauses. "Okay."

"Okay."

"But, Danny…" She stops. Silent but still thoughtful.

But Danny what? Do I want to be with her? Yes. Do I want to live in Israel? Yes. So what, what? What more is there? Is she the reason I want to live in Israel? No. Yes. Partly. Why does it matter? "What?" I prompt finally, but she shakes her head, brushing away the dangling deliberation. Her jaw straightens.

We drive in silence. It is not awkward. With Safia it's all about the back and forth, the repartee, with Hayley there was endless chit-chat, but Orli and I...there are jokes, there's lightness, but we tend also to say a lot of stuff that matters, and we punctuate that stuff with this: calm, quiet. Orli stares out of the window and I find myself regarding the familiar North London streets in a new light. Her light. Or how I imagine it to be. The buildings, I suppose, have their own history, interesting for a foreigner. London will never be the land of the living bible but the architecture is an eclectic mix of generations, colours, styles, a fascinating fusion organically grown atop each other. For all its flashing lights and cutting edge technology, not even Tel Aviv can replicate this. There, the epochs, millennia apart, blend nevertheless into a pale panorama, and everything seems to have emerged from of a pile of sand.

"Take me to the Eye," Orli says suddenly, as though I've been talking out loud. "I want to see the whole of London."

"You mean the wheel? Now?" I've never been on the London Eye. I don't even know how to get there.

"Yes, why not?"

Hayley would never have suggested something so spontaneous. Not at this hour. I type *London Eye* into my Sat Nav and we drive. Past my road, through Regent's Park and across the river. Orli points out most of the sights on route that for me are ordinary and so invisible. As we arrive, I point out Big Ben. The line is short and when we reach the front, Orli insists on buying the tickets, counting out her carefully acquired currency.

It is almost dusk and there are only a few other people in our capsule – presumably the views are better in daylight.

But the city is illuminated by a million tiny dots of different hues: street lamps, brake lights, stark neon office windows and soft bedroom glows. It looks magnificent, magical, elegant, and in the calm of our capsule, 450 feet above the emptying, rain-cleansed streets, it is possible to forget the plague of people that will emerge in the morning, swarming into tunnels, across pavements, up and down buildings, all over each other, like rats. And that I am usually one of them. And that the city feels like a giant cage. With Orli, up here, it is possible to forget this.

"So this is your city," Orli says, more to herself than to me. "It looks like you."

"How can a city look like me?" I laugh.

"It has your confusion."

I raise my eyebrows.

"It's beautiful," she explains. "And very interesting, but it doesn't know what it is. Over there it is kings and queens." She points at the Tower of London. "There it is space." She fingers the Gherkin. "And here it thinks it is France." She points to the gothic structure of the Palace of Westminster. "But this is its beauty," she adds.

"I'm not confused," I say. "That was a long time ago that I said that. And you'd got me drunk with that cocktail with the daft sparklers and those endless rounds of shots you ordered." We grin at each other. "I know who I am."

"Okay, if you could be any part of this city, what would you be?" she asks.

I like this kind of question. Hayley and I spent a lot of time over the years deciding which genre of cuisine we would choose if we could only pick one to live off forever, and which one outfit we would wear every day, and which superpower we would select. But this is a new one. I mull it carefully, but although there's a lot I love about London, there isn't any one part I feel really attached to, nowhere I really see as me. Which I suppose is the problem. "I guess I'd be the river," I say. "Flowing away."

181

"Changeable," she laughs. "Always moving."

"Polluted," I add. Then, placing a hand on her back, amend, "Dirty." She has been in England for a full eight hours and we have only kissed once. She laughs again, reaches for my other hand and squeezes it. "So what would you be then Miss Psycho-babble? What part of the city are you?"

"Ah, I am not really here," she answers. "I am just a scent in the air."

She is right as always. She, and everything about her, is a scent I am tracking.

We walk along the river. It is only April and the evening is cold. Even with my jacket Orli is shivering. We stop to look across the Thames and she arranges my arms around her shoulders like a coat. Resting her head against me she squeezes our interlocked hands. I like this gesture. She does it frequently now and though we haven't translated it aloud I feel it to be a secret, silent hello, a quiet promise of union. Or else she is checking I am still there.

"Danny," she says softly, still gazing across the river. "Danny, I want you to wait."

I drop her hands.

"Not forever. I want you to come. You know I want you to come, but-" She reaches for my hands again, squeezes them. "There are things to talk about." Orli's eyes seem clouded, looking at me yet past me too. Perhaps it is the murky Thames water. Or the evening. They are dense with something.

"I have to go to the army," I say slowly. "You know I do."

Orli shifts her gaze back into focus and her tone changes, as though she has only just started listening, as though my words have flicked a switch somewhere. "All because of what my father said?" She begins to walk along again. "It isn't a game, Danny. It's real you know."

I can't quite catch her point. "Orli," I venture. "I'm not David. You're not going to lose me."

She shakes her head. "You have no idea."

We walk on. For a good few minutes neither of us speak. But she is wrong, I do have an idea. I know there will be challenges, but they excite me. And I will be with Orli, who excites me. I think I feel her mood shifting, lightening, there is again a squeeze between our palms. Enough of this. Enough disagreement. I want to go home, to get her home; it is my birthday after all. I am about to tell her this but suddenly, Orli's palm has stopped squeezing and is slipping from mine, suddenly she is not at my side, and as I turn I see her ducking underneath the barrier next to us and her feet are on the edge of the cement, and her hair is loose and wild and she is leaning backwards, away, over the river.

"Orli! Are you crazy?"

I reach for her hands, clamping down over her knuckles gripped around the barrier. She laughs, but I press tighter and slowly she allows me to swap the metal railing for my grasping hands. Our eyes lock. She smiles, and I think she is going to climb back under, back into my arms. "Come on," I say. "Come on." Instead she leans back again, further, over the rushing flow. Now her whole weight is in my clutch, her whole life and death. Despite the cold, my hands begin to sweat. It is difficult to hold on. She bends her knees, half sitting in the air, like we are a team of gymnasts. It makes her heavier. She weighs more than I had realised, or I am less strong.

"This is how it will be for me," she says calmly, still smiling, the water roaring beneath us. "This is how close I will always be to losing you."

Our fingers are slipping. It is not funny. None of it is funny. I yank her arms and she comes tumbling forwards. I catch her body, pulling her over the barrier, her chest first then one leg and the other. "Don't ever fucking do that again."

"I wanted you to see. To see what it will be like for your family, and for me."

But I am in no mood for a lesson. I turn away and start striding towards the car. "They'll get used to it. And you'll have to as well. Fuck."

She grabs my arm and steps in front of me. "Then it really is for you, not for me?"

"I told you that already." I am still angry, my heart is still racing. "I told you."

"Okay," she says.

She doesn't apologise.

She doesn't seem to realise the danger of what she just did.

She looks pensive, preoccupied.

"Life is not a fucking metaphor," I say.

Now she reaches for my hand and squeezes it. She kisses my shoulder. "I just don't want to be the reason," she tells me again.

***

I ignore Safia's call. It's 8.45am. She'll be on her way to work, just off the tube at Covent Garden, queuing perhaps at the kiosk that sells her favourite coffee, a those-in-the-know hole in the wall, not Starbucks. We're meant to be meeting her for lunch – a third attempt to get together this week. (The attempt being made by Safia, the cancelling being done by me.) It's not that I don't want her to meet Orli. I do. I distinctly do want them to meet. But today is our last day. I don't want to waste the time we have together by sharing Orli with anybody else. That's what I tell Orli. But it's possible that I'm not ready to introduce her to the one fiery element of my otherwise water-logged world. I wait a couple of hours and then send Safia a text: *Sorry. Got hectic. Dinner tomorrow night?*

***

My Nana is in the kitchen when I arrive and waves to me from the window. The cobbled path to her door has been lined carefully with daffodils. Mum tells her not to, that her knees can't take it and wouldn't it be easier just to have a few

184

pots, but Nana insists on working in her tiny garden every day, despite the rain, despite the cemented plots to her left and right, flowers having given way to driveways. I remember being put to work weeding one Sunday when Mum and Dad were at a wedding and Nana and Papa had charge of us. I must have been eight or nine and I loved the ritual of it all, wanted to be part of it. Side by side, Nana would prune while Papa watered, or one would dig while the other sprinkled in the seeds and patted down. A ballet between them. I remember Nana letting me hold the hose that day and Papa showing me how to break the hardened soil with the tip of the shovel. And I remember spilling a lot of dirt onto the pathway, which I'm sure they later had to clean up and probably had to redo most of my 'work'. I might be making it up but I think that was the same summer they cobbled that pathway and so planted the daffodils. I stop for a second to admire them. A few months ago, Nana finally allowed Mum to hire her a gardener so there is someone again to mow the lawn and trim the hedges and do the jobs that require heavy instruments she can no longer lift. But I feel suddenly very guilty that it wasn't me doing the lifting, that I haven't offered to help her, that in my whirlwind of work and clubs and meaninglessness I have never made time for this. I see her still waving from the window and feel another pang of guilt. Her cold is better but she is 87 years old. It's a long journey to her house from Israel.

Tea and biscuits are presented within seconds of my crossing the threshold. The tray shakes as Nana carries it into the lounge but she'd kill me if I tried to take it from her. *Not yet redundant* is a pronouncement we have heard pass her lips so often that Gaby and I have adopted it and now say it to each other, only sometimes in correct context. The pot jolts, but the liquid inside it doesn't spill.

"This was my mother's china you know," Nana informs me as I reach forward to take the delicate cup. She speaks with a thick Hungarian accent, though she has been living in England since she was 18 and her English is perfect.

"I know, you've told me once or twice."

"Pfft," she smirks. Nana inspects the cup in her own hand carefully and tuts when she finds a tiny, hairline crack in the handle. "How is Gaby?" she asks. "It's very difficult being a bride you know."

"Oh really? Difficult choosing dresses and flowers and going to food tastings?"

"Don't be cheeky," Nana reprimands. "There is a lot of responsibility to it. The whole world is looking."

"Gaby's fine," I say. "I think. We're not really speaking."

"Why not? Daniel, this marrying for love, this is what happens now," she smirks. "This is what these young ones do." I grin and she continues more earnestly. "You mustn't always take up your mother's mantle. I know you always want to protect everybody but you can't-"

"How are you Nana?" I interrupt.

"Oh, you know. I can't complain. My legs ache a bit, and my fingers are playing up again. And you'd think the neighbours would consider turning down their television wouldn't you? I was up past eleven thirty last night with that one's racket." She nods her head towards the neighbouring wall and sips her tea delicately, her little finger raised. "But I can't complain."

I can't help but laugh gently. I lean forward and plant a kiss on her cheek.

"Such a charmer," she says. Then looks at me closely. "Go on. What is it?"

"Did Mum tell you about Israel?"

She puts down her tea. "Of course she did."

"I'm sorry I won't see you so much," I say quickly.

"This is a problem," she agrees.

"I know you didn't get to meet Orli but-"

"This is a problem too."

"Mum hates it," I say. "But-"

Nana raises her hand to stop me. "Daniel, I told her already to take her feet off your back. It is a wonderful idea."

"Oh." I'm not sure quite what I'd expected Nana's reaction to be, but this wasn't it. "Oh. Really? I think you're the only one."

"Pfft," she says again, a noise frothing in the front of her mouth like the hot chocolate she used to make us during school holidays in the years after Mum went back to work. *Toast or poppyseeds?* These were the accompanying choices to our afternoon drink. The same each day: toast with jam or poppyseed crackers with cheese. I love that noise. Gaby makes that noise sometimes, when she's talking to me. And I always keep a packet of poppyseed crackers in my cupboard; they make me think of arms wrapped around me, and games of dominos. I don't come to this house often enough, I think. I have forgotten how comfortable I feel here. Nana flaps her hand at the wall behind her. It is lined with row upon row of books and I know them well. There is half a shelf dedicated to novels, another half to biographies, a few graphic novels and a large stack on the floor of *National Geographic*s, but the rest is philosophy, psychology, history, politics. "Do you know how long I've spent reading these things?" Nana asks me. "Buber, Spinoza, Maimonides, Rosenzweig… useless all of them."

"Nana, you have just swept away centuries of philosophy."

"Good riddance," she winks. "None of them could tell me why it happened."

I stop grinning.

"Why…" She pauses. "None of them could show me the good." She stops again and closes her eyes. She does this occasionally now mid-conversation, but this time she is only gathering herself. "The only good, the only good to have come out of those camps, Daniel – it is Israel. That is it. Kaput. Nothing else. So nothing is more important. If I was young enough, I would go there myself."

"You could come with me, Nana," I smile. And for a second I imagine it, my little European Nana hobbling through the hot Tel Aviv streets with her smart winter's coat. It makes me smile again. But then I catch a glimpse of Nana, no longer talking, and not mischievously winking but somewhere else, somewhere cold, dark. These reveries are happening more often these days, but they were always there, always present, haunting, and I know I will never feel this like she does. It is real but not real. Her life, but not mine. For me a story, an echo, a single twist in my disjointed DNA.

"The china was my mother's," Nana says again. "She brought it with us from Hungary. It was all that was left in the house when we came back to it."

"I didn't know that."

"We'd had art, you know. And things. Books. Belongings."

Nana has never spoken to me before like this, and I say nothing.

"We were Hungarian. Really Hungarian. And then we were British."

I nod.

"You are leaving a great country, Daniel, you know that don't you? A country with open arms."

I nod again. "I need your ketubah," I say quietly.

Nana smiles, she points. The marriage certificate is framed in a beautiful antique wood, standing proud between Maimonides and Spinoza.

I kiss her on the cheek again and carefully remove my parchment passport from the frame.

***

Safia is oddly interested in the minutiae of the emigration process. I suppose it is pretty astounding, the help I've received. Before Nana's I drove straight from dropping Orli at the airport to the Jewish Agency (who knew it was in Finchley?), and it would not be underestimating things to say that the Agency has the process down to a fine art. Beyond filling in a bunch of forms and providing evidence of my so-far Britishness, all I really needed was the ketubah, proof that my parents are authentically Jewish, proof that I can satisfy the Law of Return. I've read about this law a lot – not in the context of it being my easy out, or rather in, but as in it being a racist policy that Palestinians are not equally entitled to, not equally able to 'return'. It comes up all the time in media analyses of the peace process. And at uni debates. It is with slight unease that I refer to it now.

"Kinda weird, isn't it?" says Safia.

I think of my Nana. "I guess. But I reckon there are enough countries where Jews have been booted out for there to be one country that always welcomes us in."

Safia scrunches her nose and raises one side of her mouth, not agreeing, not protesting.

"I have to pick an ulpan," I say.

"A what?"

"A school to learn Hebrew. It's like an intensive language course for new immigrants."

"Do you pay for it?"

"No."

"Do you pay for the Jewish Agency help?"

"No."

"They really want you to come, huh?"

I shrug. "I guess. But works for me since I really want to go."

"Yes I'm aware of that, Dan."

Safia moves her arms off the table to allow the waiter to put down her chicken. I make room for my sea bass. We are out in the evening, again.

"Was it hard saying goodbye to Orli?"

"I'm sorry you didn't get to meet her."

"Uh huh," she says, raising an eyebrow.

"I am. Next time."

"Fine."

"Seriously, I want you to meet her."

"Fine," she smiles.

Safia digs into her chicken and asks the waiter for another glass of wine. Her parents know that she does this –

drinks alcohol, eats meat that isn't halal, doesn't fast during Ramadan – but I still can't help feeling that each bite is a small act of rebellion, a way to assert that she is more St John's Wood than Tehran. I wonder, just fleetingly, what her parents would have said if we'd ever actually dated. Not that I would have. Not that I could have. Not that even chicken-eating Safia was willing to take on the 'complications'. Safia notices me staring at her fork.

"Would you like some?" she asks.

"It does look good." I pick up my own cutlery and begin to navigate my sea bass.

"So?" She offers me her fork.

"Saf." I take a bite of the fish. It needs a little more lemon. Safia watches me squeeze the slice on the side of my plate over the fillet, then add pepper. She watches me deposit a small mountain of ketchup next to my chips. "Would *you* like some?" I ask.

"It's weird that you keep kosher you know."

"Really?" The waiter brings Safia's wine. I put down my fork and reach for my own glass. "Why?"

"I mean, it's weird that you keep kosher when you're not religious about anything else. Why do you bother avoiding a bit of chicken?"

I shrug. "It's how I was brought up."

"So?"

"So it's how I was brought up."

"So you just do it, without questioning why?"

"I don't need to question why. It's just something I do."

Safia shakes her head and makes a noise that sounds like it starts at the back of her throat, gathering disdain as it moves forward. More Tehran than St John's Wood.

"What?"

"It's not a rational answer, Dan. Why? Or else, why not do all the other stuff too?"

"Because I don't."

"That's it?"

"That's it."

"That's ridiculous. You're meant to be an intelligent, thinking person."

"Not everything has to be rational. It's a gesture. At least I do something."

Safia makes the noise again. I don't like it as much as the question mark eyebrows. She takes a long sip of her wine and studies me. What is it about girls and looking? Orli does this too: looks, looks. I grin. She smirks sarcastically back. Then very deliberately she forks another piece of chicken and slowly, seductively places it into her mouth. She takes a long time to chew. Still looking. I look boldly back.

"It's really good," she says eventually. "This chicken. Sure you don't want to try just a bite?"

"I'm good, thanks."

"Just one bite?" She stabs another chunk and dangles the fork in front of my lips. Suddenly I feel irritated.

"No thanks," I say less jovially.

"Fine. You could be missing out on the most delicious morsel you've ever tasted, all because you're too stubborn to even let yourself think about why you're not eating it. But that's fine."

"I know why I'm not eating it."

"Why?"

"Because that's how I was brought up."

Safia sighs and I am about to relent, to expand, to start philosophising about the fragmented parts of my self. But then she asks, "Does Orli keep kosher?"

"No, actually," I say. "She loves prawns."

The throat noise comes again. Then a pause. Then the eyebrows. "I do want to meet her," she says.

***

191

Now

12

It is harder than Udi imagined for him to actually go. It has been a year in the making. It has been arguments and headaches and hard work. Now, at last, his ticket is in his hand and his documents are in a folder in his hand luggage and his father is starting the car for the airport and his mother is on the sofa next to him. And Udi smells falafel.

Perhaps it is the unravelling nature of goodbyes.

First, there was a Friday night dinner. As well as the swathes of cousins and uncles and aunts his mother had invited, each with their own opinion and advice, his brother Ari was there. Ari congratulated him. He also told him that he is mad and that Israel is the greatest country in the world and that he still thinks Udi should return to the army, but also he is proud. Avigail said far less. She is holding back, Udi supposes. Holding back her lecture and her disapproval, because he knows this is what she feels, but all she told him was to stay safe and to dream big, and gave him a notepad in which on the first page her kids had drawn pictures of aeroplanes and she'd inscribed a short poem that he doesn't really understand. He wishes he did understand it, because when they parted there was an uncharacteristic shakiness to her smile.

Next, there was a beach barbecue with his friends. Officially it was a send-off for Chaim too who had been promising for months to join him in London, but yesterday Chaim found a cheaper flight to Barcelona. Still, he brought weed.

"Don't go getting all British on us," Dov had said at the beach, between puffs. "No crazy ideas about driving on the left okay?"

Udi had laughed but Dov pushed on. "Seriously, Udi, things will be different in London. You're expecting this, right?"

"Of course," Udi had replied. "I know, of course."

"But really different. Here, we know how everything works. I can arrange to speak to the Prime Minister in one phone call."

"I can do it in two," Yael had chipped in.

"It would take me four," said Udi. (It is a frequent conversation of theirs, to see how many degrees of separation there are between them and the highest office in the land. Most people can do it in less than five.)

"So okay, how many would it take you to call David Cameron?" Dov had demanded.

Ella didn't come to the barbecue. He had had to tell her of course. Not the morning after he opened the envelope, despite his mother's prompting eyes, nor anytime during the three days that followed, but finally. They have been on-again-off-again ever since. Blazing rows. Tears. Sex. But now they are off and he is leaving.

He called her last night on the phone: "I still want you to come with me."

"I still want you to stay."

"What if we got married?"

There was silence, for a long time, then he'd heard her swearing under her breath, and then finally she'd demanded: "Udi, was that actually a proposal? After almost five years is this actually how you're going to propose to me?"

"No. It wasn't a proposal. It was hypothetical, I just wanted to know what if."

"Well you'll know what, *if* you ask me, Udi," she'd said, and would probably have slammed down the phone if he

193

wasn't the very next morning going to be getting on a plane for London. As it was she could manage only one further word: goodbye.

But it didn't feel like a proper goodbye. It wasn't how he'd wanted to leave things. It is no wonder that he smells falafel.

"Turn your cup," says his mother.

Oz is outside making sure that Udi's bag has been packed properly into the car, that the battery is not playing up again, that he has petrol. Udi has already done this twice. He has not slept.

Inside, Batia has brewed him a thick, muddy coffee and they have spent the past ten minutes drinking it, saying little.

"Turn your cup," she says now, and because he feels guilty he obeys, allowing the consolidated sludge at the bottom to seep down the china sides. He leaves the cup however upside down on the saucer and does not hand it to her. Resting it instead on the table in front of them, he nods, then stands up. He will not stay for her reading, which he doesn't believe, and fears might be bad.

His mother nods back at him, stands too, hugs him hard. "You will be careful," she tells him, a plea wrapped up as an instruction. She takes his face into her palms. "I will speak to Yarden. Tell him if there is something you need." Yarden is Batia's brother, Ben's dad.

"I will be fine Ima." Gently he pulls her hands away. "I can take care of myself."

"I know," she says. "This I know."

"*Y'allah*." Oz appears at the front door.

Giving his mother a final kiss, Udi accepts the container of sambousak she has prepared for him and checks his documents one more time before following his father to the car.

Oz drives. He does not speak, but he drives. Udi has not been driven by his father in many months and is not sure, in

194

the silence, what to do with his hands. He takes out his phone and begins scrolling through messages, half thinking one may pop through from Ella, but it doesn't. Still, he keeps his phone in his hands. It isn't that he doesn't want to talk to his father, he does, very much so, but he fears that words might endanger the fragile bond they have resurrected at a time when there are few moments left to fix it. The silence lasts. Over the bridge. Onto the motorway. Signs for Ben Gurion Airport begin to appear.

"It is very hard to start again," Oz volunteers abruptly.

Udi puts down his phone. His father's face is heavy, pulled downwards. This is it. The words. The breaking of bonds. A recalling of that fleeting faith. Udi remains silent and prepares himself to bear it, to bow to his father's opinion one final time.

"We had just some clothes and each other," Oz says. "They gave us a tent and they gave us food but we had no money. Our bank accounts had been frozen by the Iraqi government. Our house was taken. At the border the valuables we'd carried with us were confiscated. Young people don't know this. They think we came and we conquered, but we were turned out, we were refugees. Israel is our only home. And we came to it with nothing."

Udi stays silent. He dares not speak.

"For two years we lived in this tent. Not a hut, not even wood or tin, Udi, just soft material separating us from the sun. I was lucky, I went to school for one more year and then I went to the army. It was better than the tent. Even when there were wars, and there were lots of wars, it was better than the tent." He reaches a junction and turns towards the airport, cutting in front of a car on his left. "After that I went to the kibbutz. Of course you know this is where I met your mother." The driver of the offended car has pulled up by their side and is swearing at Oz loudly, but Oz is almost smiling now. "We worked very hard. It took us much time but slowly, slowly we saved money so we could buy a small

195

patch of land and build a house. Our house, Udi, this is where my tent was, on this same bit of land. I built it. I helped to build Israel."

They have reached a junction and Oz looks directly at his son. Here it comes, there is only one way the conversation can go now – the entreaty to stay, the obligation to do so, the duty. Apprehension seeps back into Udi's stomach.

"I am proud, Udi, that you should want to do this for yourself," says Oz. "To make something for yourself. It is good."

Without meaning to, Udi claps his hands. Loudly. The sound reverberates in the small car.

"But it is hard, Udi."

"I will work hard," he speaks finally.

"I know you will," says Oz.

The airport comes into view. Udi would never have guessed that it would be his father driving him here, his father giving him these parting words, his father believing in him. He reaches out and squeezes Oz's shoulder. It still feels strong. Oz places his hand on top of Udi's. He nods. Udi returns the nod. And smiles. And as he opens the door to the car, that smile between them holds. Udi breathes in deeply, a hot, dry breath full of the future before him, the one he has his father's blessing to find. Still smiling he turns towards the airport. At last he is free. At last. Finally, now, in this moment. Yet, in the same moment, there is a sinking feeling. Because in his liberty he is also alone. And he cannot help thinking of Ella.

Inside, Udi joins the long security queue and, without Ella, feels immediately impatient. He hopes this sensation is fleeting because otherwise it is an anti-climax. Like waiting for his first army assignment. After the months of training, preparing, readying, he'd wanted it all to be worth something, he'd wanted to do something, but waiting was all there was to do. Waiting. For the purpose. For his purpose.

The queue moves slowly and after a while Udi lays his bag on the floor in front of him, kicking it forward inch by inch. While he waits he checks his documents again and fiddles with the shrapnel that is always in his pocket. Four female security officers are controlling the queue, three of them younger than Ella, though not as beautiful. Ella again. It occurs to him that she would be surprised to know how much he thinks of her. It occurs to him that he should tell her. But perhaps it is too late for that. There is a pang in his chest. A physical pang. But he forces his attention back to the travellers in front of him. It is easy to tell the tourists apart from the Israelis. As they are questioned they grow flustered, acting suddenly as if they have something to hide, the innocent whitewashed with guilt. *I've been in Tel Aviv on business*, he hears one young man saying. *Yes, I have family here. In uh, Herzliya. Their name is. Jesus what is it? Fischel. Yes, I am a member of a synagogue. Hendon Reform. No, I don't speak Hebrew. Yes, I can read it, I learnt it, but I can't speak it, I mean I can't understand it. No. No. My rabbi is called…um…oh, Jesus, sorry, I can't remember. Yes I am a member I just can't remember. I've been here three times. The last time was 2003, no 2002, no 2003. Yes I am sure. Yes I am a member of a synagogue…* Udi cannot help but laugh. The officers are not interested in the answers, only in the manner with which people respond. It is the surest of all airport security – people talking to people; machines do not know what is at stake. Udi is always interrogated closely. He has an Iraqi surname so the officers take special note. Today it feels like the final obstacle, the final barrier to his escape. But suddenly he is through. And his bag is through. And he has his ticket. And there is nothing else in his way. Udi is unable to quite believe it, to believe that this is it, that he has done it, and he has an urge to turn around, to cast one last look back. Because he is not coming back. He knows this with certainty. So he looks.

And behind him, she is there.

She is staring at him as though she has been standing in her spot for some time. Now she lifts her hand and waves. He waves back. She walks forward a few paces. He covers the rest of the distance. "What are you doing here?"

"I forgot- I forgot to tell you something."

"What?" His tone comes out aggressive. He doesn't know why. It is surprise, he thinks. Surprise and pleasure at seeing her, and desire. And caution. "What?" he repeats, more softly.

"I forgot to tell you that I love you, Udi." She pauses. Not with uncertainty, but as though all at once she is entirely sure of herself, and of him, he who is leaving. "And that I'll come. Not now, but when I'm finished studying, if you still want me to, and if you still like your London, I'll try it." More tourists brush past them, and more Israelis, more bumps in their path. "I will come," she repeats steadily.

In the midst of the airport bustle, the midst of the watching people, Udi has an urge to sweep Ella into his arms and lean her backwards and kiss her. He should do it. She would love him to do it. But he is afraid. Not now of guns and bombs and men who wield them, but that if he takes hold of her now he will never let go. Instead he reaches into his pocket where as always the shrapnel sits, warm from being handled, and he gently presses the hard pieces into her palm. She knows what they are. He has told her – only this one story and only part of it – but enough for her to understand.

"Bring them with you," he says. It is the nearest he is able to get to a promise.

***

It was light already. They had walked through the night but now it was light and Udi had expected to see something. To see something change, something different.

"Okay," said his commander. "So as you know we've been in Gaza for 20 minutes now…"

As you know.

Udi hadn't known anything. They hadn't been told anything. And the transition had been seamless. He could look behind him and still see Israel, still see the skyline, still see the place he was there at dawn to protect.

Arriving in London is the same. The plane is a microcosm of Israeli society and while he is still on board he feels as though he has not yet left, not completely. Israel sticks to his skin. Even as he walks through the halls of Heathrow he feels it like sand between the toes.

He could see rockets being sent out from the land in front of him, flying to the place behind. To houses with Israelis in them. He was not just walking towards something, he was going to do something good. He believed this. He had a reason.

He has a reason.

If something were going to happen, it would happen.

If something is going to happen, it will happen.

He begins to prepare answers to questions he worries he might be asked by border control, he invents stories to explain problems the officials might find, he digs into his bag and retrieves Ben's phone number. His legs burn.

But he is not even delayed. His papers are inspected, approved, stamped, and he is ushered past the customs desk. Then he is in baggage reclaim locating his minimal belongings and all at once he is ambling through the green-lit corridor with nothing more to declare.

Ben is waiting for him. They greet each other and hug fiercely. Ben is dressed in jeans and a shirt but he seems more tailored than Udi remembers, his shoes are un-tattered, his face shaven, his watch expensive. He tells Udi how excited the family are to see him, how his mother has been cooking for two days straight. Udi asks about work and when he will begin, but Ben tells him to relax. He'll take him to his flat tomorrow, he says, show him the restaurant, show him everything, but tonight he is not to think about work.

Tonight he is only his cousin who his parents are longing to see.

The smell of rice and sambousak hits Udi as soon as he enters the house. The next thing to strike him is the noise, the familiar sounds of chattering relatives, kids running wild, and pots and pans clanging together, announcing the feast.

A strange sensation builds inside Udi. He is not sure if it is excitement or foreboding, comfort or anxiety, ease or utter panic. Yarden and his wife, Gail, greet him warmly, and in the same breath tell him that his mother wants him to call. Dutifully he takes out his phone and heads into the hallway. He should call. He is an adult and he is here and they did not in the end stand in his way. He should call, he owes them that. But the feeling persists, and he has only just arrived and doesn't yet know what it means. Besides, he doesn't want this, whatever it is, to be explained to him by the dirty, crusted remnants at the bottom of a coffee cup.

**

The days that follow are filled with both action and inaction, an unhurried frenzy of introduction to his new life, the pace of which requires some adjustment. Ben takes Udi to the restaurant the following morning as promised, but not until after a late breakfast that stretches on until midday. The delay disconcerts Udi and makes him think of his father. When they arrive however, he loves the place at once. The restaurant has a hip, urban vibe with a traveller theme. South American music plays through the speakers, the walls are covered with maps, photographs, and souvenirs from far off lands, and the food, served by young, trendy waiters is a fusion of international cuisines. Ella would like it too, this food, these booths, this retro chandelier. It is a Monday but the place is packed. Udi feels an unusual sense of peace amongst the hubbub and finds himself brimming with ideas. He is introduced to the waiters and kitchen crew who will be working under him, and to the manager who will be moving to the new restaurant. They arrange for Udi to shadow him the next day, to show him the ropes, but neither Ben nor Jonny appear to have any doubts in Udi's abilities. Udi wants to prove them right, to begin, to start, to do. But Ben and Jonny don't want to loiter here. The restaurant is only a preamble to the rest of what they want to show him: first a car parked outside and then the flat. They lead him upstairs, apologising about the smell from the restaurant kitchen and the noise from the diners. But it is perfect. The bedroom is larger than his one back home, there is a spacious open plan kitchen/living room already fitted with appliances and furniture, a small but modern bathroom with brand new tiles, and there is air conditioning. Udi laughs when he sees it.

"Here you have air conditioning!" His cousins are wearing t-shirts and sandals but the temperature is cooler than some days in an Israeli winter.

"Soon you'll think this is hot," Jonny warns. "Anyway, it's a heater too." And he shows Udi the switch that turns the blowing air effortlessly from cold to hot.

***

Driving on the left takes more thought than he'd expected, largely because most of the time he has no idea where he is going and the Sat Nav doesn't seem to speak to him until it's too late. He finds himself frequently swearing at the voice that tells him to 'make a U-turn' and after a while doesn't bother to turn her on. Instead he talks to Ella on speakerphone who, amused by his misdirection, consults Google Maps. Fortunately, Udi learns fast and in any case the drivers aren't as impatient as they are at home. His first trips are to places of necessity: the bank where, after an elongated discussion with the manager and the arrival of Ben who vouches for his credit, he sets up his first English account; the post office where he applies for a British driver's license; the mobile phone shop where the family and friends he lists are Ben and his family. After that he begins to venture further. It is a Saturday afternoon when he drives the greatest distance he has navigated so far, to meet Ben 25 minutes away at a shopping centre. He takes a wrong turning only once and parks in the multi-storey car park.

Because he is late he hurries: slams the car door, barely notices where he has parked it, and strides towards the entrance. It is raining outside and he notices the smell of dampness that has seeped into even this covered building. The smell is satisfying. A wetness that reminds him how far he has travelled from the dust. It adds an invisible boost to his step and he bounds through the rows of parked vehicles, slipping easily through the spaces between them.

Until just before the entrance, Udi stops.

There is a pillar between him and the man he is watching, and he conceals himself behind it. The man is only stepping out of his car, but there is something about the way he is moving that seems unnatural, deliberate, disconcerting. The man is bearded and sandaled, and wears a kufi atop his head. Udi observes in silence as the man moves quickly around to the back of his car. He opens the passenger door. But Udi sees no passenger. The man reaches inside – carefully, purposefully. Udi can feel his muscles tightening, preparing. He glances around the car park for a security guard but cannot see one. He will have to act himself. Udi breathes quietly and takes a step forwards, revealing himself just a little from behind the pillar. The man glances up and notices him but doesn't stop, reaching further, faster. Udi contemplates wrestling the man to the ground. He contemplates shouting. Running. But before he can decide, the man has stood up again exposing the careful package he was reaching for: a baby boy. The man straps the baby to his chest. And nods amiably.

For perhaps the hundredth time in days, Udi shakes his head. The disparity between his assumptions and reality makes him feel ridiculous. He must adjust, he tells himself.

Be British, like his father decided to Be Israeli. But at the entrance to the shopping centre it happens again because what faces him there is unthinkable: nothing. There is no guard, no gun, no search and no metal detector; only open doors. The place is crammed with busy shoppers. If there were an explosion, hundreds would die. He cannot fathom it. He tells Ben he cannot fathom it. That it is crazy. That Brits are crazy. But Ben argues that it is the Israelis who are crazy, that in Israel the constant security makes him feel not protected but unnerved. Later that day they stray into the same conversation again. Ben is taking Udi clubbing with him and they ride the tube to Piccadilly. Again there are no security checks though their carriage is full with people, races, suspicious-looking bags. There is even one bag unaccompanied, propped up against the barrier by the door.

"Whose is this bag?" Udi asks loudly as soon as he spots it. "Who owns this bag?"

There is no answer. Some of the people turn to stare at him as if it is he who's insane, a few catch on to his anxiety and glance around for the owner, but most simply ignore him, burying their heads in Kindles or conversations more important than the imminent ending of their lives. "Whose is this?" Udi repeats more firmly, moving towards it, and finally a few passengers begin to take note.

"Udi," Ben says. "It's fine." But Udi is already reaching for the emergency stop lever.

"Does this bag belong to anybody?"

At last, the owner looks up from his newspaper. He does not answer but angrily leaves his seat to pick up the heavy bag and returns with it to his place, heaving it onto his lap. "Wasn't blocking anyone," he murmurs under his breath, before re-opening his paper.

Now, the rest of the passengers have lost interest but Udi cannot grasp their complacency. "Why don't you check?" he demands of Ben. "You should check. It would be so easy to bring a bomb here."

"There was a bomb," Ben replies, hushing him.

"I know. So you want another? Why don't you check?"

"If we change our way of life, they win," Ben answers flatly.

"If you don't, you die."

"It's not like that here, Udi."

And it's not. Here, in London, where the absence of security is so salient, Udi sees it afresh. He sees himself afresh. And he feels an intangible freedom he has never before tasted. It is unfamiliar in his mouth. The flavours of Israel and England twist on the tip of his tongue.

***

Now

13

Gaby had not expected to feel this way, this unsteady. Friends
had warned her about nerves before walking down the aisle,
and she doesn't have those. She's seen plenty of movies about
cold feet to await that with calm readiness, but her feet have
remained positively toasty. She loves Pete. *Loves* him, with a
certainty that should crush unsteadiness. So then what? She's
not even, today, worrying about her brother.

Now that she realises this, Gaby's mind clouds. Daniel is
so stubborn, so blindingly stubborn, and naïve, and stupid.
He thinks things have changed over there, that it is no worse
than in London. But it is only days ago that three teenaged
Israelis were kidnapped by Hamas. Gaby, no longer a
teenager, cannot bring herself to speak to him.

Orli sits by herself half way up the congregation. On one
side of her is Pete's cousin Archie and from under the flower-
decked chuppah Gaby notices him glancing repeatedly at the
beautiful blonde. Orli is beautiful. And brilliant. And on the
surface of things she is on Gaby's side, at least about the
army. But there is something else.

Daniel stands a few feet away next to Nana, dutifully
wearing the lilac cravat Gaby and her mother selected for
the ushers. For a second he catches her eye, and he smiles, a
beaming smile Gaby remembers from his barmitzvah when

he'd stood on the bimah and glanced up to the gallery of girls; but this time Gaby doesn't reciprocate. Perhaps it is simple self-protection. Perhaps unconsciously she is trying to detach herself so that she will care less. Whatever it is, she refuses to think about it now. It is her wedding day, after all.

Gaby returns her gaze to her moments-away husband. Pete is grinning, in a mischievous, proud, triumphant way. Like they have pulled off some kind of magic trick. Now you see it, now you don't. A tangible weight of anticipation emanates from the watching congregation, but Pete remains composed, unruffled. In the end, they have chosen a fusion of traditions: the chuppah, the circling around the groom, the stamping on the napkin-shrouded glass; but English vows – the familiarity of the words making Gaby feel giddy, as though they are play-acting and the marriage is not quite real – and no rabbi, rings straight onto the fourth finger, no ketubah. Both sets of parents seem uneasy with the mix, glancing both across the chuppah at each other and to the congregation for assurance, each feeling they have dared too little and too much. Pete however reaches out for Gaby and they interlock their fingers while the officiate talks of their union until finally, they are allowed to kiss, and of course it is not a magic trick, it is real, and this too is not what has made Gaby so unsteady.

Pete stops to shake Daniel's hand as they make their way down the tunnel of bridesmaids and ushers and out of the sumptuous room that Gaby and her mother have spent months designing. But Gaby doesn't look at him. She can't.

'Well?'

'Well what?'

'Three Israelis captured, probably dead.'

'Not dead, the IDF will find them. And right on the border, Gaby. I'm not going to live on the border.'

'Dan, if you join the army, where the hell do you think you'll be?'

'I'm sorry, Gaby, but I'm not changing my mind.'

'Then I'm sorry, Dan, but I can't forgive you. I won't. And I don't want you at the wedding.'

Of course she hadn't meant it, that last bit. Ironically their mother had been the one to patch things over, make sure he was actually going to attend. At least he is here.

She doesn't want to make a scene, doesn't want to embarrass him, but she slips past his extended palm. Out of the corner of her eye she can see Orli getting up, moving forward, sliding her hand into Daniel's instead.

Gaby and Pete pose for photos. She tries again to shake her mind free from the unsteadiness. It isn't fair to Pete for them one day to look back at these most wonderful of captured moments and for her to remember, probably secretly, that as she smiled down the lens she was also worrying – though not about Pete who remains, unshakeably, a can't-live-without-him kind of love.

Can't live without him, and won't, and would never want to despite any sacrifice. Any loss. Not that she has felt it as a sacrifice. Yet. But will she?

This is it.

This. This is what is bothering her, far too belatedly.

The master of ceremonies calls them to dinner and they enter the room holding hands, just as at any other Jewish wedding. Music strikes up, just as at any other Jewish wedding, and the guests stand and clap just as at any other. But then she and Pete make their way to their seats and not to the dance floor. And it feels quiet. There is no Jewish hora music to begin the night with a sweaty, frenetic outpouring of enthusiasm. There is no swarming of guests onto the dance floor. There are no hectic circles. She and Pete are not holding a white cloth between them and being hoisted atop chairs onto the shoulders of their male friends and relatives and her brother. There are no shouts of Mazel Tov.

There is a jazz band, as they have planned. There is Sinatra, Armstrong, Simone. Smooth and cool, as they had wanted, as she had wanted. But the fairy lights dotted around the room remind Gaby of her mother's Shabbat candles, and of herself remembering them while drinking eggnog and looking at a Christmas tree. And for the first time, at least consciously, Gaby allows herself to understand that if she wants her own children to cherish Shabbat candles in this way then she will have to light them. And although religion in general and Judaism in particular remains irrational to her, antiquated, divisive, the archaic practices surely doing more to exclude than unite, Gaby worries that should she suddenly want to resurrect them, she might be too late, or, on her own, not enough.

She thinks about this through the starters and main course. She thinks about this through the toasts, smiling not at Daniel but just to the left of him as he proposes their happiness. She thinks about this as the band expertly drums in the opening chords to the first dance and Pete leads her by the hand to the dance floor, twirling her in the way they've been practising. And she thinks about it as their song ends and other couples begin to litter the room with spinning examples of easy solidity. Her parents' back and forth jigging is perfectly in sync. Pete's parents waltz elegantly around the edges. They haven't, she supposes, ever had to practice.

Pete rescues her from her thoughts with a kiss. "What's the matter, honey? Faulty flower arrangement?"

"I'm just taking it all in." She returns his kiss, leaning into his chest, reaching around his neck. His smell is steadying.

"You sure? You can tell me if something's wrong. I am your husband after all."

She looks up at him and giggles. "So you are." They dance silently for a moment before she speaks again. "I was just thinking about the music. I was thinking we should have had a few Jewish tunes after all. Maybe."

"I thought you didn't want them."

"I didn't think I did. But maybe that was just to spite my mother." Pete twirls her gently again, hands behind them, meeting in front. "How would you feel if I wanted to light candles on a Friday?" she asks him. "Or send our kids to Hebrew classes?"

"Honey, you know I'm happy to do as much or as little of that stuff as you want. Is that what's bothering you?" he laughs. "We can eat gefilte fish every day of the week for all I care. So long as I can still have a Christmas tree."

Now she laughs, spinning out again, and suddenly feeling lighter. "Not even I like gefilte fish."

They pass their arms over their heads and spin back into another embrace, practised but perfect. She can feel the photographer loitering nearby but she doesn't let Pete go, she is happy for this moment of oneness to be captured. Pete however pulls away. He has spotted Daniel dancing nearby with Orli. Without consultation he waves them forward and cuts in, sweeping Orli away so that Gaby is left standing alone with her brother. Pete gives her a penetrative look as he melts into the crowd, and dutifully, Gaby turns to Daniel. Her brother offers her his arms. She hesitates.

"Remember when you made me dance with you at Auntie Netty's wedding?"

She hesitates again so Daniel exaggeratedly reaches for each of her hands and places them in his.

"We were so awkward," she relents.

They begin to sway. "Completely."

"I was 13 and thought I was totally grownup. You kept treading on my feet. Netty looked gorgeous."

"You look ten times more gorgeous," he tells her. "Gaby, Mazel Tov."

The words echo in Gaby's heart. She feels something release in her chest. And tears welling. "Dan, I wish you weren't going," she says.

"I know."

"I don't want to lose you."

"I know."

"Dan…"

"What?"

"I wish I was up on a chair."

Daniel stops dancing and looks first at her, quizzically, and then around the room.

"Dan," she says.

But Daniel only grins. "Not yet redundant," he whispers in her ear, before dropping her arms and diving into the crowd of dancers where within moments he has grabbed their father, uncle, and various others of their male relatives, and seconds later she and Pete are holding a white napkin between them and surfing the crowd on a pair of chairs, while the men below chant the hora music she'd imagined she wouldn't miss.

***

Then

14

Kaseem has not seen Dara for almost a week. She has exams and is studious. Sometimes she sits in the backroom of the shop and studies while he fixes computer parts, but if he attempts to distract her she warns him away with an unyielding glance from underneath the fringe she has recently cut in. It is one of the things he admires most about her – that she knows her mind, that she will not be stopped or swayed from her ambitions, not even by him. And she is full of ambition. She is 16.

Kaseem was unsurprised by this confession. He had watched her building herself up to it at the end of their camping trip, propelled by the actuality that in the coming days she was not beginning the army but returning to school. Of course he had guessed. And it is irrelevant to him anyway. At 16 she is already the most complete person he has ever known. She doubts of course, like every teenager, like every person, but her fears are not about who she is, or what she believes, or what others will think of it, but in whether the world will live up to her expectations, her highest of hopes. He sees how much she wants it to, she tries to cajole it, to cajole him, and he loves her for this; but the strength that seeps out of her soft, bronzed skin is not a casual commodity and others are often lacking. He is lacking. She does not realise how rare a thing she is.

Kaseem realises it, and he can feel himself smothering her. Clinging. Controlling. Or trying to, though Dara will not allow it. For the past week she has refused his entreaties to take an afternoon off school and when, last time they met, he suggested she not drink alcohol, she ordered a second beer to prove, he assumes, that she will not be cowed by principles other than her own. It doesn't bother him really, that she drinks. Nor that she wears bikinis and short skirts and lets her hair flow freely; it is a modernity he has tasted during his time at university, and wants. Besides it is how he first adored her. But to his surprise he is finding that the closer they become, the more it does bother him when other men stare hungrily at arms and legs and breasts that should be reserved for his eyes only. He does not know why. It is not as though he had imagined a future with Dara, it is not as though her integrity is his to protect. His fling with a Jewish schoolgirl was never meant to be more than a fleeting thing.

Perhaps if he did not perceive himself to be one of them – the other men who stare at her. Perhaps if he could cling to the self he was six months ago when he left university, when his esteem was flying like a rocket, when he had professors and peers and a piece of paper that proved he was educated, tipped for greatness, different from the rest. Now that piece of paper is worthless. The frame his mother bought in which to hang it cost more money than the illustrious degree has earned him, and it is a daily humiliation. One he fights by working all hours at the shop, applying for job after high-tech job, and yes, he recognises it, dangling Dara like a piece of gold upon his arm. He dreads the day that she will look up from her wilful adornment and see what he now sees: just another brown face with nothing to distinguish it. She begs him to paint, but he cannot bear for her to see the feelings that a careful brushstroke of colour would expose.

The previous week they were in a café on her side of the city. *Her* side because this is where her home is, where she goes to school and to hospital and to the theatre with her parents who also play out their lives in this broad vistaed vicinity. Kaseem has spent time in this area, with university friends whom he spoke to in Hebrew or English, or even one or two in French, and who marvelled at his abilities. He has been to the cinemas and tasted the weak coffee and seen inside the tall, permission-granted buildings. But at night, he has always returned to the place in which he was born. The place that is his. Even if he could afford to, he would not move to Dara's shinier location; his ambition is not to hunt new treasure, but to polish the rusted jewels he already owns. The East of the city, where his mother lives, and his sisters wait for husbands, and his father breathed his last breath, and Kaseem sleeps and has dreamed, this is his home, and thus, the café where he sat with Dara is on her side and he was, as always, just visiting.

Dara had ordered a tuna salad. The waiter was young with sandy hair almost the same golden tone as Dara's and a slow, snaking smile that slithered carefully across his face. Kaseem disliked him even before he spoke. He disliked the way he moved confidently between tables, and tucked a pencil behind his ear, and brought them water and olives before they asked for anything, presuming he knew them, presuming he knew what they wanted, presumptuous enough to smile at Dara who smiled back. Even as the waiter wrote, he looked not at his pad but at her. Dara, as usual, was wearing a tight pair of jeans and a low-cut vest top with a jumper thrown over the top that was too large and so fell tantalisingly off her toned left shoulder. Her hair had grown even longer than when they'd first met and was draped in an untied bunch in front of her chest, the newly cut fringe playing with the lashes of her eyes. Underneath the table, she had slipped off her trainers, as she always does when sitting, more comfortable in the summer months of sandals and exposed toes. She had been trying to play footsy with him, trying to make him smile. Kaseem however had not been in the mood for smiling. He'd had another job rejection, the computer shop was not doing well, money was running out, and his mother had been nagging. He therefore studied the vast menu with an expression that curled doggedly into a scowl and Dara told him that he looked like the colour black. He said nothing.

The waiter in contrast, smiled broadly, silkily, lightly like his hair. "Just a salad? Nothing else for such a beautiful girl?" he asked.

And Kaseem had exploded.

Quietly.

A slow, measured fury.

He did not slam his hand on the table but he pressed it firmly into the wood. He did not punch the young, obnoxious, Jewish usurper but he raised his chin defiantly towards him. He did not swear but he took a deep, pacifying breath of the cigarette he was smoking before, and with a gentle menace he knew Dara had not yet witnessed, he snarled: "What the fuck are you doing?" It was a controlled, familiar anger.

"Excuse me, but I'm not talking to you," the waiter had responded immediately, holding up his hand. "I'm talking to the beautiful girl." He smiled at her again.

Now Kaseem stood up but Dara touched his arm. "It's fine, Kaseem," she told him. "I'm fine."

"You see, Kaseem, she's fine," the waiter repeated. "Sit down, Kaseem, we are only talking."

Kaseem could feel Dara imploring him to rise above it, to sit down, to calm down, to be more than the waiter expected. "Don't you fucking tell me to sit down," he said, louder, shrugging off Dara's hand and leaning his face closer to the waiter's. "Don't you presume to tell me anything."

"Stop it," Dara said quietly.

"Yes, Kaseem, stop it," the waiter goaded.

"And you stop it too," Dara commanded, louder. Both men now turned towards her and her eyes flashed. She jerked her jumper back up to her neck. "Can't you see I have a boyfriend?" she flung at the waiter. "We are not *talking*, you and I, I am ordering. And I want a tuna salad. With a Coke please."

At this, the waiter had huffed, and reluctantly written the order down on his pad, and now Kaseem had smiled. Returning to his seat, he had placed his hand on Dara's and tried to stroke her delicate, un-manicured fingers, but Dara was no longer jovial as she had been before and removed her palm from the touch of his skin and pulled her half-trainer-clad feet beneath her, unwilling to make contact now even with the parts of herself she trod upon. "What do you want, Kaseem?" she said wearily, her tone assertive but tired, like that of a fatigued mother fed up with refereeing her squabbling brood. It made Kaseem feel petty, and small, and angry all over again.

"I'll have a coffee. Black."

"Of course." The waiter smiled, not writing it down but sticking the pencil behind his ear. "But just a coffee? No food for you, Kaseem? Nothing more?" And they both understood the allusions. *No money* for something more is what he meant. No prospects, no future, no right to be sitting in an expensive café in a nice part of Jerusalem with a beautiful, Jewish girl.

"Fuck you," Kaseem spat, loudly this time with a flick of his hand knocking his menu to the floor. He glanced at Dara, but this time she did not stay his arm, or ask him to be calm. Instead, her feet half in and half out of her trainers, she walked straight out of the café.

Kaseem followed. Feeling foolish and indignant. Hating the waiter for his smug prejudice. Hating Dara for making him feel so inadequate. Hating himself for being so. Her long hair swished freely in time with her pace and for a fleeting second he imagined himself yanking it and her to the ground. How easy it would be. How satisfying. To rub dirt in the face of something so righteous. But in picturing her face, he saw at once her soft, compassionate smile. And hated himself again. The heels of her trainers folded underneath her step as she strode into the distance.

Eventually, stopping at the entrance to a park, she looked around to see if he was there and paused just long enough for him to catch up with her. When he did, he bought two coffees from the vendor just outside the park gate, and followed her in. She had wanted, he presumed, a quiet, neutral place in which they could talk, but as soon as they were inside it was obvious to them both that the space was too open, the sun too bright, the children on the playthings too high-spirited for their dark, brooding tensions. Eventually they found a bench in the shadiest corner and sat at separate ends of it, fondling their hot, plastic cups. Dara's full lips were pursed together, her cheeks were flushed by the winter chill, her skin had lost the bronze of the summer months and in its paleness looked fragile and innocent. A china doll. Kaseem wanted to put his arms around her, to bring her close to his chest, to feel the store room tug of her own arms around him that made him feel needed and worthy. But a scowl worried her brow and kept Kaseem on his side of the bench. Finally, because one of them had to, he spoke, but he hadn't prepared the words and hadn't intended them to be wrapped in the tight, angry tone that shot out of his mouth and hit Dara's porcelain defences like sharp rocks.

"You heard how he insulted me, Dara. You heard him, and you expected me to do nothing?"

It was meant to be an apology but Dara's scowl deepened. Her eyes hardened. "You were rude, Kaseem. And aggressive. It wasn't necessary."

"Well of course *you* would think that."

"What's that supposed to mean?"

He'd meant because she never used swear words herself, because she saw the world through her rose-tinted glasses, because she was delicate, and innocent, because she was only 16.

"You mean because I'm Jewish? Because I'm like him? Because I'm racist? I thought you knew me better than that. God, Kaseem, you carry such a heavy chip on your shoulder, you can hardly breathe beneath it. You don't see what's really happening. I thought you were different."

"Different from the rest of the fucking Arabs you mean?"

She froze, her eyes brimming with hurt. "How can you say that to me?"

"You mean after you've slummed it with me? Come on, Dara, admit it, I can see it in your eyes. You're so confident of yourself, you think you're so open-minded and perfect, but you still see a stinking Arab when you look at me. An uncivilised, backward man who embarrasses you in cafés. You don't see what your people do to make me act this way."

"*My* people?"

"Yes."

"*My* people?"

Her eyes had grown smaller than Kaseem had ever seen them and the hand in which she held her coffee was shaking. She looked as though at any moment she might explode, or weep, and again Kaseem was overwhelmed with a desire to put his arm around her. His Dara. His Compassion. But the words continued to slip out of him, like a threaded yarn, the pattern old and fixed and deeply sewn. "Yes," he repeated.

Dara opened her mouth and then closed it. Whatever she had wanted to say to him she was reassessing. Tears brimmed in the corners of her eyes and she set down the coffee, crossing her arms in front of her chest and lifting the hood of her sweater over her head, turning away, retreating from him. Kaseem felt a sudden panic. He was losing her. She was losing her faith in him.

"You are the racist one if that's what you really think," she ventured finally, twisting back to look at him, scrutinising his eyes as though she was trying to find the truth swimming within them. Giving him one last chance.

Kaseem breathed deeply. He was not used to the women in his life making him struggle to explain himself. It was tiring. He felt tired. And reprimanded. The thought of the waiter taunted him, the waiter with his smug, underhand insults, his arrogant smile, and his hair that matched Dara's. Kaseem clenched his fist. But Dara was still watching him, waiting, hoping.

"It's not what I really think," he said finally.

Dara kept looking at him. He bowed his head. And Dara began to weep.

Now Kaseem moved closer to her and took her hand. She was so young. He pulled her into his chest. She wrapped a long arm around his waist.

"I'm sorry," she whimpered. "I know things are difficult."

A little way off in the park, two young Jewish boys wearing yamakas chased each other through the bars of a climbing frame, clambering higher and higher, one after the other. Elsewhere, a group of girls around Dara's age laughed loudly at an inside joke. And Dara and Kaseem, each other's insiders, held on tight and dared not move. Only outside the park was the peace broken. It was rush hour, and the traffic made noise and stirred up dust around them.

"I need a job," Kaseem said.

And sitting back from him, though still gripping his hand tightly, Dara replied, "I may have one for you."

They have now not spoken for almost a week. Because of her exams and her study and the argument, but also because they have arranged for him to appear by coincidence on another outing in her part of the city. He loiters outside the electronics shop, waiting, as planned.

He has not imagined what her father will look like. She has spoken of him only briefly, as a provider of either wise insights or bad jokes, both of which she happily recycles, but she has not discussed what he does, or what he wears, or the colour of his hair, or what Kaseem might think of him. Kaseem wonders now, vaguely, anticipating more acutely the quiet enthusiasm of Dara's smile when she sees him there, faithful to their conspiracy. When they appear however, Dara gives away nothing. Her arm linked through her father's she is all vivacity, her eyes and laughter and chatter turned with enthusiasm towards him. Her father meanwhile is unhurried, lethargic precision – one foot in front of the other, slowly, purposefully, assuredly, dominating the cobbled pavement. Dara's eyes barely flicker towards Kaseem's as they pass, but he smiles. There is no need he realises for her to check his complicity; their trust is unflinching.

Kaseem takes out his bag of tobacco, rolls a cigarette and smokes it before entering the shop behind them. He gives them time to examine the computers, time to engage the Russian owner in a conversation about installation, time to talk about the security system also needed, time to get to the crux of the matter which is the cost, time for the two of them to barter, for Dara's father to pretend that he needs a moment to think, for him to retreat to the far side of the shop where the cables that the owner has agreed to throw in for nothing are shelved and where Kaseem is carefully standing, time for Kaseem to turn to Dara's father, who has her eyes, and quietly excuse himself for overhearing but suggest in perfect Hebrew that with his Hebrew University education and his need for work, he could do the job himself at a far cheaper price.

He hates himself for this. For the pretence of chance. For the pretence altogether. For the stereotype he is fulfilling. For not, in front of Dara and her father, being able to present himself as himself, nor as Dara's boyfriend, nor as a self-made, self-reliant man.

***

It is difficult for Dara to stay in her room doing her homework when she knows that just a few feet away, on the other side of the wall, Kaseem is there in her house, in her home, taking instructions from her father. She imagines briefly how it might be if her parents knew about them. Would they still allow Kaseem into their house, invite him for dinner, eat with them on Shabbat, crack jokes? Would her mother analyse him? Would her father take him aside and talk politics? Would her brother get out his guitar and play him a song? She paints the scene in her head. She would use blues and yellows and other peaceful, life-loving hues. But then she hears a hammer and some kind of drill, her mind is flooded with black, and she senses the impossibility of her daydreams.

It is not only now. Ever since their camping trip this black sensation has been growing, creeping, though she tries to push it far to the back of her mind and use it only in her art. It is as though distance from the city exposed it to her, like one of those paintings you have to stand far away from to see. Jerusalem is not good for them. It is heavy, a heavy place, the whole weight of history and fighting and accusation and clashing ambition balancing on their backs, falling too often between them. Not at night. When they talk late in the computer store room, he lifts her up with the sparkling treasures of old family tales, or art he has seen, or computer technology that will revolutionise the world, all of which he shines for her so that they are illuminated, an extension of him. And he touches her so expertly. But the day always returns. And in the day, when the realities of their separate existences come crashing and smashing like bombs and bulldozers into their lives, his shoulders are no longer reserved for her alone to curl up against and lean upon. Instead, they carry the hopes and very survival of his family, of his whole generation it sometimes seems, and though they are broad they are not broad enough. He has begun to stand with a slight stoop.

Once, a few weeks earlier on her way to school, Dara saw him standing with some other Arab men on the side of the street. He was wearing the shirt that she knew he saved for interviews and he had combed down his hair. She hid behind a tree across the road and watched him. Smoking. Talking. Waiting. He waited for a long time, such a long time, until eventually a passing car pulled to a stop, and then he and the other men hurried over to its window, offering their services – computers, wiring, carpentry, building, carrying, anything, anything. The driver took his time haggling down the small price for their labour and then selected one of the men, not

Kaseem. His posture stooped a little more. And Dara felt a deep wrench in her stomach as he stepped back onto the pavement to wait for his next opportunity to beg a job far beneath him. His eyes dulled. She knows better however than to offer him money. Pride is perhaps the only thing he still has in abundance. Pride, and talent, and intelligence, and soul. All of which are useless.

Dara puts down her pen and stands up from her bed that is a soft-seated mountain of books and pens and small canvasses. She is meant to be studying geography, she has an exam in two days, but when she is not drawing she feels fidgety and incomplete. Kaseem does not know quite how much she draws, or quite how significantly he is a part of it, but his guidance has set her technique years ahead of the others in her class, and the inspiration of him has made equal transformations to her style. She can capture emotions now. Soft strokes of her brush rush the page with feeling. Feeling for him. Sometimes she no longer even thinks about what she is creating, ideas and images and shapes and colours seem to come to her of their own accord, fighting for precedence, her task merely to choose them; like a forbidden love. Dara has been doodling without really looking while flicking through her geography textbook and listening for sounds of Kaseem. She looks down now at the canvas that has, in standing, dropped from her lap onto the floor. It is a strange, imprecise arrangement of interlocking circles, connected and separate. She throws the drawing onto the growing pile next to her desk and moves over to her wardrobe where she stares into the mirror and studies her reflection.

Her skin has paled in the winter weather but she does not apply bronzer. It makes for a greater contrast between her hair and her skin and she thinks this makes her look interesting. She wears dark colours to emphasise the clash. She has lost weight without intending to, the price of love she imagines, noting the intestinal turmoil of the past months, and her jaw bones are more defined than before, her cheeks less rounded, less baby-faced. But this, she decides, is the only physical change since Kaseem. It would not be possible for her parents to guess that she is no longer a virgin, that she has committed treason, that she has given herself to him.

Dara pulls on one of her brother's jumpers that, since returning from camp that summer, he no longer fits into, as though they fed him only on sun and beef. It has a hole in one elbow that makes Dara think of her little brother running around wildly. But suddenly he is not so little, and not so wild, and not so young. She smiles. Over the summer he has become a contemporary again. It is good for them. They talk once more about everything – or almost everything – and she has begun to rely again on his opinion, his insight, his advantage in this that comes from knowing her so well. Though lately he has been exploiting this resurrected status. He asks her all the time where she has been, tells her she is getting too thin, rifles with curiosity through her sketches. He is careful however not to say such things in front of their parents and fortunately they do not notice the details as much as her protective little brother does. She bunches up his baggy sleeves and opens the door.

In the hallway, amidst the work area her father has constructed as his home office, Kaseem is laying underneath a desk scrutinising a bunch of inter-tangled wires. "Not that one, not that one," her father is saying over and over, directing Kaseem who is breathing deeply, Dara can tell, to disguise his impatience. Customers, Kaseem has told her before, always interfere. They think only of the outcome, trying to impose their narrow end game upon his delicate task without comprehending the benefits of getting there carefully, in the right order, with every leftover dispossessed wire accounted for and made good. She loves the way that he talks even of wiring – everything he does is with thoughtful, artistic diligence, as though the electrics of a computer are a beautiful philosophy of their own. His skilful fingers slide quickly between the knots and the computer on the desk pings abruptly to signal that it is alive, ready for work. "Okay, okay!" Dara's father shouts, waving his hand at Kaseem to stop, anxious that with an ill-considered move he will undo his good work. Presuming Kaseem's stupidity? No, Dara decides; her father is simply of an older generation, not computer-friendly, not aware how easy somebody with Kaseem's youth and intelligence can make an apparently insurmountable undertaking seem.

"It works," Dara says, emerging from the doorway and daring a glance at Kaseem who is now sitting up underneath the table, pulling down his t-shirt that with his manoeuvring has risen slightly up his chest.

"Yes. Finally. Kaseem here has worked his magic. We officially have Internet," her father replies. "Now we just have to connect your mother's office. And Kaseem says he can install that animation software for you. And we have a few other jobs before we're done."

"That sounds like it will take some time," Dara smiles.

Her father frowns. "Is the drilling disturbing your study? Dara is taking exams this month," he explains to Kaseem proudly. "She has been very busy. She has had to do a great deal of research. Every day she goes somewhere in the city doing, what did you say? Surveys? Questionnaires?"

Dara nods, remembering the 'questionnaires' she and Kaseem gave each other in the store room: Which part of my body is your favourite? Why did you first notice me? How many times have we kissed? "379," he had answered, then kissed her again. "380, 381…"

"I barely heard the drilling," she reassures her father, pecking him on the cheek before slipping past them downstairs. It takes all of her will power not to look back at Kaseem who she knows is equally carefully not looking at her.

For the next week Dara does not concentrate on her exams but listens to the noises that Kaseem makes in her house: the tapping of his slender fingers on the keys of the computer, the buzzing of wires, the increasingly extensive conversations he has with her father. She can tell that her hard-to-impress father is indeed impressed by him; he has always appreciated ambition and focus, and Kaseem has both. Dara's brother too loiters near where Kaseem works and talks about football or music. One evening her mother invites him to stay to dinner. Kaseem is enchanting them all. But that is because their guards are down. Dara is not fooled into believing that she could ever tell them the truth, she is not so naïve as to think they could ever accept Kaseem as more than an exceptional worker but also as her lover, her one true love. She is not fooled, but still she hopes for it. And she draws. Kaseem being close makes her create with an even greater intensity and for the first time she is not wholly critical of the work she produces. She does not feel dwarfed by the juxtaposition of her abilities with those of the man who has influenced them. She is able, suddenly, to truly capture the light. She would like to have another go at the canopy outside the computer shop. She would like to ask Kaseem to stand again in the shadows there, appearing for her from amidst them.

One evening Dara's brother flicks through the growing pile next to her desk and suggests that she send a selection to some small galleries or magazines. The next day he buys a bunch of appropriate publications and dumps them on her bed. She does not quite believe that there is any point, but sends off a few, just in case.

In between drawing, and small patches of study, she takes breaks to make herself a cup of tea or warm a pita, and she offers food to Kaseem, couched in niceties that seem appropriate and unrevealing. They find it more and more difficult not to smile at each other, not to launch into eager conversation. It becomes a game, almost. But Dara notices how gratified Kaseem seems when her father compliments him or cracks a joke, how proud and affirmed he is, and she fears that he is beginning to imagine himself within their sphere, that he will press her, soon, to tell her parents about them, and when she refuses, he will be crushed. The thought of this makes her smile less often, but Kaseem grows ever more daring. On his final day on the job she stands in the kitchen waiting for the kettle to boil while he leans casually against the doorframe. Her father is sitting at the table leafing through a pile of documents, reading each sheet carefully before placing it within a card-covered file. Dara pours her father his tea, adds the two sugars she knows he prefers, and places it on the table in front of him with two small pastries arranged like wings around the cup in the saucer.

"Would you like sugar, Kaseem?" she asks then, knowing he takes three, but enquiring for her father's benefit as she fills another cup and prepares another assembly of sweet accompaniments.

"Yes, please. Three."

Dara feels Kaseem watching her as she delicately stirs the liquid and makes a final adjustment to her display of pastries.

"It is a rare talent to make such small things so beautiful," he says as he takes the saucer from her. "The whole world should be this way."

Dara laughs and her father looks up.

"They are only pastries," she says quickly, her stomach tightening, coiling, but Kaseem speaks again.

"Everything we do is an extension of ourselves." He smiles. Winks.

Now Dara's father puts down his papers. His tone is jovial, but his words are not. "Kaseem, am I paying you to stand around my home and drink tea?" he asks him.

Kaseem stands up straighter. The notion of a joke hangs in the air but he is unsure, off-guard.

Dara can only watch helplessly.

Kaseem shakes his head. "No. I'm very sorry. I'll get back to it now." Carefully, he places his un-drunk tea and un-disturbed sweets back on the kitchen counter. Her father watches. Dara opens her mouth to protest but does not know what to say and so in the end says nothing. Kaseem doesn't look at her. He casts his dark eyes down to the floor beneath her feet and hastily retreats from the room.

Dara's father glances at her but says nothing.

Dara says nothing.

From the next room there is the sound of a drill.

Hours later, Dara is back in her room, finally studying, sinking amidst her bed of books, when the door opens. Kaseem slips inside. He shuts the door behind him. Dara smiles conspiratorially but he does not speak. Instead he starts fumbling with his belt, unbuckling his jeans. Dara laughs and begins to stand up, but Kaseem grabs her shoulders and guides her forcefully back onto the bed. "Your father has gone out," he whispers, pulling impatiently at her own tight denim.

"But-"

"Be quiet," he tells her, and heaves her backwards, the spine of one of her books digging into her ribs, a newly completed canvas crumpling beneath her elbow. Kaseem yanks her top over her head and shoves her bra to one side, not bothering to undo it. He pulls her jeans and knickers to her knees and leaves them dangling there. Then he pushes himself inside her. His eyes are darker than ever. He grunts heavily. Dara attempts to adjust her position beneath him and strokes his chest to move him slightly to the side, but he seizes her wrist and pins it firmly to the bed, the book jabbing into her ribs again, over and over. She does not know what to do, what to say to him, how to act. The aggression scares her, but she feels a need to acquiesce, to apologise for her father, to atone for him, to assuage Kaseem's humiliation. She doesn't speak, but she feels tears welling silently behind her eyes until abruptly Kaseem stands up and by her hair pulls Dara into sitting. Heavy droplets now trickle down her cheeks. She glances up but Kaseem tilts her face downwards and steers her head towards him. Her mouth is suddenly full and he coaxes it forwards and back until she submits to the urgent rhythm. Occasionally he jerks forward and she has an impulse to retch, but obediently she continues on and on, barely able to breathe until finally he pulls back, and pushes her down and falls on top of her again.

"A condom?" she manages to whisper. But Kaseem ignores her. And within seconds he is finished. And standing up. And pulling up his jeans and re-buckling his belt and moving towards the door. And altering everything. Before he leaves, he turns briefly, but he says nothing.

And Dara says nothing.

And in a few minutes, from the next room, there is once again the sound of the drill.

***

Now

15

With each day that passes Udi feels a glorious, impalpable dissolution of stress. In less than a month he is sleeping, sometimes without the need for a spliff. The summer is cool, fresh. Even on the hottest days there is a breeze that makes him feel a forwards momentum, no longer standing still, no longer treading sand. Attempting to remember his father's advice he tries to Be British: resisting the pull of kosher delis in Golders Green where everybody speaks Hebrew; nodding at but not talking to people in the street; standing in line. He has even got used to no security guards. But he doesn't want to shed his Israeli-ness altogether. In England, it is like having superpowers. Chutzpah, others call it. All Udi knows is that in the army he said yes and he did, but in life: rules, regulations, good manners – these are the qualities of the weak, the cringing, the disempowered. They don't get a take-away nut stall set up in the restaurant and make it the sole biggest profit-driver. They don't persuade a little old Lebanese man to exclusively stock them with the best hummus he has tasted since arriving in London. They don't buy Ella a ring.

She has no idea. Now that her semester is finished she is coming to visit, a trial before she hopefully makes the move for real. But he has given away nothing. Their conversations over the past days have been practical – plane times and days he has off and what she should pack. Or tentative – where his brother has been sent, how involved he is in Operation Brother's Keeper, what the chances are for three teenaged Israelis who are most likely already dead. Although look at Gilad Shalit, she keeps insisting, there is a chance.

It is strange to be away from Israel during a time of such national dismay. He can't help imagining Ari somewhere in Hebron, going from house to house, searching, looking, watching, hopefully with somebody watching his back too. He can't not think of the families of the teenagers who were kidnapped by Hamas while hitchhiking home, clinging to any hope they can. He can't pretend he doesn't know that amidst all of this, Avigail will be standing shrouded and supplicating on street corners. At least she no longer seems shaky. Her articles have been doing the rounds and are bolder than ever, audacious, full of criticism of the Hannibal Directive, full of shame for the revenge murder of the Palestinian teen, and the demolition of Palestinian homes, and the sweeping arrest of Palestinian men, full of words others won't speak. Words he is not sure she should be speaking. But even without this to rile him he can't not feel the seed of something, the promise of escalation, that reliable cycle of prodding and prodding and prodding, and then response, retaliation, catastrophe. Even the international news has a whiff of it.

But he is not there.

He has a restaurant to run and suppliers to change and cousins to repay. And a nut stall. And it is possible, he discovers. It is possible for him to detach, to block out, to live.

To live. The sense of satisfaction is unexpected and extraordinary. Ben and Jonny have allowed him complete managerial control and tell him often how impressed they are. They even said he can hire, and he has done so: a 25-year-old Egyptian named Tadaaki studying for an engineering degree at UCL. They met in a café where they both ordered Assam tea instead of English Breakfast, with baklava not biscuits, and then after briefly establishing their countries of origin, and warring histories, Tadaaki asked Udi where the hell he could find a good falafel because all of the ones he'd had in London tasted like shit. Now Tadaaki works evenings at the restaurant but they often meet there for lunch too, or an early breakfast before Udi opens up. Neither mind that the meat Udi serves is neither kosher nor halal. They finish every meal with tea and baklava. Tadaaki is the first person Udi tells about the ring.

It was a Saturday when he decided, four days before Ella was due to arrive. He was not working but woke early and went for a jog on Hampstead Heath. He does this often, or he cycles; he has brought with him that need to be active, to do, to not waste precious minutes. His mother would be pleased, though he does not like to think of her, pleased or otherwise. He does not like to think of his desertion. It has only recently occurred to Udi that even if he travels back to Israel every couple of years and his parents sometimes come here, even then he can probably count the number of times he will see them again before they are gone. In order to avoid addressing this fact he speaks to them as infrequently as possible. It is hard not sharing his success with those who would most cheer it, especially his mother, strange to have removed from her, along with his laundry, the daily inspection of his soul. It is like dressing without a mirror. But even without consultation he knows that his mother would be happy he is not sitting in his room lacking occupation and purpose. Besides, he loves the soft, un-crunchy grass underfoot, and the way the refreshing air laps around him when he is moving, bathing his lungs.

Despite the relative coolness of this particular Saturday he arrived home sweaty and in need of a shower. He does not wear shorts so for most of the way home from the park his long joggers had stuck to his skin. In his bedroom they were the first thing he peeled off before switching on the TV

– to MTV, not news, even now – and removing his equally sodden t-shirt, kicking his trainers into the wardrobe. After turning on the shower he returned to the bedroom to pump up the volume of the music before getting in. It was then that his phone rang. Ella. He picked it up, easily, without thinking. Then smiled at this not thinking, this progression, this lack of need or desire to hide.

"Where were you so early?" she had said before hello. "I called you an hour ago. Don't you sleep anymore?"

"Actually, I'm sleeping well, Ella. I'm sleeping well." He could hear her smiling down the line at this. Understanding the magnitude of it. "But I was running," he continued. "I went to the park."

"Ah, it's because you're missing another activity," she told him. Now he smiled and she heard it. "I am so excited to see you, Udi."

"I am too."

"I saw your mother yesterday."

Naked, Udi sat on the bed. "Oh?"

"She gave me food for you."

"Oh."

"She asked me to tell you Ari is okay. Not to worry. And to call her so she can tell you this herself."

Udi turned down the volume on the television. "I know. Of course Ari is okay."

"Your mother said he has enough deodorant to last him a decade! It's going a bit crazy here. The whole country is sending the soldiers care packages like this. And there was a bunch of anti-Arab graffiti down by the port, not that you can blame people, but- I just hope to God they find those teenagers soon."

"So how is everyone?"

Ella had paused then and Udi could hear the slight consternation at his lack of interest. But he didn't want to hear, to be drawn back in. He couldn't. Usually she didn't want to either. But she was there. And he was here. A voice

231

sounded in the background on her end of the phone. Her mother. It made him think first of making out with Ella in her bedroom while her mother was downstairs cooking. And then it made him think of his own mother again. His own mother, and his father, and his somewhere soldier brother. "I have to go, Udi, Ima is calling me."

"Okay." He had prepared to put down the phone then but hadn't in case Ella had only paused as she still did sometimes, not meaning to say goodbye, waiting for him to offer something. This time it was she who offered him.

"Ari is fine, Udi. And so is Avigail. And so are your parents."

"I know. Of course I know."

"Your mother misses you, but she is pleased for you."

"I know."

"Okay." Ella paused then, again.

"Okay."

And again.

"I'll see you in four days," she'd said finally.

"I love you, Ella," he'd told her.

Silence again.

***

At the other end of the line, Ella had sat in a humid room with the dead receiver in her hand wondering where Udi's sudden proclamation had come from, ruminating over whether she should call him back to tell him that she loves him too, because of course she does, worrying that without such a response from her he may feel rejected or snubbed, and he may think again. Worrying. Worrying. Hoping.

***

The ring sparkles with promise in his hand. It is a small diamond mounted on a thin gold band. Two days ago

Tadaaki and Ben had both accompanied him to Hatton Garden to choose it and the jeweller had offered them three equal seats while he brought out this ring for their equal examination. Udi hadn't noticed it at first but since he has been in London, more and more, obscurity masked as egalitarianism is something he revels in. Nobody blinks at him here, nobody – or at Ben or at Tadaaki. A hundred different ethnicities and religions and cultures rub up against each other in the bustle of passion and apathy, and he is just another shade of brown. The same as his wealthy British cousin and his determined Egyptian friend. Emancipated. At last he has freedom to be just another, another undefined person in a city full of them. At last he has liberty to be not part of an occupying, dominant force, not a citizen of an ideological nation of whom good examples are required. And at last he has license to feel no responsibility, no duty to be restrained, to be neither better nor worse than the rest. At last. It feels wonderful, though he hadn't even realised this was a thing for which he was longing.

Udi closes the safe and transfers the ring from his hand into his buttonable jean pocket. He has showered, tidied, and dressed in a freshly laundered shirt that Ella once told him makes him look like Vince from *Entourage*, who she loves. Ella's flight is due to land at ten past eight. At six, Ben and Jonny meet him in the restaurant. At the sound of their shouts up the stairs Udi carefully picks up a thick brown envelope he has removed with the ring from the safe and closes its seal.

"There's the man!" Ben enthuses as Udi appears from the stairwell. "Are you going to do it now at the airport, or later?"

"At the airport," Udi replies. "Straight away."

"Big day," says Jonny.

The three of them sit at an empty table and ask one of the waiters to bring coffee. Udi sees Jonny glancing at Ben. They are wondering why they are here, why Udi has requested they meet.

"So, everything okay?" asks Jonny slowly.

"Everything is fine." It is hard for Udi to articulate quite what he wants to say, to cast aside jokes, to speak to them unlike kids, unlike cousins, unlike what they have always been, but he is determined. "I just want to say to you both," he starts. "That I know how much you have done for me, and I appreciate it all. And I want to give you this." He throws the brown envelope at Ben.

"What is it?" Ben fingers it tentatively but Udi only grins so Ben unpeels the seal, pulling out a thick wad of well-thumbed notes.

"It's rent. I have a job, thanks to you, so I can pay rent. And don't argue, I want to. And I can afford to. My bosses pay well, you know." He grins but immediately both of his cousins make to protest. He interrupts them. "Take it or I'll hit you," he says, reverting back, raising his hand in a mock threat, relaxing them.

"Okay, okay," Jonny says, feigning fear. "Thank you."

He pockets the envelope and when they stand to hug, Udi notices that though Jonny will always be the older brother, the years have unravelled or caught up or merged or rearranged themselves, because this time, next to Ben, he feels neither old nor young.

The airport is the furthest drive that Udi has so far made in England, but he declines Ben's offer to accompany him. He wants to do this alone. Besides, he has been Being British pretty well. He knows to approach roundabouts from the left, he knows that the fast lane for overtaking is on the right, he knows that nothing is sign-posted properly. Other drivers do seem to swear at him with some frequency, but he is good at that too.

Ben has written out directions for him in case the Sat Nav goes awry and Udi leaves plenty of time to make it to the airport. He wants to be there waiting. With a sign. And flowers. And a kiss. It's corny, it's like the stupid romantic movies Ella adores. She will love it. Udi imagines her brushing her

234

tumbling dark hair out of her face when she sees him, smiling with surprise, then giggling as she leans forward to smell the flowers where inside one of the buds, she will discover the ring. He can almost hear her laughing already. He can almost feel her wrapping her arms around him.

The motorway however is bumper to bumper. There are road works a few exits before the airport and for miles ahead all lanes are at a standstill. Udi hoots impatiently, setting off a chain of responsive sounds, but there is nothing he or any of the other trapped drivers can do. Some have even clambered out of their cars to walk their dogs on the verge.

Ella will come out and find no one.

Udi manoeuvres onto the hard shoulder and quickly speeds along it until he reaches the exit a few hundred metres ahead. He intends to pull over once he is off the motorway, to consult his Sat Nav for another route to the airport, but a few cars have followed his example and are tight on his tail, hurrying him to make a decision at the roundabout, urging him to turn left or right. Both ways are jammed with traffic and he refuses to be delayed further by making the wrong choice, so at the edge of the roundabout he switches on his hazard lights and puts the car into park, ignoring the raging drivers who swerve around him. Now that he can concentrate, he manages to instruct the Sat Nav to avoid the motorway and another route of side roads and high streets pops onto the screen. It promises to get him there with five minutes to spare. Udi turns off his hazards and signals right. He is about to move but a red beamer at the exit to his left inches out, unsure whether Udi is moving now or still sitting. Udi flashes his lights to make it clear that the beamer's driver should stay where he is, Udi is going, moving forwards, Ella is waiting and he is on his way. He squeezes down on the accelerator.

And that is when, for the first time in many weeks, guns explode inside his head. Red flashes before him. A toxic, rancid stench invades his nostrils. And all at once he is tumbling fast and hard through the air, then lying flat on hot sand while cold, metallic arrows whiz past his ears, numb his burning body, and with their terrific sound, obliterate the light.

***

Now

16

I take the tube home. It's my last time so I breathe in the experience with a conscious, deliberate nostalgia, but I won't miss this. For six years my morning commute has been defined by it: jostling elbows, surly faces, sweaty bodies crammed so tightly against train windows and each other that, although I know it's trivialising to do so, I would often think of carriages on their way to Auschwitz. Or the images shown once in school assembly by the Animal Rights society. Night-time journeys were even worse. Now that I think of it, perhaps this is what it all comes down to – the tube, lulling us, lulling us, lulling us into a state of apathy, detachment, acceptance. Softly moving underground. Bullets in the dark. Occasionally at night there were encounters with drunkards who shouted obscenities while the rest of us pretended we couldn't hear. Or beggars making the same tired plea to each carriage, trawling for money, for food, for anything, for a sign that we who kept our eyes firmly on our papers or Kindles or mobile phones were not ghostly apparitions already dead, but alive. I look up at my fellow nightriders now. Perhaps for the first time. There is a small group of middle-aged women bedecked in caps that have been decorated with ears and horns to resemble livestock. They are carrying placards: STOP LIVE EXPORTS. STAND UP FOR SHEEP. I will never be able to understand that strength of feeling. That pull, fierce enough to get people off the sofa and into Hobbycraft for marker pens and pieces of card, then onto the streets of Westminster where they are fervent and angry, authentically angry, enough to be there, sometimes in the rain, travelling home late with sodden placards. Not that I don't like sheep. I'm sure I'd be suitably appalled if one of these ladies told me about export conditions. Every time I drive past the Falun Gong vigil outside the Chinese Embassy, I'm full of admiration-

The train jolts to a halt in West Hampstead. As is habit, I immediately pull out my phone. There are three messages. One is from an old university friend who has just heard I'm leaving and wants to meet for a farewell drink. The second is from Orli telling me not to call because she's going to be painting all night but that she'll call in the morning when I'm no longer a soul-selling banker and finally free. This last part makes me smile. But the third message is from my mother, left at around five o'clock in the midst of one of her panics: she knows I'm moving to Israel, she's not trying to stop me, but am I really sure I want to quit such a good job, and perhaps I should just speak to my boss before I go, just to lay the ground for a possible return, just in case. And am I eating?

I shake my head. Mum has continued to worry and chastise and guilt and support and admire and smother in equal doses ever since meeting Orli. It's as though she can't resist the stereotype of 'Jewish Mother'. Sometimes I'm sure I can hear an ever so slight tinkling of humour in her lectures and it makes me wonder if she's aware of this role fulfilment, if perhaps, actually, it's all done in jest, or as a performance. But when I challenge her she refuses to agree. 'No, Daniel, my heartbreak is not one big game. Thanks for asking.' Although it's almost ten thirty I call her as I walk home, assuring her as she answers that my boss doesn't hate me for leaving and has indeed promised me an open door. 'That's nice, Daniel,' she says. 'But have you seen the news?'

I stay awake most of the night playing on my iPad, the news flickering away on the TV. I put my family and Orli into their astronaut suits three times. Orli asked me not to call and by now I know to heed such requests, familiar enough with the change in temperament that comes from disturbing her amidst a flurry of creativity. But I need to talk to her. Just after six in the morning I hear the familiar shuffling of Robert's feet on the way to the bathroom, his cupboard doors opening and closing, toast being burnt, coffee being poured, and then the hurried sounds of Robert grabbing his briefcase and dashing out of the flat in the usual, sudden realisation that he is late. Even today I take pleasure in the unprecedented luxury of not having to get up, not having to repeat the same unthinking routine I have observed religiously for over half a decade. I find myself out of bed however less than an hour later. My shower is long and fanciful with scented tubes of stuff I've collected as freebies over the years and will not pack with me to take to Israel. I'm killing time. When she's painting, Orli works into the small hours and may not rise 'till noon. Ambling into the kitchen in my tracksuit bottoms I make a coffee and spend a long time concocting a green juice made largely from spinach and avocado, and an omelette. This is the first day of a new beginning and I am pleased with my healthy start. I take my breakfast into the living room where again I switch on the TV. But of course this is a mistake. I still haven't spoken to Orli but the news is buzzing with her. Or rather not with her, but her home, her scent.

Overnight there's been an escalation. It's been bubbling for weeks. First the hunt for the kidnapped Israeli teens who we now know were killed almost instantly. Then the revenge attack on the Palestinian boy. Then rockets, and incursions, and yesterday 80 Hamas rockets were fired from Gaza into Israel and now the Israeli Air Force have attacked around 50 targets in the Gaza Strip, and it feels like only the beginning. I had to do a bit of googling to find out about the Gazan rockets, the official news is focussed almost entirely on Israel's actions. But I need to know the 'aggravating factors'. The defence. It is certain that I will need one, this a fact I learned alongside other studies at university, though it wasn't a classroom based lesson. I picked it up walking past a demonstration that was calling for the boycott of my diminutive Israeli professor, and another time noticing pro-Hezbollah graffiti scrawled over a Jewish Society notice board, and seeing a cartoon in the *Guardian* of a giant fist dripping with blood having punched a small child, a fist emblazoned with Stars of David, like the one I wear around my neck. Now, every time there is tension in Israel I feel myself holding my breath, both hoping and not hoping for a substantial enough 'reason'.

There are visuals of Palestinian homes reduced to rubble.

And of crying children.

And Israeli jets in the night sky.

I can't finish my omelette. My juice is too green.

I want to check Orli is okay. Or rather, I want her to tell me that everything is okay, and will be okay.

My phone rings.

"Are you watching this?" says Gaby. "Have you seen what's going on?"

"Hi Gaby, how's married life?" I attempt to say lightly. She has been back from honeymoon for three days.

"Well they're at war, Dan. You're going to a war zone."

"Gaby, calm down," I say automatically, though all night a tightness has been building in my stomach. "Tel Aviv's nowhere near any of it."

"They'll end up calling up reservists."

"I won't be one yet."

"This time. This time. For God's sake, Dan, can't you see this isn't an event, it's a way of life? You're moving to Israel, fine, I get it. Just wait a few months."

"Gaby, listen…" I begin. But she is not listening. She has slammed down the receiver and is probably dialling Mum because a few minutes later my phone rings again and it is our mother. Despite my lay-in I am suddenly overcome with an overwhelming fatigue.

***

Gaby waits until the office is empty before accessing Facebook. She hasn't been back long and her desk is littered with cards of congratulations. There is also a newly framed picture of her and Pete on their wedding day, a cliché she has amusedly embraced. She finds herself glancing at the image often. She opens her news feed. They are not really supposed to use social media at work but everybody does. Besides she has her own office, carved out in a glass corner overlooking the cobbled surface of Middle Temple Lane. Nobody will notice, or care. But she is staying late anyway to meet Pete in an hour and prefers to read the message she hopes has arrived alone.

Gaby reached out to Avigail Shammash a week ago. She is the jewel in Gaby's collection. Ever since Daniel announced his intention to move to Israel she has been collecting everything she can: articles, information, a million contradictory truths. She doesn't know what she intends to do with it all, really, wave it in front of Daniel until he will see? But it was sometime amidst her first thrust of research that she stumbled across an article by Avigail Shammash. Bold. Brave. Provocative. Feminist. Gaby has been following her blog ever since, but she has only just reached out. Over the past week they have exchanged a flurry of communications. In the last one, Gaby made a proposal. Now, as she moves the mouse to see if there is a reply, she notices her wedding ring sparkle. As though bizarrely dazzled by the light, she finds herself pausing to wonder how long she and Pete will wait before trying for a baby. She wonders if Daniel would come home for the birth.

241

She wonders if he will have a child, if he will live to have a child, if such a child would also join the army.

She clicks. The message is there.

Gaby, thank you for your invitation.

It is tempting to accept. Today we had three sirens. My girls were at school for the first of them but I couldn't bear it so I collected them and now they are home. Bedtime was difficult. You must understand our kids play in the streets here. I know in America, in England, you worry about children being taken and teenage thugs and muggings and things, but our children play in the streets. Now though, they are scared the noise will come again and we will have to run again to the shelter. They are scared next time it will be more than noise. My youngest wakes up in the night crying and even though I bring her into bed with me her body is clenched and trembling. Some of the Arabs here in Jerusalem are rooting for Hamas. Yesterday there was anti-Arab graffiti at the bilingual school here – it is a Jewish and Arab institution. Words of hate on this institution of tolerance. It would be a good time to take the children away, to come to London and speak to your group. I was asked by one of your universities last year, but then there were boycotts, and I was cancelled. You know my brother is there already, in London? But of course I must stay. This is the time to stay, and to speak. I do not believe we will be hit, not really, not in Jerusalem. This is what I tell the girls. And also that we, Israel, we are doing far too much hitting. Far too much killing. We are killing so many.

Of course when I say this now, when I write this, I am hated. Somebody wrote 'Death to the Left' under one of my articles online, and there were other things. The newspaper asked me if I need security but I think no. What message would it send my girls: if you speak you must be protected? No, we speak to protect. That is the problem here. They say if we question, if we mistrust Israel's need for such force, then Hamas will win and Israel will cease to exist. But they do not see that if we don't question, Israel has ceased to exist already.

It is getting crazy.

I used to think we had to fight the extremists on their side only. Yes we had some too, but few, and marginalised. There is a growing religious influence, you know. I remember recently there was a Simchat Torah celebration in the army and female soldiers were ordered to leave it, ordered to dance in a separate area. Soldiers! But it is everywhere. In the government, in the IDF. On the buses.

My friend is a university professor. She expressed empathy for the Palestinians in an email to her students and now she has been rebuked. Another friend, this one teaches high school, asked for a minute's silence in her lesson in memory of the hundreds of Gazans who have already been killed. The head teacher told her 'Shame on you. What about our boys?'. But what about empathy? It didn't used to be like this. Something is happening here. It is us versus them now, like McCarthy, or Stalin. We are losing our ability to see another side, to just recognise the suffering there, let alone to take responsibility for it. And those of us who try are silenced. Well I won't be silenced.

I don't know what 'us' I belong to now.

I do not really know you so I can tell you my secret. I am pregnant. Again. It is very early, I don't know yet if it will be a girl or a boy, this time, but there will be another life. And I cannot bring this life into this country without trying to remind our people of who we are and what we set out to do. Israel is the best place in the world for kids, you know. They play in the street still. But for the first time I don't know if it is the right place to bring new life.

If you are happy, I will come when this war is over. By then there will be a bump to see and I will try to skip the queue at the airport!

Avigail

Gaby sits for a moment to re-read the lines. She is disappointed, but of course it makes sense for Avigail to want to stay, to stand up, to make a difference. Gaby hopes that if she was in the same position she would do this too. Is this what Daniel is doing? She allows this thought to permeate for a moment. But no, it isn't his fight. Avigail is trying to change her country from within. Daniel is flocking to it blind to what needs to be changed. He has been blinded. By something. Not a wedding ring. So perhaps by the bright desert light.

***

The thing about time is you need stuff to fill it. I gave myself a month. A month of nothingness. A month to prepare. A month to (if I'm completely honest) fulfil my romanticised notions about the adventures I might have if I ever stepped off the treadmill. Besides, I figured there'd be loads to do – packing up, selling up, closing up, catching up. But it turns out that I don't have that much stuff, forms don't take that long to fill, and as for bank accounts and council tax and utilities bills – it turns out it's a few phone calls, it takes one dedicated morning, one morning to dismantle one's life.

This is all a long-winded way of explaining that I've spent an unusual amount of time over the past week eavesdropping on other people's café conversations and trawling through Facebook. Which is not the healthiest thing to do if you're a Jew amidst an upsurge in antisemitism.

Antisemitism. I check myself sometimes, check that I am serious about this bulbous, stick-in-the-throat thought. Are people not just anti-Israel, or what they perceive of Israel, because of the conflict, because of what they understand Israel to be doing? Are they really anti-Jew, anti-me? I check, but no, I mean it, it's there. For now mostly words, but words ubiquitous.

I wonder what Nana would say if I told her that I feel it here, now: That what I see happening is nothing? That it is everything?

I am afraid to ask.

I keep telling myself I'm being paranoid. And of course it could be a subconscious passed-down survivor-syndrome-incited post-assimilation paranoia, but I swear it's everywhere.

Because Israel is everywhere and suddenly everyone is an expert. Everyone. Although they have no context of the history of the conflict, no idea of the geography of Israel's tiny Jewish dot surrounded by swathes of Arab land, no understanding of the political goals of the various parties. There are pictures of dying children and that is all it is necessary to know. 'We are all Hamas now', apparently.

Hamas. Who not only want to destroy Israel, but want to kill all Jews everywhere. Kill me. This is who all these British bleeding hearts align with?

They like to say so. Loudly. As though it is the latest fad to show off. #hateblamekillthejews.

Before this fad, I had indulgently filled my month with coffees and dinners and lunches, but now, at each and every one of them, Gaza trips off tongues, and as we dine and sip and converse, I find it harder and harder to swallow. And I get that feeling, that old teenage apprehension that I will be talked about as soon as I am gone.

As a child it wasn't like this. With the exception of Mr Pike and his 10 per cent off, and the one time in the supermarket that I heard a woman tell her husband who was comparing prices of wine, 'Don't be a Jew', my North West London world consisted of Jewish school assemblies, kosher butchers, Adam Sandler, Ben Stiller, Jerry Seinfeld. I don't know if it ever even occurred to me that people in Britain, in my country, might consider being Jewish as a thing, an unusual thing, a bad thing.

It's like being a goose. Imagine you're an egg, just laying around the barn with a load of other eggs and you hatch out with all the others, and since all the others are chickens you assume you're a chicken too and everybody calls you a chicken. But as you grow up and get oily feathers and a slightly longer beak you start suspecting that perhaps you are a chicken but, maybe, well not quite a chicken. And then one day the farmer comes in and says, 'Hey goose!' And he's pointing at you, and he asks, 'Goose, what the hell are you doing in here with the chickens?' It's a bit like that. I see my friends holding back, holding themselves back in respect of my goosishness, tempering their thoughts, not trusting me with them. I know it is for fear they might offend, they probably imagine they are being sensitive, but they don't see that this very assumption is part of the prejudice: I am Jewish therefore I must blindly support Israel.

Prejudice. Am I really saying my friends are prejudiced? Yes, that's what I feel – prejudiced against, ostracised somehow, branded as something outside of their commonality. I have felt this way only once before, in 2006 during Lebanon. Maybe that's what started me thinking, noticing. Maybe that's what began my slow unravelling of wholeness.

I feel bad for these friends. I'm sure they too feel persecuted, stifled, by me.

Far worse are the ones who don't show restraint. These are the people who make me feel that irrational loyalty the first group assume, that inexplicable need to defend, that urge to look at pictures of Gazan children and not speak the sickness I am feeling. Around Friday night dinners I speak it, we speak it, explore it, argue over it and rarely agree. But these debates are like dirty linen, not to be laundered in public, with stains not suitable for the scrutiny of a clean, scathing world.

One Facebook friend I went to school with posts articles almost hourly about the disproportionate force, the trapped Palestinians, the civilian deaths, the Israeli aggression. Countless others comment on the thread concurring. They use words like 'appalling' and 'inexcusable'. I can't help reading and feeling riled. Silently. Riled by the ignorance, the bias, the hypocrisy. One afternoon Robert pops up half way down one such thread attempting to voice the Israeli point of view: Hamas have been firing rockets into Israeli towns for weeks; they've been building tunnels from which to launch attacks; they use their own children as human shields; Israel must have the right to defend itself. But he shouldn't have bothered because within minutes there is a barrage of responses: *Hamas' rockets don't kill people; the Palestinians are desperate; the force is disproportionate; it's the Palestinians' land.* And then somebody calls Gaza a prison camp, and the next person comments that after what 'they' went through the Jews should know better. And suddenly that feeling that has been rumbling underneath everything pushes ever so slightly more to the fore, like a splinter under the skin, the sharp end poking violently through, swelling the flesh around it, but not visible enough to be pulled. I try but I can't quite grip my discomfort. It's not that I don't wish people in Gaza weren't dying. It's that all these people here, these people who are so angry, so up in arms, so ethically superior, they don't say a peep when the problem is in Syria, or the perpetrators are Boko Haram, or the Saudi regime, or China. It is only Israel, only Jews, only us, only me – we are the chosen ones. We, because people don't bother to differentiate between Israeli and Jew. Or do and don't realise Hamas don't. And don't understand what they are trivialising. Like my Nana as a teenager, with a shaven head and a tattoo on her arm. And that's why no matter how jarring the attacks, I won't criticise Israel like Gaby does. And I won't stop posting the saner articles emerging from the US press. And I won't hesitate to de-friend Facebook acquaintances.

Breathe, says Orli. It's not black and white. Even after David she won't blame a whole people and she won't blindly support her own. Her new series of paintings is about division and though she isn't yet ready to share the details she talks about internal versus external schisms, she talks about truth, the spring of truth, the way it fractures, the impossibility of it remaining whole, un-tempered. She says Gaza is hell on Earth.

But Orli does not live in Europe. Her identity is not splintered like mine. She has the luxury of a sensation of wholeness to observe division from.

I am unsure whether my apprehension about seeing Safia is because of the political divisions I anticipate between the two of us, or because of my dreams. I haven't seen her since the night of the un-kosher chicken, but she is the only person who seems to have picked up on the fact that I have way too much time on my hands. She has consequently been sending me an array of amusing texts and I'm sure it's only as a consequence of this that for the past three nights in a row she has appeared in my dreams. Not doing anything sexual. Or even interesting actually. It's my regular anxiety dream and totally ordinary – me in an exam hall at school suddenly realising that I have neglected to do any revision. It doesn't take a psychologist to understand that that's about Israel, a concern that I haven't prepared, that I'm not ready. Except in my waking state I am ready. Every time I speak to Orli I know this with ever more certainty. And I wouldn't even think about the dream if it weren't for Safia being in it. But it's weird, she's just there, sat at the desk next to me beavering away at her own exam, but every few minutes sparing a glance in my direction, asking with one raised eyebrow if I'm okay.

Of course I'm not going to tell her. Telling somebody they were in your dream is akin to confessing a secret obsession. But I don't tell Orli either. And that makes me feel like I'm hiding something, like I've done something disloyal, and just the whisper of that idea creates a peculiar tension. I'm not sure now how to be with Safia. Coffee feels like a preamble. An overture.

She has the sofa. And the paper. And the coffee.

"Well thanks so much for joining us." She shuffles a little across the leather to make room.

"Sorry. I came from Mum and Dad's – traffic." I kiss her hello. Her hair is down and I catch a whiff of what smells like not quite strawberry but-

"Extra milk, extra sugar, extra foam." She nods at the coffee she has bought for me.

"Coffee of champions." I take a sip. "Thanks. So, what's going on?"

"Nothing really. Had a friend's engagement party. Went to a great exhibit at the Tate. Crazy busy at work – oh hang on, sorry, that was insensitive, you're unemployed aren't you?"

"Gainfully so," I grin.

"Sure, that's why you're texting me every five minutes."

"It's that or watching daytime television." The second I mention television I wish that I hadn't.

"Best avoided," says Safia. Then a pause. Then, "Kind of disturbing viewing at the moment."

"Yes." I take another slow sip of my coffee and pick up the menu, though I know all the dishes by heart and am not planning on ordering anything. "It is."

"Does it not bother you? Going there now?"

"There's always something happening."

"Yes." Safia looks at me carefully as I pretend to study the food selection. "There is." She pauses for a moment and I prepare myself for the conversation, this conversation, the Gaza conversation, it seems we're doing this. But instead Safia asks abruptly, "How's Gaby?"

"Gaby? She's fine. Fine. Angry with me still, but fine. Happy with Pete."

"It's funny that she's so liberal and you're not."

"I'm liberal."

"No you're not." There is a peculiar focussed look in Safia's eye.

"Are we having the kosher conversation again? Is this because you saw me eyeing up that guy's bacon?"

"*You'd* never marry someone who wasn't Jewish, would you?" says Safia. She leans forward so that her elbows are

249

resting on her knees, her chin in her hands. With her head angled slightly to one side I catch another whiff of her hair. Strawberry vanilla?

"No," I say. "I wouldn't."

She sits back. "You realise that's racist, right?"

"Uh, no."

"Well you're determining somebody's worth by accident of birth. You're deciding who is and who isn't good enough for you based on their race, religion, whatever, so…"

"Not isn't good enough, just isn't Jewish."

"You hear yourself, right?"

Her tone has a slight waver to it. It is uncharacteristic of the jocular way we usually debate. "Saf, come on, you're exactly the same. You know you'll marry someone Muslim."

"Not necessarily."

"Really?"

"Really."

I look at her sarcastically, but she doesn't laugh. "Huh."

"What?"

"Nothing. I just- I always thought that was the case."

"Nope," she says.

There is a strange pause between us, until a woman standing next to me accidentally brushes my head with her handbag. She apologises but she is part of a small huddle of people who have gathered next to our sofa. The café is busy and they are eyeing our almost empty coffees. If Orli was here, she would probably just tell them straight out that we aren't leaving.

"Food?" I say to Safia. "Another coffee?" Safia nods and I get up to order at the counter. There is no need to consult her for her preference – she will have another black coffee and a goat's cheese salad minus the beetroot with sourdough bread. I select a fishfinger buttie. There is a short queue and I watch Safia as I wait. She has reclined back against the sofa. She flicks through the paper for a few minutes and then thumbs her phone, scrolling through something that makes her brow crinkle. Is she angry at me? In the mood for a debate? I arrive back at the table with the coffees and, disappointed, the hovering crowd edges away.

"Territory reclaimed," I say.

"Hmm." Safia takes the coffee.

"What?" I sit down.

"It just feels a little David and Goliath doesn't it?"

I laugh. "There were four of them! How can it be- Oh hang on, am I David?"

"Not the sofa," she grins. "Idiot."

"Charming."

"Israel. Gaza."

"Oh." I pause and spend a long time carefully dispensing sugar into the top of my cappuccino so that it makes a tunnel down to the liquid below. The barista has created a heart in the foam and the tunnel looks like an arrow through it. I look at Safia and take a deep breath. "How do you figure that?" I ask her.

"Um, unarmed children against the might of Israel's army?"

"You mean terrorist group bent on destruction versus democracy wanting peace?"

She makes the Noise of Disdain, as I have coined it, the one that starts at the back of her throat, gathering momentum as it's released.

"Anyway, I don't remember David picking the fight."

"Are you serious? Your side aren't the ones being bombed." Safia pulls her hair roughly into a pile on top of her head, removing the strawberry vanilla (watermelon?) sweetness.

"No, my side are just the ones being referred to as 'my side'. Israel doesn't equal all Jewish people you know."

"I know."

"Jew and Israel aren't synonymous."

"I know that, Dan."

I know she knows, but I can't stop. I am like a wound spring. "And if you really want the David and Goliath metaphor that's fine, except you've cast your characters wrong, Israel is David. The mass of hostile Arab countries surrounding the tiny dot on the map that is Israel, is Goliath. The rest of the world including our stupid press and idiots on Facebook who like slamming Israel for defending itself, is Goliath."

"See, Israel is your side."

It's possible that there is a smile amidst Safia's goading, but still I can't halt myself.

"Do you have any idea what kind of antisemitic crap is going round at the moment?" I take out my phone and start searching for deleted Facebook threads.

"Don't be so paranoid, Dan. You're talking to a post-September 11th Muslim here. Care to compare the prejudice?"

"That doesn't make this invalid." I am still searching but keep clicking onto the wrong app.

"No, but it puts it in perspective. Come on, Dan, you're being a little dramatic."

"I don't think so."

"Do you actually feel worried by it?"

"I feel very aware of it."

"Does it worry you?"

I give up on the phone and concentrate on Safia. "Yes."

"Really?"

"Yes. Not as in my actual safety, right now. And I don't think the government's about to make me wear a yellow star or anything. But as in how people secretly feel about Jews, how integrated we really are, how safe our future. My Nana was a middle-class Hungarian you know? Her father was a university professor. I know now it's mostly just words, but remember where words can lead. It's definitely another reason to go."

"To Israel."

"Yes, to Israel."

Safia shakes her head and makes the throat sound again. I seem to be hearing it more and more frequently.

"Hamas started this," I say.

"So Israel should finish it? Just, fuck them?"

Safia eyes me pointedly and puts down her coffee. She opens her mouth to say something else, but then stops. She takes a breath. I can see the struggle of restraint. Now she raises an eyebrow, opens her mouth again, and I have the distinct feeling that she is about to say something heavy, something true. I know Orli thinks there is no one truth, only versions of it, fractured, splintered, reflected or refracted by experience and culture or something like that; but still I want to hear Safia's truth. Just then however, of course, our food arrives. Safia closes her mouth, looks away from me and accepts her salad. She concentrates hard on unwrapping her cutlery from its napkin case, then carefully drizzles on the dressing. We both take pains to talk to the waiter who after all our Sundays knows us by name. He tells us that in a few months the place is closing for a refurb. While I can, I tuck into my fishfinger buttie. A small trail of tartar sauce escapes the bread and leaks down my finger.

"So cultured," Safia says, with a half-formed, half-sure smile.

"I didn't want you to feel uncomfortable." I point to her coffee stained teaspoon which has somehow made its way onto the white denim of her lap.

She picks it up and tentatively prods my leg with it, uncertain of our level of playfulness. She says something about a mutual friend who is issuing an all-white dress code for her wedding. I laugh and say that we better practise our table manners. Forwards. Backwards. We exchange nothings. As we talk, she dabs with a napkin at the stain, but the mark remains. It is a small tarnishing of spotlessness.

***

Dad is bringing boxes. We've never been one of those families where the mother pops round to her grown children's places to pot plants or decorate cushions, and Dad isn't handy so he's never offered to put up a bookcase or drill holes for picture hooks. Their support comes in the form of forthright candour – elicited or otherwise. And the impetus is on us, the children, to remember to make visits home. 'If they don't,' so says my mother, 'Well then they never loved you anyway.' Today however, Dad has insisted on bringing the boxes. He has taken a day off for it and driven himself to the storage company to collect them before meeting me at the dealership where I am selling my car. Dad waves as he pulls up and I slip into the seat beside him before doing a double take and stifling a laugh.

"Uh, hello Reb Dad."

"Daniel." Dad nods as though nothing is unusual.

"Do I actually have to ask the question?"

"What question is that?"

"You're wearing a yamaka."

"Yes."

"Why are you wearing a yamaka?"

"Ties in nicely with my jacket, don't you think? Blue."

In my lifetime I have seen Dad don a yamaka only at synagogue, at simchas, when we do the prayers at home on festivals, or sometimes if we have guests for Shabbat dinner and Mum nudges him towards one. Never, ever, to a car dealership. Dad turns off the Edgware Road towards Golders Green. I've attempted to fill the final three weeks before I go with at least one thing a day that I'll miss. Today it's my favourite deli's bagels. And Nana. Mum has collected her and is meeting us for a bite before we get packing.

"It feels like a time to not hide," Dad says, turning to me with sudden concentration so that I have to wave my hand to direct his attention back towards the road.

"You've never hidden, Dad."

Dad keeps his eyes ahead and nods to himself. "I'm glad you think that. I hope that's what you do think. I haven't meant to hide. Integrate, assimilate, contribute, yes, reach out to others, but not hide, that's the thing."

"You haven't."

"Maybe I should've kept kosher after all, done some things that marked me out but- I don't know. Anyway, I just want people to see Jews right now. To really see us here, working, living, along with everyone else. So what's a little hat?"

"You're an atheist."

"I'm a Jewish atheist," Dad corrects.

I smile as he tilts his blue yamaka slightly, pleased with his linguistic agility, and I can't help but think of the time he burst into the school staff room to confront Mr Pike. I have that same 12-year-old feeling of awe, that strange sensation of seeing my father just for a second as an outsider would. His rainbow grey hair sticks up around the blue yamaka like decorative tissue paper in a shop display.

"Did you hear about France?" I ask him.

"Disgusting," he nods.

"It's like it's been there the whole time, just bubbling below the surface, and now that it's cool to slam Israel, the antisemitism is just exploding."

"Not so much here," Dad clarifies. "It's not as acute. I think people are still making the distinction, still-"

"Apparently loads of French Jews are moving to Israel."

"I don't think we need an exodus from London quite yet," Dad says as he manoeuvres into a parking space." Don't make that an excuse, Dan," he adds. "You go because you want to go."

"I know. I do want to."

He nods again.

"Did you hear about the sign in Belgium?" I say. "In the café? Dogs are allowed but no Jews."

"It's important to remember these are isolated, crazy incidents," Dad says.

"Do you think that's what Anne Frank's Dad told her?"

"Dan…" Dad shakes his head and pats his blue yamaka as he gets out of the car. I grin. There is a horror movie element to our discussion and I'm being a little facetious. I am scared, but not really. There is some amount of revelling in the dreadfulness of it all. A detachment. As though the horror really is only on a screen somewhere, a director's lens between us. Disbelief not quite suspended. Still, I see Dad glancing around with uncharacteristic apprehension as we make our way towards the deli. We are in one of the most Jewish neighbourhoods in the UK, where Jews are most numerous, most safe. Most visible.

Nana and Mum have ordered. Nana gets low blood sugar and Mum gets impatient, and we are admittedly 20 minutes late. Nana is talking to Sadie, one half of the old Polish couple who run the deli, argue non-stop and are the only people I know other than my Nana who are fluent in Yiddish. I love listening to them: the guttural clatter that sounds like an exaggerated stage whisper, or a list of ingredients for some kind of stew. Nana is two years younger than Sadie and Sadie calls her *bubula*, meaning baby. Nana's face is alight, enhanced I suppose by this position of relative youth. I kiss her on the cheek as I sit down next to her and lean across the table to kiss my mother. I smile at Sadie too who pats my hand absentmindedly before grasping on to it as though she means to tell me something in just a moment. For now she is busy telling Nana that it is her wedding anniversary today – she and Moshe have been married 64 years and tonight they are going dancing. I sit with my arm above my head as she clings onto my palm but eventually Sadie releases me and as her arm lifts away I notice, as I have noticed many times before, the dark stain of imprinted numbers. No matter how many times I see this I cannot help but feel startled, and uncomfortable, as though I have mistakenly picked up her diary. Nana always wears long sleeves so it isn't something I otherwise see. I look away. On the wall behind the counter there is a photo of Sadie and Moshe winning a ballroom dancing competition back when they were mere whippets of 70. Next to it is a faded black and white picture of the two of them in 1945, fresh off a refugee boat to England. They met on that boat. It was called *The Atlantis*. So is the deli. Sadie signals to a young Israeli waitress to take Dad's and my order. I go for the classic, a smoked salmon and cream cheese poppyseed bagel with lemon and pepper, and an Israeli salad. Mum is already tucking into the same, though she has removed the top half of her bagel so as to lessen her bread intake. "Sold the car okay?" she asks between mouthfuls, but I can tell that she too is listening to the glorious back-throated, life-coated exchange between Sadie and her mother. We all are. We are so consumed by it that none of us notice the two men wearing hoods who enter through the open door behind us.

None of us notice that one is carrying a spray can and a knife, the other a bat.

None of us see until glass is shattering down into bagels and challah bread.

And Moshe is standing statue behind the counter.

And a red swastika is bleeding across the wall next to the words 'Free Gaza' and ruining the photo of Sadie and Moshe's arrival to their English safe haven, and their ballroom win.

And it is exactly like a horror movie. The lens shaking to give that naturalistic edge.

Rewind. Go back.

That's the thing about movies, or books, or events that happen in your head. Paranoid imaginings. You can replay them, spot new tangents, catch glances and objects and clues you hadn't noticed before, in real time, in reality.

Like the volume of the crash. A shattering, not dissimilar from the glass underfoot at a wedding, but louder, far far louder, echoing in the ears. A shard of it struck my jacket. No blood, no wound, but an unexpected impact that took my breath.

Like the feeling of paralysis. Did I hunch? Did I cower? I know I did not stand up.

Like the way a falling blue yamaka looks like a puddle in the air.

Like the feeling of terror. A bit like suffocating.

Like my father's uncovered head, fragile and grey. His lined hands raising to protect it.

Like my mother's voice hurtling through the instant.

Like my Nana sitting still and tall and dignified, her lunch on her lap.

And then the sudden sound of an alarm.

And the look of disgust and hatred from the man who turned first towards Moshe and then to my shrieking mother.

And Sadie staying standing.

And me still not standing up.

It is only after the men have raced out of the store and are half way down the street that a few customers belatedly chase after them. It is as though it has taken a minute for our collective brains to understand that what we have just seen is real, here, now. Not a movie. You can almost see the cogs turning, forks still hovering mid-air near mouths. But all at once we are up and chasing. I follow because Dad has gone and because I am a man and cannot remain sitting, but even before we have stepped out of the door I know we aren't going to catch them. Even if we did, we aren't going to restrain them because what are we going to do really? Beat them up? Clearly not. We jog down the road for a bit to make a good showing then sigh dramatically when they jump into a waiting car. One of them extends a fist out of the window, and we throw our own arms around and do a lot of pointing while we call out the number of the car's license plate to each other. By now my adrenalin is pumping. I am standing, moving. We all are. There are five of us by the side of the road, strangers except that everybody looks a bit familiar and actually I think one of the men is related to Robert. We're not quite sure what to say to each other but we seem to have got stuck on the word 'unbelievable'. I've noticed this before, you hear it on the news all the time: an event is reported and one word starts to stick to it –'tragic', 'shocking', 'unprecedented'. Everybody starts referring to the event the same way, as though none of the other adjectives quite encapsulate the proper emotion, or as though the chosen descriptive is part of what happened, a noun not an adjective: Tragic Crash; Shocking Scenes; Unprecedented Flooding. Disproportionate Force. Disproportionate Force. And it becomes not a description or an opinion or a feeling but a fact. Israel's force? Disproportionate. The five of us are still stuck on 'unbelievable', and we say it over and over in different ways all the way back to The Atlantis.

There, a police officer is already talking to Sadie and Moshe and a handful of customers. I hurry over to our table, kissing Mum's head and squeezing Nana's hand as I sit down. I want to reassure them, to be their protector. But when Nana keeps hold of my palm and holds it against her cheek, and Mum reaches for my other hand, I realise that my face must have betrayed fear or shock or panic, or they must have noticed how I didn't stand, couldn't stand, because the women are fine, it is my own heart that is racing.

Of course nothing happened. Not really. Nothing devastating, nothing to anybody's person. It's all just stuff and symbols. And it's not like I've never been around violence before. Throughout my early twenties there were the usual bar fights and argy bargies with bouncers, as a teen there were muggings (I had my phone stolen three times between the ages of 15 and 17), just last year at Costco I almost got pummelled by a huge tattooed guy who decided I'd pinched his parking space, and don't forget the time I got bottled. But all of those things felt random, accidental. And, 'It began with words,' said Nana.

Dad stoops to reclaim his yamaka from the floor.

Now I stand up. Now. And sidestep like a warming up boxer. And can't breathe.

Perhaps Gaby is right, what am I going to do, talk Hamas to death? Imagine astronaut suits? Throw a punch an hour late?

But at least in the army I'll be trained, and have a gun, and know how to use it.

Not that I want to use it, except if my family is threatened. If astronaut suits turn out not to work. If people hate us that much...

"Come on, Dan," Dad says eventually. "Boxes to fill."

He is at my flat until late, long after the packing is finished. We order pizza for dinner. I ask him if he remembers Mr Pike. I demonstrate to him that I have recently realised I can still recite my entire barmitzvah portion. We pause for a moment as we carefully roll into a tube the painting of me created by Orli. He hugs me for no reason. We find we are again stuck on the word 'unbelievable'. Before leaving the flat, he dons his yamaka. He looks older in it, vulnerable. I call out to him as he is about to round the corner and he stops to wave. He moves a few feet down the road then turns to wave again. I keep my hand raised until he is out of sight.

***

Now

17

So I went to Hobbycraft. After the incident at the deli I spent four days writing 'letters to the editor' that I never sent, five nights constructing ever more indestructible astronaut suits, including one for Orli, and then I came up with this. It's ironic really – there's finally something in London that I want to get up and shout about but that something only confirms to me that I want to leave. I'm an outsider anyway, it seems, London won't miss me. The discomfort this triggers in me sticks in my throat. A nervousness creeps into my muscles. Even so, there is something enlivening about caring, about identifying a problem, a wrong to right, a chance to make a difference. I remember being a kid and stumbling for the first time upon Teenage Mutant Ninja Turtles, being overcome by the unnerving, thrilling sensation that under my radar there had been a whole world out there, with superheroes and villains and all the glorious trappings of boyhood obsession, and now I was privy to it, clued in. I feel a bit like that. Though in this case there are villains on both sides, and real victims, and superheroes that are few and far between. On Facebook there is an article going around that lists every one of the Palestinian children who have been killed. It makes me think of the American nurse in Jaffa who told me to take a trip. Of his Palestinian girl, bright as anything. She'd be there now. In Gaza. What was her name? The article gives each child's age and their cause of death: *Ziad Kamel Hamad, age nine, immediate on air-strike; Adam Abu Mustafa, age 16, immediate on air-strike; Farah Hasan al-Breem, age 12, died later of asphyxiation.* The list fills four pages. I cannot bear to read the names, but I also cannot bear the article's blatant manipulation of emotion. Of course the deaths are tragic. Of course. But why are they happening? Surely that's the point? I bought blue markers and have turned my placard into an Israeli flag with a small British one in the corner, and the words: *Free Gaza... From Hamas.*

I thought maybe Gaby would come with me after she heard about the deli. She had that look when we told her the story, the same one as when our cousin Simon unceremoniously dumped her best friend, or when she overheard two teenage girls on a bus making digs at a fat woman, or when she noticed the guy in Fenwick slipping electronics into his bag. It's a look of indignation. It's a look that ushers forward consequences. It's a look she's inherited from Dad. But she wouldn't come. "It's not the same thing," she said. "It's a different argument." And she forwarded me a bunch of articles by some leftie Israeli journo. So I am standing only with Robert at the Pro-Israel rally.

Carrying the cardboard flag, I have a new appreciation for the black hats. Underneath my shirt sits my Magen David, as always. A platinum star, the ancient symbol hammered to look industrial and edgy, Jewishness made appropriate for fashion. I've had this particular necklace since I was 21, I take it off only if I swim and I barely notice the weight of it just below my collar. But there have been times when I have been aware, and have patted my shirt to make sure it is safely covered in cotton. Now there is no ambiguity. The placard is twice the size of my head. We are loud and proud.

Orli says there have been demonstrations in Israel too. She hasn't joined them and she says she feels selfish to have stayed home, to have looked inwards to her art. But I assure her that her work has greater reach, that it says far more than even the loudest of our rallying voices. Still, our voices are loud. Robert and I join the back of a blue and white crowd. There is a sense of being on tour, or at a football match. Our numbers bolster my nerves. We sing first the Hatikvah and then the British national anthem. Then somebody with a guitar and a microphone begins 'Oseh Shalom'. The words are in Hebrew but everybody knows them – we hear this song time and again at weddings and other simchas. I don't know the full translation but shalom means peace. Peace. That word reverberates again and again down the Kensington street, the melody soul stirring, hopeful. Peace. It is so moving to be here. I feel that for once, for once, I have connected to something real, something important, something that is a part of me. I want to stand up for Israel and defend it, with deeds as well as my raised voice in song.

I take a picture, add a moody filter and send it to Orli before in a moment of awareness realising that when we spoke about the protests in Israel, I never asked what they were about, which side she would have stood on. "There is no one truth," she said to me again today. "It is as vulnerable as land. As partial as history books." I make a mental note to ask her later, which side she has selected.

On the other side here are those that hate us. Not the other side of the street – blue and white floods both flanks of the Kensington path. But down the road, a little away from where I am standing the police have cornered off an area where there is a counter protest. There are maybe 40 or 50 people, it is not frightening and nothing like the swell of 15,000 who protested against Israel yesterday. The opposing group here is small, much smaller than ours, and the police seem ready for attempts to cross the barrier. Still, there is the same venom, the same aggression, the same violence that I watched with horror on TV. I was at Nana's for some of it. I could feel her sadness, see her remembering. For me it is novel to be so directly, so publicly hated. Novel and uncomfortable. But

263

for her... She went to a march once, she told me. Or rather, she was made to march. I hear a chant: 'From the river to the sea, we will fight until we're free'. To the sea. Not to the green line. Not to the 1967 borders. See, that's the whole problem in a nutshell. They don't want their own state, they never have, they want to destroy ours. Ours. I know I am not yet a citizen but I feel proprietorial. Of course many of the counter-protestors won't realise what they're chanting. They are focussing on dead children and freedom, not geography. But their bleeding hearts are being exploited. To bleed mine.

I turn back towards the sea of white and blue, the voices uplifted. But my sensation of hopefulness has been tainted. I feel cowed by the chants, paralysed. Why do they hate us so much? The missiles of course, but... I find that I have stopped singing. I stand amidst the swathes and I watch the waving of flags, the cheers, I hear a speech starting, but my mind is elsewhere. I am zipping up astronaut suits and fiddling with straps on helmets.

I am aware that my fixation with this is a little obsessional. But there are things I like to do. Things I sometimes have to do.

In Israel I'll be doing.

Gaby doesn't understand this.

Safia would.

Orli? It's strange, Orli gets me in a way nobody else has and nobody ever will, she sees me, sees through me. But sometimes I feel like she looks at my quirks as though they are creases to be ironed out. Perhaps they are. Perhaps they're like the baseball cap I wore every day as a teen and still don sometimes on Sundays – boyish traits I've somehow neglected to shed. But Safia has known me since I was still a boy-man. She recognises those quirks as part of me. She knows there are reasons for them, some irrational.

I understand why she's irritated by the whole kosher thing. It's not logical and she is. The marrying a Jew thing too. But it's too complicated to explain. Too messy. Too difficult. And that's the thing about Orli – I don't need to explain it, she gets this stuff, she feels it or knows that I feel it, and sees it, and paints it, and with her painting shows me how to see.

But I am still dreaming about Safia. Last night she was sat in the exam hall in a state of semi-undress and I woke up with a boner. I guess it doesn't help that I have seen her naked. It makes the image so much more detailed. So much better. Not that I actually think my subconscious is telling me that I still fancy Safia. I know that I love Orli. And Orli is clearly the logical, simple, straightforward option, not that I even have an option. My attempts however at decoding the dream have led me only to the following: Safia is undressed, exposed, so there's a truth/secret/issue that she is exposing that I am attracted to? And that is…? Basically I don't have a clue. Other than knowing that I need to see her again before I leave. There are things that feel unsaid.

My thoughts are interrupted by a kerfuffle in the street. A counter-protestor has attempted to break through the barrier and is being marched back to his section. Other than a megaphone he isn't carrying anything threatening, it seems unlikely that there was anything physical he was going to do, but in my mind I see falling blue yamakas.

The man is shouting through his megaphone. Anonymous bravado: he wears a hood, and sunglasses, and one of those typical terrorist-looking scarves, and is bearded; it is impossible to make out any defining characteristics, I cannot see the emotion on his face. The image however is violent, or strikes me that way. And now I listen: "*Allahu Akbar!*" So nothing new.

And then something new: "*Heil Hitler.*"

Heil Hitler.

It is like a punch to the gut.

I am in the deli again looking at a swastika. I am in a movie. Or a history book. I cannot speak. But I am not the only one who has heard him. A few on our side boo. Others, like me, seem stunned into silence, this perhaps their first real, up-close encounter with an attitude we know exists but not where we live, not in our schools nor our work, nor our lives. Somebody near me shouts an insult back and around this man there is a flurry of V-signs, again like a football match, a co-ordinated wave, but this time we are disoriented, not in sync and quickly it peters out. I think of my Nana and the number I never see on her arm. I think about whether the police have checked the other counter-protestors for weapons. I wonder how easy it would be for somebody else to break through the barrier, this time with a knife. Robert glances at me uneasily. This unease, of course, is what the megaphone man intended.

The police however are efficient and he is returned to his section, cheered by his supporters. Behind him, somebody holds up a hand-written sign: *Hitler you were right*.

Another gut blow.

Seriously? Seriously? People think this?

I saw stuff on Twitter about this kind of thing at yesterday's march, but it is different seeing it not on a screen but right here, just feet away from me. I cannot look away. But on our side of the barrier somebody is speaking through a microphone.

And suddenly, there is a siren.

I duck down. I haven't been listening to the speaker's preamble but the siren was planned, it is part of our protest and I know what I'm meant to do. For us it is a simulation, but it is what Orli has been doing for real – running, hiding, living like this. It is important to show onlookers that Israelis are victims too. Do they get that? Do they even try to? Do they spare a moment to imagine random, unpredictable murder? We all kneel on the ground. I think for a moment about having to dash to a bomb shelter myself, what that would be like, what that will be like. I can't pretend I'm not shitting myself. I tell people it's the same everywhere now, terrorism is everywhere, and that's true but not true. Because the thing is the threat is not made up. Rockets come. Often. Bombs too before the fence. There's a real, relentless reason why Israel has to act. Why does nobody see that? I look down. Beneath my feet there is a sticker: *Israel is a terror state*. I hadn't noticed these stickers before but when I scan the pavement I see they are everywhere. Left over from yesterday's pro-Palestinian protest but still here, it feels, to taunt us. To hate us. To despise and revile us. "Shame on you," somebody shouts to us from the small counter contingent.

I look up. Down, up, loathing everywhere. The voice however did not come through the megaphone and I can't see who shouted, who had to shout though our moment of solemnity. At least in Israel you know your enemy. I look again but still I can't see the person, the fellow Brit. I keep looking, and suddenly, just a few feet away from the Hitler sign, I do see someone.

She is at the back of the crowd.

She looks almost like an off-duty model.

I am too far away to tell, but she probably has one eyebrow raised.

***

Now

18

At first, all Udi is aware of is the whiteness. The walls are white, though sometimes he thinks he is looking not at them but directly at the sun because he feels hot all the time and it is hard to breathe. The sheets are white, though it is difficult for Udi to turn enough to see them. And when he opens his eyes and glimpses sometimes Ben, sometimes his mother, and always Ella hovering nervously at his side, their faces too have lost all colour. It is a pure, uncontaminated whiteness that he slips in and out of as the days pass by.

He has never seen sand like it. He stands at the window and looks out, across Gaza. Soft waves caress utterly white beaches. Shady huts are roofed in palm. They are in a Nice House. It has white rendered walls with yellow shutters, a curved side roof giving way to an arch behind which there is a gate and a garden, with a dozen colours of carnations. Inside there are flat screen TVs and designer furniture and hidden lights casting a stylish glow. They came in through a hole they blew in the hallway, like in cartoons where the animals run so fast they leave rabbit or roadrunner or coyote shaped outlines in walls slightly to the left of open doors. But the doors may be booby-trapped. Under the floorboards of this house they have found an IDF uniform, grenades, AK rifles, a press pass. They have already searched the place next door, a house with no walls, no shutters, and no flat screen TVs. That house looked as though it had been half way through building when work just stopped, stopped, a home incomplete. Now, open to the elements the floors were disgusting, there were cockroaches and rats, and unprotected beds staring out into the collapsing city. But the beach is beautiful. And white. Udi would do anything to get there. He would fight through all of Gaza to reach it.

The pain comes later.

Back at base his commander calls them into a room and explains they are going back in, into Gaza. That evening a little orthodox guitar-playing kid arrives with his father in a car filled with people handing out wet wipes and sports drinks and deodorants, and he plays them a song, his childish, hope-filled, sure voice ringing out across crowds of fatigued soldiers, and the whole of Udi's unit joins in, letting themselves believe the music, feeling full of purpose and pride, and apprehension too but hey you could lose a leg in a car crash; dancing on shifting sands. Their job is to find the target and blow it up. The same as the previous day. He is in the front squad. His role is to clear the building and so far it has been everything he'd hoped, exactly like in action movies – darting around corners, pointing his gun, giving the all clear. But now they are headed to another part of the city. There are people. Not women and children, but men, and any man still here, here where they have been warned not to be, is here for a reason and that reason is to kill them. So they are alert. They walk through the night. Gaza's sky is lit up but still there are dark, narrow passageways where they must send ahead their toys. The toys don't make it. There are blasts, exploding metal that but for their technology could have been flesh, but still it is like playing a video game – they choose the correct weapons and they clear the level. On to the next.

Next is a house in whose wall they don't make a big enough hole to enter. Another kind of explosive is needed to open the back door. It's in Udi's backpack. To save him the trouble of taking it off, Mordechai goes to unload it. But no, says Tomer, go to the passageway at the side of the house, don't stand in the garden, it is too open, too unprotected, prime pickings. Udi agrees. He makes to move. Shimon and Tomer are already half way there. But Mordechai calls him back. The side passage is far away, it will take time, time for Hamas, if they are inside, to escape. So far it has been a clean run. They have already found two tunnels. Countless weapons. They have not yet had to point their guns and actually shoot. And besides, God is on their side, says Mordechai. It will take one minute, he says. Udi hesitates. His instinct is to follow Tomer. But Mordechai is already opening the backpack, *Trust me*, and pulling out the explosives, *Trust God*, pulling them out and up, and up, and up, and they are moving up, flying, hurtling, exploding.

The pain comes later. First there is yelling. And confusion. Have their own explosives gone off? No, or Udi would be dead. But then what? What? He has had training for this, they have prepared for every possible scenario, but in his mind he had always won, he always wins. He has not imagined himself lying here, not shot, not hit by a bullet where he could at least see a person and shoot them back, but floored by something else, something more. He is unable to tell if his body is still attached to him or which part of it is melting. And now he can feel his legs burning, burning, burning.

The pain comes later. First it is mainly in his chest: a bruised lung, the doctor will tell him. With every breath he feels himself on fire and not even the refrigerated water or ice chips the nurses bring him do anything to put it out. Then it is a searing, deep throbbing that both shoots down his leg and is ever-present in an insistent, raw ache. He has vague memories of being lifted on and off gurneys, of entering what he thought was a coffin, and of briefly lying on a cold metal table surrounded by masked attendants before slipping back into his white existence. The doctor will later inform him that he has been operated on; that his leg was broken in such a severe open fracture that they were forced to insert a metal rod to hold the shattered parts together, that he was lucky not to have lost it, that he is lucky to be alive. But for now all he knows is the pain. When he smiles at Ella, she bursts into tears.

She is not wearing the ring. This is all Udi can think about during those first glimpses of her face that he takes back with him into the whiteness. Did she refuse him? Did he ask her? Does she know?

Tomer stands next to his bed, his face sombre, ashen. "You're okay," he says when Udi opens his eyes. "You're burned, but you're okay. Fucking roadside bomb, Udi. Thank fuck you crawled out of there. Thank fuck they didn't shoot you while you were on fire. Thank fuck you saw their shooter. You got him, you know. Thank God."

"Mordechai?" Udi whispers.

Tomer hangs his head. "Nope."

A young boy is next to his bed. He carries candy. His mother is behind him. A stranger. Where is his own mother? "This is what you are fighting for," the unknown mother states, pointing to her child then placing her hand onto his. "Thank you," she says. "Thank you."

Tomer remains next to him with his message of death. Death on one side, life on the other. Where is Ella?

He cannot piece together the jumbled memories. He remembers her crying and him shouting; he remembers pain and noise; now his own mother screaming, banging on his bedroom door, and another time sitting silently, accusing him with her gaze; then Ella again, this time smiling, her lips still pursed; giggling; and then once more the pain.

He cannot stop it. He wants to stop. Stop the chaotic pushing and shoving inside his head, go to a place more retiring, more calm, cooler, and ask Ella, where is the ring?

Ben provides the answer. On the third morning in hospital he appears clearly at Udi's bedside. Ella has gone. "She's at my mum's. Sleeping," Ben informs him when he sees Udi's eyes opening. "Your parents are here too. My God, Udi, talk about scaring the shit out of us. We thought that was it you fucking cooney."

Udi laughs painfully and Ben calls for a nurse who helps him to sit up. "What the fuck happened?"

"You're a crazy Israeli driver, that's what!" Ben says. "You had a car crash on the way to the airport. Another car drove straight into you. He says you flashed him to go."

"To stop," Udi begins, but cannot really remember. "Ella, how did she…what did she…is she…"

"She's okay. I picked her up from the airport. You might be needing this though." Ben reaches into his pocket and produces a dented box. He opens it.

"Still perfect." Udi grins, reaching his hand out to take the sparkling diamond, before glancing up at Ben. "Still perfect."

Ben says nothing. He wears the same look that Tomer once did.

With some difficulty, Udi pushes himself up a little in bed. He glances around the room. There is a drip attached to his arm, but he cannot see anything revealing. He looks down at his body but it is under a sheet. There is pain but the pain is everywhere. "What's the diagnosis?" says Udi.

"You should probably speak to the doctor," Ben answers.

"*Y'allah*, the doctor's told you, no?"

"Yes."

"So tell me. How long? How long 'till I'm running round the Heath?"

There is a pause before Ben answers. Finally, he looks Udi directly in the eye and shakes his head. "Udi…"

Unconsciously, Udi reaches to touch his leg.

"They want you to go back, Udi, to Israel."

"What?"

"You almost lost your leg and they say you need a lot of therapy on it, and that- Udi…"

Udi has stopped listening. His head is suddenly full, loud, deafened by noise.

"Udi-"

"And why must I do that in Israel?" he snaps.

"Well I suppose you don't have to but the doctors say Israel has an advanced set-up for this kind of...rehab, you know, for limbs. I guess because of..."

"Because of the army. And the bombs."

"Yes."

"There are lots of injuries like this," Udi muses. But it could happen in a car crash. He laughs obscenely. Then pauses again before turning back to Ben. "And Ella? She wants to go back?"

"I don't know," Ben says. "I think she just wants you to get better."

Udi shakes his head and fingers the ring in his hand. "I'm not leaving."

The doctor confirms what Ben has told him. He needs months of intensive rehab on his leg and even then they cannot promise he will ever regain normal functionality. He will probably never run. His lungs are less serious – painful but not chronic. He was lucky. He will be okay. Still, the doctors tell him that the Israeli set-up is first class, better than what he will be able to access in Britain. He would be crazy, they tell him, not to go back. He tells the doctor it is true then, he is crazy.

Ella appears just as the doctor is leaving. His mother is with her. Both are brimming with tears. Batia rushes forward. She strokes his face fervently and kisses his cheeks. "Udi," she breathes. "Udi. We were so afraid. We were- Thank God. Thank God."

Udi looks up. Ella is standing in the corner making way for his mother. She has so far said nothing. Udi winks at her but she does not move. She looks terrified.

"Your father's on his way," Batia continues.

"Abba's here?"

"Of course he's here."

"Where is he?"

"Jonny took him to see the restaurant." She smiles as she says this. "You have been doing well, Udi."

Udi looks to Ella but she makes no movement. "Yes. I was."

"But of course. We knew that you would," says his mother.

"Ima, I'm going to stay."

For a moment Batia says nothing, then slowly, carefully, she sits on the side of his hospital bed and summons Ella to stand next to her. Ella moves forward tentatively, in silence she flanks his mother. "It is not what I saw, Udi."

"You saw this? You saw this?" Neither of the women respond. "You saw this in my fucking cup?"

"No," Batia corrects. "I saw a journey, and it was a circle. I saw that you will come back."

***

Ella waits until Udi and his mother have stopped blaming each other for their separate despair, she waits until Batia has stopped crying and waits until Udi's mother has left the room to find a doctor to corroborate her decree that he must return with her to Israel, before finally she reaches out to touch him. To touch him again. He doesn't know that she has already stroked his face, kissed his wounds, smelled his neck. He doesn't know that she has sat by his bed for the past three days, or that sometimes, when no one else was there, she has curled up carefully in it, warming herself in this cold country with the heat of him.

For days she has been unable to uncross her arms from her chest. She has walked around numbly, frozen in this posture of defence, paralysed by fear and shock, and the cold. Ben tried once to make a joke of it when she wrapped a hospital blanket around her shoulders, telling her that it was summer, it was hot, but she could only shiver in response and he brought her some tea.

It is not how she'd imagined her first glimpse of England. Her grand arrival. In her head, Udi had not been bruised and cut and broken. He had been alight: with confidence and success, and love. He was in love. With her. He'd finally said it. But when she'd walked through the arrivals gate at Heathrow and been greeted not by Udi but by his too predictable absence, her first thought was that he'd forgotten her. She is haunted by this thought now. She'd been hoping for more, hoping he was finally ready for more, but it would not have been so unlike him. And her anger was quick. Anger and then disappointment, and then fear. She was alone. She had his phone number but only his, and her mobile didn't work in the UK and it took nine attempts on a payphone for her to figure out the dialling code, and then, of course, there was no answer. A wild fury consumed her, a hatred sprung from frustration, a desire for him to suffer as he had made her, exacerbated more and more as the lonely airport hours passed. She left message after angry message on his mobile – messages she has now deleted – and by the time Ben arrived she had been hysterical. Now, she is unable to stand the thought that while Udi was lying unconscious in a wreckage that she can't stop imagining, she was practically wishing him dead. She wonders if Batia saw this too, in a cup, if this is why she has always disliked her.

"Ella," Udi says, winking at her again and ushering her closer. "So, what do you think?" He points to the bruises on his face. "Do you still like me?"

Ella laughs painfully through pursed lips, determined to make up for it all, to be strong. "Udi, how you look isn't important," she says. "Only thank God you're okay."

"Ah, but it's very important," Udi says, taking her hand and placing it on his scarred face. "It's very important that you still fancy me."

"Okay, I do," she hurries, forcing a laugh. "Now stop touching your cuts, how do you feel? The doctors say you can try to get up if you feel ready. We can get you a wheelchair and-"

"Don't you want to know why it's important?" he interrupts, not letting go of her hand.

"What are you talking about, Udi?"

"It's important, because a woman should always be attracted to her husband." And suddenly, between their pressed palms, she feels a warm, round object. Slowly she looks down, and she sees the diamond. "Marry me, Ella," Udi whispers through his bruised lips, and she doesn't giggle, but her tears are answer enough.

They do not look up when a nurse enters the room to check on Udi. They are locked together, finally with the certainty of forever, despite the uncertainty of everything else. If they draw back it will be necessary for them to talk, or at least to look into each other's eyes, and then they will be forced to address again the question of where they will live, how they will plan their future, and she will feel a need to tell him what is happening back home, what has begun. So long as they remain linked, bound and blinded by this embrace, it is not requisite to look beyond it. They hold tight, pulling in opposite directions.

Finally it is Batia who disturbs them. She has a doctor in tow and Ella moves aside so that Udi can sit up to listen. He reaches however for her hand, which she provides gladly. As their fingers interlock, Batia notices the ring and Ella catches just a hint of a smile flit across her face, though neither woman says anything. They stand silently to the side as the doctor repeats the news they have already delivered, but in a package more littered with medical terminology and detached objectivity, wrappings more persuasive. Udi nods along as the minutiae of his injuries are detailed, the facts laid out, the prognosis stated. His face betrays concentration but not despair, and when the doctor re-iterates that Israel is better equipped to deal with Udi's kind of injury, both Ella and Batia look hopefully towards him. They intend to be sympathetic, supportive, caring, but it is hard not to appear gratified. Ella is sure that there is a reason for his accident, Batia is sure too, they have discussed it – the reason of course is his return to them. And they are sure that some day Udi will see it this way too. But not today. For although Udi is still listening to the doctor, and still sitting upright, his broad frame seeming strong and powerful in the narrow hospital bed; all at once his shoulders begin to shake, and his head shakes, and when Ella moves forward, he has to rub his chest before he can say to her, in a trembling, pleading voice she has never before heard, that he doesn't want to leave, that he can't.

Ella hesitates, but only for a second. At the sight of his tears she is filled with an urge to make a protective fence around him. She uncrosses her arms. "Okay."

"What?"

"Okay, we'll stay. We'll do the rehab here."

"You don't want to go back to Israel?" Udi asks, glancing also to his mother who says nothing.

"Of course I do, but more than that I want to be with you. Your life is my life," she tells him, and untangling his fingers from her own she reaches to her neck for the locket she wears every day underneath her shirt, and opens it into his hand. Four pieces of shrapnel fall out. They are discoloured now, and cold from lack of touch, but as hard as ever.

***

Now

19

The annual Jewish Giving campaign dinner comes at a timely moment. Think the Oscars. Wait, think the Oscars without a red carpet, without the Hollywood starlets, without Billy Crystal or Steve Martin, but with almost the same attention to fashion and at least as good food. After all, it's Josh Berger, the crème of kosher catering.

Dad and I go to the event together every year. He has supported Jewish Giving since its inception almost 25 years ago. Mum even volunteered for a while at one of their day centres, and every time I watch a campaign film I am struck by the elderly or the ill or the previously alone who describe how their lives have been changed. This night is how the charity stays afloat, how it manages to do its work, this one night of appealing to the community. But the chatter this evening is not about Jewish Giving, not about this year's big-name host, not even about who has or hasn't appeared as mutton dressed as lamb. We are talking about the conflict. About the impact of the conflict. About the state of European Jewry.

As the reception comes to a close, chatter continues, but the master of ceremonies ushers us into the banquet hall for the meal. I am seated next to Dad. Most of our table's guests are family friends but on the far side are three men I have never met before. One is an older chap, silver-topped, at least a generation older than Dad. The second is closer to his age, heavy set, skin slightly grey from too much smoke. And the third I estimate to be somewhere in his late 30s. He is sharp and well-gelled and on second glance he looks familiar. After a while I realise that he was one of the organisers of the Jewish Security training course I took part in almost a decade ago. I recall his heavy East London accent, the uncanny knack he had of turning completely normal speech into a swear fest, and his passion for protecting the community. Tonight, this seems like an important thing.

He catches me looking at him and I nod. He raises his glass before lowering his head into conversation with the man to his right. I cannot hear their exchange but all three of these men exude an air of toughness, roughness, not quite smooth despite their impeccable suits and shined Oxfords. Though they have done nothing to suggest it, when I study them I get a whiff of menace. Dad has clocked them too and I notice all of our friends sitting with a little extra swagger. In the light of recent events, there is a vicarious pride in having these men as part of our group. That's strange I know, pride in thuggery. But it's like having a famous relative or owning a renowned work of art – gratification from the affiliation to something that we ourselves are not.

It's not that all Jews are gentle. Google 'Jewish mob' – Meyer Lansky, Bugsy Siegel, there you go. Or look up Jewish boxers. And nobody's going to suggest that Israelis are weaklings are they? Even from my own crowd of friends at school we had our one or two loose cannons. But generally speaking, generally, we're not fighters. We love our mothers, and don't want bruises for meetings, and so long as there's food don't bother too much about the drink that might set others going, and besides, we care too much about our faces.

Clive. I remember his name: Clive.

Starters are smoked salmon and beetroot. This is followed by roast beef and veg, and then a pause before dessert for the campaign film. It is as heart-wrenching as always. It ends with the story of an elderly gentleman who first lost his wife to dementia, and is now suffering the early stages of it himself. They were both Holocaust survivors. They never had a family. Jewish Giving is giving. Immediately on the film's finishing, envelopes are passed around with pledge cards for each guest. Clive looks at me and nods. Now the 'surprise' music act that is never a surprise, this year Kathy Sledge. Then the desserts. By this time many of the diners have left for journeys back to the suburbs, to sleeping children or dogs that need to pee, the outpouring of emotion and determination and cash complete. Dad turns to me.

"Ready to go?"

I nod and stand, but across the table Clive ushers me over. I feel presumptuous introducing myself, as though Clive really is some kind of celebrity, but he looks at me hard as our palms meet. "Do I know you?"

"I think I did a course you ran a while back. You're Clive? From the security course."

"Ri-ight. Your name's…"

"Dan."

"Of course, that's it, been fucking with my head all night. Dan the man." He turns to the middle-aged man next to him. "Dad, this here's Danny-boy. Did the security training jobby."

"Pleasure to meet you."

"And this here's my uncle Charlie."

I turn to the older gentleman. He has the look of an old English rock and roller. Lined, weathered, but with a boyish twinkle. Silver hair but full and lustrous. A scar down his left cheek. He grins. "Coming to the club with us are you then Danny?"

I look to Dad. He already has on his jacket and shakes his head, jerking his thumb softly towards the door, but I can't think of a reason to say no. Besides, tonight I feel connected to everyone, particularly to these men who are here supporting the community and teaching us how to protect it. We are connected, united, by heritage and responsibility, and shared dismay.

In the cab, my phone rings. Orli. Even now, so many months after we first met, I feel that tiny bubble of excitement when I see her number flash up. I know it can't last forever but I love that it still happens. I can't wait until I am able to see her every day.

"It's finished," she says.

Her voice is breathy, excited, triumphant. She has been working on the same painting for weeks, struggling with it, changing it, starting again. Since the conflict began the entire colour scheme has changed twice, she says. I still don't know the subject though she talks ambiguously, and I have no idea about art terms, but I have sympathised over her quest to capture a truth. *A* truth. Not *the* truth, she reminds me. Even so, depicting even one version has been eluding her.

"Mazel Tov," I tell her. "I knew you would do it."

I did, but I also feel a little relieved that she finally has. I know that's wrong. I meander and over-think constantly so why shouldn't she? But Orli's indecision over this painting has been unsettling to me. Normally she is so sure, so straight. I saw it that very first night next to the sea, her ocean eyes brimming with bright blue insight. Even after David died and everything was off kilter, that space beside her un-fillable, still her sadness was clear, it had direction. But lately she has been talking about the heaviness of direction, of choosing paths. This painting has paths. She says it is a portrait but it also has tracks, footsteps, and there is truth she says on both sides. If you don't run so fast that you miss it. She has been a little fixated with running. Running forward. Running away. She does not want me to run away. I keep assuring her that I'm not running away, I'm walking with purpose. Now that the painting is finished, I hope she will regain her sense of purpose, too.

"I'm going out to celebrate," she enthuses.

"Who with?"

"Everyone. How was your evening?"

"Still going." I am talking quietly so that Clive and the others won't hear. I like them, but I wouldn't want to introduce them to Orli. They are immersed however in their own banter and are paying no attention to me. "So when can I see the painting? Do I finally get to know what it's really about?"

"The dinner was good?"

I smile at her diversion. "The dinner was good. I'm going now to a club with some new friends."

"Enjoy."

We are about to say goodbye when suddenly I remember: "Orli, what was the protest you wished you had gone on last week?"

"Against the government's actions?"

"Against?"

"Of course." She pauses. "I know you feel differently. Israel is complicated, Dan. You will see."

"Orli," I begin.

"There's never a reason," she interrupts. "For hatred. Danny, the reason is only the excuse, only the justification, only the beginning. They took my brother, but I won't let them take me too. I will never let them take who I am."

"Well you're more noble than I am."

Clive looks up.

"It's more complicated than that." In the background on her end of the phone, I hear first Orli's doorbell and then the sound of Ittai's voice. "Everyone's arriving," she says.

"Okay."

"Okay."

We both linger over a silent line.

"Danny, I've been painting Muaz." Her voice has lowered. I know that for her this is as revealing a confession as she can give. "It's going to be one of the central pieces."

"Muaz? Can I see it?"

"Not yet. The series needs balance. There's another side. To all this, to everything." She takes a deep breath and I feel for a moment that she is about to tell me something important, something big. But then Clive laughs, loudly, the cab is filled with rowdy hilarity, and the moment is broken. "Anyway, I'm going to Jerusalem tomorrow. I need to do some sketches there."

"Jerusalem? Not East Jerusalem?"

"Maybe."

"Not now. Orli, that's not sensible. You're not going alone?"

"I need these sketches, Danny."

"Orli, you have to be careful." Despite the fact that I am soon to become a citizen, the mention of certain places, certain circumstances, still triggers an outsider's apprehension. Like Mum and Gaby with the markets and street-side cafés, and buses. True Israelis cannot live this way and I force myself to exhale. I imagine her waving her hand at me dismissively.

"Bye, Danny," she says. And I don't argue. She would not listen to me in any case. She is sure, she is strong, she is true.

The bouncer at the door to the club shakes the hands of my three companions. We have arrived at the entrance of an exclusive, old English, private members club and they are clearly regulars. They stride ahead of me, Clive stopping to have a word to a hostess, shaking hands with a passing waiter, comfortable and familiar. I however am struck by the grandeur of the deep red and brown upholstery, chocolate-coloured chesterfields forming separate clusters around mahogany table-tops, chandeliers dripping from the ornamented ceiling, fire-places, marble pillars. I imagine this to be a place where chess has been played, pipes smoked, whisky devoured. We sit in our suits and it strikes me that to an outsider we have passed ourselves off – Jews, immigrants, so integrated, so at ease, as English as the next man. Not geese but chickens.

Charlie waves to a waiter who hurries towards him and takes his order of champagne.

"You'll have some bubbly, won't you my boy?" Charlie declares, not really as a question, clapping his heavy hand onto my leg. His smile dances but his eyes are weary. I feel a surge of gratitude for not having had to battle the world as I imagine he has. A pulse of admiration.

"Sure. Thank you very much."

"So." His voice is gravelly. It makes me think of smoke and old movie stars, and mobsters. "What's your game?"

"Pardon?"

"What do you do, Danny-boy?" He sits forwards in his chair, a certain whimsy in the way he caresses his champagne flute – just a finger and thumb on the spine, the other digits dancing merrily.

It is the first time I have been asked this question since I left the bank. I recall Orli asking me the same thing, then rapidly following it with an entreaty of why. And Gaby asking me what I'll do now. And Safia, back when we met at uni asking me what I wanted to do afterwards. And Hayley already knowing. It would be liberating to answer with the truth: nothing. Right now I am doing nothing to define or label me. To give me away. Just a deep void awaiting definition.

"I'm moving to Israel," I choose as my reply. "Next week."

"Danny-boy," Clive's Dad, Sid, interjects. "You're going to the old homeland? Eretz Yis-ra-el? What are you gonna do over there then? Property? You should get into property. I tell you, a lot's happening out there."

"Just not near the border." Charlie laughs, patting my leg again. "Not unless you've got good rocket insurance. Fucking Arabs."

Fucking Arabs? I feel my smile freeze into a contorted grimace. Did I hear right? Fucking Arabs? Seriously?

The old man is oblivious to my bewilderment and laughs at his own joke, sipping his champagne, fingers raised. None of the others bat an eyelid. Perhaps I did mishear. I must have misheard.

"There's a hell of a lot of business to be done out there," Sid continues. "Clive and I were over last month having a look, weren't we mate?"

Clive nods. "Fucking overrun with buggering Russians now. And wanking French. Well that's only gonna get shittier now isn't it? I'm telling you, there's a market there for some cunting cheap housing. I could set you up with a couple of contacts if you want?"

"Um…" I say.

Clive is eager to write the names of his contacts on one of his business cards, and I give him one of my own. "Ignore the bank stuff," I say, writing my personal email on the back.

"Fucking free fucking man," he grins.

I can't help laughing.

"So," says Clive. "Are you a Gooner?"

We talk for a long time about football, property prices, football again, Charlie's pretty young girlfriend who's 30 years his junior, the potential advent of mansion tax, 'Ed buggering Miliband', *House of Cards*, football again. By the time the second bottle of champagne arrives I've all but forgotten the previous jarring comments. I feel again the bonding sensation of earlier, the conviction that despite their relative coarseness, these men are all Jews, like me, with the values I assume we share. Just as it will be in Israel. No hoodies to avoid when walking past an estate. No yobbos in the pub waiting to start on anyone who dares to look. The waiter pours a glass for Charlie to taste and approve, which he does, and they raise their bubbling glasses.

"L'chaim gentlemen," Charlie declares.

"L'chaim," I agree. "To new friends!"

"To wanking cheap flats in Israel!" Clive adds.

"To a year of success and safety," Charlie says solemnly

and I nod with equal solemnity. It is impossible to ignore what is going on. It is no longer below the surface. "May we all feel safe on our streets, in our homes, in our professions, and on the fucking television," Charlie continues and I nod with them all again. "Up the Jews eh, and down the fucking Mussers!"

This time I have not misheard.

The others laugh raucously and clink glasses, but I don't know what to do.

In my hand is the champagne bought for me by Charlie, I am seated on the luxurious leather of the exclusive club to which I have been invited as a guest. I cannot speak. I cannot be so rude as to speak, to object. But I cannot say nothing. It is right there in front of me: the beginning, the justification, the reason, the excuse. Not even the biased British press coverage, nor the deli, nor the rockets can give license to this. Hatred for a whole religion, culture, people? Isn't that what we're fighting against?

The conversation moves on. I have said nothing. Now it is too late. Clive is asking me something but I remain stuck in that previous moment. Spiralling suddenly backwards over the past months. Reminded of that turmoil I felt for so long at the bank, that sense of fraudulence, of miscellany. I am a Jew, but not like the black hats and not like Gaby and not like these men; a Brit, but not like those who march against me; and an Israeli, but not yet. I am nothing and everything, every part of me watered down, clinging like a leech to the skin I am trying to shed, burrowing into the fresh layer I am attempting to grow. Insisting. And I am too British-ly polite to reject any of it. I put down my champagne flute on its coaster.

"Thank you for a lovely evening," I say, standing.

"Off already are you?" Charlie asks. "Can't handle the bubbly eh? Well good to have met you, Danny-boy. And good luck in the homeland."

The rest of the group break off from their heavily gesticulated conversations to add their farewells, but

I negotiate an obstacle course of chesterfields, almost backing into the fire to avoid making physical, palm-pressed goodbyes. Charlie however stands up to see me to the door, and although every fibre of my being wants to turn from him, tell him how backwards and prejudiced and wrong he is, no matter his toughness and his experience, I cannot bring myself to refuse his extended hand.

Over the days that follow, I find that it is no longer with nostalgia that I bubble-wrap my life. Instead I cut through boxes and tissue paper with the dissection that I feel myself. I can't wait to go. I can't wait to get away, to no longer be confronted by the mess of my own identity, my Britishness, my passivity, this part of myself that I despise. No IDF soldier would sit when he should stand, stay silent when he should speak. But the days filter slowly like sand in a timer. I hardly speak to Orli and this prolongs the grains further. But she is in Jerusalem, painting, finding for herself some element that is missing. I wonder what she is doing there. How she is collecting her ideas, her inspiration. I wonder why she has turned off her phone. I wish sometimes she would let me share the process, let me in on her thoughts before they are there on the page for everyone.

I have attempted to explain to my family my own thoughts, again, but they still don't understand. I think they had imagined that the conflict was divine intervention, God conspiring to devastate an entire region all in order to make me stay at home.

Safia has not asked for any more of an explanation. We've texted but she has been busy with work. We haven't met. We haven't talked about the protest. The more I think about it the less sure I am that it was her. Perhaps it was my own projection. Perhaps it was because of the dreams. Perhaps even if it was her, there is nothing to be surprised by, saddened by. We don't agree but of course we don't agree. Of course we don't agree? It is complicated and too hard to unravel.

It was Charlie and not me who spoke against Muslims. But I said nothing.

Safia did not create the Hitler sign. But she stood beside it.

In her texts she asks after Orli. She asks about my flight. She says she will be at my party to say goodbye.

**

Now

20

With Ella at his side there is nothing Udi can think of that could persuade him to return to Israel. So he will have to travel a little further to the treatment centre, so he will have to wait a little longer between sessions, so there might be slightly less hi-tech equipment; so then he will work that much harder on his own. It is not a high price for freedom.

Batia has begged him to reconsider. He feels guilty for her distress, for her continued distress, and sorry for Ella whom his mother shoots with barbed glances, but actually she seems distracted in her persistence, or weary of it. She spends a lot of time on the phone. In any case his father is on his side. Oz has seen the restaurant, and he has not joined in Batia's pleas. They have not actually spoken about it directly, but yesterday Udi overheard him on the phone to a friend in Israel telling him that England has done his son good. Udi would stay if only to hear more of this approval. He would stay for a million reasons smaller than this.

It is a Thursday when Chaim calls. Udi is still in hospital and growing restless. He has hardly been out of bed in weeks and doesn't even have a TV or Wi-Fi for Ben's iPad to occupy him in the small room he shares with another patient. He has books and some old magazines, but mostly his time is filled with talk. Often he dozes or just lays back and listens to the familiar, throaty, Hebrew vowels that fly back and forth across his white-clad bed. His family have become something of a joke at the hospital. There is an Israeli-born doctor in his wing and he pops in every day to visit what is now in jest referred to as 'the Israeli quarter'. Udi has heard a few muttered insults from passing nurses when this doctor or his family are about – something about it being another occupied territory, something about wondering whether Palestinians in Gaza get as good treatment as this. But he knows that there will always be those who hate Israel, and most of the staff are friendly and welcoming and blessing-sent. He has just finished physio when Chaim calls. His family are out having dinner somewhere nearby so he is alone in his room, examining the scars down one of his legs and the pins that remain in the other.

"I'm coming to England," Chaim announces. "I heard what happened you crazy fuck. I'm coming to see you. Should I bring shesh besh or cards?"

Udi laughs. "Bring both. I am so fucking bored."

"I heard your leg is fucked."

"It's nothing, a tiny scratch." Udi's leg aches as he says this.

"So you're staying then?"

"Of course."

"That's smart," Chaim tells him. "You should. I'm coming too. I need to get out."

Udi pauses. He had expected his friend to remind him that Israel is the greatest country in the world. "What's news at home?" he asks.

"You know, it's the same," Chaim replies. "Except everyone's in Gaza. Dov's based near your brother I think, on the border. He says they've been in twice and are going again."

"What?" Udi pulls the phone away from his ear.

"This week maybe."

"What? Why are they going *in*to Gaza? And why the fuck is everyone there? Dov's done his service this year."

"Udi, they're calling up everyone," Chaim answers. "There's probably a call up waiting for you. Ask your mother."

Udi peers out into the corridor and sees not his mother, but Ella. She is standing holding a doggy bag of restaurant food but has suddenly frozen, her arm suspended in rigidity on the door knob. He waves her to come in but she darts away in the opposite direction. "Chaim, what the fuck's happening?"

"How do you not know? Even *I* watch the news for this."

"Chaim, *y'allah*."

"Fuck Udi, we're at war."

"We didn't want to upset you," begins Ella. She has returned with Ben and his mother, a team. "We wanted you to concentrate on your recovery."

"Who is there?"

"Your brother," Batia replies starkly, cutting as always to the heart. "He called us this morning. So far he is okay."

"Tomer and Shimon are there also," Ella adds. "Your unit was called up practically on the first day. Dov too."

"How could you not tell me?"

Ella touches his arm in apology, but Udi is not really angry at them. He is angry because all at once his head is full with much more than whiteness. All at once he is back in the bunks with Tomer, he is patrolling the fence with Shimon, he is in the dark, in a bush, in an explosion, his legs melting. And all at once, he wants to go home.

He wants to go home?

How did he not foresee this? After all of it? The months and months of planning and longing and dreaming and working. He knew there would be another war, there is always another war. But he didn't expect to feel this, this... "Is there a call up for me?" he asks.

Batia nods. "But of course you can't go."

"Udi, the doctor says you won't be able to go to the army again," Ella tells him. "Not in combat. Your leg will never be strong enough."

"Thank God," mumbles Batia in Hebrew.

He sits himself up straighter and punches his frail leg. "Where my brothers go, I go."

"You can't," Ella repeats gently.

"Thank goodness you can't," Batia declares more firmly. "Udi, can you not see this has been the reason for it all?"

"Ima, there is not a reason for everything," Udi shouts. "I am a fighter. How can I not fight for the land for which my friends are spilling their blood? For the land that has my blood already? I have to do something. I know I can do something. It's my duty. I cannot just sit here!"

"You don't have to sit here," Batia replies. "You can come home, to Israel. You can help the country by living in it. You've done your fighting, now do your living."

This is the very least that he will do. This, suddenly, is as to nothing. "Call the doctor," he says to Ben, ignoring the two women who seem so happy in his impotence. Ben nods and stands up from the chair at the back of the room from which he has been listening to but not understanding the heated Hebrew. "Tell him I need to make arrangements to finish my treatment in Israel."

Both women smile, but Udi refuses to indulge them. He will, he knows, forgive them their feminine fears and tugs on his existence, but not yet. "Where is Abba?" he demands.

Only his father will understand the mixture of pride and shame he now feels. He is returning to Israel, but not as a soldier, as something less. It is a cruel trick: that distance from his homeland, and danger to it, are what it takes to make him know the bond it has already scorched irreversibly onto his heart through so many years spent in the heat and the sand.

When Oz arrives at the hospital that evening he says nothing about Udi's change of mind. There is no reprimand, no words to suggest disappointment or Udi's failure, no accusation of a deficiency in resolve. Oz sits for a long time in the chair next to Udi's bed, first listening to Udi, then in mutual quiet, and then finally, he speaks.

"In Iraq, my family were called Jews," he tells Udi slowly. "In Israel I am called Iraqi. Here in England, I am Israeli. But you know Udi, only this last one I truly am. These other things, they are just a part of me. Israeli is the whole of it. Sometimes you must be outside to know where the inside is."

It is the first time since Udi was a boy that he has looked at his father and wanted, with that resolve of the young, to be like him. His lined face seems suddenly full of experience not fragility, his unmoving principles a product not of obsolete thinking but truth, his judgement not criticism but love. Udi opens his mouth, but he cannot think of anything to express the admiration he feels, so in the end, he simply holds out an open palm. His father takes it. "Good," Oz says. "*Y'allah*."

***

The practicalities of reversing his immigration are far less arduous than was the task of securing it. In just a few phone calls it is possible for Udi to eradicate all evidence of his life in London until all that is left are his memories, and a shattered leg, and the nut stall.

Ben helps him to tie up the last of the loose ends. There is money in his bank account that must be withdrawn, a credit card bill bearing the cost of Ella's ring that must be settled, a mobile phone contract to terminate. The flat above the restaurant is cleared by Jonny under Ella's direction: his clothes packed neatly away in a single hold-all; his notepad, filled with plans for the restaurant, placed with the few books he owns in a canvas bag Batia has produced from somewhere; and the pots and pans and other homely items he has accrued delivered in a large brown box to Ben and Jonny's mother

293

who promises to get a good price for them at her next car boot sale. There is no car to return to his cousins. Udi worries about this. He makes phone call after phone call from his hospital bed to the insurance company which tells him that they cannot yet make a payout because there is still dispute over which driver is to blame. Udi cannot wait. He does not want to leave England in debt to his cousins but the doctors have made arrangements and he is booked on a medically supported flight back to Israel in two days time. Besides, he cannot bear to be here when the world is collapsing there. Ben thinks he is mad. He cannot understand why a war, sirens, terror, why this should be what makes Udi want to return. But who can explain that kind of a call? How can he describe the urgency with which he feels it? It pumps through his veins, he tells Ben.

They watch the news now constantly on a portable TV. They worry about Ari. They worry about their friends. They worry whether it will ever be possible to contain a people consumed by so much hate that they dig underground and hide rockets behind children.

They worry too about Avigail. It takes days for anybody to tell him but he had already found it strange that she had not been on the phone harassing him, mothering him, smothering him. Then one afternoon there is a flurry of other people's phones buzzing and his parents excusing themselves and finally it is Ella who explains. Avigail has – as he knew – been against the war from the start, and now Ella tells him that she has been writing more articles, attending protests, becoming a Voice, a Voice Against. She pushes, pushes people to think and question and condemn. Her blog posts have been going viral. Oz, says Ella, has been ashamed. He has not been speaking to her and even Batia could not support the strength of her dissent. Yes, think of their humanity, Ella had overheard Batia telling Avigail in one of their many phone conversations, care about their children, want to help them, but not at the sake of our boys, her boy, Ari.

But now Avigail is in hospital. There were counter-protestors at a recent demonstration, says Ella, and Avigail was followed home by an angry right-winger. She was beaten with a flagpole. She was bruised by white and blue.

Udi cannot stop thinking about her. He imagines Ezra bringing the kids to the hospital to see her. How will he prepare them to see her bruises? (And why, it occurs to Udi, is she still in hospital for just bruises?) How will he explain to them that the person who did this to their mother does not represent the whole, but that that person is part of the whole, and it is this whole that their soldiers must protect from others who would destroy it? And that those who seek such destruction are not a uniform whole either: they are four-year-old girls, and women with metal under their dresses, and men with guns and bombs and pebbles and dreams and tunnels and rage and pride and determination. And that the right-wingers can't see this and their mother can, and that is the problem. And that the Palestinians won't distinguish either, but would kill Avigail in a heartbeat, while her bleeding heart for them makes those on her side doubt, and blame, and makes Israel vulnerable, and that is the problem too.

At night he thinks of Avigail lying on the ground while an enraged patriot stands above her, and he thinks of Ari, and of the dead kidnapped soldiers, and Palestinian boys on beaches, and his friends. He imagines Shimon chasing another cross for his gun, of Tomer restraining him, and of both of them missing his third pair of eyes, his trigger. He feels he has let them down, wide awake he dreams of it, and in the dark he longs for the heat of the Israeli air to suffocate the coldness of these images that come to him in the English night. Only during the day does he manage to doze. The doctors say this is not unusual after a trauma and prescribe him sleeping pills. He is therefore asleep when, the day before his departure, Ben appears in his room.

The nurses gesture to Ben to be quiet but Ben hovers silently next to Udi's bed for only the briefest of moments before dragging the plastic hospital chair noisily up next to it and coughing loudly into his hand.

"Fuck yourself," Udi murmurs squinting through half open eyes at his grinning cousin.

"*At tachat shel dog mishuga gadol!*" Ben retorts with the Hebrew phrase Udi taught him the day before – something about being a crazy, big fish's arse. "Wake up you cooney, I've got news."

"Is it Ari?" Udi sits up. He had been watching a news bulletin before he dozed off and was sure that the Israeli soldier in the footage looked like Ari. He was alive, but limping.

"No," Ben says. "Sorry. But it's good news. I had a call today from the driver who went into you."

"Oh?"

Ben has never had a good poker face and is struggling to contain his excitement. "He wants to make you an offer. There's a big dispute apparently between your insurance companies and it's going to end up going to court, and this guy's worried he's going to get stuck with a huge fee at the end of it. So basically, he still won't admit blame 'cos he maintains that you flashed him to go, but he did go into your car, and it was your right of way so…"

"So what?"

"So he's offered to pay you a settlement, so long as you drop your insurance claim."

"How much is the settlement?"

Ben has come prepared. He hands him a piece of paper and Udi unfolds it sceptically. He is interested to see the price tag affixed to his leg.

"Well?" asks Ben after a long pause. "What do you think?"

"I think… I can pay you back for the car…"

Ben laughs. "You can do more than that you cooney!"

"I can buy a flat in Tel Aviv," Udi says slowly, the recognition gradual, layered. "I can open a business even. Maybe a restaurant. Maybe by the shuk. And I can do something else. I'm going to do something, really do something, something to, I don't know, educate or, reach out, or, help... I can't fight so I have to do something now, you know? It's not built yet, Israel. After all. Sixty-six years, that's nothing. I could... Fuck!"

"So you'll take it?"

"Fuck!" Udi exclaims again.

He breathes deeply. It hurts his recovering lung but the pain tells him the moment is real and he cannot help but smile at the thought of Ella's face when he tells her. She will try of course to be restrained. She will try to be respectful of his injuries and what he has lost. She will try not to show how glad she is to be going home, with him, with a future that will not be interrupted by a call up in the post. But she will not be able to conceal her joy completely. Eventually she will give it away. Eventually she will call her mother in Israel whose voice Udi will hear careering above pots and pans and other sounds down the line of the phone. And eventually she will giggle. And they will be free.

**

Then

21

Everything he does is in apology. Kaseem cannot take back those violent, vengeful moments, nor rid his mind of Dara's tear-streaked face, nor forget the utter humiliation he felt at the hands of her father. No matter how hard he tries he cannot assuage his loathing for the man, he cannot stop wishing him ill. But he can try to make up for these things, for these ugly feelings. And that is why he finally takes a manual job laying cables on a construction site. He knows it is an end to his ambition, to his family's hopes, to their way out of the stone-walled circle her people have built around him. But he takes it, in apology.

His mother has been nagging again. She wants to know if he is going to marry this Jewish girl, if she will become a Muslim, if she will cover her legs, and if not, when he will stop this nonsense with this whore and turn his attentions to the women who truly need him, and look after him, and will remain. It is a choice, she tells him: his family or his whore. He tells his mother to be quiet and to make his dinner, but the roof of their house is leaking, it needs to be fixed, and they need more space, and he is the man of the house and it is his responsibility to take care of it, to take care of them. And she reminds him of this again and again. He applies, for the fifth time, for a permit to extend the house, and for the fifth time he is rejected, and so he shouts at his sisters who have not yet found husbands and for whom there is even less work than there is for him, except for menial, demeaning positions that he will not allow them to accept. Dara tries to be sensitive, she brings treats and leftover meals so that he can save his money, but this humiliates him further and his mother is insulted that Dara does not want to eat her food. So although Dara comes as often as before, they spend more and more time in the cramped store room, or in other small crevices of the world where they can be alone, saying things that mean nothing, and avoiding the realities around them. Despite everything, it is to Dara who he turns. It is she, still, who is the light of his day. It is her youth, her talent, her strong, compassionate, passionate soul. It is this and only this that lures him out into sun-baked streets and keeps him from the desperation and anger he is sure would otherwise consume him from inside. She is a butterfly in his hands, a species of another world, a flash of colour he can never quite hold. It is Kaseem's greatest fear that one day soon he may be forced to open his palms, and let her fly free.

Dara assures him that he is her inspiration too, her foremost passion, both in her heart and in her paintings. Her paintings. A talent grown to mock him. A small gallery has agreed to stock some of her work – a gallery! She is 16. When she shows him her hanging pieces they shock him with their honesty and insight. She is extraordinary. It makes him feel both proud and ridiculous. Yet she begs him to paint her. To teach her more. To at least let her paint him. Instead, he sells every canvas of his that he can, to tourists who buy them because they are authentically Arab and want to hang this slice of his soul above their sofas, and he takes his brushes and easel and expensive paints that he bought when he was still studying to an art shop near the university. And then he splits his money into two piles, and with one of them buys bricks, and cement and the materials he needs to build his mother's extension.

For the next month, it is how he spends his evenings and weekends and snatched spare moments: clambering up and down the side of their small house. He is building, permit or not. He will create a fresh, airy room at the top of the house that in being higher feels closer to heaven, more clean, more pure, less coated with the dust of the city. Sometimes Dara helps him, though lately she seems loathed to pass bricks or carry things that are heavy, as though her enthusiasm for the project, for him, is waning, and so she will only help in small ways, lifting things that do not tax her. He says nothing but his mother notices too, and tells him, and if he takes a break to walk a little with Dara then he returns to recriminations and the accusation that for a lazy Jewish girl, for a piece of meat, for a whore who does not help him, he is abandoning his family. Thankfully, she does not say such things in front of Dara, but Kaseem is sure that Dara can sense them. She says nothing, but she has grown quieter and often opens her soft, rounded lips as though to tell him something urgent, before closing them again without a word. There was a time when there was nothing they could not say. But it is insurmountable, this gulf of unspoken sentences and unformed explanations and unfurnished imaginings of the future. The growing silences are dark and fear-coated. He cannot express to her in words how deeply he loves her, and is sorry.

With his second pile of money, the other half, Kaseem walks one day to Dara's gallery and buys one of her paintings. He does it with cash, anonymously, so that she will not find out it was him, and sure enough that night she runs to his house brimming with the news of her first ever sale. He smiles and congratulates her, but is careful to feign disinterest and so, disappointed, she changes the subject and asks him about the progress of the extension. It is almost finished. There is a letter from the Jerusalem Municipality sitting on his bed that he dares not open, but he does not tell her about this, he refuses to ever again cause her trauma and so talks only of the positives, describing to her the new room that will be for his sisters. As he talks, he catches Dara from time to time smiling, not at his words but, he presumes, at her sale, and her happiness helps, in a small way at least, to allay a fraction of his continuing guilt.

He hides the painting at his uncle's house where she will never go. She signs her work with only her last name and Kaseem's uncle does not realise that the painting is a creation of Dara's. He thinks it is foolish of Kaseem to have spent money on art, on useless frivolity, still he accepts the canvas and Kaseem's promise that it has been produced by an exceptional young artist and one day will be worth a great deal. When it is, in return for his help with storage, they will split the reward. Kaseem cannot keep it himself, he tells his uncle, because his mother with her feminine lack of overview cannot understand such things. And Kaseem's uncle nods as he hangs it, and stands back to examine the depiction of a young Arab girl in a hijab, whose lips are painted hot pink, and who he does not realise is Kaseem's sister. Hadiyah. Kaseem, meanwhile, admires the painting with a foreboding sense of sadness. It is only a small piece of Dara hanging on the wall, but he fears that, one day, it is all he will have left.

***

Neither of them speak of what is in the past. It was one blip, Dara tells herself. It is not a representation of him. The bruise to her ribs however lasts for weeks and reminds her too often of the sudden, black-eyed aggression that shot from somewhere deep within him and was directed at her. She tries not to think of it. Occasionally it appears, un-thought of but there nonetheless, in a sketch or a painting, but she quickly sends these pieces away to one of the galleries that have begun to stock her work, or to the magazine that has not yet printed anything of hers but has asked to see more, and so she doesn't concede to looking at the innermost fears of her soul.

She goes to him as often as before and he is gentler than ever. He has found a job. It is not high-tech and it is not well paid but it is better than what he earned at his uncle's shop and she knows that at least this means he no longer has to stand on street edges. He is happier, she thinks. He has even been with her once to the gallery on her side of the city where two of her paintings were then hanging. He, more than anyone else, is who she wants to share this accomplishment with, but she understands his occasional disinterest, she knows it is difficult for him to toast the triumph he once dreamt of for himself.

She has not yet told him that she is pregnant. She has told nobody. Her breasts are swollen and she has been feeling tired and sick, and she has missed two periods and taken a home test that was positive, but her stomach is not showing and she has not been to the doctor. She is still 16, and unmarried, and too young to get married, and unable to marry Kaseem. She would qualify for an abortion if she went to the committee, but she does not think she wants this. It is not because of some deep, religious ethic, but because holding this tiny life inside of her, even though she cannot yet feel it, leaves her unable to consider anything but keeping it alive. It is already a part of her, and of him. Nevertheless, a small part of her resents Kaseem for his carelessness, for doing this to her. And she imagines that he will see a baby as only another stress in his already difficult existence, another mouth to feed. She does not want to be Kaseem's stress. She wants to be his light. She wants him to illuminate her in paint.

He will not. He refuses even to dig out his easel and grows angry when she suggests it. There is no point, he asserts. It is not helpful to remind himself of what will never be. At first she tried to coax him, but now she is growing tired of his stubbornness, his jealousy. He is not the only one who has had to make adjustments. She understands acutely now exactly what it is like to have compromised dreams. She feels it every day at school. Never again will she be like

Naomi, or Rachel, or any of her carefree friends; Kaseem has stolen this liberty from her, he has drunk her last drops of childhood, he has exchanged it for a store room, and secrets, and whispered words, and everything that is him and for which she would willingly make the trade over and over and over.

It is his fault.

But she cannot tell him.

The words stick in her throat and choke her with an anguish that she finds she can only release through paint. Blacks and oranges and deep, swirling purples; brown skies and red sand and shadow people, the way things really are. In class she is distracted and draws endlessly on her pencil case, highlighter pen and black ink. Naomi and Rachel, who by now have lost interest in East Jerusalem and make trips into Tel Aviv instead, want to know why she is suddenly so pensive. Dara's brother too asks her constantly what's wrong, refusing to be fobbed off with unimaginative laments about homework. He takes her to the cinema and makes her eat dinner when their parents are too immersed in other people's minds, and watches her closely. But it is only to blank paper that she is able to speak. Until, one Thursday, Dara arrives home from school to discover an envelope addressed to her from the magazine. They have received her latest piece and want to publish it. In fact, they say they want to use it on the front cover and include a cheque for the privilege. Dara feels her stomach leap, and she is not sure if it is because of the baby, or because of the news, but nonetheless she places her hand on her belly and savours the rare, joyful sensation. And she thinks of Kaseem.

It is already dusk by the time she arrives on his side of the city. The dark, intertwining streets still make her nervous, but she has navigated them enough times now for familiarity to lull her into a temporary sense of safety. She no longer notices the crumbling walls, the dirty gutters, the overpowering stench.

She feels these quirks as a part of him, or the path to him, and thus it is a terrain she loves.

She will tell him both things, she has decided. About the magazine and about the baby. His life is hard but still he can appreciate what is good. He is not her husband, but still he can be a father. They cannot be together, but still… She feels a rise of hope in her chest and trains her eyes downwards, forcing herself to see the pot-holed track. The letter from the magazine sits folded in the back pocket of her jeans. Her breasts throb.

Dara turns the corner into the road where Kaseem lives to find a commotion. People have spilled from their houses into the street and are floating in angry rings, leading like crop circles to the source of their fury. Up the hill. Towards him. They speak in Arabic and Dara cannot understand what they are saying, what has happened, but they gesticulate violently and Dara pushes through the throng amid hot, scathing stares. One man shouts something at her but she ignores the words that she doesn't understand anyway and hurries forward. She wonders if she has stumbled upon a Muslim festival she wasn't aware of and shouldn't be intruding upon, or if there has been a riot, or a fight, or a death? She starts running. And then suddenly, she sees.

Kaseem is standing amongst the rubble. His mother is sitting within it. His sisters – embarrassed by their inside wares being on display, as though their hijabs have slipped or their knickers are showing – gather pots and pans and clothes and bathroom soap. All the women are wailing. Around them, Kaseem's diligent work of the past month is in pieces; the bulldozers have done their job. The newly tiled roof lies in shambles on top of their kitchen table, the old front wall is half-collapsed and the room inside it open to the dirt and dark of the city. The bricks Dara once passed him, one by one, lay broken. The extension might never have existed. The house too. Rice scatters the ground like shattered glass. A pot of water is on the stove, still boiling. Soon it will overrun.

Kaseem is staring blankly into the distance. He does not at first see her as she picks over the ruins towards him, but his mother does, and his mother screams: "Whore!"

Dara freezes. Kaseem turns.

"You have done this. This is your fault. You, trying to Judaize him, you all trying to Judaize us!"

"Ummi-" Kaseem interrupts his mother, and he raises his hand. But he does not say anything to defend or admonish, he does not move, either towards her or to Dara. Only others have moved – the angry, watching people who are now watching Dara. Eyes everywhere. Even Kaseem's are flashing black.

"What happened?" she asks him softly, tripping over a piece of broken brick as she steps closer.

"What do you think happened?" he snaps. "The bulldozers came."

"But you had your permit."

"Of course I didn't. Don't be so naïve, Dara. Who would give me a permit? They don't give *us* permits. I am not a Jew. I am not like you."

The people are listening now too. Watching and listening. Dara moves closer to Kaseem so that she is able to whisper. "Kaseem, I am sorry. I know this is unforgiveable." She places her hand on his shaking arm.

"Go home, you Jewish whore!" Kaseem's mother screams again, loudly, for the onlookers. "Leave him be. He doesn't need you. He does not want you." She grabs Dara's hand from his arm and throws it back towards her, her nails scratching. "You bring us shame."

Dara looks up at Kaseem. He holds her gaze, but he says nothing. It is as though he cannot find the words to either break her, or pull her back. As though he is too tired, or too confused, or too...

"Kaseem, I have to tell you something," Dara urges softly. Her stomach tightens as she feels the circle around her moving closer, and she feels an urge to cover herself.

She fumbles with the zip of her cardigan and does it up. She reaches again for his arm. To steady herself. To steady him. "Kaseem-" Again Kaseem's mother slaps her hand away and now the crowds begin to close in on them. A step. Another step. Suddenly it feels dangerous. But she is still with Kaseem and this calms her. With one hand on her stomach she reaches for him once more. "Kaseem-" He is stony-still. Looking now not at her but at the wreckage beneath his feet. He will not look up. She doesn't mean to but feels tears welling. Her hormones are betraying her. Or, he is betraying her? "Kaseem-" Her voice breaks.

Slowly, slowly, he raises his head. Hair streaked white with dust, he looks older, wearier. He looks her in the eye as though taking in a painting, etching the colours and shapes and shading into his mind, deconstructing them for posterity. He takes her hand in both of his, grasps it tight, tighter, and then, as though releasing a butterfly, he opens his palms. "Go, Dara," he whispers, beneath the hearing of the crowd. "I have to… You need to go."

His mother steps closer.

"What? I don't want to go."

Now his mother smiles.

"It's late," he says. "The light has gone."

For a moment Dara sees a flicker in his eyes. A hesitation? An apology? A signal? If they were alone she could decode it. If they were alone she wouldn't need to. There wouldn't be this moment, this world, this-

"Go!" his mother screams now, again, affirmed by her son's obedience. "Go! Go away from here!" And fortified, she pushes Dara, and Dara falls backwards, slicing the back of her leg on a broken pane of glass, burning her elbow across the rubbled floor. The watchers laugh, and some cheer in agreement. They are huddled now amidst the rubble and Kaseem is jostled away. She can still see the top of his lowered head, the hunch of his back. But in front of him other faces are stepping into the fore. Scowling at her. Spitting words she

306

doesn't understand. She wills Kaseem to break through them, to come forward, to lift her up.

Instead, Dara notices Kaseem's uncle. This time, he does not call her 'beauty', and as he moves through the crowd towards her she has an impulse to get away.

Out of the corner of her eye she sees Kaseem's sister, Hadiyah noticing the uncle too, but she bows her head and does not come forward.

And Kaseem still does not come forward.

Instead, suddenly, from the shadows behind her, it is her brother,

David,

bursting through the crowd, and shooing people from her, and with his newly strong arms lifting her up, and noticing the hand she has placed on her stomach, and telling her he is there, and she will be okay.

It is David who takes her to the doctor. It is David who tells their parents about the baby. It is David who talks about Tel Aviv and suggests the move. It is David who asks the magazine if, before her painting is printed, Dara can change her name. It is she who decides on Orli.

***

Now

22

I am ready. Two suitcases are filled to the brim. A further three boxes are crammed inside my parents' loft. I have one set of linen on my bed, one towel hanging in the bathroom, a single wash bag next to the sink ready to receive my still strewn toiletries, my phone charger and laptop sit bold on an otherwise empty desk, and there is one clean outfit hanging in the wardrobe alongside three broken hangers. I feel as if it's Pesach and I'm scrutinising the room for crumbs of old bread that I must sweep out before the new festival dawns, indictments of the past year. But no crumbs remain. All that is left is to say goodbye.

I have already survived the final Friday night dinner. Nana kept things jolly with a flood of tales about her youth, my departure a prompt for her to recall the fantastic things she was doing aged 29, or perhaps to celebrate the miracle that she reached 29. Dad and Pete put in a good showing of interest in my plans – they asked about Ulpan, about the cheap hotel I'm staying in until I find a flat, about Orli. Under the direction of Mum's unsubtle whispers Dad also asked where my rocket shelter is and if I know the best route to it and how long it will take me to get there from my hotel room.

But Mum didn't cry. The effort of this was evident in every nag that was as blunt as ever, but didn't entreat me to stay. *You know we're not a storage facility Daniel, when are you going to move those boxes? That gravy's for everyone. Eat more. And don't forget to shop properly or you'll just eat rubbish. Eat. You're wasting away.* For the first time I can remember, she made challah from scratch.

Gaby, sitting on the other side of the table from me, kept tight-lipped. We used to congregate at this very table to do our homework, attempting to distract each other with thrown rubbers or loud breathing. But now there was little to say.

"You hate me, but you love me," I grinned as we said goodbye.

"I love you and I love you," she corrected. "And I think you're blind and stupid and stubborn and selfish."

"I love you too," I told her. We hugged then, my arms over hers, and then she wriggling her arms over the top, correcting things, she the older sister, the protector, the wise one.

"You can always come home," she said, just before I reached the door. "You're English, remember, not Israeli."

"Okay Gaby," I said, not bothering to correct her, not having the energy or clarity quite yet to explain that being Israeli, whole, sure – that was half the point.

She and Pete and Mum and Nana moved with me to the doorstep, Dad already waiting in his car to give me a lift home. This is how I know I'll picture them when I'm gone, gathered together, standing sentry to home, watching me leave.

"Dan." Gaby grabbed my arm.

"Yes?"

"I'll never forgive you if you get hurt."

"Oh thanks a lot Gaby. Lovely parting sentiment." I patted her hand. "At least I'm not yet redundant!" I'd said with a grin.

But she didn't grin back and days later her words are still resounding in my head. As I drag my suitcase to the corner of the room and dig into it for the shirt I have forgotten to leave out for the party, the responsibility of her love, her worry, feels heavy. It is as if I am walking not on carpet, not atop hard, supportive concrete, but wading through something illusive and less sturdy, a surface that slips away as soon as I try to touch it, as soon as I reach out and press down for balance, a surface a little like sand.

Robert and I buy vodka, whisky, beer, wine, and a few mixers. We go to Costco and add ten trays of ready-made canapés. Debbie rushes around the flat carefully removing her female flourishes and locking them in Robert's room. I too lock the door to my bedroom where my desk is now fastidiously arranged with my passport and immigration papers.

The nostalgia hits me unexpectedly.

I am ready before Robert and Debbie so am standing on our small balcony, sipping beer and waiting for the guests to arrive when it happens. Perhaps it is the smell of London in the summer. Or the anticipation of a good night. In truth I don't know why at the eleventh hour it has manifested, but I suddenly find myself thinking of long cricket matches in the park on mild summer evenings; of football games watched down the pub; of hectic, friends-filled schooldays; gowns on graduating uni; the sound of rain on car windscreens, the wipers moving comfortingly back and forth; the vast mix of colour that fights through the grey. I know I will miss this and I am glad that I will miss it, and that I am thinking of it now. This is how I want to remember England, with this jumble. A jumble that assures me I am not being pushed, but am choosing.

Robert appears on the balcony with a beer in his hand. He hugs me round the shoulders and kisses me smack on the cheek. "Book a flight back next summer," he grins. And digs his hand into his pocket to flash a diamond at me before hurrying it away at the sound of Debbie coming to join us.

By nine, everyone is there. Or almost everyone. There is no sign of Safia. The flat however is buzzing with a bunch of my other uni friends, all the old yeah-you North West London contingent, and a few work mates. Even Hayley has turned up and enveloped me in a strong-squeezed bear hug that jolts me with its familiarity. She smiles at me in a way she shouldn't, now, but to my relief it doesn't floor me. And when she tells me that she always knew I had places to be, I feel validated, as though she had the answer all along. We talk for a good 20 minutes and I notice in her a new, interesting womanhood, a certain worldly poise. I wonder if I have changed similarly. I feel more than I once was. "You look good, Dan," she winks as she gets up to rejoin her friends, and I take this as agreement.

Now, despite Safia's absence, I feel excited. I spend the next hour flitting from one group to the next, repeating the same pat response to each of their questions: "It's sunny there," I say. As they nod I lap up their good wishes, their hugs, their familiarity. I tuck them away in anticipation of needing them later. But even amidst the warmth of it all, the rare indulgence of filling a room with people who are all there for me, even as Robert brings out a surprise Bon Voyage cake and everybody cheers and claps me on the back, even now, right at the summit of the evening, I find myself thinking of the heat of the Israeli tarmac, and the unyielding beat of Tel Aviv, and of Orli. As soon as I get a chance, I slip away from the crowd.

"Why are you calling?" Orli demands when she answers the phone. I am standing just inside the door to my bedroom, the key in my hand. Outside the music is pumping. "Danny, you are supposed to be at your party."

"I am at my party. Almost. There are two inches of wood between me and my party."

"So it's not good?"

I laugh. "It's very good. Aren't I allowed to think of you?"

"You'll see me tomorrow. Tonight you should see them." She says this earnestly. "Danny, you will miss it you know."

"I know." I sit down on my bed. "But I'm still thinking about you."

"Go back to the party, Danny," Orli says, but I can hear the smile in her voice.

"Are you painting?" I lay flat on the bed, noticing the blankness of the ceiling, not even a crack for interest.

"Actually, I'm finished."

"Really? The whole series? Can I see?"

She pauses. I can hear her thinking. But she is finished, finally, and after a moment she agrees. For lack of paper I use my hand to write down the web address where she has uploaded the images, and the password – they are not yet ready for the uncensored world, but she has unlocked them for me.

As we say goodbye, the door to my bedroom creaks open. I expect Robert and turn with raised hands, ready to atone for sneaking away. But it is not him.

Safia closes the door behind her. She wears a long white dress, ruffled at the bottom and streaked green, as though she has been sitting in a park somewhere. Her arms are bare, her hair loose and a little dishevelled.

"I nearly didn't come," she says, as though noticing the query in my eyes.

"Why not? I'm glad you did."

"Really?" She releases her hand from the door and takes a step into the room.

"Of course really. Why would you think I wouldn't want you to come?"

She is carrying a large tote bag, a leather jacket threaded through the handles, a book poking out from underneath. The book makes me think of her reading and that makes me think of her in the exam hall in my dream. She lifts the bag from her shoulder and places it on the floor. "I saw you see me," she says.

I know of course what she is referring to, but feign innocence.

"At the protest, Dan. You saw me at the protest."

"I wasn't sure it was you."

"And now that you are sure?"

It feels strange standing like this, no glass of wine or cup of coffee in our hands or other prop to suggest we are just chatting, just killing time, not talking about something so difficult. "Well I already knew we feel differently, about that."

I see her looking around the room for somewhere to sit. There is a chair, or the bed. She selects the chair, glancing briefly at the forms on my desk before looking back up. "We do."

"I didn't love the fact that you were standing next to a sign lauding Hitler."

"I didn't make the sign."

"I know that."

"And I don't agree with it."

"I know that."

"But I also don't agree with you."

"Yeah." I sit on the edge of the bed facing her. "Likewise." For a moment we say nothing more. The image of her there at the desk is disorientating me. I feel as though I am slipping between dreams and reality. "Look, does it matter?" I attempt to say light-heartedly.

"No. I guess not." She picks up my passport and opens the photo page, grinning with an overt attempt at joviality at the image of 19-year-old me. "It doesn't. Except. Except that-" She looks up. "I can't fathom your blindness."

I take the passport from her hand, close it and settle it back onto the desk. "Just because I think differently, Saf, it doesn't mean I'm blind."

"You're blind."

"To what?"

She takes a deep breath then exhales loudly. "To reality."

"You know real Israeli soldiers are dying too, right? And real rockets are flying into Israel, right?"

"To the presence of choices. To the responsibility of actions. To the prejudice of not caring, or caring only about your own."

"I don't only-"

"And to me."

I narrow my eyes. "To you?"

"Oblivious." Safia picks up one of my forms and studies it.

"Saf, what are you talking about?"

She says nothing but rolls her eyes to the ceiling and shakes her head.

"Saf?"

The form lands heavily back on the table. "Dan, you fucked me, and then you met Orli, and that's it?"

"You ignored me for weeks! You said it was too complicated!"

"It is complicated!"

"So?"

"So that doesn't mean it's not worth attempting. But you wouldn't anyway, would you? Because I'm not Jewish. Just like you don't care about Gazans because they're not. It's screwed up, Dan. And it's killing me because if nothing else you're still meant to be one of my best friends, and I, I just can't rationalise that prejudice."

On the bed, I am still reeling from the revelation that Safia was interested in a relationship. I feel myself trying and failing to process it, like a broken parking meter, attempting to slot this information into a receptacle that lets it fall straight through. I see her waiting, waiting, waiting for a response, an explanation, a statement of intent. But I don't have one. "Safia," is all I can say. "You're being spectacularly unfair."

"Okay, Dan." She stands up. Shakes her head again. "There's no point in arguing anyway. I just wanted to say goodbye. And good luck." She bends down now and kisses me lightly on the cheek. I smell strawberry-vanilla…mango! The scent bounces across the taut air. I sense her lingering and I am surprised by an urge to reach out, to pull her closer.

"I'll miss you, Saf," I say.

Safia straightens. "I'll miss you too."

She turns to go and I stand up, watching as she bends for her bag and hoists it onto her shoulder. "You don't have to leave," I say, coming towards her, part of me feeling a vague guilt at even saying this yet wanting desperately for her to stay, and the other part wishing she would exit faster. My wholeness fragmenting.

Safia doesn't respond but she raises a single eyebrow, hovering.

I feel like we are locked in this moment for a long time. Eventually, I grin, stupidly.

Safia reaches for the door handle. She opens the door.

I want to make her stay. I want her to help me analyse the moment, what led us to the moment, what led us together, and apart. I want her to sit up from her own exam and give me the answers. But it is too complicated.

"Be careful, Dan," Safia says. And then she is gone.

Later, when the last of the revellers have departed, I return to my room. I sit at my desk in the chair Safia occupied a few hours earlier and open my laptop, hurriedly copying Orli's web address and password from my hand. I have been thinking about her pictures ever since I spoke to her, and more so since Safia left. I need a reminder, an uplifting vision, clarity. A myriad of images appear in miniature. I have seen most of them before, all but the final Jerusalem two, but I click on each in order, hungry for the whole.

Here it is: Division. First is the picture of me. About half way through there is Muaz, Orli's non-nephew. There are another ten or so portraits and images. I study each of them. As always I am impressed by the depth of Orli's painting, the way each one hits in waves, first the aesthetic, then the emotion, then the cerebral challenge of thought. There is something about the way Orli channels the light, as though illuminating ideas beneath and above her subjects, forcing the viewer to look there, to look harder. I feel confronted as I scroll through them, but, as I near the final few, alongside the perfectly articulated sense of division, I taste hope. We have talked about the theme extensively now, Orli and I. I always argue that division is divisive, simple as that, and so deconstructive, distressing. But Orli maintains that division leads to space, and space leads to renewal, and with renewal comes hope. I feel that hope now. I hope because of her, because of Israel, because of what both represent: strength and straight-shooting, wholeness and direction, passion and possibility. Clarity and substance. Truth.

Orli says there is no such thing as one truth.

Yet my feelings for Orli are clear and sustaining.

Safia makes me feel fragmented and undone. Though I keep picturing her standing there, her hand on the door.

I click on the penultimate image, the first of the Jerusalem two. This I suppose is where that building feeling of hope will be fully released, will soar. I hold my breath in anticipation.

But I'm not sure what I'm looking at. The bulk of the landscape is in shadow and shades of dusty, rusty brown lap across and over each other, swirling, refusing to settle for the eye. Slowly however, a light-coloured shop front comes into view, a canopy above it, a cobbled path winding away, and in a subtle, almost invisible corner, the outline of a man. There is something strong and disconcerting about this lone figure, something powerful and challenging, though his frame is practically a blur. He is both young and old. Bold and weary. Strange and intimately familiar. I'm not sure how to feel about him. About this painting. Not hope after all. It is a jolt in the journey. I sense it is intended to elicit expectation or desire, an obscure promise just out of reach. But I feel only uncomfortable, apprehensive, and full of an odd, illusive fear.

I open the second image. Unlike the first it is at once vivid and in full-colour, yet, there is a quality about this one too that is unsettling. From inside the screen the face of a young Arab girl in a hijab gazes out. Her hair is covered, her stance is demure, but her face blazes with defiance and her lips are painted hot pink. There is a peculiarity about it unlike Orli's usual work, something unfinished perhaps, unknown, uncrafted. Raw. But it is as hypnotising as ever and I can't stop staring at it. The face captivates me. And unnerves me. I have a nagging feeling of familiarity, déjà vu, I can't escape it, and suddenly I realise that I'm not crazy, I have seen it before. I click on the earlier painting and there it is, I am right. It is the eyes. The girl in the hijab has the same eyes as Muaz.

I don't know why this realisation packs my gut with a sudden dread.

There has always been a dark space around Muaz, I tell myself. Even around Orli. I have never been privy to the mysterious details that creep from her soul into her art.

But who is she, I wonder. Who is this girl? A sister? A cousin? An aunt? Does Muaz know there is somebody in East Jerusalem with eyes like his own? There is much, I realise, that I don't yet know. And Orli hasn't told me. But the unknown always illicits trepidation. That is all. That is all this is. That is why panic is scrambling silently inside my head.

***

Now

23

The Israeli quarter of the hospital moves in convoy to Heathrow. Before he goes, there are last visitors: the Lebanese hummus man, some of the restaurant staff, Taadiki. Taadiki doesn't mention the war but he brings baklava. It is a fitting gift. The Middle Eastern pastry is a last taste of England, a last mingling before there is a need to separate out, to distinguish, to define. He will take this taste with him, he will remember it, summon it perhaps.

At the airport, everyone is there to see Udi off, even Chaim who arrived at this same airport the day before and is now staying above the restaurant in Udi's old flat. Ben and Jonny promise to look out for him, and to make a trip to Israel soon. To see the restaurant Udi is going create, they say, and to steal his ideas for their own. But after the jokes and the jibes and the final affectionate exchanges of obscenities, they hug with heavy arms and a recognition of all that has passed.

Ella and his parents are travelling with him and stand next to Udi's wheelchair in the queue for the check-in desk after the others have departed. The camaraderie of this is at once a comfort and a disturbance. Liberty swapped for kinship. But it is not a choice. And it is not a mistake. It is an undeniable imperative.

It takes a long time to get through security. Udi is allowed to skip the queue with Ella because of his medical situation, but Oz and Batia are forced to remain in the line and so they all wait, on separate sides. Heathrow feels more familiar this time around. Armed police officers are everywhere, queues are moving slowly, more bags are being checked. Still, the place emits a fragile innocence, as if it doesn't yet know the depth of the danger ahead. The laxity makes Udi feel unsafe, but he both pities and envies this naivety he is leaving behind.

He is asked to board the plane first, before even the First Class passengers, and despite the circumstances takes a mischievous pleasure in this, as though he is returning home a conqueror. He has only been assigned an economy seat but it is in the front row where there is extra leg space, and his supplementary oxygen is being stored nearby. His lung is mostly recovered now but the hospital has given copious instructions for him to follow. He is good at this still. Ella and his parents sit further back. It is a full flight despite the conflict at their destination. Typically, Ella and his mother make a fuss and try to change the seating arrangement so that they can be close to Udi, but the airline staff insist, and in the end it is neither of them but a young man around Udi's age who sits in the empty chair next to him.

"Wow, that looks painful," the man says, pointing to Udi's elaborately plastered and strapped leg. "What did you do?"

"Car crash," Udi replies. The man nods and Udi picks the in-flight magazine out of the pocket in front of him.

"You're Israeli?" the man asks.

"Yes."

"You're going home?"

Udi thinks about this. "I guess so. And you? It's a strange time to take a vacation to Israel."

"I'm not taking a vacation," the man replies. "I'm making aliyah."

Udi looks at the man afresh. He raises his eyebrows.

"Daniel," the man says, offering his hand and grinning.

"Udi," he replies.

They talk sporadically throughout the flight and at length. At times they are interrupted by films or by visits from Udi's family, and by the meal for which Udi orders the regular chicken dish and Daniel is given his pre-ordered kosher plate, but conversation returns. For both of them there is something intriguing about the other, something either opposite or parallel, as though the other man holds a part of the truth they have been trying to grasp, or a different truth, or a light to illuminate it.

Daniel is consumed by the British response to the war; he sees antisemitism everywhere, but even watching the bleakest of bulletins Udi was unsurprised by it. "The Arabs are smart," he tells Daniel. "Of course they want this opinion in the world, this sympathy. If I were Arab I would want Israel too and if I were English I would feel sorry for them. But nobody knows what's really happening. And nobody in England really cares. They go out and they shout for a bit and then they go home and go to bed and get up in the morning and go to work. And the Arabs don't really care what you guys think anyway. It's us they're getting at. Israelis. They want to get into our heads, into our mentality. They want people like my sister to make us think we're doing something bad, that we don't have a right. They want to make us forget what we're fighting for and why we need our own land and the reason that Israel was created. But once we do that, Israel is over."

"Do people think that?"

"Some do. Sometimes I do. But you can't, you know? You can't look for the nuance. If a soldier thinks that what he is doing is wrong, it's over. He will sleep when he's supposed to guard, he'll sit down when he's supposed to be training, and when there's a war and people at home are protesting against it he'll wonder who he's protecting. And then there'll be bombs in our markets again and guns in our faces. Our biggest enemy is ourselves, and the Arabs know this. Hamas know this. They know they can't beat us unless we don't want to win."

"But we do want to win," Daniel says uncertainly.

Udi shrugs. "You say yes and you do."

"Huh?"

"I don't know. Maybe you reach out. Maybe you get four-year-olds together and get them to make peace in the sandbox."

"You think there can be peace?"

Udi shrugs again. Across the aisle he sees a group of Haredis stand from their seats to pray before the plane's final descent. Daniel's face has dropped. Udi has unsettled him.

"You know I'm talking crap, right?" Udi grins, surprised that he has actually been lured into talking politics, and that there is a part of him that wants to. "Israel is all about the nuance," he says. "Anything is possible there. And that's the truth."

And that is the truth.

He didn't push a four-year-old girl, but she was still pushed, they were still pushing. And that's the truth too.

And Gaza is a shithole. And that's the truth.

And Israel's had a big hand in it. And that's the truth.

And the Palestinians are desperate. And that's the truth.

And some of them are murderers.

And they are all punished.

And somebody kidnapped three Israeli kids.

And somebody burned a Palestinian in revenge.

And rockets were fired.

And missiles were launched.

And Israelis ran to shelters.

And Gazans lay dead.

And it's all the truth. Black and white. And tit for tat. And no nuance. And nuance in everything. And nobody looking for it. And everybody knowing. And nobody seeing. And still this feeling that he must go home. And do something.

But Udi cannot understand why anybody on the outside would volunteer for any of it.

"You know, the only way to make a fortune in Israel is to come to Israel with a bigger fortune," he says, turning towards Daniel.

"I have enough money," Daniel replies.

"Nobody drives Mercedes convertibles," Udi warns.

"So I'll drive a Subaru."

"You may have to fight."

"I want to."

"You could be killed."

"I know."

"You are crazy," says Udi, banging his fist on his good leg.

"There is also a girl," grins Daniel.

The Haredi have returned now to their seats and the hot tarmac below is coming into view. Udi's chest tightens. He is unsure whether it is the injured lung or something greater. He turns once more to his new acquaintance. Daniel's face is awash with emotion: elation, excitement, apprehension, naivety, fear, hope? He is not yet hard around the edges. He is like a lamb.

"Israel is the greatest country in the world," Udi concedes, and Daniel nods, gratefully, his assured grin returning.

Before they can say anything more however there is a screeching of brakes and the plane bumps to the ground, both men listing in their seats until at last the great machine comes to a halt. Scattered rounds of clapping break out within the cabin in gratitude for the safe landing. The Haredi are silent in prayer.

"So," Udi begins again.

Daniel looks up.

"So what is her name?"

"Orli," smiles Daniel.

And Udi laughs. "Orli. This means 'light'. No wonder. Everybody is blinded by the light."

The seatbelt sign is turned off. Daniel stands up and Batia and Ella can be seen pushing up the aisle towards them. The door is opened and a surge of heat thrusts its way into the cabin. Waiting for his wheelchair, Udi remains seated. He can already taste dust in the air. Daniel has his bag. Udi nods, a nod he hopes will convey luck, and Daniel reaches over to shake Udi's hand, but a man behind Daniel huffs impatiently and before their palms can meet he is carried away in the throng of flip-flopped masses, everybody already shoving and jostling, lurching forwards.

***

During the 2014 Israel-Gaza conflict, more than 2,100 Palestinians and 72 Israelis were killed.

Acknowledgements

There are many people I would like to thank for their help in creating *Chains of Sand*:

Ofir Nakar and Amazia in particular gifted me with invaluable insights into life in the IDF. I am also indebted to Rube Backal, Ben Mason, Joshua Raif, Gili Rosenheimer, Ora Seidner and Spencer Gelding at Beit Halochem, and Noam Zamohi.

For reading many different incarnations of this book, I am grateful to: Anna-Marie Collier, Jane Fields, Naomi Gryn, Rachel Rushbrook, Nikki Saunders, Anna Seymour, and Geraldine Wayne.

My brilliant agent Donald Winchester has provided immeasurable editorial help, and guidance at every step. And I am indebted as always to the Legend Press team, especially my fantastic editor Lauren Parsons who has championed my writing from the start.

I would also like to thank my family – Jeff, Geraldine, Anna-Marie, Damian, Zeb, Olivia, Joab, and the extended Wayne and Kattan clans who have supported me throughout. In particular, James, my husband and rock. And our daughters, to whom this book is dedicated.

We hope you enjoyed *Chains of Sand*, the first fictional address of the current Israeli-Palestinian crisis.

This novel follows Jemma's debut, *After Before*, which was longlisted for the prestigious Baileys Women's Prize for Fiction, longlisted for the Guardian Not the Booker Award and shortlisted for the Waverton Good Read Award.

'Rich, haunted, gripping, painful and beautifully entwined'
Ruth Padel

'A powerful novel. Its characters will haunt you long after their stories have been told.'
Naomi Gryn

'A fearless and meticulously observed examination of pain transformed by the redeeming power of friendship.'
Vanora Bennett

Here's a first chapter sample of *After Before*:

Chapter
One

She said her name was Emily. It had always seemed easier for English people to pronounce than Emilienne, and she refused to offer this part of herself, also, for sacrifice.

"Okay, do you have any cleaning experience Emily?" asked the thick-necked, white woman behind the desk. She shuffled the forms in front of her, impatience spilling into Emily's pause, but it wasn't a simple question to answer. The woman said it so easily, rolling off her tongue as smooth as the flesh beneath the skin of a sweet potato, the same as most of the words Emily had had thrown at her over the years: stupid, ungrateful, cockroach. Emily's mind ran over the dirty floors of her flat that she hadn't so much as threatened with a vacuum; then to the sparkling windows and door knobs in the house she'd cleaned and lived in once, belonging to Auntie; then tentatively to the dark puddles of blood she'd scrubbed from her father's floor.

"Yes," Emily decided upon. "I have experience."

Her smile was gummier than she would have liked, and there was a gap between her front teeth, but it was important always to smile. It conveyed honesty, familiarity, trust.

"Do you have references?"

"No."

The woman sighed. "So you have no experience." Tutting, she scribbled out the tick in what was now the wrong box on the registration form.

"You asked about experience, not references," Emily clarified anxiously.

But the woman only smiled, as though such ignorance was what she expected. Emily smiled back at her. Ignorance didn't matter. Auntie had told her once. What mattered in this country was a willingness to work, to get down on one's knees and scrub stains out of floors too low for English girls. "You'll be cleaning commercial properties," the woman continued, lists of products and rules and company policies suddenly undulating out of her like a well-sung nursery rhyme. Obligingly, Emily nodded along to the beat until she noticed that the woman had paused and leaned forward. "Can you remember all that?" the woman was prompting, smiling again, her over-padded wrists escaping the cuffs of her green blazer. The colour made Emily feel sick. The flesh made Emily feel sick. The woman's gritted grin made her feel sick.

"Yes," Emily nodded.

The darkness of her skin seemed untidy against the neat, white piece of paper the woman pushed across the table for her to sign. Her hand shook as it hovered over the box where she was supposed to form the letters of her signature. It shook, and she shuddered, and her stomach grumbled queasily.

Outside, Emily wrapped her scarf around her neck. It wound three times and sat like a woollen brace that she rested her chin upon. Already the beginning of September, the first chill of winter was beginning to seep through the air into her bones and she knew she would be cold now until April at the earliest. It was impossible in this country to warm up once the cold was inside you and she would never grow used to it. But the scarf helped, and she liked the barrier it made between her long, skinny neck and the elements. Auntie used to try to get her out of the chunky knits she clung to and into more feminine shapes, but that was before she'd caused Auntie and Uncle so much distress, and they preferred her to disappear not just inside baggy clothes, but altogether.

A bus roared past Emily's right shoulder, her bus. She ran to catch it and smiled at the driver who paused long enough for her to clamber on and touch her Oyster card, but then accelerated with a jerk that threw her sideways. Emily was athletic once, strong, but now she was always a little unsteady on her feet and had to clasp the rail in order not to fall flat on her face.

She swung rail to rail down the length of the bus until she found a spare seat, avoiding eye contact with the other passengers who were just as furtively avoiding eye contact with her. It had been a shock when she'd first arrived in this country to find that people didn't greet each other in the street, or on the bus, or talk if they could possibly help it. Sometimes, sun-streaked instinct still got the better of her, but if there was anything she truly loved about England it was exactly this - the anonymity, the ability to live unnoticed, unidentified, undefined. There was a pleasure she found in the vast hoards of people whose names she didn't know, rushing obliviously past each other. There was comfort in the uniformity of floor upon floor of council housing like that of the building she lived in, her room on the fifth indistinguishable from the rest. There was tranquillity in the busyness of people's lives, in their individualistic pursuits and their self-obsession. There was isolation. Escape.

Emily alighted at Golders Green station. Her flat was still a 15 minute walk from there but she needed some groceries and preferred to buy them from the bigger shops with hundreds of customers rather than from the small convenience store on the corner of her road. She'd only been a few times but already the owner knew her face and asked her questions like, 'No avocados today? How about mangoes? I have perfect mangoes, you don't like them?' and, the week before, 'Where are you from?'

She picked up a basket outside the front of Tesco and dipped into the shop. She had exactly £4.73 left in her purse so had to make her selection carefully. The money needed to last until the end of the week and it was only Wednesday. Reluctantly she made her way towards the canned goods aisle and selected a tin of economy beans and some corn. Next, she found a loaf of bread that had been reduced in price because it was already at its sell-by date, and tore three bananas from a bigger bunch. Longingly she eyed the avocados but here such fruits were exotic and expensive. Emily picked up a small, hard one and quickly slipped it into her coat pocket. At the counter the cashier greeted her politely but without recognition, and Emily smiled. Rubbing the bunch of carriers between her fingers to separate them, she packed her few items into two bags so that the heavy tins could be divided and she could prevent the plastic handles from carving out valleys in her thin arms on the walk home. She always carried bags over her arms instead of in her hands. When she used to go shopping with Auntie, they would walk home with fifteen bags between them, and Emily would carry ten of them, each one balanced carefully an inch or two away from the next, all the way up her scrawny forearms, the skin pinching together as if she, like the avocados they'd bought, was being tested for ripeness. That was at the very beginning when she was grateful to Auntie for coming to her rescue, and naïve still to the reality that real rescue wasn't possible simply by escaping a place. Memories weren't rooted in the soil.

Emily realised now that Auntie had loved her then. She hadn't been able to feel it at the time but identified it later, like so many things, in its loss. They had done well to put up with her really. They managed it for three years and she knew even as it was happening that the screaming and the silences and the disappearances would one day amount to a final straw. Gradually, Auntie began to raise her voice at her, and Uncle hit her once. Which made everything worse. She wasn't surprised when they told her to leave. She told herself she felt safer that way anyway: alone, and running.

A white van was parked in front of the entrance to Emily's

building. As she rounded the corner, she studied the men bounding in and out of it, unloading boxes. In Africa, they would be surrounded by people: newcomers were objects of curiosity to be scrutinised and assessed. *He who has travelled alone, can tell what he wants,* went the proverb, one of many that even after so many years, Emily was unable to rid from her mind. But the proverb held a truth, and it had felt natural for her, in another time, in a place that no longer existed, for strangers' stories to be tested and repeated, inquiries encouraged, questions asked. Emily shifted her shopping bags higher up her arms and walked past the van without a word.

The lift was broken again so she climbed the stairs, trying not to breathe in too deeply the stench of urine and beer. It amazed her still that a flat had been found for her so quickly, had been given so freely, by a nation who barely looked at each other in the street. Auntie had explained to her once about welfare, about asylum, about how she and Uncle had claimed both before the day came that with a job, and a passport, they needed neither. She'd told this story with pride, gratified by the distance they'd travelled, and though it wasn't due to a similar sense of aspiration, Emily always remembered this, and didn't mind sometimes having to hold her breath on the stairs. By the time she reached the fifth floor however she was gasping. Stopping at the end of the corridor, Emily rebalanced the shopping bags and dug into her handbag for her key. She always did this - stopped, prepared, felt the consoling piece of metal in her palm. An instrument of safety. Of power.

Emily looked up. A little way down the corridor, the door of the flat next to hers was ajar, a box propping it open, male voices inside. Emily had only ever seen the flat's occupant once, but she knew it to be a tiny, hunched-over old woman who seemed not to have any visitors and made noise only when her kettle occasionally whistled. Probably, Emily considered, the woman had died, because it was plain that the foreign voices she heard now were those of the men from the van, who it appeared were moving in. Emily wondered, briefly, how long the woman had laid dead next to her, whether her decomposing body had started to smell, who had found her; but then she heard footsteps on the stairs and quickly covered the last few feet of the corridor to her door, locking it carefully behind her.

The room was minute, the only windows facing directly onto a small courtyard with buildings so closely crammed around its edges and to such heights that it barely let in the light. Emily breathed deeply. She liked it this way. Rat-like. It was useful to be so far removed from the illumination of light, the transparency of sunlit days. Quietly, she unloaded her shopping, slipping the stolen avocado out of her pocket and onto the countertop to ripen, and placed a slice of bread into the toaster. She knew she shouldn't really eat the beans that night, but she was hungry so dug around under the sink for her solitary pan and, with a knife, pried open the tin before sense could change her mind. The dark red contents gushed with satisfying, hearty thickness into the pot. As it heated she opened the tap and let the water run until it was cold, then held a tall glass under it, allowing it to overflow, still finding pleasure, and promise, in this small excess.

When it was ready, Emily carried her meal over to the cushion in front of the TV. In a moment of charity – or pity, or guilt – Auntie had let her take it with her from the room she'd once slept in, along with the clothes Auntie had paid for over the years, and a wad of ten pound notes folded together and pressed into Emily's hand with a look of exhaustion at the door. Now the TV was Emily's biggest distraction from the dismal reality of everything else, and the floor in front of it had become a place from which she could watch laughter, glamour, optimism, frivolity, extravagance, romance, hope, dreams, success. She wished sometimes that she could be one of the happy people inside the screen, or even one of the girls who worked in the café around the corner that sat outside on their cigarette breaks, making jokes and throwing back their heads, light beaming from their eyes. There was a time when she would have given anything for that brightness, that spark, but the darkness that filled her seemed impossible to escape. Her anger was impossible to escape. Misery was impossible to escape. And for the most part, she no longer tried to.

Footsteps hurried past her door then returned a moment later, doubled and slower. Emily placed the remnants of her meal on the ground in front of her, turned off the TV, and slid from her cushion onto the floor. Lying flat she could make out the large, trainer-clad feet of one man walking backwards, and the sandals of another moving forwards opposite him. They were carrying something. The one wearing sandals was dark-skinned, though not as dark as Emily, and the wiry hair on his toes sprouted wildly, impervious to suggestions from the sandal straps of where they should lie. He called out to the other man in front of him and both pairs of feet stopped. Emily remained flat on the floor and listened to the muffled muttering between them in a language that wasn't English and that she didn't understand, then after a while the feet moved again, and disappeared from sight.

Emily began to weep.

It crept up on her slowly sometimes, and then there was time to make a cup of sugary tea, run a bath, or find some distraction on TV, but other times it hit her like this, abruptly. Angrily she hit back at the hot tears streaking down her face, but they only ran harder from her nose in polluted floods. She hugged her knees to her chest and forced herself to sit up, but then her mind wandered beneath the sink to the razor blade she had attempted to hide there, underneath toilet roll and toothpaste. The scar below her fringe throbbed, dizzying her. Her stomach tightened and contracted. Afraid that she might be sick she turned further onto her side, but couldn't muster the energy to reach the toilet, or even the bin in the corner of the room. All she could do was remain low on the ground, clinging to the hard, worn, reassuring carpet, until it was over.

When finally it was, Emily dragged herself back onto the

cushion in front of the TV. The last beans on her plate were cold now and sickened her. She felt weak and listless. Her throat was dry and her head pumped after crying for so long, but she couldn't be bothered to refill her glass at the sink. She switched on the TV. A nature programme investigating the life of insects filled the screen and she changed the channel quickly. Now Jeremy Kyle appeared in front of her, arbitrating the trivial, meaningless, wonderful disputes that were enough to drive the families on the show apart. Emily curled her body inwards, hugged her knees to her chest again and rested her head on the cushion. When her eyes closed she was in a field of sweet potatoes, in a shallow dirt valley between the straight lines of crops, her face crouched next to the soil, her breath unsteady and unreliable, caterpillars taunting her from underneath the leaves.

She opened her eyes.

Another blink and there were voices screaming her name, shouts raised to a gruesome, fever pitch in exuberant anticipation of finding her. Darkness was in her mouth, dry, soil-smelling darkness. It scratched her eyes and covered them.

She blinked again. Her view cleared and suddenly, in the distance, she spotted her mother. Emily scrambled up. She ran towards her, fast, faster, her legs and arms flooding with acid, but somehow, the distance seemed only to grow. She shouted, but no sound came out. She waved, but her movements were slow and minuscule. She ran. But with every metre she covered, her mother fell further away, and the more she ran, the more pain filled the older woman's eyes, until finally Emily stopped and saw that her mother, on her unreachable plane, was undressed, and unhelped and unflinching.

Emily opened her eyes once more.

Her mother was gone.

Jeremy Kyle screamed on in comfort.

Come and visit us at www.legendpress.co.uk
Follow us @legend_press